Praise for Laurie J. Marks's Elem

Fire Logic

★ "Marks has created a work filled with an intelligence that zings off the page."
— *Publishers Weekly* (Starred Review)

★ "Marks is an absolute master of fantasy in this book. Her characters are beautifully drawn, showing tremendous emotional depth and strength as they endure the unendurable and strive always to do the right thing, and her unusual use of the elemental forces central to her characters' lives gives the book a big boost. This is read-it-straight-through adventure!"
— *Booklist* (Starred Review)

"A deftly painted story of both cultures and magics in conflict. Marks avoids the black-and-white conflicts of generic fantasy to offer a window on a complex world of unique cultures and elemental magic."
— Robin Hobb

"Cuts deliciously through the mind to the heart with the delicacy, strength, beauty, and surgical precision of the layered Damascus steel blade that provides one of the book's central images."
— Candas Jane Dorsey

"Laurie Marks brings skill, passion, and wisdom to her new novel. Entertaining and engaging—an excellent read!"
— Kate Elliott

"This is a treat: a strong, fast-paced tale of war and politics in a fantasy world where magic based on the four elements of alchemy not only works but powerfully affects the lives of those it touches. An unusual, exciting read."
— Suzy McKee Charnas

"A glorious cast of powerful, compelling, and appealingly vulnerable characters struggling to do the right thing in a world gone horribly wrong. I couldn't put this down until I'd read it to the end. Marks truly understands the complex forces of power, desire, and obligation."
— Nalo Hopkinson

"Most intriguingly, about two-thirds of the way into the book, the low-key magical facets of her characters' elemental magics rise away from simply being fancy "weapons" and evoke—for both the readers and the characters—that elusive sense of wonder."
— Charles de Lint, *The Magazine of Fantasy & Science Fiction*

"An exquisite novel of quiet charm. *Fire Logic* is a tale of war and magic, of duty, love and betrayal, of despair encompassed by hope."
— *SF Site*

Earth Logic

★ "The powerful but subtle writing glows with intelligence, and the passionate, fierce, articulate, strong, and vital characters are among the most memorable in contemporary fantasy, though not for the faint of heart. Definitely for the thinking reader."
— *Booklist* (Starred Review)

"The sequel to *Fire Logic* continues the tale of a woman born to magic and destined to rule. Vivid descriptions and a well-thought-out system of magic."
— *Library Journal*

"Twenty years after the invading Sainnites won the Battle of Lilterwess, the struggle for the world of Shaftal is far from finished in Marks's stirring, intricately detailed sequel to *Fire Logic*.... Full of love and humor as well as war and intrigue, this well-crafted epic fantasy will delight existing fans as surely as it will win new ones."
— *Publishers Weekly*

"Rich and affecting.... A thought-provoking and sometimes heartbreaking political novel."
— *BookPage*

"*Earth Logic* is not a book of large battles and heart-stopping chases; rather, it's more gradual and contemplative and inexorable, like the earth bloods who people it. It's a novel of the everyday folk who are often ignored in fantasy novels, the farmers and cooks and healers. In this novel, the everyday lives side by side with the extraordinary, and sometimes within it; Karis herself embodies the power of ordinary, mundane methods to change the world."
— *SF Revu*

"It is an ambitious thing to do, in this time of enemies and hatreds, to suggest that a conflict can be resolved by peaceable means. Laurie Marks believes that it can be done, and she relies relatively little on magic to make it work."
— Cheryl Morgan, *Emerald City*

"*Earth Logic* is intelligent, splendidly visualized, and beautifully written. Laurie Marks's use of language is really tremendous." — Paula Volsky

"A dense and layered book filled with complex people facing impossible choices. Crammed with unconventional families, conflicted soldiers, amnesiac storytellers, and practical gods, the story also finds time for magical myths of origin and moments of warm, quiet humor. Against a bitter backdrop of war and winter, Marks offers hope in the form of various triumphs: of fellowship over chaos, the future over the past, and love over death." — Sharon Shinn

"A powerful and hopeful story where the peacemakers are as heroic as the warriors; where there is magic in good food and flower bulbs; and where the most powerful weapon of all is a printing press." — Naomi Kritzer

Water Logic

★ "How gifts from the past, often unknown or unacknowledged, bless future generations; how things that look like disasters or mistakes may be parts of a much bigger pattern that produces greater, farther-reaching good results—such is the theme of Marks' sweeping fantasy, which reaches its third volume with this successor to *Fire Logic* and *Earth Logic*."
— *Booklist* (Starred Review)

"The third installment, after *Fire Logic* and *Earth Logic*, in Marks's "Elemental Logic" series, explores the relationship of water, an element that travels through space and time, to those people who share its qualities or who oppose its power. Finely drawn characters and a lack of bias toward sexual orientation make this a thoughtful, challenging read that belongs in most adult fantasy collections."
— *Library Journal*

"Frankly, it's mind-bending stuff, and refreshing.... I haven't read the previous two Logic books by Marks so this was like a flashback to my childhood. Interestingly, while there was some character history that I missed, from what I've seen of Marks' writing style, I didn't necessarily miss much explanation anyways. The world is presented as-is, and of course all the people in it know what is going on and why. I found the book quite intriguing, since Marks does have some unusual magic going on, and there's certainly no overkill in the infodump department."
— James Schellenberg, *The Cultural Gutter*

"This is a genuinely original and subversive work of fantasy literature. It's the real thing: capable of changing the world, or at least the way you see it. . . . there's the depth and mythic sweep of Ursula K. Le Guin's Earthsea novels, with a seasoned, mature sense of a world where adults make hard choices and live with them.

"Marks's characters are real people who breathe and sleep and sweat and love; the food has flavor and the landscape can break your heart. You don't find this often in any contemporary fiction, much less in fantasy: a world you can plunge yourself into utterly and live in with great delight, while the pages turn, and dream of after."
— Ellen Kushner

"Picking up the threads left loose at the end of *Earth Logic*, Marks's third Elemental Logic tale weaves three story lines through her tapestry of a war-torn world whose elemental forces are dangerously out of balance. . . . Marks plays the fantasy of her unfolding epic more subtly here than in previous volumes, and the resulting depiction of intransigent cultures in conflict, rich with insight into human nature and motives, will resonate for modern readers."
— *Publishers Weekly*

Air Logic

Elemental Logic: Book Four

LAURIE J. MARKS

Small Beer Press
Easthampton, MA

This is a work of fiction. All characters and events portrayed
in this book are either fictitious or used fictitiously.

Small Beer Press
150 Pleasant Street #306
Easthampton, MA 01027
smallbeerpress.com
weightlessbooks.com
info@smallbeerpress.com

Distributed to the trade by Consortium.

Library of Congress Cataloging-in-Publication Data

Names: Marks, Laurie J., author.
Title: Air logic / Laurie J. Marks.
Description: Easthampton, MA : Small Beer Press, [2019] | Series: Elemental logic ; book 4
Identifiers: LCCN 2019006516 (print) | LCCN 2019008423 (ebook) | ISBN 9781618731616 | ISBN 9781618731609 (alk. paper)
Subjects: | GSAFD: Fantasy fiction.
Classification: LCC PS3613.A756 (ebook) | LCC PS3613.A756 A37 2019 (print) | DDC 813/.6--dc23
LC record available at https://lccn.loc.gov/2019006516

First printing 1 2 3 4 5 6 7 8 9 0

Printed on 50# Natures Natural 30% Recycled Paper by the Versa Press in East Peoria, IL.
Text set in Centaur MT.

For my found daughter, Anna Williams.

Song of the Four Elements

The way of earth is to make and till
Earth needs fire to enrich its soil
Earth wants air so its storehouse fills
Four elements for balance.

The way of air is to judge and prove
Air by earth can be beloved
Air needs water so it can move
Four elements for balance.

The way of fire is to see and know
Fire with earth can be renewed
Fire needs water to ease its woe
Four elements for balance.

The way of water is to change and sing
Water needs air for its lightning
Water wants fire for divining
Four elements for balance.

Four enemies, or four friends
Four elements to tear and mend
Four elements to begin and end
Four elements for balance.

Prologue

Four enemies, or four friends
Four elements to tear and mend.

The southern coast of Shaftal is a maze of peninsulas, inlets, and hidden harbors. It is the ocean that has shredded the landscape to rags, some say. But others say that the land's many fingers are stealing space from the sea. In that region, two hundred years ago, in the morning of a beautiful summer day when nearly everyone was working in the fields, a tremendous earthquake happened. There were many injuries and some deaths, when people were buried in the rubble of stone farmhouses. Tadwell G'deon happened to be in the southeast already, and people soon brought the severely injured people to him. The G'deons of Shaftal usually heal with great discrimination; but on this occasion Tadwell healed everyone who reached him alive, including farm animals. He worked day and night until he was gray with exhaustion, and still he worked, ignoring the Paladins' pleas that he lie down and rest.

An account of this earthquake can be read in any history book. But that Tadwell G'deon had caused that earthquake was known only to the border people who saw him do it: two fire bloods, Arel na'Tarwein and his kinswoman, Zanja na'Tarwein of the Ashawala'i; and several water people: Grandmother Ocean, and various members of her Essikret tribe. Tadwell had been made angry because Grandmother Ocean had meddled with the course of history, and because Zanja na'Tarwein had stolen a precious book from the library at Kisha. But once his temper cooled, he was ashamed of what he had done.

Tadwell's lover, Arel, like Zanja in her own time, was the speaker for the Ashawala'i. Arel became cold and distant, and soon left the House of Lilterwess to return to his home in the northern mountains. Summer became autumn, and then winter came, and Tadwell thought he would never see him again.

One day in spring, after mud season had passed, when the barren twigs of the trees began to be decorated by tufts of brilliant green, Tadwell worked in the kitchen garden of the House of Lilterwess, planting cabbage seedlings he had started in the solarium when snow still covered the ground. In spring, earth witches, normally stubborn and predictable, often became restless and changeable. But Tadwell continued doleful, irritable, and solitary, and even the simple pleasure of planting did not delight him. Then he looked up with surprise from the wet soil, for a familiar, long-absent person had stepped into the garden.

Tadwell and Arel stood facing each other. Then Arel squatted down and took a seedling from the basket and planted it.

They worked together for an hour or more before Tadwell finally spoke. "You seem recovered from that weakness of the lungs. I worried you would fall ill again during the bitter mountain winter."

Arel did not reply. Since he often complained of the Shaftali people's constant chatter, Tadwell remained silent for another long while. He turned to get more seedlings and found Arel gazing at him. It struck him how much Arel na'Tarwein looked like the thief, Zanja na'Tarwein, except that his warrior braids were intact and tied in an intricate knot that he had trouble doing for himself. Sometimes, though, Tadwell had seen his hair loose, kinked from the braids and hanging past his waist, his only clothing.

Tadwell sighed and looked away. He said, "The lexicon stolen by your kinswoman has been returned to the library where it belongs. I have thought for many months about what you said, that your kinswoman must have been compelled to steal the lexicon for reasons she could not say. My own behavior was far less honorable than hers, when I killed some of my own people, destroyed a portion of my own land, and lost the esteem of the one whose opinion matters most."

He returned to planting cabbage seedlings, joylessly.

Arel continued to work beside him. Only when the seedlings basket lay empty did he speak. "I have taught my people a new song."

He straightened his back and began to sing. Although Tadwell knew that Arel was a poet, he had never heard him sing. He sang in his own language, but Tadwell could understand how sweet and sorrowful the song was. When Arel finished, Tadwell rubbed his face dry on his shoulder. Arel said, "If I am very lucky, then someday Zanja na'Tarwein will hear that song, and will understand its meaning."

Time and knowledge travel forward. Zanja had traveled backwards in time and thus knew secrets normally concealed by the current of time, but she had not revealed her knowledge of the future to anyone, not even to Tadwell himself. To keep a secret from a fire blood like Arel, however, is not a simple matter of holding one's tongue. Tadwell said, "Zanja told me that she was a ghost from the future, but that is all I know. I can't guess what you're saying to me."

Arel's hands, sprinkled with grains of dirt, rested on his knees. Zanja also had possessed this physical stillness.

Arel said, "I believe that the water witch transported her against time because the witch needed a tremendous change to occur, and she knows that Zanja is a hinge of history. If Zanja is a hinge of history, she tried to steal the lexicon because it has been lost in her time and is sorely needed. So I have sent my song to my kinswoman—it will journey from one singer to the next, until, long after I have died and become dust, Zanja hears it. You can do the same thing with the lexicon, Tadwell, because you are the G'deon."

Tadwell looked at his hands, still the blunt, powerful hands of a stone mason, though he did that work only for pleasure now, or to escape the problems of Shaftal when they seemed too tangled a knot to untie. He said, "The artists and scholars already are making an accurate copy of the book, which will take a few years. When that work is complete, I intend to secure the original book against harm and leave it for her in an obscure place. I must trust that fire logic will reveal its hiding place to her."

Arel turned his head, and his sharp features were softened by a smile. "She will know someone who lives at High Meadow Farm in Basdown. She told me this."

"Will you travel to Basdown with me, when the book has been copied, and help me to hide it for her to find?"

"Years from now, when the copying of the books is complete? Yes, I will."

Arel offered his hand, and Tadwell clasped it, and they rose up together.

Part One: Earth

The way of earth is to make and till
Earth needs fire to enrich its soil
Earth wants air so its storehouse fills
Four elements for balance.

Chapter 1

"I want to stay up all night," Leeba said as she walked with her father, J'han Healer, to the great room.

"Tonight is the shortest night," he said. "Between sunset and sunrise are just a couple of hours of darkness. Even the sun is exhausted from lack of sleep."

"I *know.*" At nearly age seven, Leeba knew everything worth knowing, but her parents had entered into a conspiracy to exasperate her with needless instruction. Today the streets of Watfield were filled with rare pleasures—there was music, and puppets, and people on stilts, and games, and prizes, and sweets. J'han had said he would take her, but—he always said "but"—first they must play the mouse game.

"I want to stay up all night," she said again. She wanted to see the sun set, and stay awake until it rose again. Things happened between sunset and sunrise—she was quite sure of this—things wonderful and terrible, things always kept secret.

"I'll make a bargain with you," said J'han.

He was always making bargains with her. But those bargains were never fair, because he always made her do something she hated before he let her have what she wanted. "What?" she said sullenly.

He glanced down at her with mock concern, and she knew she was in trouble. "Oh, Leeba, are you feeling poorly? Are you having a bout of grouchiness?"

J'han would insist that the cure for grouchiness was solitude. Leeba might declare a hundred times that she wasn't grouchy, but her father wouldn't believe her unless she didn't act grouchy. So she smiled at him, smiled so big her mouth practically reached her ears. "I'm not grouchy!" she said, which was very hard to say when she was grinning like a clown she had seen once—only *his* grin had been painted on his face.

He laughed. "Oh, you're not grouchy! Well then, this is the bargain—you can stay up all night, but you must take a nap this afternoon. Think about your answer while we play the mouse game."

They stepped into the great room. That room looked different every time Leeba saw it, but it was always big. Today the walls, which in winter had been shiny with ice even when a fire burned in the fireplace, were hung with swags of greenery and flowers. Yesterday the room had been noisy with hammering, but today the musicians' platform was finished, and Karis was lying flat on the yellow wood, peering across its surface, holding a plane in her hand. Scattered over the platform were dozens of wooden ringlets: the lumber was growing curly hair. Leeba ran over to collect some of the curls. She tried to straighten one, and it broke. Why could wood go from straight to curly, but not from curly to straight?

Over by the far wall, Bran and Maxew were talking, and both of them were invisible. Leeba saw them, but no one else could see them—she could tell. She didn't like Bran. Every time he came into the bedroom to clean it, he hid her lizard, and she had to look for it for hours. Sometimes she thought it was gone forever, and she cried. J'han had asked Bran to leave Leeba's toys where they were, and Bran said he was just putting things away. But the worst thing he did was he made J'han believe that he wasn't hiding Leeba's lizard on purpose. Now, every morning, Leeba took her rabbit and her lizard to the air children's room, because that was the only room that she knew Bran never went into, and every night she took them back to her bed again.

She hoped that Bran wouldn't play the mouse game today. But if he did play it, maybe she could punch him in the face and make his nose bleed.

Karis swiped the plane across the wood, and a curl spun out, tight as a scroll. Then she heaved herself up to her knees and hugged Leeba. Her shirt was speckled with sawdust and smelled like a carpenter's shop. "Leeba bird, how tall you've grown! This morning you scarcely came to my waist, and now you reach my shoulder!"

Leeba began to laugh so hard she could scarcely talk. "You're on your—on your—knees!"

"Oh! Well, I think I'll stay on my knees. I'm so tired of being tall."

She was happy today, Leeba thought. She was not happy very often any more. None of her parents were—not even Medric. "J'han is taking me out to see the holiday."

"Then why are you still indoors?"

"He says we have to play the mouse game."

Now Karis didn't look as happy, because she didn't like the mouse game, and refused to play it with them. She wouldn't even play the parent who only had to say, "Leeba, come to me right away!"

"Leeba, come to me right now!" said Kamren, who was a Paladin like Emil. That was strange—Kamren wasn't one of her parents—but Leeba ran to him as fast as she could, and hid behind him. He held his hand open at his side—he *did* know how to play the game.

She couldn't see—she wasn't supposed to even peek out. But she knew it was Medric who said in a fake mean voice, "Give me that little girl!"

"I will not," Kamren said, "for I am an avowed Paladin and will spill my life's blood in her defense. For she—"

Leeba noticed that his fingers were outspread, like the legs of the spider. She made her muscles ready, like Zanja had taught her. She also must imagine what she wanted, to escape out the door, and hold it in her mind like a picture.

"—is precious to Shaftal, as are all children, who—"

He closed his fingers into a fist, and Leeba ran.

She heard Zanja shouting: "Run, mouse, run! Run! Run!"

She heard a sharp sound of weapons clashing together, and it scared her, even though it was just pretending.

"Ow!"

"Hey!"

"Help!"

Everyone except Karis was pretending to fight.

Never yell or scream, Leeba reminded herself. She ran, folded over with her arms tucked in, dodging this way and that, like a mouse. People tried to grab her. She didn't know who was supposed to be a friend or an enemy, so she avoided everyone. A Paladin ran at her, and she dodged, and the woman fell down.

There were people crowded around the doorway. She heard Zanja, shouting, though it sounded like she was laughing too. This was a time for Leeba to slow down, then smash through with all her might. Leeba bent herself over and aimed between the legs of the people who blocked the doorway. She banged her shoulder hard into someone and heard a shriek. People grabbed at her shirt, but she yanked loose. She was through the door. She ran down the crooked hall, and now she was supposed to yell: "Help, Paladins! Help!"

Zanja was right: yelling for help did make her feel more scared.

Everyone in the great room was clapping, cheering, and laughing. "Little Hurricane, come back!" Leeba went back, and the Paladins were sheathing their weapons, and Emil, Zanja, Medric, and J'han crowded around her and told her how well she had done.

Zanja said, "Remember to keep as low as you can. What do you do if someone gets hold of you?"

"Fight!" Leeba cried. It had been scary, but fun-scary, and she was still excited.

Karis picked her up. Leeba was big now, but Karis was very strong. She hugged her. "Leeba bird, go have a holiday with J'han."

"Karis, come with us! You can have a holiday too!"

Karis had become the G'deon, which was supposed to be a good thing. But bad people were trying to kill her. She could only go outside if a lot of Paladins surrounded her, to protect her. Karis said, "I'll have a holiday when we catch the bad air witch."

She wasn't happy anymore.

On the Festival of Short Night, the people of Watfield strung the trees with little lanterns and lit a bonfire in every square. In the house Karis called Travesty because so much was wrong with it, people crowded in to offer their good wishes. In the sweltering great room, Zanja na'Tarwein and Emil Paladin danced, clasping each other by the waists, twirling madly, so the still air became a wind. Later, they leaned together, panting with laughter, sharing a cup of cider.

"That is an extraordinary sight," gasped Emil. "Is Gilly trying to teach Clement to dance?"

"Or is it the other way around?"

"The incompetent teaching the ignorant!"

"But which is which?"

"I believe you have drunk enough cider." Emil took the cup and drained it dry.

The gray-dressed general and her secretary once again attempted a simple figure, but even though both were gazing intently at their feet, they managed to entangle them. Clement staggered; Gilly fell to one knee, and Seth, who seemed to be instructing them, laughed until she herself nearly fell over.

Zanja felt the friendly pressure of Emil's shoulder ease away. She said, "If you dance with Clement, it will be an act of charity. But dancing should never be a chore."

"No sacrifice is too great for Shaftal," said Emil, grinning like a boy.

"Wait—your hair is half out of its tail!"

"How correct you are, as always." He began picking at the knots in the leather ties that held his iron-gray hair.

She pushed his hands away and undid the ties, saying, "Whose knots are these? Not yours—Medric's? Don't soldiers learn how to make a knot square?"

Emil laughed. No one could teach Medric anything—no one but Medric.

She combed his hair back with her fingers and tied it properly. He bowed mockingly to her, then walked to Clement and bowed to her with apparent sincerity. The huge room was so noisy with music and laughter that Zanja couldn't hear what he said. Clement laughed and mimicked raising a cup of tea to her lips. *But in Shaftal, reinforcements always bring tea.*

The fiddlers bowed and leapt. The drummers spun their drumsticks casually, as though drumming were no work at all. The whistlers stamped the rhythm as they played. J'han thudded past with a giggling Leeba standing on his feet. Two Paladins glided in and away: coatless, light footed, serious, each with his hair secured in a topknot by a wooden pen.

All this music, dancing, fellowship, and affection made the room too hot, too crowded, too noisy to endure. Zanja forced her way to the door and down the long hall to the kitchen, where she handed the cider cup to the volunteers who had been washing dishes for hours already. They didn't seem to appreciate the effort it had taken for her to bring the cup to them.

The hall leading to the parlor where Karis received visitors was crammed with people. Zanja spotted two babies, asleep in the arms of parents or strangers—for the Shaftali passed babies about quite casually—waiting to be held by the G'deon. Even in Meartown, when Karis had been believed to be an ordinary earth witch, they had brought babies to her on holidays. In the settlements of the border people, in the south, at the coast, and in every town she had ever visited, Karis had held the babies. Clement's baby, Gabian, probably thought Karis was one of his mothers, he spent so much time in her arms.

Norina Truthken was somewhere in that hall, keeping watch on the crowd. Zanja let her gaze unfocus and then she spotted her, for she could contradict some aspects of air logic with her own logic, if she didn't try too hard. Norina was alone, and must have sent her students to bed. She gave Zanja a sharp glance, and Zanja squeezed through the crowd to join her.

Norina said, "You must not visit the border tribes to bring them into the Council of Shaftal until we know that Karis is safe."

They had argued about this issue that morning in the kitchen, until Zanja walked away in frustration. But Norina could leave nothing unfinished. Zanja said, "You don't know how to enjoy a party, do you?"

"I danced with my husband."

"Good for you. You can cross *common decency* from your list of things to do."

"And I see that you're drunk."

"I believe I am."

Like Norina, Zanja leaned against the wall. "How pleasant that I don't resent you, Madam Truthken. I should drink too much every day."

"Drunk or sober, you still resent me."

They stood in silence for a while. Having been forced to live together, they had learned how to cooperate with each other. Fortunately, they did not have to like each other.

Norina said, "I have been wondering: What if the night of the assassins was a distraction?"

More than three months had passed since Zanja, with blood drying to a stiff crust on her bare skin, and Emil, barefoot and in his nightshirt, had stalked the invaders through the unlit maze of Travesty's hallways. Eleven people had been killed that night: Paladins, librarians, clerks, and nearly all the assassins.

"What would they have been distracting us from?" Zanja asked.

"If we were successfully distracted, how could we know?"

Zanja said, "That night haunts us like an illness that has no cure. Can't we enjoy one worry-free day?"

"Perhaps *you* can." Not once had Norina taken her attention from the slow-moving line of visitors.

Zanja sighed, and wrestled her intoxicated mind into something that resembled attentiveness. "So you're speculating that the assassins gave up their lives just to distract us? They seemed sincere to me!"

"Oh, they were sincere. But they were in thrall to the rogue air witch, whose intentions they couldn't have known."

"I'll find Medric and ask him what he thinks."

Zanja walked away. When she glanced back, Norina had become invisible again.

The ill-planned building had one unlikely, eccentric tower, reached by a staircase that for most people was impossible to find.

Zanja found it, and in pitch darkness felt her way up the narrow, twisting stairway. Like everything in that house, the steps were wrong: each one at a different height, made of stone so soft it wore away under her feet and every step was slippery with powdered stone. She counted the steps, yet cracked her head on the trap door without realizing she had reached the top.

"Who's that cursing beneath my floor?" called Medric. He yanked open the trap, and his spectacles winked with the faint light of his candle as he peered down at her.

"How can the number of steps keep changing?" she asked.

"It's not even possible," Medric said. "Oh, it's you, who steals my husband, wears him out with frivolity . . ."

Zanja climbed the last steps, rubbing her bruised head. "If frivolity tires Emil, then surely *you're* the culprit."

"Oh!" cried Medric. "Oh! Oh!" He staggered away, comically clutching his chest, and collapsed into the small room's only piece of furniture, an armchair with an attached candle stand from which poured a torrent of hardened wax. The candle that perched there atop the remains of its predecessors jiggled dangerously. Its feeble, flickering light fell upon books stacked carefully upon the floor, a tangle of cobwebs sagging from the ceiling, and a dozen unwashed windows, most of which stood open. The housekeeper, Bran, apparently had been unable to find this dirty den, and it was just as well, since his thoroughness was matched by an equally great thoughtlessness.

Zanja spotted a glimmer of gilding in the shadows. "You've been stealing my glyph cards again."

"Borrowing," he said.

She claimed the card, which lay atop the tower of books.

Emil had gathered artists to copy the thousand illustrations in the lexicon from the past: one copy for Zanja, to replace the deck of glyph cards that she had lost at sea, and a second copy for the scholars to study. Every few days, the artists gave her a card.

She squatted on the dusty floor and tilted the new card toward the candle flame. It depicted a ship, strangely shaped and oddly rigged, which flew high above a distant landscape of forest, fields, and winding river, all partly obscured by clouds. "I've only glanced at this one in the book. Does it make sense to you?"

This was how they always talked to each other, asking and answering questions, with a glyph card between them like an empty tray they endeavored to fill with understanding.

The seer said, "Arrogant indeed is the ship that sneers at its river!"

"Oh, do you mean that this illustration is about air logic? Then I don't care what it means." Music and laughter from the square below seemed far away, muted, irrelevant.

Medric said, "You're cranky. I suppose you've been talking to Norina. Why don't you avoid her like I do?"

"Because I can only avoid her by avoiding everyone, like you do. She's wondering if the night of the assassins could have been a distraction."

"She suspects the rogue air witch sacrificed five followers as a decoy? Well, our Truthken may be cold as fish and a hundred times more spiny, with a thorn bush for a heart and a dagger for a brain, but she knows her own kind." Medric rested his chin on his hand and blinked at her like a cat.

Zanja examined the mystifying Ship of Air, the ship so arrogant that it sneered at the river. "*Which* air witch is arrogant? The one who's somewhat domesticated and obsessively devoted to the law, or the one who has gone rogue and is devoted to his or her own laws?"

"All air witches are arrogant. They all love power. They all die confident that they have never been wrong. Before Mackapee, they tended to form armies of devoted followers and used those armies to destroy each other. The Sainnites weren't the first to cause bloodshed and chaos throughout Shaftal! But some air witches had the wit to fear the G'deons, realizing that their power would increase with each generation, and so decided to regulate themselves before a person of more power and less subtlety hunted down and exterminated the air children of Shaftal."

"Surely they knew that an earth witch would never kill a child!"

"But air children are not *children*."

"True enough," said Zanja. Six young air witches had come to Travesty that winter to ask Norina to be their teacher, but to call them *children* seemed ludicrous.

"And ten years after the Order of Truthkens was formed, all the air witches who refused to join had been killed, and the air witches were, as you said, somewhat domesticated."

Medric's candle began to flutter violently, and Zanja stood up to shut a window. "Your point is that they regulate themselves. But the Order of Truthkens consists of one Truthken and six apprentices. *They* can't destroy this rogue."

Medric gazed at her gloomily.

Zanja said, "We can neither attack nor defend ourselves against the air witch. So what *can* we do?"

He sat upright. "Now that's the proper way to ask questions of a seer! We cannot attack, and we cannot defend. Therefore, we will . . . do something else entirely. What, though?" He pushed his spectacles up on the bridge of his nose, peered through them at Zanja, then took them off and put on the other pair, which had been lying atop an open book. "Well, they respect the Power of Shaftal. Perhaps we should turn Karis loose and let her do whatever she does. Maybe we're helping the rogue air witch by trying to protect her from him. Or her." Medric nodded several times, each time more vehemently. Then he began shaking his head, just as vigorously.

"Well, thank you for clarifying matters," said Zanja.

"It seems like I should be more useful than I am, doesn't it?"

He hardly ever did anything useful, but more than once Zanja had trusted him with her life. So she waited for him to say something else.

He said, "I suppose you hoped for a prediction? Very well, I predict that you will never wish you had danced less with Emil."

She laughed. But he seemed serious. She said, "I'll go dance with him right now. Thank you, master seer."

"Don't call me that," he muttered. He switched spectacles and returned to reading his book.

Chapter 2

Grandmother Ocean had arrived at the day of her death. Although to her people it might seem as if she had been alive for twenty generations, she had lived no longer than anyone else, but had lived in bits and pieces, scattered between her birth in one year and her death some four hundred years later. She had never been able to swim beyond the summer of the year known by the Shaftali as *Karis 1*, and so she had long known that it was the year that her river of time would run dry. Now she had discovered the exact day.

She sat on the wet sand and ate raw fish that she cut from the bone in slices so thin that the sunlight shone through them. On this hot, clear day, the harbor's water lay still, and the children played as they had done for centuries, diving from their houseboats into the water and endeavoring to drown each other. One of those children was a water witch like her, like several others she had accidentally encountered over the years. Possibly, she had already met this child as an adult, or possibly not. Perhaps this one knew—or would know—what Ocean had done so that her people could survive in their hidden harbor.

Some months ago, she had collected seaweed floats out in the open sea, swimming with the otters whose sinuous agility mocked her splashing. She had known by then that her great endeavor would succeed, and had, in fact, succeeded, 200 years earlier, when Tadwell changed the river's flow. She gave two of the floats to a carpenter, to dry and preserve for her. Now the carpenter approached her across the beach with one of the dried floats in each hand. He had drilled a tiny hole in each of them.

Ocean's first 200 years had been eventful enough. Her second 200 years had not occurred as she remembered them. She had used up the past and had reached the end of her future. She would fill the vessels and then would devote the rest of her life to decorating them. It seemed a restful and worthwhile task.

The current Speaker of the Essikret people was named Dancing-Silver-Light, although he allowed the outsiders whose languages he spoke to call him Silver. Dancing-Silver-Light spoke with Ocean in the evening, and she asked him to send two people in boats inland on the next rising tide, to meet two visitors at the westernmost end of the salt marsh, and to bring them to her when the tide turned. "Those visitors are messengers from the G'deon," she said. "I will give them these vessels for her."

Dancing-Silver-Light said, "Less than a season ago, the G'deon swore to kill you if you interfered with her again. And now she is sending you messengers?" He laughed heartily.

Grandmother Ocean laughed with him. Not often had she been able to share such a rare and subtle joke.

Chapter 3

There are plenty of ravens in the world, thought Chaen, but only a few are enchanted. The bird that had caught her attention as it soared past, a black silhouette against the burnished sky, had already disappeared. It was not hunting for her.

Crushed shells snapped like old bones underfoot as Chaen cleaned the brush and sealed the cork of the mineral spirits bottle with wax. She had finished painting the alehouse sign, which lay on a board across two empty kegs, the wet varnish already beginning to dry in the heat. The stone walls of this sheltered yard muted the noisy city's racket and would protect the sign from dust, flower petals, and other debris when the sea breeze washed through the streets and alleys. Before sunset, it would be dry.

Now what should she do? Ten evenings in a row she had waited for Jareth at the tide clock. She had never liked him much, but his failure to make an appearance was more irritating than his presence would have been. Was he ill? Captured? Dead?

When the members of Death-and-Life Company attacked the false G'deon in her bed, none of them had believed they could fail. They hadn't considered what it would be like for her to be a fugitive, skating across the surface of other people's lives, aimless and disconnected, denied even the relief of knowing exactly when the solitude could end. From winter's end, through spring, and well into summer, Chaen had endured that strange exile. She could manage the loneliness; but without purpose or people, she had begun to feel as if she didn't exist. Little though she liked Jareth, at least she could have talked frankly with him.

She opened the back door of the alehouse and stepped into the kitchen, where the cook, dozing in a wooden chair tilted back to rest precariously against the wall, did not notice when she took a slice of bread, a piece of cheese, and a scoop of butter. She brought this simple meal into the public room. The ships had departed after many lingering days in port waiting for the weather to clear. The usually crowded and noisy room lay empty, except for the publican and the old man who always sat in the corner, and his companion.

Rain had kept Chaen from finishing the sign on time, but the publican blamed her because he believed everyone was trying to cheat him. As he approached the table, Chaen said before he could speak, "The sign is finished, and I'll hang it up before dark."

"Hmph. You'll be gone tomorrow, then."

At least he wasn't evicting her tonight. She had no money for lodging, and the city was home to many people she would rather not encounter in the dark.

Chaen sipped a cup of spring water, which was delivered in kegs, like ale, because well water in Hanishport was too salty to drink. The city sounds wandered in through the propped-open windows: peaceful sounds of children shouting in play, carts rattling past, laundry flapping on lines stretched across the street, and hammers ringing at the shipyard forge.

The old man in the corner laughed out loud. His companion, a silhouette against the glare of the window, started to leave, but paused at Chaen's table.

It was a border woman, far from home no matter which border she had come from. Her coloring was alien—raven-black hair, skin the color of wet soil, eyes that were black and lightless even with the sun shining on her face through the window. But it was her face, all hard edges and sharp shadows like a broken piece of granite, that made Chaen's fingers itch for her pencil and sketchbook.

The border woman said, "Shall I cast cards for you?"

In her hands were an enormous number of cards—glyph cards, Chaen assumed. Apparently the confidence artists had already begun to arrive for the Fair. "I have no money."

"I did not ask for money." The woman put her cards on the table, sat down, and without looking at her hands drew out a card and lay it before Chaen. "This card reveals your essence."

Glyph cards usually were cheap and crude, but this card was a piece of art. It depicted a woman standing alone in a stone-strewn landscape. She gazed at nothing, for there was nothing to see—just emptiness, and a swirl of clouds, pushed by the same wind that had torn loose the cloth that wrapped her body, and that made her hair flow across her face like water, so she seemed to be drowning. The illustration's intricate borders were composed of tiny, detailed drawings that depicted her life: a peculiar little house, a tangled woodland, a hilly landscape, a harbor filled with oddly rigged ships, an island in the ocean, a rugged coastline, a battlefield cluttered with corpses. That life caged her in the wasteland.

"What glyph card is this?" Chaen asked.

"The Wilderness."

The name was wrong. It should be called Waiting for a Dead Man. "I have never seen this card."

"It is unique."

"You invented it?"

"I stole it."

"If the entire deck is like this, I don't blame you for stealing them."

"Will you ask a question?"

"Do you think you can tell me what to do?"

Perhaps the woman could not recognize sarcasm, for she began casting cards onto the tabletop. She cast a dozen cards, each one intricate, beautiful, and unrecognizable. Chaen scarcely glimpsed each image before it was covered by the next. Then, as swiftly as the woman had cast the cards, she gathered them up, tied the pile with a leather cord, and tucked it in her satchel. "Leave the city right away," she said.

"What?"

"That is your answer."

The border woman rose and walked away. The door let her out into a blaze of sunshine. She passed in front of the windows, and was gone.

What a strange, presumptuous woman.

Chaen had never been interested in the arcane art of glyph interpretation, but she doubted that a dozen cards were necessary to generate that simplistic advice about Chaen's difficult situation. Leave Hanishport right away? "I'm not going anywhere," she muttered.

She cleared her dishes and went out into the glare of sunlight. The bright rhythm of a metalsmith's hammer rang like a bell in the shipyard, and the sweet, rotten, salty scent of low tide rode the back of the sea breeze that had just started to freshen. She headed for a tailor's shop down the street, where the shop sign was so faded that scarcely a ghost of the original paint remained.

Chapter 4

During the years Garland had wandered Shaftal, he had done all sorts of work on the land, although it was a rare day that he didn't wind up in a kitchen eventually. He had herded sheep and butchered pigs in the south; he had cut hay, cleaned milking barns, and picked fruit in the east; he had plowed, seeded, and harvested fields in the north; he had cut logging roads and hauled iron ore in the west; and he had shoveled snow or hoed weeds everywhere. Now, whenever he set out to prepare a meal, he remembered that the raw ingredients in his kitchen had come there due to the labor of many others. He had become the cook for the government of Shaftal, and each councilor from every region, and each member of every order, had been raised, fed, educated, and supported by a family, which in turn was supported by a network of families, not one of which could survive without the land. But not until Garland came to Hanishport did he realize that the people of Shaftal also relied on people in far distant lands; not for food, metal, or timber but for the raw material of imagination. The ships that from a distance seemed as calm and elegant as seabirds, and that up close were gigantic cradles crammed with frantically working sailors, came into the port loaded with cargo that spawned inventiveness: gorgeous fabrics, exotic woods, fruits that tasted like sunlight, and spices that by their scent alone caused Garland to dream of dishes no one had ever cooked before.

The dirt under their feet was different, too, Garland thought wryly as he swept the vacant house again. He was the only one to come and go through those doors, and as soon as he stepped in, he took off his shoes. Yet the floors were gritty with sand, and he could sweep until his arms fell off and the floor would never come close to being clean. When he had swept as much as he could endure, he put on a hat, for the sun was hot and blindingly bright, and went out to hoe weeds, as he had done for a short while every day ever since he decided to move into the derelict house, because he could not claim it unless he made improvements and repairs. In case his work with the weeds went unnoticed, he also had painted the front door a deep, greenish blue that matched the water of the bay that lay immediately on the other side of the little-used road.

At a sound like the creaking of a gate in the wind, Garland looked up from his unpleasant labor. A raven was walking along the eaves of the house. "Are you hungry or thirsty?" Garland asked it, as he would ask any visitor. The bird soared to the ground and walked ahead of Garland to the back door, where it waited patiently while Garland brought out a pan of spring water and some food. The bird was a speechless guest, for Karis's ravens had lost the ability to talk, and it carried no written message either, because Garland couldn't read. Its presence was the message: Karis and the government of Shaftal would arrive tomorrow. "I'm so glad they're almost here," he told the raven. "Cooking only for myself seems pointless."

Garland's work with the hoe had cleared the old wagon path to the side-door for water deliveries, and the water seller was there at the crack of dawn, delivering a barrel to keep the water in. As she waited for the kitchen barrel to fill with water from her wagon, she chatted with Garland about the weather and about the latest ships to arrive at or depart from Hanishport—two topics that must be discussed, Garland had learned, in every single conversation—then she brought up the subject of the Hanishport Fair, which would begin in a few days. She said that she could suggest where his family might find the best company of players, the best music, the best ale and wine. Garland merely thanked her, and she went away with her curiosity unsatisfied.

Then came a fishmonger with two crates of fish that he said had been alive and swimming at sunrise, and once again Garland had to discuss the weather and the ships while the fish were being piled onto his work table, the only piece of furniture in the entire house. "That's an awful lot of fish for one person," the fishmonger observed. Garland agreed that it was a lot of fish, and the fishmonger left without learning anything he could gossip about.

The grocer brought an entire wagonload of supplies, and the greengrocer was immediately behind him with baskets of fruits and vegetables. At least Garland only had to discuss the ships and weather once, but the two of them worked on him in concert, and he was hard put to be cordial while refusing to answer any questions. The wood seller came next, and last was a pretty young woman with a handcart full of bread, who tried flirting with him. Maybe someday he could have a lover, Garland thought regretfully, as the woman, baffled and probably offended, pushed her handcart home to the bakery.

Finally, he could cook.

He had brought a few things with him—kitchen knives, a box of spices, and a long-handled wooden spoon that he was fond of. He had bought the spoon on his first shopping trip with Karis, a sturdy spoon that fit his hand just right, was flat at the tip so it could scrape a pot bottom, and had no cracks or grooves that food could collect in. As he picked up his beloved spoon, he felt a puzzling sensation. The spoon bothered him. Something about it just wasn't right. This was not the first time he had been troubled about the spoon. Like all the other times, he examined it carefully. There was nothing wrong with it at all. So he forgot about it, and started making a stock from the vegetable trimmings and fish heads.

He was out in the yard hoeing again when the raven on the roof uttered a cry, and he went out to the front gate to watch the first wagon in the distance, making the turn from Marketway onto Harborway. Most of the travelers were afoot, walking beside the wagons, and could mainly be identified by their clothing—black-dressed Paladins, gray-dressed soldiers, and councilors in ordinary longshirts and breeches of various colors and patterns. At a discreet distance behind the wagons, a few brightly dressed, curious Hanishporters were following. Of course, in Watfield soldiers could be seen working with Shaftali people everywhere, even in Garland's own kitchen, learning trades, learning the language, and learning how to be Shaftali. But in Hanishport, as in the rest of Shaftal, Sainnite soldiers remained in their garrisons—weaponless, and with the gates ajar—dependent on the Shaftali people for their survival. Thus, the people of Hanishport had never seen Paladins and soldiers together before today.

Norina Truthken was the first to reach the gate, with the dogs panting at her heels. She took Garland's hand in hers, and he struggled not to yank away. "Garland, how are you?" she asked, with utter indifference.

"I'm well, Madam Truthken. But I've been awfully lonely. How I managed all those years without friends, I can't imagine."

"What have you been doing?"

She didn't care about that answer either. But Emil, who was within hearing, did care, so Garland gave a thorough report, as if he were a soldier again—horrible thought! When he fell silent, she asked, "Anything else?"

"I've been hoeing, sweeping, painting, and avoiding answering questions. I can't think of anything else."

She nodded and walked past him, into the house. Emil patted Garland's shoulder and followed her. Garland supposed he should stay out of the way while they inspected the quarters, so he got into the front wagon, where Gilly sat, with General Clement's son, Gabian, in a basket beside him. Different though the two men were, they had become friends because of their shared peculiarity: Gilly a Shaftali who lived as a Sainnite, and Garland a Sainnite who lived as a Shaftali. Garland asked, "Has something happened? Why is the Truthken treating me like an enemy?"

"Doesn't she always treat everyone that way?" Gilly grinned, which made his ugly face even uglier.

"I would rather she ignored me like she usually does."

"Well, nothing new has happened. I assume that Madam Truthken wanted to make sure that the other air witch didn't discover you were alone out here and use air magic to turn you into an assassin."

"Me?"

"Yow!" cried the baby. Garland picked him up and tickled him gently, and the baby shrieked happily, showing off a tiny new tooth.

"Tell the general that I'll have fresh milk here at the house every day. The dairy refuses to deliver to the garrison."

"Of course not," Gilly said dryly.

"And you'll come over for dinner whenever you get tired of soldier's fare?"

"I'll be here every day, then. Maybe I'll just move in, eh?"

"No! I'm already fitting twenty people into six bedrooms, and one of those bedrooms is supposed to be a storeroom! And only one outhouse!"

"One outhouse? You'll have a lot of people pissing into the ocean every morning! Oh, but that's not allowed."

"It's not? How do you know?"

"I used to beg for a living on these very streets. Thus I know for certain that Hanishporters will allow a crippled child to starve in the street. It's no surprise they won't help the smoke users of Lalali."

"Unload!" Emil called from the open front door, and Garland made haste to the stoop, so he could tell people where to put their belongings. "I like the location," Emil said to him. "Close to the garrison, easy to defend. Norina wishes it was stone rather than wood."

"This is the only unoccupied building in Hanishport, stone or wood."

"We'll put a bucket of water in every room, and forbid candles."

"I suppose you noticed that there's no furniture. I have a plan, but it needs to be written down."

"I'll gladly be your secretary. I just want a word with Clement before she leaves."

Emil trotted out to General Clement, who was indistinguishable from any other dusty and sweaty soldier, except for her insignia, just as Emil looked like any other Paladin except that he wore three earrings. They spoke briefly, clasped hands, and parted, Clement calling her soldiers into order for a march to the garrison, where there was certain to be a startled scramble when the soldiers realized who she was.

Emil, who like all Paladins was never without a pen, took the packet of writing materials out of his waistcoat pocket and improvised a writing table on the edge of the stoop. He dribbled water from his flask onto his ink stone, mixed in a bit of ink powder using the butt of his pen, weighted the paper with pebbles to keep it from curling, and wrote Garland's list as people passed in and out the doorway, with their dusty boots only a fingers' breadth from the paper.

Garland told the travelers where to put their belongings, while also telling Emil what to write. When the wagons were empty and had been driven away to the garrison, the Paladins and councilors convened in a parlor, and Emil handed out slips of paper that directed them to shops scattered throughout the city. Norina had recruited guides from among the spectators—those who didn't leave when they realized she was a Truthken—and the travelers set forth to convince the sellers of furniture, mattresses, linens, lamps, dishes, and lumber to donate or loan items to the G'deon's temporary household.

With the house nearly empty again, Garland went into the kitchen to attend to his pots, and the four people who had not gone out on errands sat on the empty crates Garland had been using for furniture: Emil, Medric, Norina, and Norina's student, Maxew. The dogs drank water, flopped onto the cool stone floor, and fell asleep.

"Are Karis and Zanja planning to slip into the city after nightfall?" Garland asked.

Norina gestured vaguely in the direction of the city. "They're here now."

Emil had taken an orange fruit out of the bowl to examine it. "What is this? It smells wonderful."

"How could Karis and Zanja possibly go unrecognized?"

"No one is expecting them to be here."

Emil added, "Karis said that if she couldn't spend a few hours without an escort, she'd have to kill somebody."

"Better she kill someone than that someone kill her," Garland muttered.

Chapter 5

Zanja na'Tarwein stood in a black, crisp-edged shadow that draped the western side of the alley. Soon Chaen, the woman from the alehouse, crossed the narrow opening, squinting in the light that glared from the city's white sandstone walls. When Zanja had showed her the first glyph card, her attention had focused on it like a dog upon a scent, which suggested she had a fire talent. But she did not have any prescience, or else Zanja could not have evaded her by simply standing in a shadow. Nor could the raven, briefly visible as it swooped between rooftops, have followed her unnoticed during the months since the assassination attempt.

On that bitter winter's night five months ago, while Chaen and her companion, Jareth, waited outside the house called Travesty, five of their fellows, using darts and blades dipped in snake poison, had entered the building and killed everyone they encountered, most of whom had been asleep in bed. They had missed their target, Karis, by a few hands-breadths. Had Zanja not awakened and defended her, Shaftal would now lack a G'deon, and Zanja would be a widow.

Karis had not waited in this alley as she was supposed to. Zanja followed the alley, in and out of shadows that seemed like they could have been trimmed from black paper with sharp scissors. The narrow passage squeezed between walled and fenced yards. Two buildings squatted knee-to-knee like gardeners, and their bright red window frames were propped open, curtains undulating in the shadows. Some late-blooming trees reached over the fence to cast white blossoms in her hair.

For a moment, the sweet, rhythmic ringing of the smith's hammer became a piercing sound of unbearable beauty. Then a racket overpowered it: the hollow knocking of mallets, the cries of work bosses, the clatter of shod horses and ironclad cartwheels. The alley opened onto a hectic street, where brown children shrieked, freight horses groaned, shopkeepers screamed, and a din of tools scraping, cutting, sawing, and hitting came from the shipyard.

To the right, the road climbed to a peak, over which the freight wagons disappeared. To the left, the roads sloped to the harbor—an expanse of water so vast that the open ocean was just a blue haze indistinguishable from sky. Before her there rose a skeletal ship from whose timbers people dangled, pulling themselves up and down ropes like spiders. Between her and the shipyard lay a hectic, shouting, struggling traffic of empty wagons rattling past on one side, and filled wagons creeping uphill on the other, with no break on either side as far as could be seen. She stepped into the road and skipped across—pausing, leaping, pausing, and leaping again, until one final hop took her over the dung-clogged ditch on the far side.

An old man perched upon a rickety stool in a doorway applauded her performance enthusiastically. Zanja worked her way uphill, jostled by big-shouldered stevedores and repeatedly jabbed in the back by a bundle of staves carried on the shoulder of a woman behind her. She ducked into the arched opening of a cool tunnel, where it was surprisingly quiet, except for the smith's hammer, which rang now as loudly as an alarm bell. The tunnel opened into a walled yard with a row of furnaces marching down the center. There the shipyard smiths all took their ease on stools, beneath ruffling shade awnings or in shaded doorways. A couple of skinny apprentices came through the tunnel hauling a handcart and began shoveling coal into the furnaces.

Karis worked at the one active forge. She had tucked her left hand into her belt, and her foot pressed a complicated device that held the metal steady on the anvil. The anvil was too low, and the hammer too small, but Karis was accustomed to being a giant in a small and cluttered world. She lifted the hammer and smashed it down onto the hot metal with such force that fiery bits sprayed around her, and the observers had to dance back. She turned and spoke to a one-armed man, then lifted the hammer again.

Zanja found a shady place and squatted down to wait. A heavily pregnant woman offered her a cup of fruit juice and asked, "Do you know that woman?"

"Somewhat," said Zanja truthfully. The juice was interesting: bright orange, both sour and sweet.

"My friend and I have a bet." The woman stood tilted backwards to counterbalance the weight of her belly, her hands at the small of her back. She had been squinting in the bright light for so long that pale lines radiated from the corners of her eyes like white paint on her sun-brown skin. "My friend says she's the G'deon, and I say she's not."

Zanja laughed sharply.

"I laughed, too," the woman said. "*Is every woman with Juras blood the G'deon?* I said. *And for what would the G'deon be wandering into a shipyard smithy?*"

"If the G'deon did that, it would be very odd," Zanja said.

The woman walked away to tell her friend the untruth that he had lost the bet. The furnaces, their fires renewed, began to smear black smoke across the bright blue sky. The metalsmiths were finishing their noon meals, rising up, stretching stiff muscles, and putting on their leather aprons. Karis returned the borrowed hammer and seemed to be thanking the one-armed smith for letting her try his curious device.

Zanja rose up as Karis approached, each of them unsurprised to have found the other so easily. "Have you tasted this marvelous juice?" Zanja asked.

"Yes—it is wonderful. It's from a round fruit with skin like leather that's grown in a distant southern country. The price is usually too dear for ordinary people, but a ship blown off course was forced to sell its cargo cheaply because it had begun to spoil. The entire city has been drinking this juice for a week."

"You didn't find out how to grow the plant?"

Karis laughed. "I did ask, but they didn't know."

At the entrance to the dim tunnel, Karis crouched over and shuffled awkwardly, using her riot of hair like a cat uses its whiskers, to keep from cracking her head on the ceiling. "So you met Chaen. What do you think of her?" she asked. With the racket of the street entering from one end of the tunnel, and the clangor of the hammers entering from the other, her smoke-damaged voice was nearly inaudible.

"I think she is lost in the wreck of her life."

"Like you, sometimes."

"But I follow you when I'm lost. She follows a rogue air witch who could destroy Shaftal."

"Usually, *I'm* following *you*," Karis said.

"Not today."

"Not yet, anyway."

Karis had been born in Lalali, which lay only a short walk from the port city, but she had never visited Hanishport, and neither had Zanja. They wandered the city unheeded. Zanja noticed several people with skin as dark as hers, or darker. Some were border people of Shaftal, and she wanted to talk with them but couldn't risk becoming too distracted in this crowd. Some looked nothing like her, and must have been sailors from a far country. She had never been particularly interested in the world beyond Shaftal, and today her lack of interest seemed peculiar—perhaps Medric had a map among the books he had brought with him from Watfield. They heard the famous tide clock ring to mark ebb tide, and on the quay they watched a ship sail in, while people on shore scrambled to be ready to unload it. At a smaller dock, over a fire that burned in a huge kettle, a woman fried fish directly from a fishing boat. Zanja bought two fried fishes wrapped in slices of bread that also served as plates and napkins. They ate standing up, spitting bones onto the ground.

"That is how fish should taste," said Zanja, remembering the mountain trout she had sometimes caught, cooked, and eaten at a lake's edge.

Karis said, "While you were getting the food, a man offered me a job as a stevedore."

"What kind of job is that?"

"Stevedores load and unload ships."

"Did you tell the man you're afraid of water?"

"I told him I have too much work already. I was tempted to accept, though!"

They wandered from shop to shop on Merchant's Way, amazed by the variety of things that were for sale. They paused in a spice shop with floor-to-ceiling shelves filled with jars of leaves, flowers, bark, seeds, and roots. Two customers were tasting a concoction that the proprietor had just ground for them, arguing about whether it needed more of one spice or another. Another customer came in and said, "Have you heard? Some Paladins are moving into that abandoned house on Ocean Way. And people are going about begging for furniture and lamps and such, in the name of the G'deon."

Zanja and Karis left the shop hurriedly and nearly knocked over two members of the Peace Committee, who were lugging between them a huge basket filled with bed linens. The councilors directed them to a nearby seller of bedding, and soon they and other members of their household were staggering down the hill with mattresses balanced on their heads. On the road that followed the edge of the restless water, they encountered other hot and breathless people with chairs resting on their shoulders, lamps dangling from their arms, and tables balanced on their heads. One of them was Seth, who peered between the legs of a chair, laughing at the spectacle.

People of Hanishport had gathered outside a wooden derelict of a house with the ocean sighing at its doorstep, two big dogs panting in the shade of a scraggly tree, and an extremely organized man on the stoop telling people where to bring their burdens. Seth said, "What is wrong with these people? Why are they watching instead of helping?"

Zanja briefly glimpsed their new house when she dumped her awkward burden in the barren front garden. Then the spectators realized that Karis had walked past them, hidden under the mattresses, and surged forward, but the dogs, Granite and Feldspar, leapt up to block the gate. Garland abandoned his post on the stoop to hurry Karis and Zanja into a dim front hall with parlors on either side and a groaning staircase in the middle.

Karis said to Zanja, "We've moved from a house that makes no sense to a house that's falling apart." She sighed. The weight of Shaftal had settled upon her shoulders once again.

Garland was saying, "Twenty people, not counting the dogs—and Emil said the Paladins can all sleep in the other attic room, where there are bats, and it's hot as an oven. I'm sorry I couldn't find a better house."

Karis hugged him.

Embarrassed, Garland continued hurriedly, "Norina and Emil left a while ago to seek out the city elders, who can usually be found in a tea shop just off the quay. General Clement has gone with Gilly and her escort to set up headquarters in the garrison. Medric is asleep on the second floor. Norina thinks we can risk keeping the doors and windows open today, so the sea breeze will blow through the house and cool it off. Seth has taught the dogs how to guard the doors. Do you want to see your room?"

Karis said, "I had better get my toolbox. That staircase is about to collapse."

Zanja said, "I'd like to see the room. I need to be alone."

Garland showed Zanja to a small, dark, barren storeroom adjoining the kitchen, tucked under the groaning staircase. The walls were marked by pale horizontal lines where the shelves had been removed. It had one small window that didn't look like it could be opened. "It's the only room on this floor that has a door," Garland said apologetically—Karis could only sleep on the ground floor of a building. "I wore my feet out hunting for another house, but with the festival coming, the city is more crowded every day." He added, "Someone was throwing out that bit of carpet, and I thought you'd like to have it to sit on, because the floors are always gritty with sand, no matter how much I sweep them."

When he had left, Zanja shut the door, sat on the square of carpet, and laid the assassin's array of cards upon the floor.

An hour or so later, Emil opened the door. "I'm told you did manage to cast cards for her."

"Come in and look at them. There's nothing for you to sit on, though."

"I don't see how there *could* be. Will Karis even have room to lie down in this closet?"

He knelt beside her and examined the cards, picking up each one and then replacing it exactly as it had been. After a while, he said, "Perhaps this casting will settle one question: Will the glyph cards prove useful, or are they nothing more than gorgeous artifacts?"

She said, "Don't offer again to buy me a cheap deck of glyph cards instead. I would rather not grow backwards."

"May I wish you had done a simpler casting?"

"You may. But I don't think the assassin is a simple person, and she asked me a difficult question: *You think you can tell me what to do?*"

Emil laughed, and then sighed. "So this casting might be telling her what to do. Or it might be addressing her distrust. Or it may be about your own interpretive abilities."

The little room lay silent then, but the house and stairs creaked restlessly. Zanja finally said, "No—she was thinking about this card, the Wilderness, which expresses her essence. The entire array could be an elaboration on this card."

Emil picked up the card. "I wish I had more time to study! You showed Chaen this card, and she thought something about it, a question she didn't say out loud?"

"I think that's what happened. I know it was a true casting, but I don't know what question she asked."

Emil was Zanja's oldest friend. She had first met him shortly after the Fall of the House of Lilterwess, when she had still been a child traveling with her teacher. Following the annihilation of her tribe, she had served under Emil in a company of Paladin irregulars, and he had taught her how to use and interpret the glyphs of Shaftal. When their family coalesced around Karis, Zanja began to call him, in the language of her people, *brother,* as she would call any of the *katrim*. He assisted her through the periods of madness that overcame her every summer, and she knew—although no one had said so—that one reason Emil had traveled to Hanishport rather than remaining in Watfield was to help Zanja through that madness again.

Zanja gazed at him so as to rest her eyes from the difficult, beautiful glyph illustrations. But he too was a glyph—the man on the mountain, embracing the sky in his open arms, pierced to the heart by the light of the stars. Then he became a Paladin, dressed in black, three gold earrings in one ear, pen, paper, and ink in one breast pocket, and a commander's timepiece in the other. Then he was a father, cradling baby Leeba to his chest, soothing her to sleep with his watch's quiet ticking. She watched him kill one Sainnite soldier and fall in love with another, painstakingly repair a damaged book, walk down a dusty road with a heavy knapsack on his back, and stand at the head of the reconstructed government of Shaftal.

Emil said, "My sister, are you certain this casting is not about your own questions rather than hers?"

"What are you seeing?" she asked in surprise.

He touched one card after another, saying, "Loss. Death. Boundaries. Insight. Destruction. Fire."

The pattern did describe her own life, but Zanja didn't think she had made the novice mistake of casting cards for herself. "Perhaps the assassin and I have similar histories. If Willis had been commander of South Hill Company instead of you, and if he had been able to overlook my alien features and manner, I could have followed him when he formed Death-and-Life Company. I could have ended up serving under the rogue air witch. I could have been an assassin."

"Hmm."

Emil made that sound when he was following a new train of thought, and Zanja fell silent. She picked up the Wilderness card and seriously considered whether her unlikely sympathy for Chaen was a misplaced sympathy for her own past self.

The door cracked open and Medric said, "Oh, at least *you're* not working. There's far too much banging, bashing, bubbling, and brushing in this house."

He entered, and a cool, salty breeze washed in behind him. He picked up a card from the floor and stood by the window to examine it in the light. "Why is it so blurry?"

"Wrong spectacles," said Emil, without looking at him.

Medric exchanged the lenses on his face with the pair that was in his pocket. "Oh, it's the Ship of Air again."

"Give us back that card," said Emil. "I haven't seen it before today."

Emil wasn't looking at Medric. Only Zanja saw how the seer's loose, uncombed hair filled with the light of the window. He surrendered the card, which Emil put in its place on the floor. Garland came in, set a tray of tea and bread on the floor beside Emil, and left in a rush so no one would thank him. Emil poured the tea, sniffed it, then gave it to Zanja. "Smell that. It's extraordinary."

The scent of the steam rising from the teacup transported Zanja to a distant memory: a remote Paladin hostel, surrounded by Shaftal's gathering champions, her teacher taking his ease by the fireplace, as Councilor Mabin, who was now dead, left the room, and Norina, then a novice Truthken, gathered Mabin's papers. There Zanja had stood at a window and glimpsed Karis for the first time, as she was carried away in a wagon like a criminal. In Zanja's hand had been a cup of this tea.

"You may never again taste tea as fine as this," she murmured.

Medric, who could not drink tea, took Zanja's cup, sniffed it, and gave it back to her. "You're remembering something. Who said that, and when?" A historian in his own peculiar fashion, Medric always wanted to know *who* and *when*. And, although he couldn't find a clean shirt without help, he remembered the details of other people's lives more accurately and reliably than they themselves did.

Zanja said, "It was my old teacher, the Speaker of the Ashawala'i. He and I were drinking a pot of this tea, which had been made for Mabin, who had been awake all night, writing."

Emil said, "It must have been eleven days after the Fall of the House of Lilterwess, in a Paladin hostel where Shaftal's forces were gathering to fight the Sainnites. Mabin probably was writing *Warfare*."

"Such an angry book," Medric muttered. "And no wonder."

"It was a remarkable day," said Emil. "Zanja, Norina, Karis, and I—the four of us were all in the same place, each of us unaware of how important we would become to each other, each one thinking we had been doomed by the Fall of the House of Lilterwess."

"How little things have changed!" said Medric, and Emil choked on a crumb, and Zanja escaped the downward drag of memory and burst out laughing.

It was the good kind of laughter, the kind that brings a person along the narrow edge of grief, then shows her the pathway back to firm ground, with tears on her face.

Emil sipped his tea and uttered a sound that was half sigh and half moan. "Blessed day—this tea must be priceless."

Zanja had tucked her braid into her shirt earlier to disguise her identity, for even the minor details of her appearance had become common knowledge, and now she began to pull it out—a long, slender black cord with a red tassel tied at the tip. Emil folded his ink-stained hands around his teacup. He said to Medric, "I want to ask you why you picked up that Ship of Air card. But . . . there are questions you should answer, questions you cannot answer, and questions you should not answer. If I inadvertently ask you the latter, I must watch you struggle to reply without hinting at the truth you must not reveal."

Medric said, "But how am I to know the answer unless someone asks me the question? And how are you to know the next question unless you ask the one before it? I am a ridiculous person, I know, but

I'm the only seer we've got, and to spare me from struggle is to prevent everyone from discovering the truth."

"You are correct, of course," said Emil. "But sometimes I can't bear it. Maybe I'm getting weak-minded in my old age."

Zanja and Medric both snorted. There was nothing feeble about Emil.

"Anyway," Medric said, "ask anything you like about Ship of Air—that card's meaning is hidden from me."

"But you think it's important," Zanja said.

"It's important, but it's impenetrably obscure."

"Then it must be about air logic."

"Oh, I suppose so. I'm so pressured by air logic lately that my mind feels like it can't breathe. Which is ironic."

"You have been in uncomfortably close contact with air witches since we left Watfield," said Emil.

Medric dug his fingers through his hair, which did not improve his appearance. "I hope that being surrounded by fire bloods makes *them* this wretched."

Zanja said, "Maybe this close contact will help you to figure out how fire logic can contradict, or retaliate against, or frustrate air logic."

"It certainly should be able to do that, since fire logic is air logic's opposite. But if it's possible to impede, or destroy, or undermine air logic, the fire witches of the past have neglected to mention it in any book. Maybe that was a ploy, to keep it secret from the air witches. Or maybe it's a knowledge that's unspeakable."

"Literally?" Zanja asked. "Norina does seem to think you could talk her to death."

"No, no, no, no," said Emil, beginning to laugh again. "Talking alone can't do much to her. But by knowing things that are so unlikely, irrational, and unbelievable . . ."

"You could annoy her to death," Zanja said.

"Exactly!" cried Medric. "I'm quite certain I could do that!"

A while later, Norina came to the door, with her student Maxew at her elbow as always, and found all three of them prostrated by laughter at an insane plan they had concocted for annoying an air witch to death. Norina did look annoyed. "Emil, Kamren has returned from Lalali, bringing a couple of healers with him. Karis is talking with them in the parlor, and General Clement is on her way here."

Emil got up from the floor, and Medric brushed sand from his clothing while Zanja smoothed back his hair and retied the thong that held it in a tail. He said, "I expect Kamren brought those healers because they are complaining about our plan to have soldiers work in Lalali. I would appreciate your help, Zanja."

Zanja picked up the piece of carpet to bring with her. The parlors were probably furnished with chairs by now, but, even though she had lived exclusively in Shaftal for seven years, she could not sit comfortably in a chair. She said to Medric, "And I would appreciate it if you could explain that casting to me when I come back."

"But that would be work," said the seer.

Chapter 6

FIRST ASSIGNMENT: *Why am I here?* I understand this question to have two aspects: First, why did I come here? And second, why have I remained here?

I came here to Watfield in search of Norina Truthken because I was both desperate and inspired. I had lived in a tack-room in the stable for more than five seasons because I could not bear any longer to be with my family. It was a large family of more than thirty members, and they jabbered incessantly, with their words scarcely ever in alignment with their truths, so that I was driven to distraction by their agitated and contradictory chorus. And the quality of their truths, which were trivial, irrational, and repetitive, bored and infuriated me. I had discovered that my ability to perceive their feelings, perceptions, and motivations—and thus to guess their thoughts—was not a passive gift. I could control people. The few times I did so, it gave me great glee. It also made me very unhappy, because my actions changed the people around me, my family, and it was not a good change. Before, they had been puzzled by but also half-proud of me. After, they feared me and thought about how to get rid of me. They thought about how, when I was an infant, they had debated whether to kill me, because there weren't any Truthkens they could summon to raise me and make me a student of the Law of Shaftal. Now my family knew I had become dangerous, and they regretted their softheartedness.

I wanted very much to behave correctly, and I didn't want to be the boy who lived in the stable, never talked to anyone, and didn't even join his family—who wished they had murdered him—for meals.

My desperation came from knowing that there had once been a place for people like me, but it no longer existed, and now I had no possibility of belonging anywhere or of learning how to be useful and not malevolent. My inspiration came from reading in the broadsheet that announced that Shaftal had a G'deon again. The broadsheet said, "The family of Karis G'deon is composed of people from all the old orders: Paladin, Truthken, Healer, and Seer." That night, I filled a sack with food from the kitchen, put on all my clothing, hoping it would keep me warm enough, and set out for Watfield. I did not leave a message for my family, but I realize now that I should have.

Just as I had left my home by dark of night, so also I arrived in Watfield. It was very late, but I found someone who could direct me to Travesty. There I found an unlocked door, watched over by a Paladin named Kamren, who was reading a book by lamplight. Kamren's way of thinking was strangely organized. His attention was extraordinary, but he did not pay attention to normal things. Though he was very polite, I could scarcely bear to be near him. This was my first encounter with a fire blood.

Kamren fetched Norina Truthken from her bed. She glanced at me and said to him, "There will be others."

He answered, "We have plenty of room."

She turned away, and I followed her.

Most people make a show of welcoming people when they arrive, but the Truthken didn't even speak to me. She already knew that my only reason for traveling all that way, through hunger and frostbite and bewilderment, was that I wanted to follow her. Her glance told me I would be permitted do so.

It's difficult for me to explain what I felt as I walked after her down the wide hallway. Probably all air witches since the dawn of history have felt the same way when they first met another of their kind. Someday, if I survive being a Law student, a young air witch may yearn to follow me.

I continue to remain at Travesty because the Truthken is here. She's here because of her duty, which is to observe and enforce the Law of Shaftal; but she also is here because she too has someone to follow. Norina serves Karis, has served her more than half her life, and will serve her until she dies. Karis is the person *she* follows, but she could not follow her if she were not also following the law. The law gives her a framework of principles within which to exercise her judgment, and the law defines her proper role in the world. The law is what makes her a safe person. The law tells her that her proper role is to serve the G'deon of Shaftal, even though Karis is the only person in all of Shaftal who is not subject to the law. In becoming acquainted with Norina, I also have become acquainted with myself, and so I understand that, like her, I must discipline myself every day to serve rather than dominate, and that this self-discipline will never cease to be an effort.

(I wonder, if Karis asked Norina to violate the Law of Shaftal, would Norina do so?)

Secondary Reasons:

Karis. She is both deep and guileless.

My fellow students, especially Serrain, who helps me all the time for no good reason.

Emil Paladin, even though he is a fire blood. Emil may be impossible to understand, but he is easy to trust. He doesn't mind air witches. He says fire and air are opposites because of their similarity. For fire bloods the insight comes first, and then they explain it if they're able to, whereas for air bloods the explanation comes first and leads us to a single, inevitable conclusion. Emil's words made it possible for me to see beyond my antipathy for fire logic.

The Law of Shaftal. It is rational and elegant.

The food.

Note written by Norina: *If Karis asked me to violate the Law of Shaftal, I would refuse. But she will never force me to make such a choice. You are correct that you should have left a note for your family. I trust that you have written a letter to them and arranged for it to be delivered. I am assigning you to practice the discipline of congeniality as long as necessary for you to master it, for an uncongenial Truthken will never be relied upon, regardless of how reliable he actually is.*

Note written by Anders: *Madam Truthken, I think that you are uncongenial, and people certainly rely upon you. Have you made an error?*

Norina: *People rely on me because they have no choice.*

Anders: *Please explain how I can learn to be congenial from a teacher who is uncongenial?*

Norina: *You can't. It's fortunate that I am not your only teacher.*

Book of Everything, *by Anders of the Midlands*

Norina Truthken had gone away, leaving the law students to continue their studies while guarding a practically empty house. She might be gone all summer. Even worse, she had taken Maxew with her. Of course, Anders understood why she had chosen Maxew, the eldest by three years, who had dared to own and study a *Law of Shaftal* when being caught with it could mean death. Maxew's knowledge and skill were far more advanced than that of his fellow students, and so he could assist her far more. Yet the five who had been left behind resented it very much: If Norina could take one student with her, why couldn't she take all of them?

A few days after the departure of three wagonloads of luggage and nearly forty people, Anders realized that being left behind was a lesson. For people like them, it was not at all easy to accept what they disliked. If they could not bear the disappointment of being left behind, then they certainly could not endure the torture of restraint when they knew, or thought they knew, how to properly arrange the world. However, this was an insight of the sort he had learned to keep to himself. He might write such things in this *Book of Everything,* which his fellow students were welcome to read, but that was different. Written words were sufficiently separated from active thoughts that he didn't need to worry he might reveal smugness or a feeling of superiority that a congenial person would keep to himself.

It was evening, after blade practice and supper, when the sun had crept close enough to the horizon that they could no longer study by its dimming light. The lamp had been lit, and they had abandoned their studies. Anders borrowed Braight's *Book of Everything* and leafed through it, examining her charts and analyses of the people who remained in Travesty, for he needed a new exemplar of congeniality. Emil was gone, taking with him a host of people whose names were connected to his by Braight's complex system for annotating relationships. No one who remained at Travesty was gifted like Emil, but Anders wondered if he could emulate features or aspects of congeniality that other people did enact. Braight had observed that some of the artists were empathetic; all the Paladins were courteous and curious; and the healers genuinely liked people. Perhaps he could acquire these abilities by modeling himself on one person at a time, and grappling later with how to make those separate abilities coalesce.

In his own book, he copied some names. Then he thought carefully and deliberately about Braight's sophisticated and refined ability to observe people. He said, "Thank you, Braight," and returned her book to her. She gave him a suspicious look but refrained from a sarcastic reply. Although she had noticed how deliberately he spoke (reminding himself to always be grateful and always use a person's name), she had been convinced that his appreciation was genuine.

Perhaps, Anders thought, air witches can lie to each other by a similar process—by summoning and exaggerating things that were true, and using them as a concealment for falsehood. This possibility disconcerted him so much that he hastily wrote it down in his book, so that he wouldn't risk concealing anything from Norina when she reviewed his progress. He couldn't help but think about forbidden things, so it was fortunate that only the actions and not the thoughts were forbidden.

On a dark winter day, while a snowstorm howled outside the window, the Truthken had told her newly arrived students what was forbidden and what was required. She stood at the head of the table and placed her hands on a book, *The Law of Shaftal.* It was a book she never opened, because she had memorized every word on every one of its numerous, densely printed pages.

"I will never lie to you," she said. "And you will not lie to me, or to each other. You will submit to the law as I have submitted to it. The penalty for violating these rules is death. You know there once was a time that children like you were gathered and nurtured by members of the Order of Truthkens. You know that when I accepted the six of you as my students, it was an act of mercy. But I will never show you such mercy again."

He and the others murmured hastily, "Yes, Madam Truthken."

Norina said, "Your duties begin today, at this moment. You will memorize and understand the Law of Shaftal. You will learn history, geography, mathematics, and how to ride and fight. You will complete your full share of the cooking, cleaning, and mending. You will guard this house. You will exercise your power on no one unless I give you permission. You will not use your judgment except as I assign you to do. Because my duties already are heavy and difficult, you will help me with them, so I will have enough time to teach you."

Then she had examined them, one by one. Anders had studied his fellow students also, but he doubted that he saw them as she did. Maxew, who had been a vagabond, had been given a copy of *The Law of Shaftal* by someone he met at a fair. Braight had come from the lawless region of Appleton, where she had killed someone. Serrain, from the Highlands, had been fortunate to be raised by a father with a strong air talent. Arlis and Minga, both 11, had been born days apart to different mothers in a family that transported materials up and down the Corbin River on barges.

"The six of you," Norina had said, "will create the new Order of Truthkens, if you survive."

Norina's daughter, Leeba, came into the room as she did every evening. "Greetings, Leeba," said Anders.

She mumbled something that might have been a greeting and crawled into the cupboard where she had secreted her toys that morning. J'han Healer arrived and stood patiently in the doorway. Like everyone in his family, he was accustomed to air logic and was not at all unsettled by being in the presence of five air witches. Except for Karis and J'han, who were elementally compatible with Norina, the members of her own family respected but did not love her.

"Greetings, J'han," said Anders.

"Good evening, Anders, Braight, Serrain, Minga, and Arlis. Was anyone injured today?"

They each assured him they had not been hurt, beyond the usual scrapes and bruises.

"Has anything happened that Norina would want to know about?"

It was the fourth night that J'han had asked this question. "We wish we could have gone with her," said Serrain, and Anders wished he had thought to say it. He understood that J'han was only asking for negative reports, and it had not occurred to him to answer the question differently from how it was intended.

"I'll tell her that in my next letter. But about your behavior today, toward each other and the people you have worked with, is there anything she would want to know?"

Norina would only want to know if any of them had become impossible for the group to manage, for she expected them to discipline each other, and rarely intervened. "You are like a pack of dogs," she had said once. "If you struggle for dominance, you'll kill each other, and the last one alive will starve to death. If that is your fate, you deserve it."

They told J'han there was nothing Norina would want to know.

Leeba had crawled out of the cupboard with her toys, and J'han plucked a cobweb out of her hair. "Very good," he said. "Good night, then."

After he and Leeba had left, Arlis and Minga said, "Why does the brat keep hiding her toys in our room?"

"I don't know and I don't care," said Braight.

Anders and Serrain both shrugged. Children weren't sufficiently complex to be interesting, and, as with animals, they were impervious to air magic.

"I'm going to study J'han," said Anders. "He likes people. I want to know how that works."

Serrain said, "He'll be easy to study. He is exactly what he seems to be."

Anders found it difficult to initiate conversations, and he tended to make speeches instead. He had been waiting all evening for the time just before bed, when they often practiced their conversation skills with each other. He announced, "I have learned something interesting about the old way of raising air children."

Serrain put her pen in the inkwell. "What have you learned?" She always helped Anders to make conversation. Due to her good fortune of having a father who enjoyed her company, she was skillful at getting along with people and enjoyed uncovering the secrets concealed in casual conversation. Anders frequently borrowed her book, in which she recorded page after page of failed and successful conversations, with commentary in the margins, and additional notes as she revisited and reconsidered them. This accretion of commentary made her book increasingly difficult to read, but also made it increasingly useful.

Anders said, "I learned that air children used to be fostered by fire bloods until they were old enough to begin their studies."

He stopped. Now, instead of lapsing into a monologue, he must utter a comment or question that invited reply or further comments. His fellow air children, not surprisingly, frequently lost patience when he had to pause to think in the middle of a conversation. But they all needed to practice patience with each other, so they could expect the others to practice patience with them. "I've been wondering why," he finally said.

"*Have* you?" Braight's words usually were correct, but her tone never was. "And what have you *concluded*?"

"Your sarcasm seems unnecessary," said Serrain.

"Go stick your head in a pig trough."

Braight's home, Appleton, was a lawless, violent place, a haven for bandit gangs that collaborated with the Sainnites, controlled the brandy trade, and distributed the smoke drug throughout the western regions. There Braight had served a bandit chief as a kind of Truthken, enforcing his law rather than the Law of Shaftal. She had never learned to behave properly, but she had become an expert in the complex bonds of obligation and power that unite people into groups. She should have been interested in this conversation, since she was collecting in her book everything that could be gathered about the organization, roles, procedures, and conventions of the old Order of Truthkens. She was supposed to be practicing the discipline of respect, but Anders thought she was doing a poor job of it. In everything, Braight was impeded by her ill temper.

Trying desperately to continue the conversation, Anders said, "I suppose air witches must be exposed to fire logic so we can learn to tolerate it. But I wonder . . ." He stopped himself, for he was trying to avoid speaking more than one sentence at a time, but none of the others offered to finish his sentence or ask him a question. That was interesting: half-finished sentences seemed to hold listeners in suspense. "I wonder whether we might gain something else."

Minga and Arlis groaned in unison. Arlis said, "You're thinking about Emil again! Why are you so obsessed with understanding him?"

"Understanding him will help me with my discipline."

"Oh, your *discipline*," said Minga jeeringly. "As if you'll ever be congenial!"

"I'll be congenial long before you're loyal!"

"Anders!" Serrain said sharply.

Anders added hastily, "I apologize for being unfair. You two do have loyalty to each other, and that permits you to double your intelligence."

When the Two continued to stare aggressively at him, Anders casually rested his hand on his chin, blocking his face so they couldn't tell that they were aggravating him.

Minga and Arlis were unique, according to Norina: No conjoined minds had ever been noted or recorded. They never spoke directly to each other; they both wrote in their shared *Book of Everything*; and even their handwriting was identical.

"Desist, Two," said Serrain, "Or repay us for the time you're wasting."

They had selected Serrain to keep an accurate record of wasted time, and anyone who did not desist had to repay all of them by doing their chores. Ever since they invented and agreed upon this punishment, only the Two had incurred penalties, and, inevitably, had complained about the unfairness of the punishment. Their inability to understand group loyalty also made them unable to understand group sanctions.

Anders heard Serrain's pen scratch on paper as she noted the time. The Two desisted, and Anders lowered his hand, to find them apparently fascinated by a book of history.

Serrain's pen scratched again, noting the time.

Braight said abruptly, "What could we gain by being forced to live with a fire blood?"

"Books of Everything," said the Two.

Anders restrained his impulse to remind them that he had invented the first *Book of Everything* and had brought his to Watfield with him, practically his only possession. When it was much admired by the others, although it was a poor thing, just paper sewn into a pamphlet. Emil had devoted several days to teaching them bookbinding, a craft he had learned because he loved books, as was typical of fire bloods.

Serrain had been turning the pages of her *Book of Everything*. Now she read out loud: "Fire talent may be expressed in many different ways. For example, Zanja na'Tarwein is gifted with language, and Emil Paladin is gifted with people. Both of them are presciants, and both have a talent for glyph interpretation, but Emil is better at *asking* questions while Zanja is better at *answering* them."

Braight said, "Gifted with language? With people? These seem like ordinary talents to me."

"But fire bloods know ordinary things *differently*," said Anders. "And maybe that's what makes Emil both unsettling and agreeable. He knows us differently from how we know ourselves. But his knowledge is still accurate."

He had said three entire sentences in a row, without lapsing into recitation. He was learning. But oh, what a grueling project it was.

Chapter 7

The tailor, unable to give Chaen a bed, had told her to sleep in the storeroom, among paper-wrapped bolts of plain undyed wool and linen. Expensive bundles of fine imported fabrics were arrayed on shelves overhead, and the door had an opening cut in it so the store cat could patrol for rodents. For the right to lie down in that stuffy room at night, and to eat two meals a day, Chaen would repaint both sides of the shop sign.

First thing in the morning, in the alley behind the tailor's shop, Chaen set up her sawhorses and laid the sign across them for study. The wood was ancient but smooth, without major cracks or splits. She gazed at the ghostly remains of the original paint, and the lost pattern began to emerge. In the center had stood a solitary figure, the glyph illustration known as the Artisan, which could be either a man or a woman, engaged in any skillful task, but always standing in a conventional pose, with a tool in the right hand and raw materials in the left. However, this Artisan was reversed, with a needle and thread in her left hand and a length of fabric draped over her right arm. (Chaen thought she could depict an expensive fabric, perhaps a brocade with gold embroidery, like the fabric of a coat she had noticed the other day.) The sign had been edged with a simple red border, nothing like the complicated borders of the cards that the strange woman had displayed to her yesterday: Waiting for a Dead Man.

Chaen had decided to stop lingering at the tide clock, hoping that Jareth would appear. Nor would she expectantly watch for the event that Saugus had said she would recognize, that meant she needed to be a fugitive no longer. The summer was nearly half over. She would earn some traveling money drawing penny portraits at the Hanishport Fair, then go into the countryside, seeking a prosperous farm that could hire a portrait painter for the winter. She had been an itinerant artist for much of her life; she need not put on a pretense.

The alley door opened, and the tailor peered out. "Two ships are coming in," he announced.

"Which ships?" asked Chaen, in the conventional manner.

The tailor replied with two names. Now, if Chaen had been a true citizen of the city, she would make a comment about the history of the ships, asking if they had replaced that sorry excuse for a spar-mast, or a similar sort of question. Instead, she gestured toward the ghostly figure on the shop sign. "Was this your mother?"

He blinked with surprise. "Yes."

"She was left-handed."

"She was, and people were always stopping in to tell her that the Artisan was backwards. 'If she's backwards,' mother would say, 'then so am I.'"

"And then they would order a shirt or a coat?"

"Often enough!"

"Well, you are right handed, but I'll paint the Artisan backwards. Perhaps it will continue to be lucky for you. And I'd like to give the Artisan your mother's features also."

"Sadly, she's long dead. But I have a miniature, if you can copy it."

Yesterday the tailor had behaved as though her offer to repaint his sign was scarcely more respectable than begging. Today he leaned comfortably in the doorframe as though he were chatting with a friend. He wore a loose, knee-length vest of beautifully woven wool. At breast level, a half-dozen glittering needles pierced the wool, each dangling a different color of thread. A silver thimble on his middle finger was attached to a brooch by a long, fine chain, and his index finger was deeply dented by scissors. The least interesting thing about him was his face, and Chaen hoped his mother's face had been less bland.

"What a surprise that the G'deon's come to Hanishport," said the tailor.

The pictures that filled Chaen's mind blew away like smoke before a wind. She leaned over the sign, pretending to study it, until the dizziness had passed. "The G'deon is in Hanishport? I hadn't heard."

"How could you not have heard about it? She arrived yesterday, all alone, and did some metalwork in the shipyard smithy. Those boneheaded smiths didn't recognize her, not even with a hammer in her hand! A Juras metalsmith—how many could there be?"

"Not many," said Chaen distractedly.

"Not even one! When Juras people come here to sell goatskins, they use the money to buy things made of metal: knives, needles, arrowheads. There's no metal in the southern grasslands."

"Maybe the smiths simply decided it was impossible for her to be here," said Chaen, because that's what she herself was thinking.

"And therefore all smiths are stupid! Listen, if you can get a good look at the G'deon, you could go to the smithy and offer to paint them an Artisan sign that looks like her."

"But she's a giant, isn't she? It would be a very tall signboard."

The tailor went away laughing. Chaen sat on the crate that served as a chair.

If the false G'deon was here in Hanishport, perhaps Chaen should have followed the fortune-teller's instructions and left the city. But even though Saugus had insisted on great caution, it seemed impossible that the false G'deon even knew of Chaen's existence. When others were trying to assassinate her, Chaen and Jareth had not even entered the building, because they had been chosen by lot to wait outside to help the others to escape. During the months of wandering that had followed, Chaen had not once noticed any raven that seemed to be following her. And if the G'deon had come to Hanishport to capture Chaen, then why had she not captured her already? And why would the false G'deon have come to Hanishport at all, when she could simply send the Paladins?

No one knew that Chaen was in Hanishport—not Saugus, not even Chaen's own son. The false G'deon had come to Hanishport, like hundreds of others would soon come, to attend the Hanishport Fair. That Chaen happened to be in the same city was simple coincidence.

She sharpened a pencil and began to draw. From the ghostly shadows of paint, the original pattern reemerged: not merely an ordinary tailor, but an ancient symbol of skillfulness. Chaen also had become a ghostly shadow of herself, because she was forced into unnatural aimlessness. As the Artisan's confidence took shape under her pencil, she felt herself begin to emerge from the oppression of invisibility.

Chaen would wait no longer.

Chapter 8

"Of course you have heard the news about Karis G'deon," the transfer boss said to Tashar.

Why must people talk about that woman so much, even if only to point out how mistaken were her actions, or how wrong were her positions? "What about her?" Tashar asked.

The warehouse boss, who had crouched over to get closer to the dim number, said in a muffled voice, "Why, she's in Hanishport!"

"She was on the quay as your ship came in," said the transfer boss. "The stevedore boss even offered her a job!" With her handful of transfer slips she made a disbelieving gesture, and the warehouse boss obliged her by laughing uproariously.

"How would anyone recognize her?" Tashar asked irritably. Of course, she was a giant, but so were many Sainnites, and, in Hanishport at least, groups of Juras people were a common sight in the warm season, when they came to trade or peddle tanned goatskins.

"No one did," said the warehouse boss. "That's why it's funny."

"Then how does anyone know it's her?"

"It's her," said the transfer boss, and gave him a hard look as though daring him to challenge her. He *was* tempted, but only because of his foul temper. The transfer boss was reported to all day long by people who made their living on the roads of Hanishport, and no doubt she knew where Karis was staying, who she was with, what she had done all day, and what she was eating for dinner.

"What is she having for dinner?" he asked.

"Fish, potatoes, greens, and peaches."

"Better than what I'm having."

"Are you hungry, Master Lora?" The warehouse boss sent his boy to fetch some biscuits and water.

It had been a beautiful day, with clouds scudding past on a fresh wind and the water's surface lively with wind-waves, the way Tashar liked it best. When there was tension between water and air, with the water pushing one way and the wind another, it took a true sailor to negotiate between them, to harness those forces and transform them into motion. Tashar had been in his docked boat at sunrise and had spent an hour or so restringing a line that had gotten frayed and testing it to be certain it worked properly. He had stowed his gear, including a delicious lunch, and was about to cast off when the harbormaster's girl came running down the dock. She was so out of breath she could only point, eloquently and vehemently, at a ship that had been standing at anchor, which was now unfurling a sail and ringing its bell to announce it was coming in to dock. The tide had turned, so of course the ship was coming in. But it was a Lora ship, and Tashar should have been aboard it.

Someone had misidentified the ship, and the wrong family had been informed of its arrival. Thus there was no landing permit, no manifest, no stevedores, no teamsters. And instead of spending the day in glorious solitude aboard his trim little boat, Tashar had spent it in wretched chaos.

The days of summer certainly were too few, but they also lasted too long. A person who rose at dawn could complete two days of labor by sunset but would only sleep half a night before the sun rose again. The weary transfer boss and the lethargic warehouse boss peered at the numbers Tashar had frantically scrawled on the fabric-wrapped bales as they were unloaded.

"Forty-seven," she said, and gave a slip to Tashar. He ticked the number in his notebook and put the slip in his pocketbook.

"Nineteen."

"Nineteen."

Another ship, another tic.

This idiotic process, although used for generations, assumed that those who transferred the goods from ship to warehouse, and those who guarded the warehouse, might be thieves. But the representatives of the trading family would never steal, since they would be stealing from themselves.

The warehouse boss moved to the next bale and raised the lantern so he could read the number.

"What is she here for?" Tashar asked irritably. "Couldn't she have waited for the end of shipping season?"

The transfer boss looked askance at him. The warehouse boss said, "I imagine she's here for the Fair."

I hate the Fair, Tashar wanted to say, like a child who has stayed up too late. But he was twenty years old, the age of marriage, and trading families from all across Shaftal were using the Fair as an excuse to impose themselves on the House of Lora, along with their marriageable children. Like a basket of hen's eggs or a barrel of oysters, Tashar was for sale.

"Of course, the Fair," Tashar said. But that explanation for her visit, though obvious, also seemed wrong. The G'deon—and those who advised her—were subtle and devious, determined to convince the people of Shaftal to embrace those amoral killers, the Sainnites—after the blood they had spilled, the families they had destroyed, and the resources they had wasted! After twenty years of subjection to their vile rule! With such a task ahead of her, surely the G'deon had no time for shallow entertainment.

The boy arrived with the biscuits and water. Tashar crunched and drank, and it was like washing down sawdust with the warm contents of a rain gutter. Then he pretended to recover from his foul mood. "Let's finish and go home to our families."

But Tashar hated his family. He hated them now, and he had hated them five years ago when he ran away and stayed away for more than a year. His mother had hated them too, for she also had run away, leaving her baby son to their awful care, and had never returned at all. To him she was just a vague, bright memory followed by years of absence. But Tashar knew where she was: sailing the seas that lay south of the storm wall.

The storm wall, sailors said, lay many months' journey to the south, where it stretched completely across the ocean from west to east, and was impossible to cross. Sometimes the wall moved northward, overcoming and consuming unlucky ships that traveled too near. And at other times it slipped southward, and to the northern sailors seemed to have disappeared. A lucky ship with a canny captain could risk a hasty, risky trip to a warm southern port to buy rare trade goods: certain teas, spices, animals, plants, lumber, dishware, and artisan's handiwork that could not be found in the cold north. If the ship was lucky, it might return to its accustomed trade route before the storm wall shifted northward again. Or the ship could be sunk in the storms, or, if it lay in a harbor, stranded on the wrong side of the wall.

Twenty years ago, such ill luck had trapped a southern ship, the *Tasharial,* on the northern side of the storm wall. It had journeyed all the way to Hanishport and wintered in its harbor. Everything about the ship had been strange. The wood of its hull repelled the barnacles and other sea creatures that gradually destroyed northern ships. Its sails were made of a fiber no one had seen before, and it had no cross-masts. Its sailors, who did not speak the pidgin of the northern ocean, shivered through the winter and died of illnesses that northern people scarcely noticed.

Tashar had been born that winter in Hanishport, and his mother, absurdly, had named him after that ship. When he was old enough to ask what had become of her, Aunt had pursed her lips in disapproval. "That ship came again, and when it departed she also was gone."

Tashar had thought it was wonderful that his mother named him after her secret longing. But later he understood that to her he had been like an anchor that trapped her in the harbor when she longed to be on the open sea. So when the true *Tasharial,* still trapped in the north, returned for another winter, Tashar's mother had not hesitated to abandon the child that anchored her.

The House of Lora had become the wealthiest family in Shaftal by importing the smoke drug that Sainnites used to make their slaves compliant. At age fifteen, Tashar had decided that it was wrong to bring that terrible stuff into Shaftal. But if they didn't import it, members of the family said to him, someone else would do it. Or else, they said, hundreds of people would die from lack of the drug. Did Tashar want to be responsible for hundreds of deaths? He did not, but his disquiet wasn't eased by these reasonable arguments. He pointed out that, although House of Lora could not determine the behavior of those who used the smoke drug, or of those who might take up the smoke trade if the House of Lora abandoned it, they could, and should, change what they themselves did. Aunt had decided to silence him by saying, "Tasharial of Lora, trade puts clothing on your back, food in your mouth, and a roof over your head. When you are ragged, hungry, and living on the streets, *then* you may dictate ethics to your family. Until then, hold your peace!"

She was right, Tashar thought, and left the House of Lora that same night.

By the time Tashar returned home from his wanderings, he had indeed worn rags, grown thin with hunger, and bruised and blistered his feet on the roads of Shaftal. But his aunt would have been dismayed to discover that even after his return he was dictating ethics to them—not by using words, but by using the only thing they cared about: wealth.

When Tashar walked home shortly before sunset, the tide clock was ringing the slack tide, and the fair-weather flags were snapping in a brisk evening breeze. The House of Lora was dark, except for a lantern at the door, and Tashar remembered the family had been invited to supper at the House of Samel, which was celebrating a birth or some such thing. The fountain in the courtyard sang happily to itself, and the heat of the flagstones warmed his feet as he went wearily to the door. The honey vine that climbed the fence was blooming, and moths swarmed around it, thirsty for its nectar. For a moment, Tashar loved Hanishport.

He took a cold supper to his bedroom, which also was his office. He should have been given a separate room for work, but he wanted people to be forced to knock before they entered. By lamplight, he wrote a neat but inaccurate copy of the manifest and then burned the original, along with two of the transfer slips. Two bales of smoke that no longer existed on paper soon would be carted away by a woman Tashar knew only as Stone Boots, and the proceeds of the sale would go directly to Shaftal.

Until Tashar left Hanishport at age fifteen, Shaftal had seemed more distant than Sho, the shipping harbor for tea and spices after their grueling overland journey around the storm wall, or Kanir, where rare woods at the end of long river journeys were hoisted from the water into ships, one log at a time, or the white landscape of Nimanima, where fur-dressed people dropped baited ropes at the edge of the ice and brought up fish twice as long as themselves, whose skin made a precious waterproof leather and whose oily flesh was treasured in every port. His own country, Hanishport, was the center of the world. But Shaftal lay so close, and could be reached on foot, so he went there, and learned a few things, and became what he had been all along without knowing it. He became Shaftali.

But first he became a thief.

He supposed he was still a thief, a kind of pickpocket who stole money from rich people right under their noses while they sat laughing in parlors, eating foods and drinking wine that cost more than a farm family could earn in a year. But *they* were worse than thieves, and Tashar merely took funds they never should have had, and returned the money to Shaftal. He was a righteous thief.

Of course, Shaftal had tried to kill him, by impersonal, tricky, slow ways that could only be survived by careful thought and hard experience, neither of which he possessed. Starving, he stumbled across a fair and couldn't make himself beg for food. He became a thief by accident when a distracted person dropped a coin and Tashar picked it up and kept it. He wasn't too proud to steal, he discovered. So he had lived for some months, getting better and better at theft while he trailed the caravan of merchants and entertainers from fair to fair, with only the haziest idea of where he was and no idea at all of where he would go next. Summer began its slow turn toward autumn, with the spectre of winter hovering at its shoulder. Tashar had learned some things about survival, the most important of which was the hardest to accept: no one survives alone.

He must go home to Hanishport, or die. And the feeling he had, that returning to his family would be a kind of death, must he ignore it? Wretchedly, he wandered through the Fair, past farmers riveted by a demonstration of a new kind of cider press, around the pits in which whole pigs were being roasted, down the row of hawkers whose hoarse blandishments were never for him, to the far end of the Fair, where a man on a platform was giving a passionate speech to a riveted audience while a company of players set up their scenery behind him.

It was easy to rummage through the unattended bundles. Tashar was considering whether to risk cutting one man's purse strings when someone took him by the shoulder and said something—words he would never remember—and when he came back to himself, he was sitting on the ground, far beyond the edge of the crowd, while a troupe on the platform cavorted through a silly comedy.

A bearded man observed him, and Tashar's purse was in his hand. "You were stealing from Shaftal," he said.

Tashar couldn't answer. He couldn't move. Even his common sense seemed to be in thrall: he should have been terrified, but only felt puzzled.

The man added, contemptuously, "But *I* am not a thief." He tossed the purse into the dirt at Tashar's feet.

Although Tashar could not reply, the man continued as though he had spoken. "Desperate? You weren't so desperate that you tried to find work. You weren't so desperate that you asked your family for help. You weren't desperate at all—you were proud."

Even though the man mocked him now, Tashar felt only an overwhelming desire to justify himself. The man made an irritated gesture. "Speak! But don't wear me out with drivel!"

"I don't know a trade. The farmers said I didn't work hard enough, even though my hands were bleeding. And my family disgusts me."

"So? You'll grow up. You'll marry out. You don't have to become a thief."

"They will only allow me to marry into another great house, and all of them are awful."

The man gazed at him for just a moment, but for the first time in his life, Tashar felt like he was truly known. When the man spoke again, he seemed like a different person. "Born into a great house in Hanishport? You *are* unfortunate. Which one?"

"Lora."

"That's not the house that imports the smoke drug. It is? Then I apologize for my rudeness. You certainly are desperate." Something about his words made Tashar feel itchy—not on his skin, but in a place he vaguely conceived as his mind. Then the sensation was gone, and Tashar jerked backwards and nearly fell sideways.

He became aware that a sharp rock was digging into his thigh.

He picked up his purse, and put it down again. He felt ashamed of himself. "I was a little proud," he said. "Or anyway, I thought I should have the money, because I didn't deserve to be hungry. I was self-important."

The man squatted down and gazed at him. It was a disconcerting gaze—not terrifying, though it should have been—and Tashar wondered if his will still was held in thrall, even though his body again was his to command. "Are you a Truthken?" he asked humbly, for he had learned about Truthkens from his tutor.

"There has been no law in Shaftal as long as you've been alive, Master Lora. Therefore, if any Truthkens had survived the Sainnites they would be Truthkens no longer. When I was a boy, my father took me on a long journey. He said he was taking me to join the Truthkens. Two days from the House of Lilterwess, we learned of its fall. The Order of Truthkens, the Order of Seers, most of the Order of Healers, and the Order of Paladins, the G'deon, and the Power of Shaftal, all were gone. So my father took me home again. No, Master Lora, the law was destroyed when the House of Lilterwess was destroyed."

For the first time in his life, Tashar realized that the history of Shaftal was his own history. His tutor had told him that this was so, but Tashar had ignored him, knowing that Hanishport governed itself, and the city paid the soldiers that lived nearby to leave the city alone. How stupid he felt, that he had been wandering Shaftal all summer and only now knew he was in his own country! "What did you mean," Tashar asked, "When you said I was stealing from Shaftal?"

A boy younger than Tashar approached, and the man spoke sharply to him. The boy gave Tashar a bold, hateful look and said something to the man in a low voice. We'll discuss it later," said the man. The boy insisted, and the man said, "Do as I bid you." Sullenly, the boy left.

Was the boy his son? Tashar felt a jolt of jealousy.

"You didn't listen at all to the man on the stage?" the man asked Tashar.

"I think he was telling a story. A story about a dream."

"He is Willis of South Hill. He is the Lost G'deon's general."

He spoke as though these were statements of great significance. Tashar felt as if he had been called upon to recite a lesson that he had not bothered to prepare, a common occurrence, since he spent every day that the weather was fine in a sailboat on the water. "It *sounds* like a story," he said.

"That Willis has met the Lost G'deon, and that she told him he would be victorious over the Sainnites, these things are true. But it is also true that he was dreaming, and the accuracy of a dream cannot be judged by air logic."

Tashar felt deeply disappointed, even though he never before had expected that there was a Lost G'deon. It was a children's tale, he had thought.

The man said, "Come with me and decide for yourself if Willis dreamed a true dream."

"How could I know such a thing?"

"You will know," said the man. "And we'll give you a hot supper."

Tashar wondered why he had thought the man sarcastic, when he was so kind. He went with him to a small encampment beyond the fairground. By then, it was evening, and his crew had gathered to count their money, bathe in buckets of water, and wait for supper to be cooked. They sat on the ground or on campstools made of sticks and burlap. Traveler's kits, ordinary implements like spoons and cups, dangled from their belts, but they also carried weapons—daggers and pistols. Over their heads flapped a crude flag with a glyph painted on it in red. Tashar had not studied the glyphs, but he did know enough to recognize the G'deon's glyph, which means both death and life. Saugus, the man who was an air witch, introduced Tashar to his people, and they did seem as if they had lived in a borderland where death and life overlapped, for they had hard faces and unsettling gazes, and their flesh was scarred by violence. The men's beards were untrimmed, and men and women alike had short, raggedly cut hair. When Saugus invited Tashar to ask Willis his question, their expressions became rapt, even though they must have heard him recount his vision dozens or hundreds of times.

Willis was a big man with sagging leathery skin and a restless gaze. He wore his hair long and tied back, like Paladins of the past, but he was bearded like a farmer. He squinted habitually, and his flickering gaze was oddly riveting, as though he expected a beloved visitor to appear at any moment. "I *saw* her," he said. Tashar turned, for it seemed like the one Willis expected had arrived. But the man continued, "I had devoted my life to defeating and destroying the Sainnites, and I had risen to the command of South Hill Company when the previous commander, Emil Paladin, turned traitor. But a true Paladin was sent to replace me as commander, and, like the previous commander, would not do what was needed to remove the pestilence of Sainnites from Shaftal. I abandoned South Hill Company in despair. Then my family rejected me and sent me out to starve. I thought my life was over—I wanted it to be over—and so I lay outside in a drunken stupor on a bitter winter night and begged Shaftal to take me. Instead, Shaftal came to me, in the form of the Lost G'deon. She chided me, saying, 'Do you not know that the land will always be embodied in a G'deon? Haven't you been told that a G'deon cannot die until a successor has been chosen?'"

He paused to swallow from his cup. Saugus gazed at Willis with a fixed expression of bland attention. Near him, the boy was sitting in the dusty grass. His gaze was not on the Lost G'deon's general, but on Tashar. Tashar didn't want to look into his eyes, but couldn't stop himself, and then he couldn't look away. He felt an awful sensation, like a sharp blade slicing into a finger, only far worse. The boy's face was hideously deformed, and when he opened his mouth, he had tiny, pointed teeth like a cat's, and a flickering tongue like a lizard's. "Leave now," yowled the monstrous boy. "Go, or I will kill you!"

Saugus struck the boy sharply with the back of his hand. The blow turned his face sideways and broke the gaze that held Tashar enthralled. The boy was just a boy again, a furious boy, with tears of pain starting in his eyes.

Then Saugus said something in a low voice, and the horrible immediacy of what had happened became in a moment just a dim memory. Willis had begun talking again. ". . . the Lost G'deon's pardon and said that in my hopelessness I had forgotten the power of Shaftal. But how could I have believed that Harald G'deon would fail to vest that power in his successor? No G'deon would abandon his people! Then I said to her, 'Why are you in hiding? Why haven't you stepped forward to save your people from the Sainnites?' She replied, 'Shaftal is polluted by Sainnites, and I cannot defeat them alone. If the people of Shaftal rose up against them, Sainnites would be eliminated in a single day. There are a hundred or more Shaftali for every Sainnite! But they are too fearful, and are satisfied to allow a few people to fight while the rest go about their ordinary business.' Then I cried, 'Madam G'deon, I will fight for Shaftal! But I am just one man. Won't you step forward and call on your people, and take us into battle?' Then she said to me, 'I am not a warrior—I am the G'deon of Shaftal. But you will be my general. You must go forth and create an army, and when the Sainnites have been defeated, I will come.'"

The people sighed, and Tashar realized that Willis's story was done.

"Well, where is your army?" he asked.

The people laughed, not unkindly. Willis said, "I am building the army one fighter at a time."

"I want to join it," said Tashar.

The people who constituted the harsh and seething heart of Death-and-Life Company were like Willis—hardened veterans of the long guerrilla war against the Sainnites, uprooted from their families and farmsteads, many of them survivors of families or companies that had been annihilated by soldiers. They were wounded, bitter, righteous warriors whose commitment to their cause Tashar longed to emulate.

Yet although Willis led them all, from the beginning Tashar felt a greater loyalty to Saugus. The uprooted nature of the company made it rapid, agile, and impossible to suborn. But it also made for hungry fighters, for no families fed, clothed, or sheltered them. Saugus and his crew, including Tashar, did not fight, but instead kept the army on its feet through a hodgepodge of continuing and spontaneous operations, many of them nefarious. It was Saugus who taught Tashar how to keep accounts, and how to tell lies with numbers, so that whoever reviewed the books would see no trace of theft. Then he sent him home to Hanishport, and the richest family in Shaftal became an unintentional patron of the Lost G'deon's army.

With the family wealth and contacts, Tashar could import items useful to the cause, such as snake poison. Once, he had paid an agent an extraordinary amount to convince a man from Kanir to undertake the long and dangerous journey to Shaftal. Three seasons had passed before the ship returned, carrying neither the agent nor the man. The agent had disappeared in a remote port city, the captain explained. The man had died of seasickness. "Your agent said he was a pilot," added the captain. "What kind of pilot dies of seasickness?"

At first, Tashar's covert duties had made his heart race, but he had grown weary and bored by the routine. Then, last winter, a large number of Death-and-Life fighters, with Saugus among them, had overwintered in Hanishport, and Tashar had paid their expenses. He had happened to be visiting them in Leeside after paying their rent, when an exhausted and panicky messenger arrived with the news that Willis and some forty others had been killed on Long Night. So Tashar had been present when Saugus, without any resistance or complaint, became the new leader of Death-and-Life Company.

Every window in Hanishport was open, including Tashar's own. The night breeze washed through the room and across his bare skin as he lay on the sheets. He heard the voices of his family coming home from the House of Samel. His younger siblings began laughing shrilly at something. His aunt spoke, in that piercing tone she so often employed in place of reasonable speech. Tashar covered his lamp so they would think he was sleeping. When the door slamming and floor creaking and calling from room to room had settled, he opened the portfolio of papers that he had taken to bed with him.

The first few pages in the portfolio were filled with bland notes copied from his pocketbook. Behind them he kept a sheaf of papers, written in his own hand, with diagrams he had carefully copied from the original scroll. The scroll had been translated during the winter by a sorrowful sailor who was becalmed an ocean away from his homeland. Tashar had taken the sailor to a public house, supposedly to celebrate the project's completion, but on the way, at Saugus's command, he had shot him dead and left his body in the slush of a frozen back alley in Leeside, where bodies often lay undiscovered in snow drifts until spring thaw uncovered them.

Although Tashar had read the translation many times, it still thrilled him to read it, to whisper to himself its opening phrases: *Those who sail the seas may claim the world, but they are subject to wind and waves, and inevitably surrender their lives to the waters, and sleep their last sleep in the mysterious deeps. Such sailors know that this penalty will and must be paid. But I am a sailor of another sort, for I have sailed in places that have never seen a ship of any kind, by means no one has dreamed of. Herein I will record my secrets.*

Tashar read on, and never had anyone so savored the words written on a piece of paper—not even an infatuated lover brooding over a letter from his beloved.

Two days after the false G'deon came to Hanishport, Tashar found a note hidden behind a stone in the deserted Market Common. "Evening," it said. It was signed by the portrait painter, Chaen. She wanted to meet him at the evening tide, and she had taken the coin Tashar had secreted there, which meant she needed something.

Chapter 9

The sun, newly risen above the light-burnished water of the bay, striped the dusty road with the travelers' long-legged shadows. In the near distance, dozens of fanciful towers pointed painted fingertips at the sky, and Zanja caught her breath: those ornately decorated towers were an illustration from the lexicon! She said in a low voice to Medric, who had sleepwalked beside her all the way from Hanishport, "The soldiers that built Lalali seem to have been desperately homesick."

Medric shielded his eyes and gazed at the distant towers in delight. "I had thought the cities in the lexicon were flights of whimsy! Well, what a grim place Shaftal must have seemed to my father and his fellows. So plain, so practical, so crotchety."

"Like the Shaftali people."

Nearby, Seth was saying, "What idiot builds a village upon a cliff? Just imagine the winds of winter howling in from the ocean!"

Seth certainly was the very embodiment of the Shaftal Medric had described. He began snickering like a child.

Ever since they had awakened in darkness to the sounds of Garland putting his pots on the fire in the kitchen, Karis had seemed oppressed. Zanja clasped her hand, and thought about the power of Shaftal, passed from one forceful G'deon to the next, each one with skilled hands that were stained and callused by labor. Surely all of them had suffered, as Karis sometimes did, from fear that they could not manage the burden of Shaftal.

That morning, they had traveled in a cloud of ridiculous conversations. Clement seemed to have commanded the officers of Hanishport garrison to talk with the Paladins who surrounded Karis in a loose circle, and the Paladins insisted on speaking Sainnese, despite their incompetence with the language. Some members of the Peace Committee had joined in, for they all had lived with Sainnites in the barracks of Watfield garrison as much as they could stand to do so. They could scarcely do better than to use an occasional noun and act out the verbs.

Altogether, they numbered more than forty people, a group larger than an air witch could manipulate or command, yet Norina prowled at the rear like a wolf watching for prey.

Karis missed a step. She was looking at the tumbledown wall that surrounded the town, the rusted gates ajar and sagging. A few curious children had appeared, ragged and filthy, heads shorn for lice. Karis said, "The day I left Lalali, a fiddler was dancing on the wall. He turned a one-handed cartwheel without dropping his fiddle. I wondered if people did such things in the place I was being taken, but I was too afraid of Dinal Paladin to ask her any questions."

The buildings of the village all seemed to tilt toward one side or the other, and fully half the fabulous towers had collapsed. "An entire village in disrepair," Karis said. "How much renovation can we do in one summer?"

A healer they had met with the previous evening had been watching for them at the gate and came down the road. She had been the most vehemently opposed to the plan—which she insisted on calling a proposal—for the Hanishport soldiers to labor in Lalali. Healers tended to be earth bloods, and therefore the Order of Healers needed a method for dealing with intransigence, lest they be perpetually paralyzed by disagreements. This woman seemed to have been assigned by her fellows to play the role of greeter, which forced her to behave exactly contrary to her inclinations. Clement, with her usual impeccable manners, offered a warm greeting and a handclasp that the healer ignored. Within moments, Zanja heard Clement telling her bristling officers that they did not deserve to be treated by any Shaftali with a modicum of politeness, and therefore had no right to be offended. It was the kind of conversation Zanja often wished the Shaftali most hostile to Sainnites could overhear, but they never would, because they would never learn the language.

Beyond the gates lay a vast plaza with a dry, green-stained fountain and a few pieces of appalling statuary. It could be a fine place for markets and entertainment, but it was abandoned except for the children, who ran to a curved row of cubicles and began posing for the visitors on those miniature stages, demonstrating their use as display cases. The healer sharply told the children to get down.

"I never stood there," Karis said. "I was too gawky."

"To be a lovely child in this place can't have been a good thing," Zanja said.

"To be an ugly child was terrible enough. What a foul smell!"

"J'han said the sewers were abysmal."

"Was it a mercy I couldn't smell then, because of the smoke drug?"

They walked down a wide boulevard as large and empty as the plaza, beside which lounged buildings with large porches and doors that folded back to reveal faded, but still gaudy, rooms and boudoirs. Past these, they arrived at an eating house, where the delicious scent of baking bread overcame the stink of the sewers. A clutter of ragged children sat outside, scooping porridge into their mouths with fingers. Inside, the tables were crowded, but the people ate in dull silence and scarcely glanced at the crowd of visitors. In the adjacent kitchen, the propped-open windows cast light-streamers upon a scene of chaos, people rushing about carrying pots, bowls, and mixing spoons; dodging piles of bagged flour, loose onions, crated apples, and topsy-turvy furniture.

One of the few seated people, who was reading what appeared to be a cookbook, stood up to greet them, and gestured toward the back, where the windows opened on to a weedy garden. They went outside and the healers came out, one and two at a time, wiping dirty hands and sweaty faces on striped towels, to meet Karis. Some of the healers then went with the Peace Committee and the soldiers to tour the town and discuss repairs. Karis and a few others went to a bordello that had been transformed into a hospital. Like Norina, Zanja's only task was to follow Karis: her prescience had saved Karis from assassins, and now it was her doom to watch over her.

Lalali had been created by soldiers for their own entertainment. But the truce had turned the soldiers into paupers; the brothel keepers had fled with their wealth, and the rest of the town's disreputable residents had begun to suffer from lack of food, and die from lack of smoke. Norina's husband J'han had envisioned turning the village into a place where Shaftal's smoke users could reside, be cared for, and begin to care for others during a gradual relinquishment of the drug. But the actuality had been harsh and desperate as smoke-users stole from and sometimes murdered each other while the supply of smoke dwindled.

This gradual catastrophe had filled the hospital's windowless rooms, and the few who were merely recovering from knife wounds may have thought themselves lucky. The others lay naked and starving upon filthy linens, bound by ankle and wrist to their beds, screaming for water, for smoke, or for freedom, mumbling in delirium, or lying still and silent, nearly dead. "It's not right to gaze at these poor people for no purpose," Zanja said to Norina. "I'll wait outside."

The back door led to an open sewer in a narrow alley. Flimsy buildings leaned upon each other for support, flinging out unlikely staircases like mooring ropes to hold them steady. There, amid the ashes and the tangled tendrils of wild cucumber vines, a few children listlessly kicked a bladder balloon.

Zanja retreated from the sewer and found a tiny, enclosed courtyard overgrown with exuberant vines. She sat on flagstones beside an ornamental pond, where mayflies floated over a fine mosaic of floating duck weed, and carp hovered in the thick green water like golden ghosts. One rose up to examine her, but when she failed to make an offering, it sank out of sight.

Medric appeared in the open gate and tossed her a thick biscuit. "For the fish."

"Have you been dreaming of starving carp?"

"I wish I did dream of problems that can be solved by a simple fish-biscuit!"

She tossed broken bits of the biscuit into the pond, and the carp surfaced. A dozen weird, unblinking gazes stared at them.

"Good morning, students," Medric greeted the fish.

The fish began grabbing the food. Two fought ferociously for one piece, while several pieces floated nearby, unnoticed.

"This is an awful place," said Zanja.

"Yes. I can see why the Hanishporters want to pretend it doesn't exist."

"When Karis cut herself loose from smoke, she endured agonies like those people in the hospital are enduring. The courage and desperation it took for her to do that, voluntarily and alone—"

"Thus demonstrating that she is in fact courageous, and not merely invulnerable."

She looked at him with some surprise.

"Well, a man can't always be a giddy idiot!" He squatted down beside her. "Zanja, you're afraid that when you cast the cards for that assassin, it gained us nothing. But I think the cards answer questions we haven't yet asked."

Zanja wiped her hands clean, took out the glyph cards, and from the eleven cards at the top of the stack selected Ship of Air, because they seemed to keep returning to it, and gave it to Medric. The carp finished feeding, and the water grew still.

"What causes this thing, whatever it is, to happen?" Medric asked.

Zanja's fingers plucked another card from that casting, a card she had no name for, which showed a luxurious, windowless room among the roots of a tree. She said, "Perhaps it's caused by something hidden—something living underfoot."

"What results from it?" asked Medric.

Another card. Medric looked at the image the way he looked at targets when he practiced shooting. "What is that old man? Why is he being carried?"

"Wisdom," Zanja said.

"Bloody hell," he said in Sainnese. "That's a hard hill the young man must climb."

"Do you think it's you?"

"I'm afraid that it is," he said glumly.

"So something is living underfoot that will cause the Ship of Air, which will result in you carrying the weight of wisdom up a hard hill."

"It sounds like nonsense, doesn't it?"

"No, it sounds like those bizarre conversations the Paladins tried to have with the soldiers this morning."

"Weird verbs, oddly chosen nouns, and no connections at all."

"But it was meaningful, nevertheless."

"It was meaningful enough, you mean. But this—" He gestured toward the cards. "Who or what is hidden underfoot?"

Zanja ran her fingers over the stacks of glyph cards, but she knew she would not find an answer.

"Fire logic can't gain insight into air logic," said the seer.

"But we must end this deadlock! Karis can't be trapped in inaction like this. Every day I'm afraid she'll demand to be free of her bodyguards."

They fell silent. From time to time, a carp rose out of the green water and peered curiously at them.

Zanja said, "It worries me that you chose to take this journey to Hanishport rather than remain in Watfield with your tower and books."

"I do have something to tell you," he said.

"One of your obscure commands?" He didn't reply. "Shit," she muttered. "Every time this happens, I barely survive what comes next. You told me to be buoyant, and a water witch nearly drowned me—twice!"

"I don't cause these things to happen. I just want you to survive them."

"Medric, when I was in the past time, before the extinction of my people, I did nothing to avert it."

"Very wise of you. Also very difficult."

"But Grandmother Ocean did the opposite. She changed the landscape to save the Essikret people."

"I imagine it was the work of a lifetime for her to determine exactly how her people were to be saved."

"Again and again, the ghosts of my friends and family have forced me to endure the massacre, and to walk through the valley filled with their dead bodies. They make me experience the horror of their deaths because they believe I betrayed my tribe by making peace with their killers. If they think now that I could have actually prevented what happened . . . I'm afraid that the next time they bring me into that valley they won't allow me to leave it, and I'll be trapped there."

Medric had sat on the ground, with the two glyph cards in his hand and his chin on his knees. "Would that be a just punishment, do you suppose?"

"If I have gone from being the only survivor to being one of the perpetrators? Yes."

He reached to her and patted her arm awkwardly. "If it happens, then I'll dream my way to you and rescue you. And maybe there will come a day that your dead are reconciled with you, and will cease to haunt you."

His statement seemed like a wish and not a prediction, yet Medric was always careful to avoid saying anything about the future at all, unless he meant it. Zanja clasped his hand for a moment. "Well, tell me your obscure command."

He stood up. "Give your whole self to her."

"To whom?"

He wagged a finger at her. "Your *whole* self. Remember!"

He left her baffled, as was not unusual. She sat quietly as the shadows of morning drew slowly away. Then a raven flapped down from overhead, and she stood up and followed it.

Karis was sitting on the edge of a dry fountain, writing a note on a scrap of paper with a carpenter's pencil. The Paladins who had accompanied her in the hospital waited at a distance, passing a water flask from hand to hand while discussing the new Sainnese words they had learned or heard that morning. Norina also stood back, expressionless except for a clenching of her jaw. There were some astonished healers, also, and three children who had been dying in the hospital: pale and tottering, but flushed in the cheeks by the power of Shaftal. That Karis had decided to heal the children rather than require them to endure the pain of gradual recovery was no surprise to Zanja. She asked a Paladin, "Are we going back to Hanishport already?"

"Yes, Zanja." He offered the flask, then asked about a Sainnese word the Paladins had heard but didn't know the meaning of.

She said, "It's a virtue the Sainnites especially value. It means something like the keeping of promises—but the promises have to do with identity."

Karis had given her note to the raven, who flew away with it and probably would give it to Kamren or Clement, who were still touring the village.

"Like keeping an oath?"

"It's similar, but . . . excuse me." Karis had started walking, and Zanja trotted to her, then had to keep running in order to stay beside her. "What are we doing?"

"Getting a supply of the smoke drug for the healers," Karis said.

Zanja began to laugh, which made her breathless, so she had to stop running. The Paladins passed her, then Norina. Zanja caught her breath and ran after Karis. "The G'deon of Shaftal—visiting herself upon—the great houses of Hanishport—to ask for some of that cursed, bloody drug—that stole so much of your life—" She gasped a breath. "It is absurd!"

Karis glanced at her sideways. "Not just *some*. And I'm not going to ask. The healers can't accomplish anything in Lalali until they have smoke—more of it than they think they will ever need. Without enough of the drug, they can't wean people from it. They can't take care of them—they can't offer mercy. Smoke users won't come here for help. The hospital will fail. But Shaftal must be free of that horrible drug."

The great houses of Hanishport had gained enormous power during the twenty years that Shaftal had no government. While most people had done all they could to sustain their laws and traditions despite the occupation, Hanishport's great families had behaved like children alone with a platter of sweets.

No doubt those families were worried because the new government of Shaftal had set up housekeeping in their city. They would be even more worried, Zanja thought, before this day had ended.

Chapter 10

Tashar had gone out early to meet Stone Boots in Leeside to give her the forged papers she needed to collect the bales of smoke drug from the warehouse. She was a hard, terse woman, whose face looked like it had not smiled, even once, in her entire life. Tashar had been meeting her regularly for years, and knew nothing at all about her, not even her name. In a filthy tea shop, she crouched over the cold dregs of her tea and said not a word as Tashar muttered in her ear everything he had learned about the G'deon's presence in Hanishport. "Whatever our leader wants me to do, I am willing," he finished. It was a routine statement, but Tashar genuinely wanted something new to do: something significant and heroic.

She grunted, took the papers, and left. Disappointed, Tashar returned home to get a hat, for it was developing into the sort of day that broils the skin and dries hair into straw. As he toiled down the road, he regretted that he had worn a light linen coat so he would have a pocket for his pistol. The sight of the tree-shaded Captain's Way made him sigh with relief. Then he missed a step, for a crowd was gathered at the Lora's garden gate: a few children still in nightclothes, whose parents had probably pushed them out the door to find out what was happening, but also laborers, artisans, and shopkeepers from several adjacent streets, still wearing their aprons and work gloves. What could have happened, to turn the Lora into this spectacle? Tashar found himself feigning unconcern as he approached the crowd. They parted to let him through, and he saw that five people were in the garden, all of them dressed in black from head to foot, their hair in tails, daggers tied in scabbards using knots his sailor's eye recognized that would come loose with a firm yank. Paladins. They stood in a circle around one, who knelt at the bench where low-status visitors sometimes awaited the leisure of the house, with a pen, paper, and ink stone before her, as if the bench was a desk. Stupid from astonishment, Tashar wondered what they were discussing so intently, and why they had seen fit to do it in his family's front garden. When he finally realized what this occupation by Paladins must mean, it was too late to flee, for the one who wore two earrings had noticed him and was coming over to greet him. His boots and trousers where white with dust; his shirt patched with sweat. He had traveled a long way already, though the day was still young. "I'm Kamren Paladin," he said.

"Tashar of Lora. Has something happened?"

"Karis G'deon is visiting your family," the man said cordially. "You carry a weapon in your pocket?"

"What? Oh, a pistol, because I carry money sometimes. Why is the G'deon here?"

"I don't speak for her, Tashar of Lora. You may ask her yourself. But I'll keep your pistol until we depart." He spoke as though he was doing Tashar a favor.

"Of course," Tashar said. "It isn't loaded." He handed over the pistol. "Return it to anyone of the house."

"Why carry it unloaded?" the Paladin asked.

"I've never heard of anyone who could hit anything with a pistol. *I* certainly can't." If this man were a Truthken he would recognize this. But the Paladin, amused, stepped back to allow Tashar to pass, since doing anything else would have seemed odd. Tashar went into the house.

He wished he could see what the false G'deon looked like. But it was known that the Truthken always accompanied her, and Saugus required that his people never be within sight or hearing of that notorious woman. Well, it was a large house—he would avoid them.

He was met in the hallway by two cousins. "We were just going out to look for you," said one, and the younger one said excitedly at the same time, "The G'deon is here!"

"What am I wanted for?"

"*I* don't know," said the older cousin.

"How many people are there?"

"The G'deon, two Paladins, a woman with a scarred face, and a border woman."

"The G'deon dresses like a farmer."

"Do any of them have shorn hair?"

"Yes, the one with the scar."

The family had received the false G'deon in the formal parlor, of course, the most impressive and uncomfortable of their many reception rooms, which was draped with heavy, embroidered silk, furnished with chairs upholstered in brocade, and decorated with tables of exotic wood, with carved leaves and flowers like nothing ever seen in Shaftal. Tashar acted like he was going there, but turned down a side hall and stepped into the closet with the peephole. He looked through the hole, which had a lens that provided a distorted view of the opulent room.

Tashar was looking at the false G'deon. What an ox of a woman, he thought. Hitch her to a plow and she could turn a field or walk down a tow path hauling a barge. But she was a metalsmith, supposedly, a toolmaker who did things with steel that no other smith could replicate. He looked at her hands and was shocked by how dirty they were. The muscles in her bared forearms flexed, and her hands closed into fists. Was she thinking of striking Aunt? That would be a sight worth seeing!

A murmur of strained conversation could be heard. Silence fell. Tashar's nervous uncle rubbed one cheek and then the other. His domineering aunt, smiling fixedly, said through her teeth, "You entered our warehouse?"

"No, we haven't entered the warehouse." The G'deon's voice grated unbecomingly. "But I know what's in it."

Aunt took several shallow breaths. "Madam."

"Karis."

"You are offering us the *opportunity* to donate *an entire warehouse full of smoke* to the healers?"

A person Tashar couldn't see said, "One does not speak sarcastically to the G'deon." The voice ran down Tashar's spine like a knife's edge. Everyone in Tashar's view flinched at the sound—even the false G'deon.

A woman who stood directly opposite the peephole turned her head to look at Tashar, as though she could see through the wall. It was a border woman, her hair tied loosely back except for a single braid, as thin as yarn, that looped over her shoulder, nearly to her waist. She gazed steadily at him: *I know you are there.*

"Excuse me," Aunt said. Tashar had never heard her voice sound like this, not merely enraged, but shaken. "A warehouse full of smoke is worth a fortune!"

"I suppose it is," said the false G'deon. Even in the closet, Uncle's restless shuffling and Aunt's panting seemed very loud. The big woman said, "In my house in Watfield, dozens of people work day and night, and gain nothing from it. Their food, clothing, and the house itself have been given to us. Our storerooms are full, but more supplies arrive daily from all across Shaftal. Yet the healers requested the smoke drug from you several times, and their requests have been answered with silence."

The Loras stared at the false G'deon as though she came from an unimaginably distant country.

Karis said, "One of my advisors says that the trading families seem to think they're not part of Shaftal."

"The trading families have always been independent," said Aunt.

"How so?"

"We buy and sell, import and export. We alone, in all this land! We are the wind in the sails of Shaftal!"

The false G'deon looked at the priceless rug, the polished floor, the toes of her own dusty, much-worn boots. "And so you think Shaftal depends upon you, while you do not depend on Shaftal?"

It was strange, very strange, to hear this woman utter criticisms, however mild and indirect, that Tashar had said and thought. But this was the false G'deon, who had wrongly taken the power of Shaftal and was using it to aid the murdering Sainnites!

Karis said, "The House of Lora used to import medicines, tea, and spices, but since the coming of the Sainnites, your ships have only carried smoke. Why is that?"

"This business is a risky one," began Uncle. It was an explanation that Tashar had heard many times, about how much money was invested in a single ship and its cargo, which might sink or have its cargo stolen in the year that passed between leaving home port and returning.

The large woman listened patiently, but when uncle concluded this lengthy winding-up and unwinding of his lines, she asked again, "Why does the House of Lora import smoke?"

Perhaps this was how the day was doomed to proceed. The visitor would refuse to sit down or take refreshment, and also would refuse to leave. She would ask, steadily and patiently, until she had been given what she wanted.

One of the other Loras, Nevan, had the wit to answer her honestly. "The smoke drug is so lightweight that we can fill a ship from prow to stern, and every shipment earns a profit." All this he said, with Uncle signaling him to be quiet, and Aunt hissing like a teakettle, but it certainly was no secret.

"But your warehouses are full," the woman said. "Your business is not doing well."

"They're full?" someone said with surprise.

Then there was silence.

"You want the smoke drug for the people in Lalali?" Nevan asked. "You want us to give it to them rather than sell it?"

"The healers need it to heal the smoke users."

Aunt cried sharply, "What?"

"Pardon me—my voice is weak because I was a smoke user for over twenty years. Lalali is now a hospital for smoke-users, for the healers know how to cure them."

Smoke was a potent painkiller. Using the drug in the absence of pain not only wasn't pleasurable, but it destroyed pleasure. Smoke users couldn't taste or smell, often injured themselves due to lack of sensation, and died of starvation if they weren't forced to eat. To survive for twenty years was unheard of.

Tashar looked at her more closely, curious now to know what the woman had done, or what she had known, that enabled her to survive. He noticed how blue her eyes were, and how odd they looked. Then he became aware again of the border woman's steady gaze. Her eyes were of an impenetrable blackness, and her face was extraordinary—all planes and angles—and utterly expressionless.

The false G'deon said, "Perhaps your elders remember the old way you did business, for you must return to it."

Tashar had noticed that the warehouses had been filling faster than they were emptied, but it had not occurred to him that the House of Lora was gradually being put out of business.

"We have buyers," began one of the stunned people in the sumptuous parlor. She fell silent, perhaps because Aunt had glared at her.

The false G'deon said, "Smoke users will come to Lalali to be healed, or else they will die. There will be no new smoke users." Her big hands hung at her sides, empty. The hostility and tension in that garish room did not seem to trouble her. "But we must have the smoke drug to give to the users while they're being cured."

Aunt said, "And put ourselves out of business?"

The massive woman's muscles flexed again, and her empty hand became a fist. She turned to the woman Tashar could not see. "Will the historians say that the House of Lora refused my request?"

"They certainly have refused," said the terrible voice.

"Then I am confiscating a warehouse of smoke drug for Shaftal. We'll bring some to Lalali immediately."

She left the room so abruptly that its occupants didn't even understand what had happened until she was gone. Then some of the Loras took a step as if to follow her, but her departing companions had blocked the doorway. Tashar abandoned the closet and ran to a window in the hall. He saw the crowd parting outside the gate; the Paladins running after Karis, one of them flapping a sheet of paper so the ink would dry, and one hurrying to the door with Tashar's pistol.

Tashar opened it. "Kamren Paladin," he said, as the Paladin handed him his weapon, "Does Karis change her mind?"

The Paladin's only answer was a laugh.

Tashar said, "You must spend a large part of your day running."

"She has a long stride," the Paladin said, and departed.

Karis didn't anger easily. When she knew what to do, she did it; and when she didn't she consulted her advisors. Her anger, when it did come, was terrible, but she could usually find something to smash—a portion of Travesty, for example, which she was destroying and rebuilding one wall at a time. Perhaps they might visit the blacksmith's yard again, Zanja thought, so Karis could relieve her feelings by whacking red-hot iron with a hammer. But no, Norina also was angry—a common occurrence—and when both of them were angry, there could be a shortage of judgment.

"Karis," Zanja said.

But Karis was saying to Norina, "Gilly was right."

"About what? That the sun will rise in the west before the Lalali merchants give anything away to anyone?" Norina always remembered what people said, word for word. "Or that the Hanishport people think of their city as a doorway, neither in Shaftal nor in the sea, and so the laws of neither place apply to them?"

"If that's what everyone in Hanishport thinks, we have a lot of work to do."

"Someone was watching us through a peephole," Zanja said.

They both looked at her. Norina snorted derisively.

Zanja said, "That comment you made to that woman—Aunt somebody—about her sarcasm. That was you punching her in the face."

"She did feel it."

"*All* of us felt it. I'm thinking Emil won't be impressed by your diplomacy."

"Zanja is right," Norina said. "Which way?"

Karis pointed, and they started down the hill. Kamren, walking beside Zanja, said with comic disbelief, "Did the Truthken just say you're right? We should tell Medric to put that in the book he's writing."

"Was that a pistol you had?" asked Karis.

"I took it from one of the Loras—Tashar, his name was. He carries it for protection from thieves."

At the Lora warehouse where the smoke drug was stored, the warehouse boss started to argue with Norina and then came to his senses and unlocked the door. By the time a wagon had been fetched from the garrison, several members of the Lora family had arrived. Norina instructed them in the Law of Shaftal while the Paladins loaded the wagon with bales from the warehouse.

Zanja managed to get the attention of one of the Loras, the one who had earlier explained why the family imported smoke. "The House of Lora would look better if they donated the smoke drug to Shaftal," she told him.

The man said, "We discussed it. Aunt won't permit it."

"Could you offer half of what Karis is demanding?"

"I'm Nevan of Lora. I didn't hear your name earlier."

"Zanja na'Tarwein."

"The G'deon's wife?"

Zanja would be referred to as the G'deon's wife for the rest of her life, but she said, "I am the Speaker for the Ashawala'i."

Nevan looked confused. Perhaps he knew as little about the mountain tribes as Zanja did about the far countries of the world.

"The border tribes used to send Speakers to the House of Lilterwess, to address the G'deon on matters that concerned them."

The man said, "I left my family in a state of disorder. Aunt said that, since the contents of the warehouse are Shaftal's, I was to tell the warehouse boss to dismiss the guards. Shaftal can protect its own belongings from thieves, she said."

"Does one person make the decisions for everyone in your family?"

The man sighed. It did seem unlikely that the awful woman referred to as *Aunt* had assets beyond a loud voice and an absolute certainty in the truth as she perceived it. Zanja couldn't imagine how such persons came to be accorded even a superficial respect, but she doubted that it would make much difference that Norina had bared her fangs at the woman. She said, "If you suggest a compromise to her, I don't think it will make matters any worse. Can we at least have an agreement that the warehouse will be kept under guard until tomorrow?"

"And then what, Madam . . . uh . . . Speaker? You don't have an empty warehouse to move it to."

"We do," Zanja said. Storage space could be found in the garrison, which also would solve the problem of keeping the smoke drug secure.

So they agreed that they each would try to convince the obstinate people in their families to give and accept only half the smoke drug in the warehouse. The next day, when Zanja, with Gilly and a gang of Paladins and soldiers, arrived at the warehouse with their wagons, Nevan, rather harrowed looking, was waiting to give Shaftal half the smoke drug in the warehouse, as a donation from the Lora family.

Chapter 11

According to the Hanishport clock, it was the 201st day of the year; the waxing moon was half full, and the tide had recently turned. Chaen waited, leaning against the clock's stone base, feeling its rhythmic ticking vibrate against her shoulder like a heartbeat. The long summer day had faded into blue night, and watchman's lanterns on the anchored ships cast undulating worms of light upon the moving water. On the quay, sailors carrying bags that they had filled in Hanishport's shops waited in clusters for skiffs to their ships. They talked loudly in their ship-tongue, eating suppers bought at food stalls, passing a brown bottle from hand to hand.

Tashar appeared, stepping around a knot of sailors on the corner. He walked briskly across the quay, a sturdy young man in a rather fussy suit, his coat pulled askew by the weight of the pistol in his pocket.

During the previous winter, most of the Death-and-Life Company had occupied a drafty, ramshackle building in the poor section of Hanishport known as Leeside. Tashar had been a frequent visitor, bringing money for food and rent, and occasional comforts, such as woolens, sweets, and liquor. He always seemed to expect more gratitude than he was offered, and people sneered at him behind his back. A few people had been in the direct command of Saugus even before Willis was killed, and Tashar had been one of them. But Chaen and Tashar greeted each other as though they were strangers.

"I beg your pardon for my tardiness," he said. "It has been a peculiar day."

They walked together along the quay, talking stiltedly about ships, weather, criminality, and the sorry state of the roads. Chaen saw a few distant lights where the garrison, crouching on a peninsula, kept watch on the harbor like a massive cat watching a mouse hole. That peninsula pointed its finger at a tiny island where a fire burned atop a light-tower to warn ships of the shallows. Every day, the city's skiffs rowed to that island with more firewood and returned laden with ashes.

Chaen and Tashar turned onto the Marketway, where the ditch-clearer had shoveled the day's accumulation of manure out of the ditches to be scooped into a wagon. Tashar picked his way fastidiously, but Chaen didn't pay attention to her feet: her boots had walked through much worse. The market yard lay to their right, an open space, well cobbled and clean swept. The young man hopped a mound of manure by the roadside and stepped on the wheel bridge to cross the ditch. They entered a dark yard, climbed a rickety outdoor stairway, and stood on the landing while he fiddled with a key. A warped door squalled open.

Chaen forced the door shut, fighting its stiff hinges.

The shutter of a covered lantern slid open.

Chaen rubbed her light-burned eyes. Two others awaited her on broken-down chairs, where they seemed to have been sharing a large mug of beer that had stamped circles into a dust-furred table. Chaen said, "I am a portrait painter."

"Teamster," said a young woman with big shoulders, turning her face into the light. The man, older, sun-hardened, and bulky with muscle, was a stevedore. Tashar, as always, introduced himself as a sailor, though everyone knew he was the scion of a rich merchant family. Tashar brought some packing crates from the corner, and they all sat around the table. Chaen asked if anyone had anything to eat, for she had missed supper at the tailor's shop. The stevedore grubbed in his pocket and handed her a wizened apple and the dry heel of a bread loaf.

Chaen had not felt her loneliness half so exquisitely as she felt it now, as she participated in the fellowship that only she knew had been forbidden to her. She said, "Is it a fact that the false G'deon is here?"

The stevedore said, "I saw her on the quay with my own eyes."

The teamster said, "She's living with some twenty people in the old house on Harborway just to the north of here, the one that's stood empty these five years because those vicious Sainnite parasites killed two of the family, and the rest couldn't bear to look at the garrison any longer."

"And some of her companions are Paladins—true Paladins, not irregulars."

"Yes—and don't forget the Sainnites," said the teamster. "The entire garrison is at her service, since the general is here also."

Stevedore, sailor, and portrait painter looked at the teamster with surprise. Chaen said, "General Clement, you mean? The one that killed Willis?"

"Yes, the murderer herself is here, with an armed guard of eight." Chaen felt a wave of rage, for she had seen the bodies stacked in the snow after that massacre. But she scarcely noticed anger anymore, she had been in such a fury for so long. The teamster added, "Today the G'deon's entire company, Paladins and Sainnites included, went to Lalali."

"Lalali? Whatever for?" said the stevedore with disgust.

Tashar turned to Chaen. "Portrait painter, what does our leader need from us?"

She should tell them that she was barred from contacting any member of Death-and-Life Company, lest she inadvertently lead the enemies to them. At least, she should tell Tashar that she had not been sent by Saugus, whom he idolized as fervently as the others had idolized Willis. But she didn't.

The city had begun to fall asleep when Chaen left the office, creaked down the rickety stairs, found the way back to the road, and cut across the market yard the long way, so she wound up on the downhill corner, with a vast, empty stretch of courtyard between herself and the dark loading yard. Hidden by darkness, she sat among pieces of junk that had collected around an old shed. She watched the refuse wagon work its slow way down the hill as two tenders scooped and flung the muck, and the horse, unbidden, moved forward a few steps every time it heard a shovel's contents thud into the bed. The wagon had turned the corner, the noise of the quay faded to silence, the sea breeze picked up the sweet, rotten scent of low tide, and still Chaen saw no sign that she had been followed. She stood up and slung the knapsack onto her shoulder.

At the tailor's shop, the doors were locked and no light glimmered, so she wrapped herself in her threadbare coat and lay down in the doorway. She had slept in worse beds.

Tashar kept his hand on his pistol as he went from the warehouse to an alley that was noisy with music and drunken sailors. On Artisan's

Way he climbed the hill, where, above closed shops and workshops, the windows of the second-story living quarters were open to the cool night air. He reached the stately, level road of Captain's Way, where the gardens lay silent and fragrant, and a solitary musician was playing a flute, perhaps preparing to entertain the houseguests who soon would arrive.

Even at this late hour, the road was well lit, and the walled gardens and locked gates offered nowhere for an assailant to hide. As Tashar hurried toward the House of Lora, he considered whether he was too tired to eat, and whether he'd be able to sleep if he didn't eat.

The sky's darkness clotted into a hard scab, and became a man standing before him. Tashar shouted with surprise.

"You still shriek like a baby, Sailor Boy."

"Fuck!" Tashar cried. "Why are *you* here?"

"Why not?" The boy had grown at least a head taller since Tashar last saw him, yet he remained thin as a grass blade. "I've been waiting for hours," he said. "Don't you come home for supper?"

"I'm doing that right now. And I won't invite you to share it with me either."

"I've eaten. But *you* won't eat anytime soon."

Members of the company called the young air witch "Little Wind" behind his back. No one except Saugus liked Maxew. And his mother, Tashar supposed. "Well, what has happened?" he asked.

"The false G'deon visited your family today—and the Truthken was with her. It's fortunate that you weren't home."

"I *was* home. I eavesdropped from a closet. The false G'deon stole a warehouse full of smoke from the Loras. Does our leader know that she's in Hanishport?"

A moment passed. When Maxew spoke, he sounded more irritated than usual, probably because Tashar had ruined his unpleasant surprise. "Of course he knows she's here."

"What are *you* doing here?"

"I'm keeping my own secrets," said Maxew loftily. "Your parents are extraordinarily stupid. If they had given some of the smoke willingly, she wouldn't have taken all of it."

"They never should have imported that foul stuff in the first place. Could you tell me whatever it is you're here for so I can go to bed before sunrise?"

Tashar was several years older than Maxew, but people had assumed the two youngest members of the company would be friends. Maxew had practiced air logic on Tashar—harmless tricks, he insisted, apparently believing that humiliation was harmless. His mother had noticed, and discussed the matter with Saugus. The tricks stopped, but there was no hope at all of the boys becoming friends, if there ever had been.

Maxew said, "You haven't hidden any contraband in the warehouse, have you?"

Tashar thought he might be referring to the snake poison that had been used in the assassination attempt. He had in fact hidden it that winter under some floorboards in a warehouse but had moved the remainder as soon as the ground was soft enough to for him to bury it. "There's not much left, but it's not in the warehouse."

Maxew said, "What about that other thing? Our leader said it's some new kind of conveyance. That must not be discovered either, for we will be needing it soon."

"We?"

"You and I, and a passenger."

Tashar had hoped that the first passenger on the maiden voyage of Tashar's marvelous ship would be Saugus. Instead it would be this obnoxious ass? "It's not in the city," he said.

"*Must* you be so sullen?"

Tashar started walking again, but the boy kept pace with him. "If it's not in the city, it's not very useful."

"We can get to it by sailboat."

"Yes, that will work. We will depart sometime after tomorrow, but I don't know exactly when."

"I must have a day's notice, to get ready."

"Be ready every day," Maxew replied.

Tashar turned to retort that he only took orders from Saugus. But the boy wasn't there.

As Tashar lay in bed trying to sleep, it occurred to him that Maxew might not even be aware that his mother was in Hanishport.

Chapter 12

The weather turned cloudy, and it took hours for each layer of paint to dry. Chaen killed the time by wandering the city, looking for interesting things to draw. She drew a vine with sky-blue flowers that twisted open like spills of paper, a broken wagon wheel that leaned tiredly against a stone wall, and a handcart filled with bright red potatoes in the market yard. The potato farmer left his stall to look at the drawing and offered to trade a sack of potatoes for it. She then traded the potatoes for a shirt the tailor had made for a sailor who had never collected it. With the bow and darts that had been concealed among the potatoes, she practiced shooting a sack of fabric scraps in the empty shop at night, and the skill she had developed during the winter with a similar weapon quickly returned.

The sky cleared, and in warmth and sunshine she painted the face of the tailor's mother. When the tailor saw it, he exclaimed, "Every day of her life I saw that very expression on her face! I half expect her to chide me for my sloppy stitches!" He was so delighted that he gave Chaen some pennies for the Fair, and a key so she wouldn't be locked out again.

People from near and far began to arrive for the Hanishport Fair. Marketway and Seller's Way were closed so the vendors could camp there with their goods, and on the day before the Fair, horses and wagons were not allowed on any seaside roads except the quay. Chaen thought the quay would be a good place to set up her stools and easel, so she waited in a long line at the harbormaster's office to get a license.

Fair Day dawned. Soon after sunrise, she wended through the clutter of flimsy market stalls with her easel and stool under her arms and her knapsack heavy on her back. Vendors folded away their beds, a troupe of jugglers sat drinking tea by their baskets of implements, puppeteers carefully hung their puppets behind their stage, and a food seller arranged kindling in a firepot.

No one had been allowed to set up early on the quay, and now it was a frantic tangle of stalls being constructed; hand carts of pastries, fruit, trinkets, and game pieces being unloaded; musicians arguing about the order of performance; and the harbormaster ignoring all of them as he serenely wound the tide clock with a giant key. Chaen claimed her spot on the waterside, filled sacks with rocks and sand at the water's edge and tied them to the easel's feet so it couldn't be easily knocked over, and placed a portrait on the easel for advertisement. The portrait, painted on wood, had been a gift for her mother, which her mother returned to Chaen after she lost everything in the fire. It depicted a solemn baby, surrounded by artifacts of contentment and prosperity: a basket of corn, a hand-woven towel, a piece of slate chalked with Chaen's records of which chickens were laying and which weren't, and, drooping in the baby's hand (for he would never show any interest in toys), a wooden rattle that his father had carved for him the winter before he was born. Beyond that solemn baby lay a sunlit field in which the entire family was at work harvesting wheat, and beyond it could be seen the scarlet and copper woodland, and a few softly curved golden hills. For years, Chaen had scarcely been able to look at the painting.

The musicians settled their dispute and began to play. The debris was swept away, and the vendors set up their displays even as fairgoers began to wander past. The juice seller to Chaen's left began enthusiastically shouting his wares. Chaen wouldn't have any customers that morning—people never bought portraits in the opening hours of a fair. She took out her sketchbook and drew the red-faced hat seller who paced up and down the quay wearing a stack of nearly thirty straw hats. Occasionally people stopped to look at her painting, or at the pencil drawings in her sketchbook. She told them the cost for one person or two, done in pencil or paint, and the potential customers said they might return later. It seemed like any other fair.

No one was alone, and some families traveled like geese, with a line of children suspended between the poles of supervising adults. Chaen did notice one solitary, shabby old man who bought a straw hat from the hat man, put it on over his grimy head scarf, and stood blinking with pleasure, a point of stillness in the unceasing flow of people. With a few swift strokes, Chaen added him to her sketchbook and continued to draw him from memory long after he had disappeared in the crowd.

She looked up from her drawing when the musicians fell silent. The nearby sounds gradually fell still, and she began to hear the more distant shouts, shrieks, and patter of drums. The flowing current of the crowd had become a jostling, surging movement, and there seemed to be an awful lot of people, many of whom were peering over each other's heads, and small children were hoisted to their parents' shoulders. Chaen tucked the sketchbook into the knapsack, moved the knapsack under the easel, and stood behind it, ready to climb onto the stool if she needed to. Of course her heart had begun to thud in her chest, and she began breathing deeply so her hands would be steady. "Sweeeet coooool juuuuuice," sang out her neighbor. "Sweeet—"

The shabby man in his new hat had reappeared. He bought a cup of juice and became trapped by the crowd at the juice seller's counter. The juice man climbed onto a box and peered over the heads of the crowd. "It's the G'deon! She's coming!"

The shabby man stretched up onto his toes, peering eagerly in the same direction. "Are you certain?"

Shielded by the painting on her easel, Chaen took the bow out of the knapsack. She checked that the darts were at hand, then strung the bow. She had known that the G'deon, if she came to the Fair at all, would have to cross the quay. But she hadn't expected that her wait for that opportunity would be so short.

"I see Paladins," said the juice seller. "Dressed all in black on this warm day—they must be hot."

"I suppose they're used to it," said the man.

"The G'deon towers above everyone! Why doesn't she comb her hair? I believe I'll send her a hair comb as a gift."

The man uttered an amused snort. "Make it a plain one. I hear she doesn't like fancy things."

A Paladin spoke to the musicians on the dais, who hastily moved their instruments out of the way. Now Chaen spotted the false G'deon: a towering, broad-shouldered woman with hair like a tangle of tarnished bronze wire. Chaen could not possibly hit her in this crowd. But when the woman stood on the stage, she would be exposed.

Chaen remembered what Saugus had said to her and the other assassins: *History will join hands with us.* She sighed with relief, as though the unfinished mission that had been gnawing at her for months had already been completed. Soon all would be well, and what happened afterwards would not matter.

The crowd surged toward the stage. The man in the hat stumbled toward Chaen, with the juice cup still in his hand. Directly in front of her, another man lost his footing. The man in the hat tripped over him and his juice cup went flying. The easel began to teeter, despite its weights, and Chaen grabbed it. When she looked down, her knapsack had disappeared. The man was helping the other to his feet, bowing a graceful apology, holding his new hat to his heart. Meanwhile, a woman with a long, black cord of braided hair trailing down her back stepped onto the stage. She turned and looked across the crowd, directly into Chaen's eyes. She was the fortune-teller.

"That must be the G'deon's wife." The juice man's voice sounded odd—distant, muffled.

The man who had stumbled showed Chaen the dagger that had been concealed by his linen short coat. The shabby man tucked his loose hair behind one ear, revealing three gold earrings.

Strong hands took her arms from behind. Someone took the bow.

The false G'deon stepped up onto the stage. She had a blacksmith's massive arms and soot-stained hands. Her eyes were a shocking blue. She heaved a breath, like a suffering sigh. The people cheered, but she did not look like she enjoyed being cheered at.

A crisp, terrible voice spoke near Chaen's ear. "I am Norina Truthken. You stand accused of murder. You will be tried in three days, in accordance with the Law of Shaftal."

"Get away from me." Chaen's voice seemed like it belonged to someone else.

"Are you putting me under interdiction?" the Truthken asked.

"Yes!"

The Paladins forced Chaen to turn and walk. The Truthken went ahead of them, opening a path through the crowd. Her hair was clipped close to her skull, and in the small of her back hung a long dagger in an age-blackened sheath. A raven swooped from wherever it had been hidden and landed on her shoulder. The bird looked backwards at Chaen. All these months, despite Chaen's vigilance, it had been watching her.

Slightly behind the Truthken walked a slim young man with a massive book under his arm.

It was Max.

Maxew had entered the world in silence, and he never cried at all. The midwife said something was wrong with him. At first, Chaen, and Orman, his father, carried their infant everywhere, as if holding him could cure him. But the baby struggled against any embrace, and even when Chaen gave him suck would pull away from her breast. One day, Chaen confessed to her mother that she found it difficult to like her own infant.

"I have been wondering if he could be an air child," said her mother. "In the old days, we would send for a Truthken to judge a child's elemental balance. If it was an air child they took it away, because only Truthkens could raise such children properly. But there are no Truthkens left, and I don't know what to do. I suppose we should ask the elders."

The elders determined that both Chaen and Orman had air witches in their lineages. They summoned a healer, a weary old woman with bowed shoulders and silver hair, who examined Max. She spoke bluntly to the young parents: "I am as certain as anyone but an air witch can be that your baby is an air child."

She said that air children know things that adults cannot bear to know, and have powers that few adults are wise enough to manage. She said that once Max discovered and began to use his power, he would be dangerous—at first to other children, and eventually to everyone. "Since the Order of the Truthkens no longer exists, air children usually are killed. I can do it for you. He will feel nothing—he will sleep deeply, and then he will cease to breathe."

The elders thought they should accept the gentle death the healer offered, but Chaen refused. "I will become wise enough to raise my son," she declared. A year later, the healer returned and asked again, and again Chaen refused.

Chaen had loved her contentious, hard-working family, and she had loved the farmstead that defined them. She felt that love most deeply when she painted: a busy flock of chickens, a line of people picking weeds in the garden, an ancient bucket filled with tools that were far older than the carpenter who used them. Now, when she remembered her family, she remembered a painting of them that she had done: the entire family at work in the parlor, with a fire blazing, a lamp hanging over the vast table, and everyone crowded together in the warmth and light while snow piled up on the windowsill. Orman sat on a stool playing his mandolin as a daughter of the house leaned on his knee and imitated his fingering upon a piece of wood. At his other side, the father of Chaen's second son was singing, with his eyes closed and his head tilted back, while the sock he was knitting dangled from his hand. Three older children worked sums on slates, directed by Marcena, who at the time had been recovering from a sword slash. Breve and Anda sat together as always, sharpening tools and laughing. May sat close to the fire, sewing straight seams by feel since she could scarcely see anymore and giving an occasional push to the cradle that hung from the rafters, while Arin slept within. Maxew sat in the shadows, watching this busy, noisy family in bafflement. Chaen herself was a reflection in a mirror: a smiling young woman with a paintbrush in her hand.

In the painting, the twenty-four of them were bright and dark, warm and cold, busy, contented, preoccupied, and oblivious to looming disaster. By the following autumn, twenty-two of them would be dead.

The Midlands had suffered under the Sainnites' iron rule since immediately after the Fall of the House of Lilterwess. According to Anda, the Sainnites wanted to control the road and the river so they could control nearly all of the trade. But Marcena said they wanted to control the grain fields that fed the soldiers and their horses. And Breve said that the Sainnites were so stupid it was impossible to understand them.

Every farmstead in their region sent three, four, or even five people to join Midland Company and fight the Sainnites. Anda was the first in Chaen's family to be killed.

Anda and Breve had grown up on adjacent farmsteads and became lovers in boyhood. They began working together on each farm on alternate days so that they could spend their days together as well as their nights. Such passions of youth usually burn themselves out, but theirs persisted, and their families finally arranged for them to marry together. When Chaen married into the same family, she was in love with Orman and was devoted to some of the others, but she most admired Anda and Breve. They were heedlessly brave, notoriously inventive, and ridiculously funny. When word came that Anda had been killed, all who knew the couple thought the same thing: How could one survive without the other?

Chaen wished she could join Midland Company in Anda's place, but she could not leave Max to be raised by his other parents. Max, without being taught, had already learned too much, but could not exercise proper judgment. Just as he had learned to read that winter by watching the older children at their lessons as he sat in the shelter of the shadows, so also had he learned anger and hatred from his elders. Chaen kept him out of sight when the soldiers came to help themselves to livestock, goods, or grain, because the child still spoke rarely but always said too much.

Every autumn, the fighters came home to bring in the grain and cut the hay before the mud season began. Chaen took up the scythe that had been Anda's, even though she was weaning Arin and her breasts spilled over with every swing of the scythe. Max followed behind her, shaping bundles for the sheaf-stacker. It was a good day for harvesting wheat, with a warm sun and clear sky, and the wheat stalks so dry they practically cut themselves. But the warmth also made for dirty work, and when the dinner whistle sounded, Chaen was encrusted with dust and chaff that had glued itself in her milk and sweat. As she and Max walked back to the field's edge, passing the water jug back and forth, she spoke proudly, saying, "You are doing so well and working so sturdily, keeping out of my way exactly as I showed you. What a fine son you are!"

She knelt in the stubble to wipe his face with a wet kerchief and to brush back and re-tie his hair in a tail. The summer sun had streaked his hair with straw yellow, just like Orman's hair had been when Chaen fell in love with him at a harvest dance. Max gazed at her in that odd way of his that made people feel nervous and threatened. "You don't like me, Mother," he said.

Chaen never knew how to answer him when he said such things. For most parents, it was enough to behave toward their children with love, even if they disliked their children sometimes. But if she denied to Max that she disliked him, Max would hear the lie and miss the love that motivated the lie. Chaen said, "Oh, Max, I just told you what good work you're doing."

"While you were saying it, you wished you could be proud of me all the time."

He was only six years old, and he knew people's secrets. He knew that he was disliked, and he was becoming indifferent to that dislike. How soon would he realize what an advantage it was to care nothing for what people thought of him?

Chaen said, "I will always tell you the truth, Max. Sometimes, I don't want to—but it's love that makes me want to shelter you. I do wish you were like other children. But that's my failure, not yours. I'll always love you as much and as well as I possibly can."

His gaze, expressionless and remote, seemed more animal than human.

She said, "People are anxious around you and don't know how to act. You have to teach us what you need from us, so we can do better."

She could hear Arin screaming in the distance as someone carried him from the house so she could nurse him. Her aching breasts let out a gush of milk.

"Arin makes you happy," Max said. "And I do not."

"Your brother is an easy child, and you are not. Anyway, being happy isn't what matters."

"What does matter?"

"Doing your share," she said.

Footsteps crackled in the stubble, and Breve walked past, alone. He didn't look at Chaen, which was good, for she'd have fallen to weeping if he had.

"Breve did his share," said Max. "And now he has a hole in him."

Breve sat on the wall beside Marcena, staring into the distance, his jaw working up and down as though he were a cow. The bread was hot from the oven, and there was lots of sweet butter, jam, cold salt beef, fresh-pressed cider, cucumbers dressed with herbs and clotted cream, blackberry pie. Chaen ate until she couldn't cram in one more bite, and leaned back against the warm stone wall and let her grunting baby suck all he wanted.

She was awakened from her doze by the distant clatter of shod hooves on stone: a company of Sainnites rode past. Some people stood up to look at the highway, shielding their eyes against the sun glare.

"They're preparing to steal the harvest before it's even brought in," someone said. The farmers, streaked with sweat and coated in dust from head to foot, each cursed the passing soldiers with the bitterest words they could think of.

"They are a plague of grasshoppers," said one. "They strip the plants to the bone and give nothing at all in return, not even shit."

Another said, "What we do to grasshoppers, let's do to them—a pitch fire in dry grass."

Some of what happened that last day she could hardly remember, and some she could not forget. She remembered that afternoon so vividly that she didn't trust her memory. Had someone truly said that he wanted to burn the Sainnites alive? Or did Chaen want those words to be said, because the fate that is wished on others may be the fate that's visited upon oneself?

That night, like everyone, she had slept in a stupor of exhaustion. But she awoke, and realized the house was on fire. She didn't know if she tried to awaken the others, or if her only thought was of her helpless babe. In nightmares she stumbled down unending corridors, crying Arin's name until the smoke clamped its harsh hand on her throat, scalded her eyes, and felled her to her knees. Then she crawled, thinking she heard the baby crying, following the sound from turning to turning so it seemed she must have crawled the entire distance to Wilton. Her waking memories of that horror were not much clearer, though she would never forget that she did reach the children's room, felt for Arin in his cradle, then remembered he had been in the bed with her. Already stupid from breathing smoke when she awoke, she had left him behind.

There's a kind of knowledge that opens up inside a person, a dreadful, vacant clarity that strips the soul bare, that in a single, devastating realization turns the rich clutter of one's life into a wasteland. So it was when Chaen realized she could not return to rescue Arin.

"Mother! Mother!" Max was shaking her shoulder, coughing, shaking her again. "—window," he said, and "—on the floor," and "—won't wake up."

The roaring in her ears meant she would die. She fainted, or fell down, and lay on the floor. A dreadful, vivid light writhed in the smoke.

Her son knelt beside her, gasping, choking. "Mother," he said. "Mama." He was crying. It was the only time in his entire life that he cried.

She heard others screaming. She couldn't choose to die that way. She dragged herself across the floor to the window and wrestled it open. Max told her later that they climbed down the outer wall of stones until they fell. She broke an arm and an ankle, but he only had the breath knocked out of him. She saw that the barn also was burning—a skeleton of black timbers in a tower of red flame—and black horsemen crossed the fire, chasing someone or something. She crawled toward the darkness, with the wrong son beside her.

After the Sainnites had left, and the neighbors came to see what could be saved, Max showed them where his mother lay in a thicket, her shirt charred, her hair turned to ashes.

After that, Chaen understood why Breve and Marcena had stared into the distance, dully chewing good bread as though it were grass. It was rumored that the two of them had done something to the Sainnites, an act of vengeance for Anda's death, and that was why the Sainnites had destroyed their entire family. Chaen didn't blame Breve and Marcena—she understood them.

While Chaen was recovering from her injuries, the child she had saved began to bully and torment the other children. Chaen could not make Max stop except by watching over him, day and night. She was twenty-six years old when, at winter's end, to save the other children, she took Maxew with her and became a traveling artist. Soon they were living from meal to meal, sheltering with farm animals when they could, and frequently managing without shelter at all. For three years she and Maxew wandered the land, often cold and always hungry, often avoiding skirmishes in the war that continued around them, constantly seeking households that could feed and shelter them for a while in exchange for a portrait.

One summer in Rees, a family hired her to paint a much-loved daughter of the house who was soon to be marrying out. That family had no young children for Max to bully, and they tolerated his strangeness. After the portrait had been completed, they invited Chaen and Max to remain. She began to be acquainted with the neighbors, some of whom belonged to Rees Company, and by autumn she also was a member. During the warm season, while she was fighting, she left Max with the family, so he could learn some of the things that a boy often must know in order to find a place in the world.

She killed a soldier, and then killed some more, and when she had killed or helped kill twenty-two of them she stopped counting but did not stop killing.

By the end of the following year, in every region, from mountains to grassland and from ocean to wilderness, people did their work and raised their children in a daze of fear and despair. Everyone knows what happened in Rees, how a canny Sainnite commander, informed by the visions of a Sainnite seer; had his five hundred Sainnite soldiers raze the farmlands, burn some thirty farmsteads to the ground, and, after widowing nearly every member of Rees Company, finally destroyed them. The terrified family begged Chaen to take her son and go elsewhere.

So they became vagabonds again. But now, when a thief tried to steal Chaen's little collection of coins, Chaen fought her. It was a woman, close to her own age, hardened and hungry as she was. Chaen shouldn't have had to kill her, but she only knew how to fight to the death.

Afterwards she had said to Max, "It was wrong, but I'll do it again if I have to."

And she did have to.

Chapter 13

Sometimes, when Karis preoccupied herself with important and productive work, she could almost seem happy, and Zanja could almost forget that Karis had finally been compelled to announce her existence to the people of Shaftal by Zanja's actions. But at times like this, when Karis had to act directly contrary to her inclinations, Zanja felt keenly how much of the G'deon's role had become her own responsibility, and how heavy and terrifying that responsibility was. She stood beside Karis on the stage and deliberately exercised her trust in herself. She must heed her intuition without demanding that it serve her and without worrying that it would fail. Through long experience, she had become skilled at maintaining that balance, but she had never before done it while standing on a stage, facing a packed crowd of people, any one of whom might be an enemy determined to destroy Karis and willing to die in the process.

"Wait," Zanja said. Karis nodded. Some four or five body-lengths away, between the sweaty musicians with their fiddle bows and drumsticks, and the astonished juice seller, Paladins in borrowed clothing picked up the assassin's stool and materials and followed Norina through the crowd. The people in the crowd were a blur; then they became vast collection of individuals as Zanja made sense of what she saw: farmers, shopkeepers, artisans, traders, laborers, sailors, travelers, a cluster of delighted water people, a handful of Juras people who stood at the crowd's edge, where they wouldn't block anyone's view. Off to the left Zanja spotted Medric, red with sunburn. Emil moved toward them on the right, until he was so close Zanja could have clasped his hand. Rein, the Paladin standing directly in front of Karis, was a fourth prescient. They could expect to know about any danger to Karis in that crowd, and, at the very least, to throw themselves between her and that danger. But Zanja felt no warning prickle or vague anxiety. The faces looking at Karis were not all friendly, but none of them were dangerous. Gradually, the restless crowd fell quiet; the assassin was gone. The heralds could be seen on both sides of the crowd, standing on boxes.

"This is a stupid idea," Karis muttered. "Why would anyone want to hear me talk?"

Zanja didn't argue with her, for they had resolved the matter more than a week ago. Norina could not arrest Chaen, since there was no evidence she was a criminal. In all the months Karis's raven had followed Chaen, she had pursued an itinerant, lonely, and entirely legal life. But she was the only person they knew of who might be able to betray the rogue air witch, and they had to get her to put herself into the Truthken's power. Karis had been willing to be the bait—she would have done anything to escape the strictures on her movements and actions—but had balked when the plan required her to actually give a speech. Emil had said, "We'll help you, of course, as much as you need." And Karis had said, "There's no point to it—talking doesn't change people!" But Emil had prevailed, mainly because Karis had relied on and trusted him for so long.

Emil signaled her. Zanja said, "Talk to Emil. Don't worry about the rest of them."

Karis took a breath and said, "I don't like to give speeches."

The man in front of her gave an ear-splitting bellow: "I don't like to give speeches!"

To the left and right, the heralds cried, "I don't like to give speeches!"

Medric put his hand over his mouth, and Zanja hastily looked away from him, lest she start laughing also. Well, at least he wasn't worried.

"Actions matter more than words," Karis said, and the heralds shouted her words. "There aren't many earth witches. But people with earth talent are so common that everyone knows some. So everyone knows that earth bloods hate to have power over others. Everyone knows that earth bloods are driven to fix what's broken. That's why it made sense to the people of Shaftal to have one earth witch whose duty is to mend and protect the whole of Shaftal. It even makes sense to me, although for most of my life I have wished I could give the Power of Shaftal to someone else. Someone whose judgment is perfect, who doesn't mind being stared at, and who never loses her temper. It took a long time for me to realize that the Power of Shaftal isn't only in me. It is in all the people who serve the land and not just themselves. That power is exercised by farmers who give their fields a year of rest. And by families that are too large, and so refrain from having children. And by the people who take many days each year from their regular labors in order to repair the roads. Every action of generosity or hospitality benefits the whole. These things are the Power of Shaftal.

"Now I will tell you that Hanishport is a broken place that must be fixed. Other places, like Reese and Appleton, also are terribly broken. They won't be fully mended for many years. But Hanishport must be mended now. Doing so is a difficult task, because the people of this city can't see that anything is wrong.

"This is what's wrong. More than thirty years ago, the people of the city helped the Sainnites create the village of Lalali. Now, in that village there are hundreds of people. Many of them are children without families. They are dying needlessly, in agony that few can imagine. Two dozen healers have been there since early spring. They have told me that the people of Hanishport have remained indifferent, even when the healers begged them for help. The people of Hanishport have refused to exercise the Power of Shaftal. Therefore, this city is broken.

"If you can do or give something to your neighbors, speak with a member of the Peace Committee at the house where we're staying. You know where that is, I expect. Also, on the day after the Fair ends, the Peace Committee will hold a meeting here on the quay at the morning's ebb tide. Anyone who wishes can come. Thank you for listening to me."

When she finished, the crowd was filled with murmuring, and Zanja didn't know what to make of it. Of course, Karis eagerly stepped down off the stage and was surrounded again by Paladins, lest someone on this crowded quay had a poisoned blade, or someone on a balcony or window shot a poison dart. Zanja stayed close to Karis, and Emil slipped through the crowd as neatly as Zanja could slip through a thicket.

Karis had not had the leisure to make Zanja a dagger to replace the one she had lost in the ocean, and she carried no weapon. But neither wits nor weapons proved necessary. They escaped the quay, and soon only a few excited children followed them. Emil trotted ahead to meet a Paladin, Lil, who said that the prisoner was secure and her darts had indeed been dipped in poison. "The poison must have been in the bag of potatoes," said Emil.

Kamren said, "We can find the potato farmer. But I don't know if we'll find the other people who helped her. Unless she tells us."

Karis asked, "Did Chaen interdict Norina?"

Lil said, "Yes. She seems to know the law."

"She can't interdict me," Karis said.

In the teetering house, the hall became crowded with Paladins, whose unbuttoned wool waistcoats revealed sweat-soaked linen shirts. Garland shooed them into the right-side parlor, where pitchers of cool drinks were ready. In the left-side parlor, Norina and Maxew had a street map of Hanishport unrolled on the table. A neat little dart lay in a dish.

Norina said, "I can confirm Zanja's observation that Chaen has a fire talent. But she has an equally strong air talent. Therefore this woman has been at war with herself since the day she was born."

Norina had predicted that there would be no one at all with fire talent in Death-and-Life Company, for the rogue air witch would be unable to abide such people. This dearth of fire logic might be a weakness that could be exploited. Zanja wondered if Chaen's membership in the company disproved Norina's theory, or the assassin's elemental contradiction had made her more tolerable to the air witch. When Chaen survived the attack on Travesty, she had become a kind of exile, which removed her from contact with the air witch. But of course that could only have been accidental.

Zanja was trying to read events as though they were glyph cards, she realized rather wryly. They knew so little about their dangerous enemy that the impulse to fill the unknown with guesswork was difficult to resist.

Emil said, "Someone with an earth talent could befriend her. Seth seems a good choice. But Seth was immediately involved in the death of Chaen's friend, Jareth. Would that matter to Chaen?"

Norina said, "Maxew, what do you think?"

The young man always seemed surprised when Norina asked him his opinion. This time it took a while for him to answer, as if he had not even been attending to the conversation. He said, "It won't matter.

To a person with air talent, the difference between accident and intention *is* meaningful."

"I think you are correct," Norina said. Any of the other air students would have been delighted by her approval, but Maxew always held himself aloof; whether from self-importance or from awkwardness Zanja could not determine.

Norina abruptly grabbed Karis's hand. She had been reaching for the dart. "Let me examine your hands before you touch that thing. And wash them immediately."

Karis allowed her hand to be inspected in the bright sunlight pouring in through the open windows. Norina, dissatisfied by the condition of Karis's right hand, examined the left and finally chose her smallest finger, the least likely to have any nicks in the skin. With that finger Karis touched the side of the dart, not its point. Still, Zanja's heart froze for a moment, for the snake poison was so lethal that anyone who used it as a weapon risked killing themselves with it.

Karis and Norina bent over the map together, and Karis pointed. "The poison is there."

"That's an alley. It's not in a building? Or in a shelter?"

"It's buried."

"It can't have been buried all winter. It must have been moved."

Zanja took Karis by the wrist and tugged her into the kitchen to scrub her hands. Norina came in after them. Karis said, "Don't you even trust me to wash my hands properly?"

"I understand that you want to be angry at someone, and I happen to be convenient. I came in to say something that I didn't want to be overheard. I think the rogue air witch is here in Hanishport."

Emil entered and announced his presence by clearing his throat, but Norina didn't take her gaze from Karis. "Don't go to Lalali without me. Until I return, continue to surround yourself with fire bloods, especially Medric."

Norina's warning was not for Karis, who almost always had a fire blood at her side. It was for Zanja and Emil: even inside the house, one of them must always be in the same room with her. Medric, who never slept at night, must be within call, with his pistols at hand, and the dogs, immune to air logic, would forewarn him even if no one else could.

"Will I never do what I want and need to do?" Karis said angrily.

"That's a question for the seer, not for me. But remember that none of us are doing what we want."

Norina left to dig up and confiscate the poison. That awful stuff must be rare and extremely expensive—they could hope there was no more of it in Shaftal.

Karis turned to Emil, who had missed part of the conversation but was never as puzzled as he should be. "Do you still want to be a librarian?"

Emil looked wistful. "To have quiet and solitude among a large number of books? I do, very much. But if I could have some peace while continuing to serve Shaftal, I think I would be contented."

Karis turned to Zanja. "I know you want to bring the border tribes into the council of Shaftal, and you must be frustrated that you're trapped into being my nursemaid instead."

"If you were killed and I wasn't there to protect you, I wouldn't want to live. Next summer, perhaps, I can visit the borders." But as Zanja spoke, a longing came over her, so powerful that it strained her voice, and she wavered into silence.

Karis was not a Truthken, but she also was no fool. "But," she said.

"Karis . . . I want to return to the Asha Valley. I want to go home."

Part Two: Air

The way of air is to judge and prove
Air by earth can be beloved
Air needs water so it can move
Four elements for balance.

Chapter 14

Required actions toward, and rights of, suspected criminals.
Summoning. If a crime has been committed, the elders of a community must summon a Truthken.
Detention. If the criminal is known or suspected, then the person may be detained in a locked room until the arrival of the Truthken. The prisoner is not to suffer any deprivation or degradation beyond confinement and reasonable measures necessary to ensure the safety of those who look after the prisoner.
Companionship. The prisoner must choose a friend whose duties are to be a companion, to fetch any requested items, and to verify that the prisoner is being treated properly. The friend may come and go at will. The friend may not reveal anything to anyone except at the exact request of the prisoner.
Transport. If the prisoner is detained by Paladins or by a Truthken, the prisoner must be transported by them to the community where the crime took place.
Interdiction. The prisoner may forbid a Truthken from speaking to, looking at, or being in his or her presence until the trial. If the prisoner is in the Truthken's custody at the time of the interdiction, that custody must be transferred as rapidly as possible, and in the meantime the Truthken must refrain from speaking to or looking in the face of the prisoner. Interdiction ends at time of trial.

Law of Shaftal

Chaen's captors locked her in a whitewashed room with a steep, water-stained ceiling through which she could hear the clicking of a large bird's claws as it paced along the peak of the roof. The window was just an empty frame beyond which lay the sea. Chaen could have thrown herself into the garden below if not for the rusty grate that barred her way. She shook the grate—gently, then with all her strength. It did not move at all.

The wide floorboards were soft and furred with age, but they didn't creak under her weight. The walls were shiplapped, solid. Here and there a bright nailhead attested to recent repairs. The same hand that had removed the window so Chaen couldn't cut herself with broken glass seemed to have checked and secured every board in the room. Even the two chairs and the table were sturdy, with freshly glued joints, and the mattress lay on planks rather than ropes, with sheets of heavy linen, impossible to tear.

Chaen stood in the room's center, staring out at the bright, busy harbor. Why had she not been able to leave this one task, this assassination, undone? Why had she been unable, just one time, to do as she was told? Fluently, softly, then loudly, she cursed herself, until the raven on the roof uttered a creak like a warped door swinging open, and the house sighed, and seemed to tilt as though under a heavy weight. Chaen heard voices and turned sharply as the key turned in the lock.

The false G'deon filled the doorway.

Beyond her, silent and fluid as a shadow, the fortune-teller dropped into a squat outside the door. With her were the shabby man from the quay, now dressed in Paladin's black, and a bespectacled man who peered at Chaen curiously.

Chaen had read about them, this phalanx of fire bloods. The members of her company had talked about them as though they were pieces in a game of strategy: whether Medric, the half-mad Sainnite seer, was a threat or a distraction; whether Zanja na'Tarwein had been made more or less dangerous by the extinction of her tribe; whether Emil Paladin had any weaknesses at all. Now, here they were: attentive as marksmen taking aim at a target. They were formidable.

But not as formidable as Karis. As she stepped into the room, it shrank to the size of a child's toy. Her head brushed the highest point of the ceiling. The walls groaned as she passed.

Chaen could only show her teeth and snarl, like a lap dog. "Get away from me!" Then she backed into the window grate, and the woman's fingertips brushed the arm she raised to shield herself, and it was like being spattered with scalding water.

The false G'deon spoke in a gravelly whisper. "So. You're from the Midlands. You've been injured by fire and by blade. You've survived great privation, and you know your own strength. I won't underestimate you." She moved a step back, and Chaen was able to take a breath. "But I will let you go."

"At what cost?" Chaen said bitterly, knowing the answer.

"Tell me how to find the leader of Death-and-Life Company."

"I will not."

"You'd rather die to protect an air witch, even though that person would turn Shaftal into a place that assassinates children."

"My entire family is dead. My son is dead. Shaftal already is a place that assassinates children."

"But, having seen your family die, you stood and watched while a poisoned dart narrowly missed my little daughter. That was your action, Chaen. Your choice."

"And *you* are choosing to protect the people who killed my family and hundreds of others!"

"Yes. Do you think *I'm* untouched by this vile history?"

From a distance, it had been easy to believe that this woman was a Sainnite at heart who had stolen the Power of Shaftal and now used it to defend Shaftal's dreadful enemies. But Chaen couldn't remember why the company members had discounted the woman's history of enslavement by, exploitation by, and narrow escape from the attack by the Sainnites on the House of Lilterwess. Disoriented, she said, "I know you are colluding with them now."

"I am colluding with Sainnites," the woman said, "as much as I'm colluding with you."

"Collusion? You tricked me, manipulated me, misused the Power of Shaftal . . . !"

"Exactly," she said. "The Sainnites felt what I did to gain peace, and they continue to feel it. You also will feel it, Chaen of the Midlands. And you won't escape. Now that I've touched you, I'll always know where you are, as long as you live. And I like this fact as little as you do."

"I doubt it," Chaen muttered.

The woman said, "Every day, I awaken angry. Every day, I let go of my anger, because I can't expect the people of Shaftal to let go of their anger if I can't do so. But I'll let you go, with all your scars and pain and rage, and you can curse me in the streets for the rest of your life. Just one time, for one moment, set your anger aside and take the long view, as your parents certainly taught you to do. An unbounded air witch will destroy Shaftal."

"An unbounded earth witch is just as dangerous!"

The woman's fist clenched at her side, and Chaen remembered belatedly that only a fool picks a fight with a Meartown metalsmith. But the woman didn't raise her fist, and she spoke in the same measured way she had been speaking. "Let go of your anger, Chaen, or you will be forced to let go of it."

"As you said," Chaen said bravely, "I'll die instead."

After the false G'deon left, Chaen paced the room, frantic. She kicked the walls and shook the grate. But she was trapped.

Morning had become afternoon before the key once again turned in the lock. A woman came in, glanced at Chaen's face, and said, "Oh, for land's sake, I'm just a cow doctor."

She carried a tray, trailing the scent of hot bread, brown butter, and burnt onions; a lanky woman, dressed in a longshirt of plain linen, with an ordinary sort of face, and short, stiff, unevenly trimmed hair that kept escaping from behind her ears.

"I'm Seth, the councilor from Basdown. I'm in the Peace Committee, that came here with Karis." She set the tray on the table, then took Chaen's knapsack from her shoulder and put it on the bed. "The Paladins looked through your bag and removed everything that could be used as a weapon. The rest of your things will be fetched from the tailor's shop."

She waited. Chaen, who stood at the window, where her pacing had ended, said, "Do you expect me to thank you?"

The cow doctor blew air out of her nose like a horse and sat down at the table. "That would be polite, for I'm your friend."

"What?"

"That's what I said when they asked me! Have an onion roll—they're direct from the oven." The crust crackled as she broke a roll open and buttered it with her fingers, as there seemed to be no knife. She had a way about her, a bluntness and an imperturbability that Chaen recognized.

"You're an earth blood," said Chaen. "I suppose they thought I'd trust you because we're elementally compatible."

"What would be the point in sending you a friend you couldn't get along with?"

"I don't want a friend," said Chaen.

"Really? I think no one can have too many. Anyway, it doesn't matter what you want. The law requires you to have a friend. Is there someone else who could be summoned?"

Chaen said nothing. The cow doctor bit into her roll and shut her eyes with pleasure. When she had finished the roll, she offered the other to Chaen, then ate it as well. The silence didn't seem to trouble her. "Do you want tea? It's very good—a variety so rare that no one can afford to drink it."

"I just want you to go away."

"I will. I have a lot to do. But there are two things I have to tell you." She sipped her tea, and its fragrance reached Chaen, like the scent of a meadow of wildflowers on a hot day. "First, I have to tell you about Jareth. You've been waiting for him every night at the tide clock, am I right?" Chaen didn't answer, but the cow doctor said, "Well, he's dead. He died two months ago, in a place called Essikret. First he killed my friend, Damon, and I fought with him, and he fell off a cliff and was killed."

Chaen supposed she should be startled or distressed. But nearly fifty members of Chaen's company had been killed since autumn, and one more death was difficult to care about. She said, "So he's dead. What is the second thing?"

"I'm to tell you what will happen. Your trial will be in three days, and until then, no one is allowed to ask me about you, or even talk about you in my presence, and I'm not allowed to talk about you to anyone unless you specifically ask me to. I think that's everything I'm supposed to say. What do you want? Food? Garland is a talented cook, and he's terribly kindhearted. The garrison soldiers have started to work on the sewers in Lalali, and every day Garland sends a cake to whichever company gets the dirtiest and most disgusting job. His cakes are so delicious, and the soldiers are so desperate for good food, that the companies are actually trying to get the worst assignments. Are you sure you don't want tea?"

Chaen shook her head. To refuse food might accomplish nothing, but a symbolic resistance was still a resistance.

"Well, what will help you pass the time?"

"I'd like to finish painting the tailor's sign."

"I'll ask the Paladins to fetch it. But they may not let you have your tools and supplies."

"Do they think I can hurt someone with a paintbrush?"

"Don't ask me to explain the Paladins . . . their philosophy is exhausting."

Seth sipped the flowery tea. Outside, in the harbor, there was a glow of light beneath the waters, as though a cool twin of the sun swam in the deep. Farther away, ocean blended into sky, so it seemed a ship could sail upward and slide past overhead. A tiny sailboat with an orange sail scuttled past.

Seth said abruptly, "Zanja's glyph cards—surely you find them interesting, since you're an artist and a fire blood—in fact, some people have become completely obsessed with them. They are the lost glyphs. Or rather, the ones that used to be lost. And it was Jareth who found them, though he didn't know what he had found."

Chaen didn't turn to Seth or show any interest, but the cow doctor began to tell her the entire, incredible tale. She was a leisurely and digressive storyteller, and when her teacup was empty, she had only managed to describe the ancient, lavishly illustrated lexicon, which in the ancient past, she said, had been brought to Shaftal from a distant country.

Seth bade her farewell and departed with the tray. In the road below, people stood talking aimlessly. After a while, Seth appeared and took one of them into the house.

More time passed. Then a two-earringed Paladin opened the door and politely asked permission to enter. He explained the conditions under which she would be permitted to paint. The tailor's sign and Chaen's supplies were carried in, and she painted until the light dimmed, while the Paladins took turns watching her from the doorway and the breeze washed through the room.

Chapter 15

In the weather-beaten house overlooking the harbor, there were two captives. One was confined behind a locked door and barred windows. One paced restlessly under the guard of three fire bloods, two of whom discussed glyph cards at a small table, while one dozed on the mattress. Karis swept aside the dark cloth that covered the window and looked out, much to the gratification of the people waiting patiently in the road. Karis waved politely. "Norina is returning."

As soon as Norina entered the room, Medric awoke with a start and located his spectacles by feel where he had wisely put them in a shoe. Zanja sat on the floor, and Norina sat in the chair, saying, "The poison was in a little pot with a wooden lid, sealed shut with beeswax. It was buried in an alley-yard that belongs to a family of rope-makers. They had no idea it was there. A couple of Paladins have taken it away to dispose of it. I hope they don't accidentally kill themselves."

Emil asked, "Is it too much to hope that you have glimpsed the rogue air witch?"

"If I had, our difficulties would be over."

"Except that you also would be dead," said Medric. "Little though I love you—"

"I share the sentiment!"

The Truthken and the seer usually managed to avoid being in the same room with each other. Karis said hastily to Norina, "Then why do you think this person is in Hanishport?"

"I saw Chaen's face twice—once when I arrested her, and once by accident, when the Paladins were bringing her upstairs. Between the first time and the second, something had reassured her. Who else but the air witch could have given her that assurance?"

"Suicide is a kind of escape," Emil said.

"Yes, perhaps she did think of a way to kill herself. But since I can't interrogate her, I am reduced to speculation." She added quickly, perhaps so the fire bloods wouldn't take offense, "I don't mean to undervalue speculation. But without information it has limited value."

Norina, while struggling to teach five young air witches to behave themselves, had herself become markedly better behaved. And Medric, whose rampant speculations Norina often checked with harsh impatience, lately seemed to be checking his own runaway tongue, at least in her presence.

Emil said, "Surely the rogue air witch suspects that a direct battle with Norina is not survivable, though she can't survive it either. Would an air witch risk coming near you?"

"No," said Karis, who since midwinter had been suffering greatly due to Norina's caution.

"But a *considered* risk—" Norina began.

Emil said, "A risk for what purpose? To reassure Chaen, whom this air witch has allowed to be out of contact for many months? How could the air witch have known what Chaen intended to do? She didn't have time to seek anyone's permission."

"Unless she did it in a manner that my raven couldn't observe," Karis said. "Through those people she met with, perhaps."

"That seems unlikely. Norina, if you're about to try to confine Karis indoors, I hope you'll reconsider. Won't it be enough for you to continue to guard her? You have work to do in Hanishport, but even you can't accomplish much during a festival. Leave Maxew to keep the house secure during the day, and Medric will watch over Karis at night. No air witch will get past *him* unnoticed, and he's the only person alive who can simply shoot our enemy dead with a pistol."

Zanja could see that Norina wanted to argue with him. But instead she looked at Karis and held her tongue.

In Lalali, nearly the entire garrison of soldiers was hard at work, patching roofs, repairing fallen walls, and digging new sewers. Several wagonloads of the smoke drug, a gift from the House of Lora, had transformed the hospital into a quiet and orderly place, now dominated by a clock that marked each hour with a cheerful chime, announcing that it was time for another small group of people to come in for a slightly decreased dose of the drug. Zanja was called upon to translate an extremely stiff conversation between a healer and the garrison commander, which ended in the garrison commander's admiring comment that healers were as organized as soldiers.

The rest of the day she spent following Karis, Norina, and several Paladins and healers up and down the back streets, knocking on doors and talking with the residents. She usually waited in the street, trying to study the glyph cards, but she felt restless and unsettled, hemmed in by the narrow passageways, overwhelmed by the smells, and distracted by a sensation that someone was watching her.

Once, when she stood up suddenly, she spotted the startled movement of a child taking flight. For a while, her secret observer stayed away, but then returned.

Norina came outside, glanced at her, and said, "Something is troubling you, and you haven't mentioned it to me?"

"It's nothing—a child is watching me from hiding, impeding my concentration."

"Well, I don't see why you keep trying to understand the card-casting. In three days I'll interrogate Chaen."

"But she can only tell you what she knows, which may be very little. The cards could reveal things that nobody knows."

Norina sat beside Zanja on the stoop. She scrubbed her fingers through her close-cropped hair. She wiped sweat from her face. "Well, here's something nobody knows. I have been troubled lately."

Zanja looked at her in surprise.

"You *are* the right person to discuss it with," Norina said.

Zanja was no longer disconcerted when Norina abandoned the pretense of normal human interaction. "If you say so. What's troubling you?"

"The rogue witch's tactics seem oddly ill-considered. If this person . . . Oh, for land's sake, let's pretend it's a man. If he is experienced in indirect warfare, as he must be, then his direct attack on us last winter was a peculiar waste of resources. I wonder if he *expected* the assassination attempt to fail, and if he *intended* the assassins to be sacrificed. Even Chaen was sacrificed. Emil is correct that she isn't valuable to the rogue air witch. Her dual talent makes her difficult to maneuver or mislead. I expect that in a few days I'll be using direct force on her—maybe quite a lot of it."

"I pity her."

"Yes, you know better than anyone what an unpleasant person I am."

"But for him to stage an assassination, just to get rid of unwanted people—"

"I doubt that was his primary reason for the assassination attempt. He did it to manipulate us. He forced us to devote our resources to defending ourselves against an unsubtle but terrifying enemy. I'm afraid our attention *was* diverted while the rogue air witch was pursuing a more subtle strategy."

Unnerved, Zanja said, "That attack certainly captured everyone's attention, especially that of Karis."

"Yes, and it also restrained her, to the point that she has been unable to exercise the Power of Shaftal. And it forced me into a role that degrades both of us."

Karis came out the door, talking in a harsh rasp—as close to a shout as she could manage—to a bewildered old man. "The building will fall down! You must move!"

The man cupped a hand around his ear. Norina, whose piercing voice could slice through the dullest comprehension, rose up to help.

That night, the dogs patrolled the garden, Paladins stood guard at both the doors, and Medric sat with his lamp, books, and pistol just a few steps away in the kitchen. Still, Zanja longed for the dagger she had lost in the ocean. Karis, living under such close observation, could not go outside to work at a forge. Yes, the assassination attempt had indeed prevented her from accomplishing anything of value.

Karis had flung her filthy clothing onto the floor and lay naked upon the bed.

The first time Zanja saw Karis without clothing, she had been so stunned by the beauty of her muscles that nearly a year passed before she understood how intensely and impossibly she wanted to lie down with her and press her skin to hers. But Karis had known.

Karis said unhappily, "What kind of life is this, that we must wonder every night whether or not we dare go to sleep?"

"It's the kind of life we have."

"And none of us is living as we want," Karis said.

She gazed at or through the ceiling. Her big hands lay open, revealing fresh cuts and splinters in her fingers and palms. Zanja took a pot of unguent from the table, knelt on the mattress, and lifted one of Karis's hands. She smoothed the lotion over her scratches and bruises. She rubbed it into her palms and stroked it down each of her fingers. Even though Karis's skin was coarse and hardened by work, her palms and fingertips were extraordinarily sensitive. Yet she never protected them, using them to greet thoughtful and careless people alike, sticking them heedlessly into brambles and nettles, subjecting them to the dirtiest imaginable tasks: scrubbing pots, digging sewers.

Zanja massaged the greasy, sweet-scented unguent into the palm of Karis's right hand, a hand that smashed and built, hurt and healed: a hand that might be empowered by Shaftal but also was empowered by strength, compassion, and intelligence developed under circumstances that would make most people mean and violent.

She felt the hand quiver. Karis was not asleep—not even close to it. Their hands slid across each other in the slick oil, and Zanja's own muscles contracted. A smile grew in the corners of Karis's mouth. Zanja lay upon her, and kissed her. Then, quite abruptly, she was flat on her back, and the smooth muscles of Karis's shoulders were sliding under her hands like molten rocks, and her breath was in her mouth.

Give Karis your whole self, Medric had said.

Zanja had not argued with him. She could have declared that she was Karis's lover and not her servant, but she already knew Medric would never expect her to give up her independence or her will, without which she was of no use. He had meant something else.

But it wasn't enough to merely love Karis, was it? *Give your whole self to her,* Medric had said. Duty, independence, insight, language, rage, diplomacy, patience, life itself. All of it? But no, these Zanja delivered every day, in service of Shaftal. Surely nothing had been withheld?

Except that she was lonely, broken, crippled by loss. Except that every year the ghosts returned, and Zanja felt anew the horror of being the only one, the last survivor, of her people.

She felt that slick, powerful hand on her thigh, and a sensation like sunlight flowed upward through her veins and out the top of her head. She parted her legs, grasped Karis's strong wrist, and pulled the big, slick, careful hand toward her until it slid inside of her. Like this? Zanja wondered. Was this what Medric meant? Karis began to gasp a dizzy, heady rhythm, with a small sound as though she were about to weep or to laugh.

Inside. Where sorrow hides, deeper. Where the open wounds ooze pain. The slashed sinews that once connected Zanja to her ancient people.

Why would I, how would I, give her this pain?

Your whole self, said Medric.

"Yours also," Zanja said, or tried to say. *The slow bleeding of sorrow, the injuries that cannot seem to heal.* "For you—" Zanja gasped. "Broken. For you."

Karis uttered a helpless sound. Zanja felt that distinctive heat, between her legs, in muscle and bone and the thunder of hearts: Earth magic. Karis was doing something to her, however inadvertently, and Zanja let it happen.

Hands. Breast. Heart. Whose? She couldn't tell.

Their lovemaking became very strange.

Chapter 16

When the blue afternoon began to turn gold, Seth again arrived at Chaen's door with a tray of food. "I see a shop sign out in the hall. Were you painting today?"

Chaen said, "Are you going to eat all your meals here? I wish you wouldn't."

"This is the time I have to spend with you."

"I don't want you here at all."

The cow doctor gave Chaen a level look. "Are we to have the same argument over and over? I'm already doing that with the people of Hanishport all day long. They are the most argumentative people! If my family argued like that, the cows would die of milk fever, the cheese would turn rancid, and the hay would rot in the field."

She put a steaming bowl at the second chair, with a spoon, and sat down to eat her own meal. It seemed to be a stew of fish and summer vegetables, with green herbs floating in it. There was bread too, and butter, but still no butter knife. Chaen had eaten nothing since the day before, and the stew smelled delicious. Standing at the window, she turned her face into the breeze so she couldn't smell it.

Seth said, "I never cared about glyphs, but some people were dreadfully sad that most of the glyphs were lost when the lexicons all were burned when the Sainnites razed the library at Kisha, and we were left only with the hundred glyphs in common use. Now we have a lexicon again, and Zanja will tell you that she stole it, but what really happened is a lot more complicated. She stole it, and then she was forced to return it, and then it was given back to her . . . or maybe it was given to Karis . . . and we'll never know why, because it all happened two hundred years ago."

Chaen turned to Seth, surprised and suspicious.

Seth was holding her head. "Water magic. Just talking about it makes me seasick. I might not be able to tell you this story at all."

In time, she recovered enough to butter her bread with her fingers. Chaen looked away again, but she had been captured by the bits and pieces of Seth's account and couldn't help but try to put them together in a way that made sense. "How was it given to Zanja?" she asked reluctantly.

"Tadwell G'deon put it in a box that he sealed with earth magic, and left it in the attic of my family home in Basdown. There it sat for two hundred years. I lived in that house nearly my entire life and never knew it was there."

"And Zanja stole it from your family?"

"No, Jareth stole it from my family. And he stole a donkey to carry it. That's why Damon and I were chasing him. Also, he had killed one of Karis's ravens."

Chaen said, "Since you insist on telling me this tale, I wish you would tell it like a normal person. Who did Zanja steal the book from?"

"Zanja stole the book from the library at Kisha, two hundred years ago."

For quite a while after that, Seth's mouth was full, and Chaen restrained her impulse to ask any more questions. The harbor was luminous with sunset, and music and laughter rose like the tide. Seth said, "I was with Zanja when she broke through the ice of a river we were crossing, and disappeared. And I was there to pull her out of the ocean, a couple of months later. During the time in-between, she was visiting Shaftal of two hundred years ago. If you want to know more about what Zanja did there, ask one of the fire bloods to tell you about Grandmother Ocean. Water magic doesn't seem to bother *them*."

"What a tale," Chaen said dryly.

"I'm an earth blood, Chaen. I'm never confused about the facts. I don't repeat other people's stories until I know they are true, and I don't invent things."

All day, people had arrived and left from that creaking old house, sometimes in a hurry, sometimes waiting in the road, sometimes alone and sometimes in a crowd, while the sounds of music and revelry in the city seemed like echoes from an alien country. Always, the dogs barked when someone drew near. Now, once again, the dogs made their announcement, and Seth went to the window and called to someone below, "I'll come right down!" She said to Chaen, "The lexicon revealed something truly astonishing about the history of Shaftal."

"And I suppose you'll tell me about it in the morning over breakfast," said Chaen. "But before you go, there's something I need your help with. A question about the law."

"I can bring you a copy of the *Law of Shaftal*. But it's awfully tedious. When the Truthken recites it from memory, I always get distracted by wondering how she could have memorized the entire thing, and whether she ever makes a mistake, and if she did make a mistake, how we would even know. And why anyone would memorize it in the first place."

Chaen knew how tedious the *Law of Shaftal* was. She had looked at the copy Saugus had acquired somehow, and given to Maxew, because she was curious what the law had to say about the right of Shaftali to defend themselves against a military occupation. But she had soon given up. The book had not merely been boring; it had been irrelevant, an artifact from before the Sainnites came.

She said, "I want to know if it's against the law to manipulate and trick a person into breaking the law."

"Is that what happened to you?"

"The raven followed me, and by watching me they learned my weaknesses. The fortune-teller, she told me to leave the city, and she knew I would do the opposite. Then they dangled the false G'deon before me, knowing I couldn't bear for anything to be left incomplete."

"So you think they put you in a position that you couldn't choose what to do? Well, I will ask . . ."

"Who will you ask?"

"Norina Truthken."

"How could I trust anything she says?"

"She's all there is, the only Truthken," said Seth. Her patience was beginning to require some effort, Chaen noticed.

"There was a boy with her."

"Maxew? He has only studied the law for a few months."

"Still, he knows more than you or I, doesn't he? Please ask him."

After Seth left, Chaen brought a chair to the window and sat with the cool, salty breeze washing across her face. She gazed out at the harbor and at the bay beyond, where the water at the horizon lay in darkness while the nearby water still glowed with light. The city was filled with music. Perhaps everyone in Hanishport was dancing tonight.

Maxew would understand Chaen's message. Tonight he would come for her.

Chaen and Max had been vagabonds for eight years. One day, at a fair, Max said to her, "There's a madman down by the river."

She did not look up from her drawing of the young man whose portrait would be a gift for his sweetheart. "There are a lot of lunatics lately."

The young man relaxed his far-away expression, which he seemed to think was romantic even though it made him look dumb as a cow. "That ranting man? Willis of South Hill? Keep away from him!"

"Sit still please," Chaen said.

By the time she finished the portrait, her son was gone. Two portraits later, when Chaen, on the lookout for a new patron, was eating an apple for supper, Max returned. "Take a penny and get yourself something to eat," she said, before she realized that the man who stood nearby had arrived with him.

Max said, "Mother, this is Saugus. He travels with that madman, Willis."

Chaen no longer apologized for Max when he was rude, and the stranger didn't seem to mind that a mere boy had called a friend of his a madman.

He was a clean man in neatly mended clothing, older than Maxew and younger than she, vigorous and well fed, with an odd rigidity of expression. His felt hat had weathered several seasons of snow and sun.

"Your son allowed me to buy his supper already," he said.

Max could not be fooled by false generosity. Nonetheless, Chaen felt a stab of suspicion. "That was kind of you. You must allow me to draw your portrait."

"I don't want one, and I don't have a wall to hang it on. I want to talk to you about Maxew." He sat on the stool and laid a coin on her easel. "That's for your time." It was more than she could earn in a day—in a good day.

Max said, "Take it, Mother." She handed him the coin, and he put it in the bottom of her brush box, where their savings for winter increased much too slowly.

Saugus said, "You have no reason to trust me. I'm just a stranger at a fair. But you do trust your son's judgment. Max noticed me in the crowd, watched me for quite a long while, and finally approached me. 'I know what you're doing,' he said. 'The people who have holes in them, you're choosing them, talking to them, and getting them to give you money.'"

Chaen looked up.

"You don't need to fear him," said Max. "He's an air witch, like me."

The night Arin and the rest of Chaen's family burned to death, she had lost her capacity for joy. But, through the horrors and trials of the years that followed, she had tried with all her being not to fail her surviving son. Even when she could not be what he needed, she had continued to struggle. And now, quite abruptly, the struggle was over.

She said, "Will you teach my son how to use his air logic as it should be used, for the good of Shaftal?"

"Why do you think I know what the good of Shaftal is?"

Chaen's air self and her fire self had achieved a rare agreement, and the argument inside her head had fallen silent. She did not speak, and the air witch said, "We must eradicate the Sainnites so the *people* can decide what is the good of Shaftal."

She turned to Max. "You can go with him."

Her son said, "What about you? Do you think you will return to the Midlands? You can never be a farmer again."

"No, but my mother's family will shelter me, and I'll join Midland Company."

Saugus said, "Why not join *my* company? You need not be separated from Maxew."

Chaen examined her smudged hands and paint-daubed sleeves. Then she looked up at Max, but it was Saugus who answered her silent question. "Yes, Willis *is* a madman, because he passionately believes that a drunken dream he once had was a vision. Most members of the company believe in his vision, and that belief gives them the wholeness, the virtue, and the courage to raise arms against the Sainnites. But I don't need to believe in that vision, no more than you do."

A girl interrupted them to ask if Chaen would make a half-size drawing for penny, as that was all the money she had left. Chaen said, "Go away. I am done drawing portraits."

Death-and-Life Company had been created and trained by the Sainnites themselves. They were a collection of hardened veterans who had survived awful events and continued to fight, becoming more ruthless and fearless with every passing year; a company that depended on no one's approval or good will and was not hampered by the cowardice that the Paladins said was philosophy. Even though Willis had invented a god so that he could be designated the god's chosen servant, he still was a canny commander who knew his enemy, calculated risks without being ruled by them, and rarely accepted new members. After a year in the squad captained by Saugus, which gathered money, supplies, and information, Chaen moved into positions of greater danger, eventually making it into a detachment whose members could have been the most determined, inventive, and ruthless fighters in Shaftal, were they not overshadowed by the squad of forty that was led by Willis. By the third year, the enemy that had once seemed impossible to defeat was faltering, and she began to think their cause could eventually be achieved.

Then Willis was killed, along with his entire squad, in an operation they had expected to be bloodless. And Karis came out of obscurity, declared herself the G'deon of Shaftal, and made peace with the Sainnites.

Chapter 17

Zanja awoke to a pale sunrise glow from the small window. She lay in the tangled bedding, wondering lazily what had happened.

She found the kitchen empty except for Garland, who was splashing dishwater in the scullery. She served herself sausages from the warming oven, a fat slice of bread from the loaf on the sideboard, and a cup of rather strong, lukewarm tea. While she ate, she studied an array of glyph cards on the serving counter. The parts would not cohere. Could it be that a card was missing?

Careful to wipe the grease from her hands, she reached into the satchel—

—the iron gate latched with a quiet snick. "That's better," she said, except that she hadn't said it, and it wasn't her voice. She heard the familiar sound of the dogs huffing out small, joyful exclamations, the way they did when they were with Karis. She stood up, with the dogs dancing around her, half-blinded by the sunlight glaring from the surface of the sea. She felt extraordinarily tall—

—her hand was caught in the straps of the satchel. She saw the varnished serving counter, the gorgeous glyph cards lying at a careful distance from the plate. Her hands. Her breast. Her heart.

She looked up and discovered Norina examining her in a way she did not like. "Am I losing my mind already?" Zanja asked.

Norina pierced a piece of sausage on her knife. "What have you done?" she asked.

Garland's chopping knife pounded a quick rhythm. The kitchen smelled like onions. But a moment ago, Zanja had been smelling the ocean, the wind, and the oil can that Karis carried in her toolbox.

Norina said, "I saw Karis in you. Not the thought of her, but *her*. Her awareness. Her presence. *What have you done?*"

Medric poked his head in the doorway. "Zanja? Oh." He backed out the door.

Norina slammed her knife down on the counter.

Garland glanced over his shoulder. "Norina! What if I had a cake in the oven?" He picked up a spoon as if to stir the onions into his bowl, but stopped, seeming startled, and subjected the spoon to a puzzled examination.

Norina had chased Medric into the hall and dragged him back, with her fist clenched in his shirt. "Explain!"

Medric pushed his dislodged spectacles back into place and said in a strained voice, "I'd rather not."

"My duty is to protect the G'deon of Shaftal! Explain!"

Zanja said, "But Medric's duty is to shape the future."

Norina gave her a hard look. Zanja added, "I don't know what happened last night, but I know better than to demand an explanation from a seer."

"You fire bloods may love peril and uncertainty. But now Karis must share *your* perils, Zanja. For when she changed you, she changed both of you."

"Is that what happened?" Zanja felt a growing dismay. Years ago, when Karis created the ravens to be her eyes, ears, and voice, she had put a bit of her physical self into them. When a raven was killed, as had happened four different times, Karis was diminished. Surely that loss would be far greater if the raven who was killed was Zanja.

Norina, having watched Zanja think, said bitterly, "Yes, she did promise not to create any more ravens."

"She didn't break that promise intentionally."

"You *tricked* the G'deon of Shaftal?"

Although Zanja wasn't as punctilious as Norina, she would never have followed Medric's instructions had she known what would result. Last night's lovemaking had been extraordinary. Now that she could remember it more dispassionately, it seemed obvious what had been happening when she became unable to distinguish her body from that of Karis. Meanwhile, Medric, keeping watch outside the door, had heard it happen. If Karis had been tricked, Zanja also had been tricked.

Medric already looked wretched, but she said to him, "You knew I wouldn't have consented. Were you coming in here to apologize?"

"No, to ask you to trust me."

"If something happens to me, if I'm killed again . . ."

"A catastrophe," Norina said.

Medric said nothing. He looked away.

Karis came in, with the dogs at her heels and a raven on her shoulder. She set her toolbox down with a thump and surveyed the three of them. "Are you fighting again?"

"Are we ever *not* fighting?" said Norina.

"Karis, I have to tell you something," Zanja said.

"I know, I heard the conversation with your ears." She turned to Norina. "It's done. It can't be undone." Then she turned to Medric.

"Don't ask me!" Medric cried, and fled.

The three women stood looking at each other, like friends gossiping on market day, except for their unhappiness. "Something's going to happen," Karis said. Dread strained her voice.

"I'll talk to Emil," said Norina.

"Leave Medric alone."

"Of course," Norina said bitterly. She started out the door, then turned back. "Zanja na'Tarwein, be careful with your life."

In Lalali, Norina stood guard over Karis like a furious gargoyle. Zanja could not concentrate with Norina glaring at her, so she went to the plaza, which was pleasant now that the little stages and the awful statuary had been broken up and hauled away. Sitting on golden stone, with the sun on her skin and a noisy flock of birds chattering nearby in the arbor, she laid out the array of cards and then became distracted by pointless worry about what exactly Karis had done, why Zanja had induced her to do it, and what was going to happen next.

But she wanted to be solving the problem she was prepared to solve, not some other problem entirely. Karis had wanted to come to Hanishport even before Chaen fortuitously settled there. Chaen's wanderings seemed so convincingly purposeless that it was decided to manufacture a reason to arrest her so Norina could extricate the truth from her. To find and capture the rogue air witch, that was the problem that mattered, regardless of its unpleasantness. Zanja's part in that enterprise was the interpretation of the glyph cards.

She mechanically sorted the eleven glyph cards into clusters, then re-sorted them into different clusters. Violence: a terrible animal, large as a house, was ridden to battle; paired warriors threatened each other, frozen in identical poses; a man fled a burning village, unaware that the belongings on his back also were burning; a warrior bristling with weapons was stabbed by a naked child. But did these images refer to Chaen's internal struggle with her contradictory self? It was impossible to know, without knowing what question the cards were answering.

Zanja heard a small sound. Without moving, she slid her gaze sideways. A filthy, emaciated street child, who had crept toward her across the paving stones, now had frozen, like an animal that hopes to evade a predator's notice by holding still. It was the boy who had watched her before.

"This is a difficult problem," Zanja murmured, as if talking to herself. The boy neither fled nor spoke. She said, "I'm studying these glyph cards because I am a presciant. Do you know what that is?"

"You know the future," said the boy.

She was careful not to look at him directly, lest she frighten him away. "No, the future is never clear to me. But I have feelings or ideas that won't go away, and if I pay attention to them, they lead me to more, and if I keep following them, sometimes I can discover what I want to know."

"Like a good smell." The boy's voice was scarcely audible.

"Yes. Or like feeling restless, and walking, and discovering that going one way rather than another feels better, and ending up in a plaza where a strange-looking woman is studying some glyph cards."

She glanced at him again without moving her head. His face was a mask of distrust.

She said, "Perhaps the cards are saying the assassin believes someone must be blamed. For if no one is guilty, then her pain has no meaning."

The boy stretched toward her, straining to see the cards, until he strained so far that he lost his balance. Zanja folded her hands and waited. His equilibrium regained, he cast a look at her. Then he pointed a filthy fingertip at a card. "The pain is *her* fault."

He had pointed at the Wilderness, where Chaen stood lost in the wreck of her life. "Why is the pain her fault?" Zanja asked.

The boy pointed at another card. "Because she saved only one of them."

It was the Quarrel, which showed two men standing back-to-back with their arms folded.

"What did she save him from?"

The boy pointed at the man who fled the burning village while the belongings on his back also burned.

Zanja recalled the confrontation that Karis had with Chaen on the day they took her prisoner. "She said that her son died in a fire. But she didn't say that she had two sons, and that she saved one of them? Why did she keep that a secret?"

The street child nearly touched a card, a solitary warrior, burdened by weapons and armor, being stabbed by a naked child. "The son she saved can kill her enemies," he said.

Oh, to have such pure, quick insight, unimpeded or muddled by love and sorrow! Zanja sat speechless, while the boy, his caution apparently forgotten, picked up her pile of cards and looked through them impatiently. "Where are the rest?"

"The rest haven't been painted yet, and won't be finished for a long time—years, maybe. But I have seen and remember all of them. What does it look like, the card that you want?"

"This woman, who's waiting for a dead man." He pointed at Wilderness. "She's under water."

"Is there a fish?"

"A fish—or a monster—bigger than she is."

As usual, some of Karis's tools had ended up in Zanja's satchel, including a carpenter's pencil. With it, Zanja drew a rough sketch on a piece of stiff paper that she used to protect the cards in their stacks. She could not draw well, so she described the illustration as she shaped it on the blank card. "The woman is either swimming or drowning. The fish has long teeth, and is about to bite her, but she might be about to grab it by the gills and fight it. On the shore, a bowman is aiming his arrow into the water, maybe at her, and maybe at the fish. Water usually signifies time, like it does here." She tapped a finger on the winding river that framed the woman in the wilderness. "And the fish might be the monster each of us carries within ourselves. The bowman might be her true enemy."

"He is her son," said the boy.

"Her son? Why doesn't he shoot the fish and save her?"

"Because he's her *true enemy*," he said impatiently.

"Oh. What do you think the fish is?"

A bell rang in the distance. The boy stood up.

"I wish you would stay," Zanja said.

"It's the *dinner bell.*" The boy trotted away. The soles of his bare feet were black with dirt.

"Well, of course you can't miss dinner," Zanja muttered. When the boy was out of sight, she called, "Raven!" Unless Karis had sent the bird on an errand, it would be nearby.

The raven flew down from the trellis that was covered with blooming vines. Zanja said, "That boy has a strong fire talent—he could even be a fire witch."

During the previous spring, when Zanja was making mischief in the distant past, two of the ravens had been killed, and the four that still survived had lost their ability to talk. This bird stared at her, and never had a raven's gaze seemed more impenetrable.

"Follow him. Watch over him," said Zanja.

The raven flew away. Zanja gathered up her cards and began looking for Karis.

She had not even reached the hospital when she met Karis and Norina hurrying toward her.

"What has happened?" Zanja asked.

Karis put a hand on Zanja's arm. Norina said, "Tell me about the boy."

"It was the child who was watching me yesterday. He understood the card-casting."

"Fire logic?" Karis asked.

"I told you," Zanja began, then realized Karis hadn't been talking to her. Irritated, she waited for them to finish their conversation, so she could say more about the boy. Perhaps winning his trust might be a task Medric was suited for.

Norina said, "Maybe."

"Let's bring her to Emil," said Karis.

"Will you send the raven for the Paladins?"

Now, as always, Karis would make an aggravated comment about the waste of Paladins' time in escorting her from place to place. But she said, "I don't have any paper for a note."

"The raven is following the boy," Zanja said.

"It can't follow him," Karis said. "It never saw him."

"What's wrong with the raven?"

"The raven saw and heard *you*. But there was no boy."

"It was a hallucination," Norina said.

"It was a Lalali street child, not one of my ghosts!"

"It was a hallucination, nevertheless."

Zanja said, "I felt as if I have been watching for him, just as he has been watching for me. I loved him, and this didn't surprise me. He *must* be real."

"Nevertheless," Norina began, and then fell silent. For Zanja had begun to weep.

Chapter 18

Garland was beating eggs for a cake to give the soldiers. Beating eggs took a lot of time but not much attention, so he thought about the day's problems, some of which were left over from the day before. The farmers and fishers were offering foodstuff to the G'deon's household as a matter of pride, but the Hanishport merchants, on whom they depended for sugar, salt, tea, and spices, mainly offered excuses. And Garland didn't have Seth's knack for shaming people into doing what was right—he was soft as an overcooked potato.

The house was as empty as it ever got, but still Garland needed to serve a midday meal to five people. Six, actually, because Maxew, who was guarding the door, had such an appetite that he really should be counted twice. Garland should bake something, as there would still be room in the oven after the cake went in . . .

The front door slammed open. One of the dogs dozing in the parlor gave a woof of surprise. Garland put down his bowl, glanced unhappily at the oven, and went into the hall to see what had happened.

". . . in town," said Lil Paladin, who had been sleeping in the parlor after watching outside the assassin's door all night.

"I know," said Karis. "Rane has gone to fetch him."

Several Paladins who had arrived with Karis began to move away from her. Perhaps she was feeling particularly irritated with them.

Karis wasn't embracing Zanja—she was holding her upright. Garland hurried to help her to a chair. She didn't seem to be hurt, but had a blankness and grayness to her face. "Water?" he offered uncertainly.

Norina said, "Make the tisane that J'han gave you for Zanja."

"No, don't," said Zanja. She rubbed her face. "I need to be clearer, not . . ."

Karis sighed with exasperation.

"Not all pain is evil," Zanja said to her.

"Do you think I don't know that?"

Something must have frightened Karis, to make her so irritable. Garland said, "I'll bring some water then."

It took no time at all to get cups and fill them from the water keg, but when Garland came back, Emil, apparently summoned from Hanishport, was striding into the parlor. He dropped to one knee beside Zanja, clasped her hand, and said something in a language that flowed and stopped and flowed again, like water tumbling down a hillside.

Zanja took a shaky breath and replied. Had she been weeping? She had not wept when she came back from the dead; nor after the assassinations, when Garland had wept all morning while washing her bloody footprints from the hallways.

Garland handed Karis a cup of water, and she looked at it blankly, so he took it back again.

Emil said to Zanja, "I'm not sure I understand you. There was a boy? And what did Karis see?"

"She says he wasn't there. He isn't real."

"But your ghosts *are* real."

"He wasn't a ghost."

Emil sat back a little. "What was he, then?"

"A street child of Lalali."

Garland, holding still lest he become a distraction by clearing his throat or scratching a bug bite, abruptly became aware of Karis's pungent stink—not the honorable smell of hard work, but the fetor of Lalali's dreadful sewers. But Emil smelled like boiled eggs and clean linen—he must have visited the bathhouse that morning, which used water from a hot spring.

"What did the boy look like?" asked Medric, from the stairs.

They all looked at him with surprise. For Medric to be awake in broad daylight was extraordinary, and probably important. That made this the second important thing to happen today. Garland didn't know yet what the first thing was, but it had left Norina even angrier than usual, which meant it probably had something to do with fire logic.

Zanja said, "He was filthy and barefoot. His shirt was torn, his hair was trimmed to the skull. For lice, I suppose."

The stairs creaked, even under Medric's light weight. At the bottom of the stairs he paused to remove and polish his spectacles. "And his face?"

Zanja pressed her fingers to her eyes. "His face? I don't know. Why does it matter?"

"So you can't remember his face? How I envy you!"

He came into the parlor. He would need some hot milk and toast, but Garland remained rooted in place. "Your boy is a dream guide," Medric said.

"Zanja wasn't asleep," Karis said.

"Dream guides aren't guides to dreams; they *are* dreams, and they enter the waking world to offer guidance. *The Way of the Seer* describes ten different types of dream guides. Zanja, you have been visited by the Lost Son."

What good is a guide who is lost? wondered Garland.

Emil, still kneeling, still clasping Zanja's hands, said to Medric, "By *lost,* do you mean *bewildered*? Or *mislaid*?"

"I mean *unfulfilled possibility*. He's the son Zanja will never have."

Norina said, "So he's an embodiment of her intuition? She was just talking to herself?"

Karis said, "Will he come again? If every visit leaves her grief-stricken . . ."

Medric gazed at Zanja, not the way Norina did, as if she were an exasperating puzzle, but more like Emil, with understanding, admiration, and a profound affection. These three fire bloods, born ten or more years apart, of three different peoples and languages, never seemed to misunderstand each other. Maxew, on the other hand, who had vacated his chair by the door and, in his desire to get away from the fire bloods, crammed himself into a corner, seemed bewildered and even frightened of them.

Zanja had bent forward so her forehead rested on Emil's hands. Now she straightened and said something to Emil. She looked more like her usual alert and composed self, although still burdened by sorrow. She said, "Thank you, Medric."

Norina wiped her sweaty face with the tail of her shirt, and for just a moment she seemed like an ordinary person—one who was tired to death. "Upstairs," she said. "All of us. Maxew, Garland, you too."

Garland would have to start the cake and heat the oven all over again. But this didn't seem like a good time to object.

They crowded into Emil and Medric's stuffy bedroom, where disorder on one side and order on the other coexisted in unruly harmony.

Medric said to Garland in Sainnese, "We are invincible!" So soldiers always shouted when going to battle.

"Be serious," said Garland. "The enforcer has no humor."

"If I had to be serious I would go mad." Medric patted Garland's shoulder affectionately, then dropped onto the tangled bedding and curled there like a sleepy, mangy cat.

Medric became more peculiar with each passing day, thought Garland.

Zanja, put by Norina into Emil's chair, gazed up at her with no apparent trepidation, as few could do. Karis, Emil, and Garland were forced together by the tight quarters, while Maxew once again crowded himself into a corner. Norina looked closely at each of them, before settling her gaze on Zanja.

"What have you not told me?" asked the Truthken.

Garland felt a peculiar impulse to shout, *My spoon has something wrong with it, and I don't know what it is!* Then he felt almost as if someone had spoken to him, telling him not to waste people's time with such nonsense. But no one had spoken. There was just Maxew, moving his gaze away, shrinking into the shadows.

Zanja said, "I'm not concealing anything from you."

Again, Norina looked closely at each of them. Garland felt deeply unsettled. The Truthken asked, "But what have you not said?"

Zanja replied, very politely, "I find you humorless, rigid, and unimaginative."

Norina said, "Yes, what else?"

"Apparently, I have powerful longings that I'm unaware of."

"What else?"

Zanja shut her eyes.

When they were getting ready to leave Watfield to come to Hanishport, J'han had said to Garland, "Zanja never complains. But watch for a crease in her forehead—here, between her eyebrows." Now Garland saw it: the mark of an excruciating headache.

"Norina, I'm weary with sorrow."

Karis said, with stifled fury, "Why are you doing this?"

Norina glanced at Emil, and Garland knew he would speak next. They had a peculiar partnership, those two. Emil said, "Karis, no harm has been done."

Karis began to speak, but he shook his head at her. She wiped her sweaty face on her filthy shirttail—how fortunate that the laundry had delivered clean shirts today!—and didn't say anything at all.

"Zanja, do you have a headache?" asked Garland.

She sighed. "Yes."

Karis started forward with an exclamation, but Zanja caught her hand before she could heal her. "Medric, can you go with Karis to Lalali? So I can stay here with Emil?"

Medric blinked at her. "Yes," he said doubtfully. "But what did the Lost Son tell you? I must know, or I won't go anywhere."

"Excuse me," Maxew interrupted, with unusual diffidence. "This headache is significant somehow. May I ask what it means?"

"It means I was kicked in the head by a Sainnite war horse," said Zanja.

Befuddled, the young air witch turned to his teacher. She said, "What Zanja knows is all connected, all equally true. Insights are facts, understanding is a lightning strike, images are events, the pains of the past are the pains of the present. To her, this chaos is perfectly sensible, although to us it is irrational."

The boy seemed just a boy, for once: confused by contradiction, suspicious of his elders, and impatient with everything.

"She was injured eight years ago, and the injury is healed," explained the Truthken. "But to her, the past is always present."

Garland knew that Zanja felt this old pain again every year, on the anniversary of her people's massacre, when for ten or twenty days she lost her mind. He had never witnessed her annual madness, for he had been in this family for less than a year. What a year, that contained the significance of a dozen or a hundred years! But he understood more about Zanja than her favorite food (cheese and bacon grilled on toast, with a cold cup of cider): she was a restrained person, often silent, very private. Norina might find Zanja exasperating, but she knew better than to mention her madness.

Zanja had taken the glyph cards out of her satchel. Medric got up and walked eagerly across the mattress, fumbling to put the correct spectacles on.

To Garland, written words were as mysterious as they were to Leeba. But he liked looking at the glyph cards. These particular cards had reappeared at odd moments ever since they arrived in Hanishport, sometimes studied by Medric, Emil, or other fire bloods in their company, and sometimes only by Zanja. But now she used them to illustrate a story: An assassin once had two sons. One son had died in a fire, and the assassin blamed herself for that, although it wasn't her fault. The second son had grown up to become a warrior. Now the assassin was in danger of drowning, or being eaten by a monstrous fish, from which her son could rescue her. But instead of shooting the monstrous fish and pulling her out of the water, he would shoot her and let her die.

"Is that all?" asked Medric

"The boy heard the dinner bell and ran away."

"How do we get him back?" Medric asked.

Zanja looked askance at Medric, and he said irritably, "Yes, I'm a seer and a scholar and all that, but I'm not *useful*."

Emil said, "You're as useful as you need to be. You could think about the problem of getting the Lost Son to come back while you help Karis with the houses that are falling down and the sewers that don't drain."

After everyone had left, Zanja fetched her little rug. It was the surviving corner of a much larger rug that probably had been cut into pieces when its center wore through. The fragment of pattern implied the whole, so that whenever Zanja carried it from one place to the next, she hauled a ghost carpet that only she could see. She sat upon the carpet piece and watched Emil tidy the bedding. "Why did Norina want everyone to be in the room while she examined me? Was it just to humiliate me?"

"Zanja, my dear, she wasn't examining *you* at all."

Medric had turned one corner of the tiny room into a rat's nest of loose papers, books and candles, and clothing. In the opposite corner, Emil's supply of paper was tied in a packet of waxed cloth, his well-used pens and bottles of ink were decently organized in a tray, and the letters that had caught up with him that morning were weighed down by a large seashell of remarkable beauty. Between these two shrines to ink and paper, the mattress on the floor seemed almost irrelevant.

Now that Karis had eased the pain of the headache, Zanja felt dull and distant, as though she were walking in a fog or suffering from a fever. Her stupefied gaze followed Emil as he moved through Medric's half of the room to pick up a book from the floor and use it to weigh down a pile of loose papers. Then he opened the window, and the room began to breathe. Air flowed through the open door, into the hall, and out the windows on the other side of the house, tangible as water. Emil sat at the table, which now glowed with sunlight, and looked down at Zanja with one iron-gray eyebrow cocked.

"She wasn't examining me?" Zanja said. "Then who was she . . ." But of course Norina had been examining all of them.

Emil examined the nibs of his pens, one by one.

She said, "You're worried, my brother."

"You have a dream guide," he replied, "which means you need guidance." Zanja could hear the faint, rapid ticking of the watch in his waistcoat pocket. "I have been called any number of things in my life, but no one has ever said I'm unimaginative. Yet I can't imagine the circumstance in which you would not know what to do. So, yes, I am worried."

After a while, Emil took a letter from under the shell and read it out loud to her. A man in Appleton, the city of bandits and thieves, had written at length about the wrongdoings of the Sainnites. He wanted Emil to visit there and see for himself. In fact, Emil planned to do that very thing later in the summer, but he wanted all of the residents to be taken by surprise. "Obfuscation?" he asked. "Or brevity?"

She helped him draft the letter, and then another letter. So they spent the afternoon in a manner that had, for them, become routine.

The light began to dim, and the house became noisy with people. Hanishport exclaimed with music, and at least two different companies of players raucously blew their horns, announcing the imminence of the opening scenes. Out on the water, to mark a historical event, skiffs were gathering to wait for sunset, after which they would tow a ship, decorated with a thousand burning candles, back and forth. The rowers, at least some of them, were not very sober.

Zanja read Emil's last letter back to him, and his pen moved in dry, rhythmic scratches as he wrote his own words in his copybook. Then she folded the letter for him to address and seal.

"I've never wanted a child at all," Zanja said, "and yet I have one, and I love her dearly. Why would I grieve a lost son?"

Emil rested his chin in his hand, smiling down at her. "Because your sorrow is the sorrow of the ages."

"I have sorrow enough of my own!"

"Oh, sorrow is rationed, is it?" He stretched his writing-cramped hands, and then his back. "Zanja, in our youth, you and I both accepted strictures that we continue, more or less, to live by. You still cross boundaries, though the tribe whose path you blaze is not your tribe of birth. And, despite the changes in Shaftal—and despite my failed efforts to retire—I'm still a Paladin, a valiant protector of the right to think bad ideas."

Despite her melancholy, Zanja laughed.

"We choose to be what we are, and every choice entails regret. You and I are Leeba's parents because at one time we thought we were free to choose her. But if Karis were to bring home a wailing baby from Lalali, we would unite in refusal to be parents again. We are unsuitable: I am doomed to grow ancient without becoming old enough to retire, and you are doomed to die, or disappear, or do some other inexplicable thing, every season or two."

"Why do you bother to guard me from that, if it is my doom?"

"My dear, guarding you has allowed me to wrest a prize from the claws of the future: a quiet afternoon with you."

Emil's indirect affection still was too direct for Zanja. She said, "If you met your lost son, would you grieve?"

"Oh, my dear!" Emil began to laugh. "I wouldn't even be surprised! I could have a dozen sons! To be a Paladin was once a *very* pleasant business."

"But no one entreats you into her bed anymore? Surely the women of Shaftal still want to bear a child of your character and intelligence!"

"Flatterer."

"Braggart!"

"Oh, no, no, no. Surely my dozen sons together aren't the equal of your singular dream son. What true child would make himself so useful?"

"Not Leeba."

"Certainly not! Our plans are irrelevant to that child, as they should be . . . Oh, was that the bell?" Emil sighed, but Garland's bell rang again, and even the most important man in Shaftal could not ignore that summons. He rose from his chair, clasped Zanja's hand, and lifted her to her feet, as he had done hundreds of times before. They went down to supper, Zanja dragging the ghost carpet behind her.

Chapter 19

"Did you ask that boy my question?" Chaen asked Seth in the morning, when another night had passed without a word from Maxew.

Breakfast was fruit, pastry, and tea, which Seth ate with appetite. Ravenous, Chaen stood at the window looking out so she wouldn't watch Seth's every mouthful.

Seth said, "Yes. It took work, though. He and Norina are usually together in the evening, attending one meeting or the other. I finally managed to catch him alone in the back garden, by the outhouse. I asked him your question, about whether the people who tricked you were violating the law. First he said he had to ask Norina. When I told him you didn't trust her, he said that under the law there are degrees of responsibility. At the same time, he said, regardless of your circumstances or what other people do or say, you are responsible for your own actions."

Chaen had wanted to find out if Maxew was still in the city, and perhaps also to jog him into action by reminding him of her peril. But her son's words were chilling. If they were a message to her, it was a message of blame, as if he criticized her for falling into the trap, even though he would have lauded her had she succeeded in killing the false G'deon. "But I didn't ask him if I was responsible."

"And I told him I didn't think what he said was relevant, but he insisted that he was answering your question, and that he had nothing else to say. Are you certain you don't want me to ask the Truthken?"

"She was there when they put together their plan to trap me! She either told them it was lawful or else she didn't care if it was lawful or not!"

"You sound a lot like a Truthken yourself. But you don't understand very well what drives a woman like her, if you think she just uses the law as a tool for her own ends."

Chaen heard the distinct sound of Seth's empty teacup being set in the tray. "Anyway, I doubt you'll learn anything else from Maxew.

Maybe he obeys Norina, and maybe he's making an effort to behave properly, but he never does one little thing more than he's required to do."

Chaen worked all day on the tailor's sign, painting layers of color and applying gold leaf to the border while the paint dried. The scrollwork was gorgeous; the gold leaf would be brilliant on any sunny day; and the artisan conveyed a serene and tireless competence. Then she had finished it, and the Paladins carried it away.

Now the day was ending, and she entered the eddy of time that most people filled with cooking and conversation. She heard the ringing of the supper bell. Through the window, she saw a distant players' procession marching toward the stage on the quay, blowing horns and ringing hand bells to attract an audience to their performance. She saw a cluster of soldiers sauntering leisurely down the road from the garrison. One, not in uniform, walked beside a woman soldier who carried a bundle against her body as though it were a baby. It was the strangest sight Chaen had seen in many years.

As they drew closer she could hear them speaking their odd, stuttering language. The ugly man made an expansive gesture. They laughed loudly, and the woman's bundle uttered a shriek. It *was* a baby.

Chaen sat down in the chair. In the garden, the dogs barked, then fell silent, and Seth's voice said with pleasure, "You've come for supper." Chaen looked out the window again and saw Seth clasping the soldier's hand and kissing the baby on the head.

When Seth came upstairs a short while later, Chaen would not talk to her.

Seth sat down and ate—it was some kind of pie, its crust scattered with herbs, stuffed with vegetables in a brown sauce. As she ate, she told Chaen a great deal of trivial information. After she put down her spoon, she continued to talk, then said she was still hungry and ate Chaen's pie as well. She discussed various meetings of the Council of Shaftal, gave a lengthy history of High Meadow Farm in Basdown, recounted some recent events that Chaen already knew about, and then began to discuss cow diseases.

"Why did that soldier have a baby?" Chaen asked.

"Now I know to start with the cow diseases next time!" said Seth. "The baby is Gabian, the son of General Clement. She got him in the usual way—the usual way for soldiers, that is: she bought him from a woman who could reasonably claim the child was fathered by a Sainnite."

"I thought Sainnites send their children to—" Chaen stopped, for the Children's Garrison stood empty now, except for the ashes of forty members of her company who had gone there to rescue the children from the Sainnites. "That woman was the Sainnite general? The one who engineered the massacre at the Children's Garrison?"

Seth put down her spoon. "Yes. She's done some terrible things."

"And you treat her as your friend?"

"When I share her bed, that makes matters difficult and complicated. But being her friend is easy. When you meet her, you'll understand."

"Meet her? Why would I do such a thing?"

"How could you avoid it, since I'm both a friend of yours and a friend of hers?"

Chaen had misjudged Seth. Anyone who could tolerate such contradictions in herself must either be very stupid or very deep, and Chaen had not thought she was either.

Seth said, "I never finished the account of the lost glyphs. Unless you'd rather hear more about cow diseases?"

Chaen said bitterly, "Do tell me more about that ancient, unreadable book for which people have taken impossible journeys, gone through all sorts of trouble, and even died."

"People do say the book is valuable and important. But if I could bring Damon and Jareth back from the dead, I would happily throw that book into the ocean."

Chaen thought two lives was a small price for such a treasure. And she would never even be in the same room with it. She was contradicting herself again, she realized: her air self dismissed the book while her fire self longed to see it.

Seth continued, "When we looked at the book—Karis, Zanja, and I—we saw landscapes, people, animals and clothing, all alien to us. But Karis and I recognized some of the plants. Soldiers are mad for flowers—it's an odd thing that most people don't know, unless they've been in a garrison. Their gardens are full of flowers that they brought with them from Sainna—and some of those flowers are depicted in Zanja's lexicon. So she showed the book to some old soldiers—she speaks their language, of course—and they told her that the places and landscapes are in Sainna."

"So the book came from Sainna," said Chaen impatiently. She couldn't see why it mattered.

"The book has been in Shaftal for at least four hundred years. It didn't get here by itself—Sainnites brought it here. They stayed here, with their book. And they became us."

Chaen turned and looked at Seth. Not only did Seth seem to actually believe this absurdity, but she found it amazing and wonderful. "Seth," she said. It may have been the first time she had said her name. "You are not my friend. This is the last night of my life. Please go away and leave me alone." Having said these pitiful words, she realized that they were true. Maxew was not going to rescue her, and tomorrow she would be executed. She was as good as dead already, and she had known it ever since she was captured. Throughout the dreary days, as the city drank, sang, and caroused within her hearing, she had been in grieving for her lost life.

Seth picked up the tray and left.

Restless, and miserably hungry, Chaen paced the room. She had gone hungry for much longer than this, usually because she had given her share to Maxew. But then she had deprived herself for a purpose, and now she just did it from petulance, or pride. Nothing she did—nothing she had ever done—none of it had made any difference. She might as well have eaten that pie Seth had brought upstairs for her.

As the house fell quiet, the carousing city became even louder. Yet Chaen heard clearly the sound of the stairs creaking all the way to the third floor, then a murmur of voices, and a Paladin tapping on the door. "Are you awake, Chaen? You have a visitor."

The door opened and admitted the fortune-teller, the false G'deon's wife. With the light behind her, the woman's remarkable face was nearly all shadow, traced with light on her chin, the bridge of her nose, and one cheekbone. "May I have a lamp, Kamren?" she asked the Paladin.

"No, Zanja, we can allow no flame."

"But it's for a glyph card."

The Paladin spoke with his comrades, then gave Zanja a lit candle and stood in the doorway to keep watch on them.

Zanja said to Chaen, "I need an artist. I will trade you, one glyph card for another."

She offered Chaen the glyph card, the one that depicted a solitary woman in a featureless landscape, framed by the events of her life. When Chaen didn't take it, Zanja squatted down, spread the tail of her longshirt on the floor, and put the card there. Beside it she put a piece of plain, heavyweight artist's paper. On it was a sketch, drawn with a dull pencil, and a glyph that had been added later, after the pencil had been sharpened.

"You certainly are no artist," Chaen said.

"That's why I need you. Will you draw this card? If I give you this one in exchange?"

Chaen picked up the sketch. The three figures were badly placed, making the picture too static and balanced for so tense a scene. It depicted a struggle of indecision: The man wanted to shoot the fish and save the woman, but fear and hatred overwhelmed his love. The woman struggled not to drown, but her will was weakened by her longing for the peaceful stillness of the water.

"What is this illustration called?" she asked.

"I'm afraid we must write its text before we can read it. What would *you* call it?"

Death of Memory, thought Chaen. But she would not speak such powerful words to a presciant who was her enemy. "What would I help you to accomplish, if I finish this card for you?"

"I think it has been accomplished already. But I don't want to carry such a poor drawing with my cards."

"No—it wouldn't be right," Chaen said absently.

To fit so complicated an illustration into so small a space, Chaen would have to use an ink pen for the details. Once again, the Paladins would have to watch her work, but they had proven unobtrusive before, which was surprising since she could hear their voices constantly when the door was closed.

"Can I leave this sketch with you?" Zanja's question had been carefully worded, so Chaen needed not promise to do anything.

"You may leave it with me," Chaen said. And she would do the drawing, she knew.

Zanja stood up, and the candle flame was extinguished by its movement through the air.

Chaen worked on the tiny painting by lamplight late into the night. When she finished, the Paladins took her pens and brushes and left her alone. She sat awake beneath the window as the waning moon sailed in a sea of rippled clouds. By the time it sailed out of her sight, the festival racket of the city had fallen silent. Chaen should have been leaving Hanishport in the caravan of vendors heading for the next fair. But even if she hadn't been tricked and arrested, she still wouldn't have escaped, for the false G'deon's raven would have continued to follow her. She would have continued in a state of suspense, like an unfinished painting, until she became too peculiar to live among people and finally died of cold or hunger, another of winter's nameless casualties. Perhaps it was better that she die now.

The night grew old, and the starlight-silvered harbor ceased its restless rippling and lay quiet as a mirror, reflecting the face of the sky in a frame of dark, rocky coastline.

She heard the distant tide clock ring for low tide. The Paladin named Kamren quietly opened the door to check on her. "Oh, pardon me. You're still not sleeping? May I bring you a tisane?"

"No."

"Would you like a lamp and your pencils?"

"Yes, if you'll then leave me alone. Do you really think I'll stab myself with a pencil, or set the house on fire?"

"We don't know what you'll do," he said reasonably.

"But I want to draw, and I want to be alone."

"I regret to say that you cannot have both."

"You regret it? Then why not allow it? Haven't you sworn to follow your conscience? Especially when your conscience contradicts what you're commanded to do?"

She wanted him to argue with her, but he laughed. "Everyone knows better than to command a Paladin. I do regret this necessary cruelty, but we have agreed that you must not escape or kill yourself.

One of your companions did die in our custody. All of those who guarded him had been present on the night of the assassinations, and perhaps we let him die because we were angry, and not because it was right. To exercise judgment, Paladins must be detached, even when we're grief-stricken, or angry. It's very difficult to do."

Chaen thought that she herself was insufficiently detached. But how could she not be angry with her own people—and especially with her own son—for failing to rescue her? To Kamren she said, "I should have known better than to ask a Paladin a question."

"May I ask *you* a question? Many Paladin irregulars like yourself have said they want to study philosophy and take the Paladins' vow. Will they be able to abandon bitterness?"

"They should be proud for having bravely fought the Sainnites during Shaftal's years of darkness!"

"Yes, they certainly should. But now the G'deon, who speaks for Shaftal, expects us to return to the old way, the way of judging people by their merits, and not only by their failures. Do you think that would be possible, for someone like yourself?"

"Leave me alone," Chaen said.

Perhaps she fell asleep, or perhaps when the key turned in the door again, she was so despondent that she could not raise her head from her arms.

In Chaen's memories Maxew was a child, but he spoke to her now with a man's voice. "Mother?"

She leapt to her feet. She could scarcely see the slim, blurry shape that stepped into the room and set down a candle. "Max!" She ran to him, and he suffered her embrace. "I knew you would come!"

"It is conventional to say so, when a hope has merely been realized."

"I *hoped*, then. What have you done to the Paladins?"

"They think they're awake, and won't realize they're sleeping."

"Max, I don't know what to do. The false G'deon put her hand upon me, and she said she'll always know where I am."

"You can't ever escape her," he said without apparent concern.

"So you've come to tell me that I must die tomorrow?"

"You know that already. Mother, why did you remain in Hanishport? Why did you make that foolish attempt on Karis's life?"

"If I had succeeded you wouldn't call it foolish!"

"Three fire bloods and a Truthken were guarding Karis. You could never have succeeded." He had never learned to control that scornful tone, though it gained him only enemies.

She said, "Our leader thought it was possible this winter past, when he commanded us to kill her."

"You're like the others," her son said abruptly, with inexplicable bitterness. "To be convinced to do anything, you must be told a tale in which you are the only one who can make the world right."

She couldn't see his face clearly in the flickering light of his candle. "Why do you say that? I always did my part as willingly as I could, and you know that more certainly than anyone!"

"Willingly? Resentfully, you mean."

She drew back from him, dismayed. How many times had she reminded Max that what mattered most was how people acted and not what they thought? Yet he raged at Chaen's impure purpose as though she intended to offend him. That she had always told her son the truth, even when the truth seemed unspeakable, should have been enough. Had their mutual understanding been a fabrication? How many times had he concealed the truth from her? Was he doing it now?

Max surveyed the room until his candle illuminated the painting of him as a child, which lay on its face on the table. Chaen had used it as a drawing board, and the glyph card of the drowning woman, drawn with ink and painted with watercolors, was still pinned to it. He glanced at the card without interest, then looked at the baby on the other side. "The Truthken hasn't seen this portrait of me, has she?"

"No."

If he noticed her dull tone, it didn't seem to trouble him. "She'll know it's a portrait of an air child. I'll take it with me."

"Leave the glyph card," she said. "If it's gone, Zanja will wonder."

"And yet you don't understand why I'm angry with you!" He yanked out the pins and held up the card, pointing at the image of the warrior on the riverbank. "This card told her that you have a son!"

"She hasn't even seen the card!"

"But she *imagined* it because you allowed her to do a card-casting!"

"I didn't even know who she was! And she did the casting without—"

"Be quiet!"

Chaen's lips moved without sound, not even the whisper of air. Never before had Max used his power on her.

"Zanja will tell Norina Truthken what the cards reveal to her. And the Truthken will ask you questions, which she can compel you to answer. I can only be safe if you forget me. You will forget me now."

Inside her skull, a screaming began. Yet her son's voice said, "Forget me. Forget that you gave birth to me. Forget that you nursed me and raised me. Forget that you saved me from the fire."

He named every event, and every year. Inside the curved walls of her skull, she screamed with pain, and then forgot what caused such agony. His eyes became darkness, and he became a stranger. Then she was alone, and had always been alone. The door was and had remained locked. She lay upon the floor, abandoned by her memories. The empty room spun around her.

The door opened later. Paladins came in. Cool fingers pressed her throat, then felt her head. "I think she just fainted," said the woman. "She hasn't eaten or drunk anything for days."

They lifted her onto the mattress and covered her with one of the heavy linen sheets. Her flesh was leaden, her thoughts spinning fragments, debris in a dry wind. The Paladins discussed whether they should awaken someone, Karis or Seth. In the end, though, they left her to sleep.

Chapter 20

How to Initiate a Conversation:
1. Select a topic/condition that's mundane, commonplace, and affects everyone, such as: (a) Weather (ranges from terrible to lovely); (b) the roads (usually bad, sometimes surprisingly good); (c) the season (compared to past years); (d) the fruits and vegetables (flavor, freshness, ripeness).
2. Shape an inquiry so the answer is implied, such as: (a) Did you notice (topic/condition)? (b) Don't you think (topic/condition)? (c) I/we experienced (topic/condition)—did you also? (d) Isn't (topic) (condition)?
3. The conversation partner first replies with a direct answer, then asks a return question that mentions a previous subject but turns it into another direction. Then, the first speaker responds in a similar manner. Example:

Person 1: Isn't the weather dreadful today?

Person 2: It's terrible. But the cold should be good for the cabbage crop, don't you think?

Person 1: I hope so. Wasn't the cabbage soup awful?

Person 2: It wasn't as bad as the tomato soup. What do you suppose made it taste so bad?

From Book of Everything, *by Anders of the Midlands*

"Don't you think those blackberries were delicious?" Anders asked.

Of course, the Two groaned, and Serrain answered, "Yes, they were delicious. Do you think that they were bought at yesterday's market?"

"They probably were from the market," said Anders. Now he must ask another question. Why had Serrain asked where the berries came from? Oh, of course. "Did your family pick their own blackberries?"

"Yes, we did—every year. The children and old people used to go out in a big group, and we would come home with a tremendous amount of berries. We would sugar them to preserve them, and the next day we would make jam."

Then she said, "Isn't it wonderful to eat jam on Long Night?"

The Two could not endure this inane conversation any longer. But an exercise in polite conversation must be politely interrupted, so one of them said sarcastically, "Oh, yes, it's wonderful!"

Then the other said, "Has anyone else noticed that something is wrong with the Paladins?"

The Two might sneer at Anders's gambits, but they also had used one.

It had been a hot, dull day. After the early morning blade-fighting exercises, a Paladin named Corvil had read philosophy to them, and then an old woman who had once taught in the university, before it was burned down, lectured to them about history. A healer demonstrated how to splint a broken limb, which they then practiced on each other. Serrain and Anders had studied law and kept watch on the nearly empty house while Braight and the Two went out riding with a horse master. Then came evening blade-fighting exercise, and they ate supper cooked by two of the artists who were engaged in the enormous task of copying the lexicon. Braight had been in a foul temper and had taken her plate to the schoolroom, where she had stood watch alone while the rest of them ate supper and practiced civility on the people who remained at Travesty while the government of Shaftal was decamped or dispersed. After eating, they had clustered at the western windows of their workroom, cramming history for an examination until the light faded. Now the lamp over the table was lit, and soon the Paladin who had the first night watch would walk past and tell them to go to bed.

Braight was still in a foul mood. Anders didn't know why; perhaps she had fallen off her horse and the Two had laughed at her. She said,

"You two would do anything to avoid studying. Are all boat people as lazy as you are?"

Norina had assigned Braight the discipline of generosity, and Anders didn't think she was making much progress. If they were to form the new Order of Truthkens, though, they must help each other to learn. He said, "If the Two suspect something is wrong, they are right to tell us about it."

Braight glared at him. He glared back at her until she turned to the Two and said sarcastically, "Arlis and Minga, how brilliant of you! Do explain more about your intelligent insights!"

The Two spoke antiphonally, which normal people found disconcerting.

"Something about the Paladins' thinking isn't right," said one.

"But it's not that their thinking is bad," said the other.

"It's more like they're avoiding a certain sort of thinking."

"Or maybe they're not supposed to think about certain topics."

"But they don't seem aware that they're doing it."

They seemed to be *trying* to be brilliant and insightful, a reaction to Braight's sarcasm that Anders had never expected. Apparently, implying incompetence could inspire people to prove their critic wrong.

Serrain said, "I noticed something odd about the Paladins also, but I just thought they had a secret of some kind."

The Two said, "A new secret? A secret that they keep from themselves?"

"I know, I should have thought about it further." Unless Serrain knew someone was lying, she didn't tend to interrogate people or problems; therefore she had been assigned the discipline of skepticism. She added, "But it didn't seem a guilty secret—it seemed more like a duty."

Braight said, "No messages have come from Hanishport. Whatever this new duty is, the Paladins have taken it upon themselves."

"Oh, and you notice every little thing that happens!" said the Two.

"She does," Anders said, which was true. Also, saying so prevented Braight from starting another squabble. He asked, "Do you two think the Paladins received a message?"

"No," they said.

"Then what has happened to make the Paladins assign themselves a new, secret duty?"

"Whatever it was, it happened yesterday."

Serrain said, "Well, what things happened recently that seem out of ordinary?"

This investigation was merely an exercise, but when Norina read about it in their books she would commend them for it. And it was a game—the only kind they actually enjoyed playing. Serrain had already been writing in her book, so now she dipped her pen and began a list, saying, "The milk delivery was late." The others said what they could remember, which was quite a lot, as they were observant and had excellent memories. A councilor who still resided in Travesty had come down with a cold. At supper, one of the librarians had complained about the glue they were using for book repairs. One of the artists had asked if anyone had remembered to request that the Hanishport party bring them some more gold leaf. The second–story floors had been washed. There was a thump in the night, like a heavy book being dropped. When the list nearly filled a page, Serrain read it back to them.

All of these trivial events could signify something important, but to investigate such a long list would require several days.

"What *didn't* we see?" Anders asked. To observe the absences, the vacancies, the things that should be there, the questions that weren't being asked, the gaps and the silences, this much-hated exercise had frequently been assigned to them by Norina as a tool for causing a pattern to become clear.

Serrain began a new list. Many events were not happening because the government of Shaftal had moved to Hanishport, and they agreed that they wouldn't try to list them. Then they discovered they couldn't list the questions that weren't being asked, because they spent nearly all their time with each other and had no idea what anyone else was discussing.

"*That's* why we should spend more time with stupid people," said Braight, and wrote it in her book.

They listed the people they hadn't seen, and then crossed out those whose absence they could explain. They were left with three: J'han the healer, Leeba, his intolerable daughter, and Bran, the housekeeper.

Braight began reading from her book. "J'han is aged forty-three and is Norina's husband of eight years. He gets along with her because he has an earth talent, like most healers. He is one of fifty-two true healers in Shaftal. He didn't go to Hanishport because someone had to stay home with the brat, but he certainly wanted to, because the transformation of Lalali was his idea. Should I tell you about his mutual obligations? Are they relevant?"

The Two said, "He's probably on an errand for the Healer's College and took the brat with him."

"We can ask one of the healers," said Serrain. "The Two should do it, because they need to practice politeness."

"Braight is more impolite than we are," they said.

Braight said, "That was an extremely impolite thing to say."

Anders suggested that they draw lots. The Two drew the slip of paper with the dot on it and immediately began to complain, even though there was nothing more equitable than drawing lots. Anders warned them that they were wasting everyone's time, and then Serrain suggested that they talk about Bran, the housekeeper.

Braight said, "The floors have been washed, so he must have been in the house. Why have none of us seen him?"

There was a silence.

"How did he get in?" asked the Two.

"None of us are shirking guard duties." They all knew this to be true.

"During the night watch?"

"Too dark for house-cleaning."

They looked at each other, baffled.

Braight stood her book up, facing outward, so they could see Bran's chart. In its center, Bran's name was in a circle, with the names of Travesty's residents scattered around it, with their relationship to him described by symbols that Braight had invented. It appeared that every resident of Travesty was either obligated to Bran, or answered to him, except Norina and the five of them. It was not unusual for air witches to avoid obligation, but it was odd that Maxew had *not* avoided it.

"What does *that* symbol mean?" asked Serrain. "Between Maxew and Bran?"

Braight peered over the top of the book to read her own notes. "Hierarchical obedience. I've never actually seen Maxew with Bran, but I noticed the effect. I used to think it was the effect of Norina on Maxew, but I've noticed it before, when she wasn't even here, and I think I have eliminated all other possibilities."

Braight's ability to perceive how people affected each other was both subtle and accurate, but in this case she was relying on logic, not observation.

Anders said, "I don't understand how someone could have such a strong effect on so many people but make no impression on six air witches. I'm sorry, Braight, but I think your chart may be wrong."

Braight asked, "Why has Bran had no effect on you?"

"I've never even met him."

"Neither have I."

"Me neither," said Serrain.

Minga and Arlis shook their heads.

"And if we assume that Norina hasn't met him either . . . how is that possible?"

Braight said, "Maxew may have admitted him to the house the first time he came here, and after that, Bran could have come in through the kitchen."

The front hall was guarded by the air witches, including Norina when she was not busy with other duties. The kitchen door was unguarded but barred, opened only by Garland to receive kitchen deliveries. The housekeeper should never have been admitted through that door, but possibly it had happened.

"I'm not satisfied," said Braight. "I don't see how it's possible for someone who is here so frequently to never be seen by any of us."

Perhaps they had seen him but didn't know who he was. Perhaps he simply didn't frequent the parts of that vast house that the air children spent their time in. Perhaps he did the housework at night, by lamplight. These possibilities could all be investigated.

The Two were losing interest in the game. The hall clock sounded the hour, and the Paladin appeared with a lamp in one hand and a book in the other. "Bedtime for the law students," he said amiably.

"Orin Paladin," Serrain said, "does Bran come in at night to do housework?"

"At night? Not that I know of."

"Have you seen him in the last few days?"

"I'm not sure," said Orin. "You know how it is with ordinary things—you don't really pay attention. Go to bed now. One must sleep to learn."

They left the room and went down the hall toward the main stairway, and the Paladin continued to his post in the front hall. When his light was just a faint glow on the wall, the air children whispered fiercely to each other.

"Did you see that?"

"What is he concealing from us?"

"I don't think he knows he's concealing it."

"What?"

"I don't think he knows," Serrain said again.

Anders thought she looked pale in the dim light. Perhaps he looked pale also. "How could he not know that he's concealing something?" he asked, although he knew the answer. But he was hoping that one of them would suggest another entirely believable explanation.

No one spoke. Silently, they climbed the stairs and went to bed.

During morning blade practice, at breakfast, and during a lecture on botany that was attended by most of the healers, the air children also conducted their investigation. They sat for their examination, and Anders suspected that none of them would perform as well as their history teacher expected. Then they scattered, each of them with additional matters to inquire into. They missed lunch, but when they reconvened later, Serrain brought bread, butter, and fruit from the kitchen, and they talked while they ate.

Braight confirmed that no messages had arrived from Hanishport or anywhere else. But she had looked in every occupied bedroom and had found a raven in one. Maybe the raven had arrived with a message, or maybe it was resting or injured.

Over breakfast they had asked about J'han and Leeba, but no one seemed to know where they were. The Two had gone to the healers' common room and asked about them again. The healers had become irritated, which was unusual. Even more oddly, they expressed no curiosity about J'han's absence.

No one had noticed Bran in the last several days, and the air children had asked every resident of Travesty and several other people as well. But some of the answers had an ambivalent quality, which was peculiar since they were asking simple questions of fact. Also, the children had asked what Bran looked like, and although there was agreement about his height and build, there was none about his face, not even on whether or not he had a beard.

No one had dropped anything heavy during the night, but others had been jolted awake by a noise—a thud or a bang.

Serrain and Anders had gone into the room J'han shared with Norina and Leeba. The bed was stripped of linens, and even the blankets were missing. Leeba's stuffed rabbit and wooden lizard were not to be seen. J'han's pack lay on the floor, with a few pieces of clothing in it. The floor was clean, and the room smelled faintly of soap. Anders found, under the table, the toy lizard's tail, broken, as if it had been stepped on.

He showed it to his fellow students: evidence of something, or evidence of nothing. Anxious and frustrated, they gazed at it, a brightly painted curve of wood in the palm of his hand.

The Two said, "It's impossible for Bran to avoid us, so that we never even catch a glimpse of him."

"*You* avoid *me*," Braight said. "If you didn't have to be with me, I would never see you at all. How do you do that?"

"Never mind how," said Serrain. "Why?"

"Because we don't like her," said the Two.

"I mean, why would Bran avoid us?"

"Why are all of you avoiding the truth?" said Braight impatiently. "Do you think that avoiding it will make it less true?"

Anders felt deeply unhappy. This was why people feared and disliked Truthkens, he thought, because we know and say things like Braight was about to say. But he wanted to be a Truthken, so he said, "How Bran avoids us is by using air logic. Why he avoids us is so we don't realize he's an air witch."

In the silence that followed, Anders understood something awful, and for the first time in his life made a deliberate decision to refrain from revealing it, not in speech and not in writing. He understood that he and his fellow law students could lose everything—the future they worked for so diligently, the purpose, the principles by which they governed themselves, and their lives. Also, he knew that, regardless of what came next, he was going to take an action that was the exact opposite of what he had promised Norina he would do.

Chapter 21

Two entire trading families had crammed themselves into the House of Lora for the fair. Tashar shepherded a half-dozen young people to taverns, performances, exhibitions, boat trips, and gardens, while pickpockets and scalawags buzzed around his charges like flies around a corpse. After the last night, he gladly put them into their carriages and saw them depart.

By the dim light of dawn, Fair Day sellers hurried to pack their wagons and flee ahead of the crowds that would soon choke the roads. A few lone travelers wandered vaguely or drunkenly from one conveyance to the next, begging for rides. From the top of Artisan's Way, Tashar could see halfway across the harbor. He longed to take his sailboat out onto the glowing water and spend the day in aimless solitude, pushed lazily about by the wind and the waves. But a Lora ship lay at anchor in the distance and must not wait another day to be unloaded, even though the stevedores and teamsters were dissipated, possibly not sober, and unlikely to work with any energy even if they responded to his summons. Tashar slung the records box over his shoulder and began the long trudge down the hill, to rouse the labor captains, pay the docking fees to the harbormaster, and hire a skiff to carry him to the ship to check the cargo.

The sun's blinding edge peeked coyly from behind a fiery, gilded scarf of cloud. The air lay still and heavy, and in the water's surface Tashar could see the reflected coastline, the streamers of clouds, the wheeling white birds. He shielded his eyes against the light, but still there was a shimmering before him.

The shimmering became Maxew. The massive book he carried under his arm bent his thin frame sideways. He said, "I'll meet you at the boat just before sunrise tomorrow."

"Tomorrow the weather will be unsuitable," said Tashar. He had been quite startled, and felt an empty triumph that he had not cried out with surprise.

"Oh, are you weatherwise now?"

"I'm not, but the harbormaster is." Tashar pointed toward the quay, where a string of flags hung listless in the glare. "Those flags say it will be hot, with light land and sea breezes. But what we need is a cool day, with moderate winds."

"The weather doesn't matter. We must depart at dawn."

"Nothing is more important than weather!"

They were arguing in the middle of the road, where any stumbling drunk could hear them. Tashar said, "Why can't we delay a day or two?"

"Are you reluctant to leave your comforts? Or the false power of the Lora name?"

"I am reluctant to row all the way across the bay, only to die in a spectacular wreck!"

"So you're a coward also?"

Tashar had stolen a fortune from his own family, and every day for three years had been at risk of discovery. Tashar was no coward, and Maxew knew it. It seemed childish of him to try to behave as if they were still boys, battling for the time and attention of their teacher.

Maxew was giving Tashar a sour look. Tashar supposed it wasn't pleasant to know what people were thinking, but Maxew only had to behave better and people's thoughts would soon be more friendly. Tashar said, "I'll meet you at the small craft landing tomorrow at first light. Maybe the dawn breeze will carry us far enough from shore to catch a wind. If not, I hope you can row."

"How hard can it be?"

"Hard. It could peel the skin from the palms of your hands."

Maxew shrugged. "You have supplies? And money?"

"Of course." He would check his sailboat today, to see if the lock on the hold had been broken and the supplies pilfered. And he would check the water cans, in case the water had soured or the seams had sprung a leak. "I'm expected on that ship," he said.

Maxew disappeared. Of course he also remained, but Tashar would soon forget that fact and start behaving as though he were alone.

He spoke—loudly, in case Maxew was walking away. "But the portrait painter's trial is today. Why are you waiting until it's too late to rescue her?"

Tashar continued his downhill trudge, still speaking in a low voice to remind himself that Maxew could be walking beside him. "You are responsible for your part of the plan, while I am responsible for mine, and we are to know as little as possible about each other's part. But sometimes this ignorance could become a problem. For example, my, uh, unusual conveyance has certain requirements and limitations . . ."

He stopped muttering, as he had drawn close to a busy family with two young, whiny children, all hard at work tying down the contents of a wagon. One parent cried, "Leave me alone! The sooner we finish, the sooner you can have your bread!" The other two adults, who seemed equally short-tempered after so many hot, sleepless, and busy days, bellowed at the children to get to work.

Then Tashar spotted Maxew, quite a distance away, trotting to catch up to a somber procession of Paladins that was entering a pub, while the publican stood at the door in a crisp new apron, looking anxious. Tashar glimpsed Chaen, Maxew's mother, dully climbing the steps. Maxew, head lowered in humility, spoke a few words to a woman whose shorn head Tashar could scarcely see behind the shield of Paladins. The Truthken!

A crowd of exhausted revelers, driven out of Thieves' Alley by the harbormaster's strong-arms, stumbled drunkenly into the road. Behind this cover, Tashar stepped into a doorway. When he peeked out some time later, the Truthken was gone.

That evening, in the woodstove that warmed his bedroom in winter, Tashar burned all his papers, even the translation of the instructions for sailing the new ship. He wished he could destroy the ledgers also, but they would not burn easily. Well, as long as the ledgers sat innocently on their shelves, his family, when they realized he was gone, would merely assume that Tashar had come to harm. Many months could pass before they recognized the scope of his thievery.

During the festival, he had collected the contents of his various caches throughout the city—a difficult business to conduct while herding giddy house guests from place to place. Now his mattress was lumpy with gold, gunpowder, and pistol balls, but he was so exhausted that he slept anyway, until the distant ringing of the high-tide bell woke him before dawn. He went quietly out with his burdens. He would never set foot in that awful house again.

Chapter 22

The Paladin opened the door. Seth came in with a last food tray of pastries and tea. Zanja followed her, inscrutable.

Chaen seemed to have slept in her clothing. Seth spoke, her voice muffled as if by a fog. "The Paladins told me you were awake most of the night, and then you fainted. Drink some tea. Eat some bread or an egg."

Zanja was looking at the glyph card that lay on the table with its pins scattered around it. Chaen wondered vaguely what the card had been pinned to. She said to Zanja, "It's not quite finished."

Zanja stepped out of the way. The amiable Paladin brought in Chaen's supplies, and she used the small muller to make a tiny bit of red-clay ink. She had practiced drawing the glyph in her sketchbook. Two quick movements of the pen and it was done.

"It will take half a day for the ink to set," she said.

Zanja asked, "Will the woman in the water be rescued, drowned, eaten, or murdered?"

Chaen shrugged. She could remember that while she worked on the illustration she had been driven by pity and anger. But now it seemed like the swimmer's fate had already been executed.

As the sun pulled itself up from the water, it glared upon an ill-humored city. A sobbing girl in stained clothing scrubbed a stoop; rubbish collectors cursed the contents of their bins; a ship's captain shouted at the harbormaster; a shopkeeper used her broom to swat awake a couple of drunks snoring in her doorway. The Paladins escorted Chaen to a shuttered tavern near the quay. From blinding sunlight she went into darkness. Gradually, the faces of the witnesses, illuminated by oil lamps, became visible in the gloom: an odd collection of people that the Truthken might have selected from the street as light dawned. They sat in a restless, crooked row. At a long table, oil lamps illuminated the paper on which a man of astonishing ugliness scratched a few words with his pen. A young man came in after the Truthken and also sat, and began to study the closely printed pages of a large book. Nearby, the seer, his hair wildly disordered, used the tail of a very wrinkled shirt to polish his spectacles. Beside him, Emil wore black, his gray hair tied in a tail and his three earrings glittering in the lamplight. And the Sainnite general, equally neat and polished, stood beside him, so rigidly still that she scarcely seemed alive.

The Truthken addressed the witnesses. The Paladins had left Chaen standing in the middle of the room, and the witnesses seemed to prefer to look at her rather than at the Truthken. Additional people sat behind them, all of them gray-haired—Hanishport's city elders, thought Chaen. The young man at the table turned a page of his book, and Chaen guessed that the Truthken was quoting the Law of Shaftal from memory while he followed along in the book.

Chaen felt a warm hand touch hers: Seth was standing stubbornly beside her.

The Truthken seemed to be finishing her dull recitation. "I am Norina Truthken. I studied the law in the House of Lilterwess, and swore my oath twenty-five years ago, witnessed by Councilor Mabin. By that oath I now affirm that the Law of Shaftal is exactly as I have recited it. By that law I now declare that only the truth may be spoken in this room until this trial is concluded. Do you have any questions?"

The witnesses shook their heads and did not dare speak.

The Truthken turned. Chaen understood why the witnesses squirmed under her gaze. "Chaen, you stand accused of intending to murder Karis G'deon. Whatever questions I ask, you must answer."

The impact of her command was not subtle. How could Chaen continue to breathe? Why did her heart keep beating?

"Do you understand what you are accused of?" The Truthken's voice seemed far away.

Chaen's mouth said, "Yes."

"Say your name."

"Chaen of the Midlands."

"Do you affiliate yourself with a militia that is called Death-and-Life?"

"Yes."

"Three days ago, did you intend to kill the G'deon of Shaftal with poisoned arrows?"

"She is not the G'deon of Shaftal."

"I am referring to Karis, a Meartown metalsmith of great stature. Do you know who I mean?"

"Yes."

"Did you intend to kill her?"

"Yes."

"Why?"

"To finish a task. So that the lives of the six who died trying to accomplish it wouldn't have been wasted."

"What was their task?"

"To kill the false G'deon, to make way for the true G'deon."

Now came a silence, and Chaen gradually realized that she had been restored to her body, and she was bitterly angry: angry at herself for her weakness, and angry at the Truthken for doing that horrible thing to her so casually.

The Truthken said, "Chaen of the Midlands, I condemn you of murderous actions. By the Law of Shaftal, you now must choose your penalty. You may be executed now, by my hand. Or you may submit yourself to me, to be changed."

Chaen said, "I choose death."

The Truthken drew her blade.

Seth cried, "No!"

"Get out of the way," Chaen said.

Behind the two somber, silent generals, there rose a shadow. Its head brushed the ceiling, then turned to the light. Karis. Her voice rasped in the horrified silence. "Madam Truthken, Shaftal requires that Chaen live, and be changed."

"The choice is mine, by law!" Chaen cried.

The Truthken said, "But at any time, for any reason, the G'deon's word supersedes the law."

"But if the G'deon is false, then her word must also be false!" Chaen turned to the young man who she supposed to be a law student. Surely, since he was young, he would perceive this illogic and injustice! But he put a finger on a page in the book and read from it: "At any time, for any reason, the G'deon's word supersedes the law."

The Paladins took Chaen out of that place, and the sunlight struck her in the face. Her trial had not lasted much longer than it takes to eat a turnover.

Once again in the bright room with the grated window, the Paladins stranded her like flotsam on a rocky shore. A bell was ringing in the far distance, and the ship that had been standing off shore with its sails furled hoisted a flag. Nearby, Chaen heard muffled voices and a restless creaking of the old bones of that weathered old house. In a storm of glowing dust motes, a spider spun a shimmering thread.

The lock turned, the door opened, and the Truthken said, "Sit down."

Chaen sat in the chair by the window. She did not know whether or not she obeyed by choice, or because she had no choice.

The Truthken sat in the other chair, at the table, between Chaen and the door that stood ajar. Beyond it, Chaen thought, the air student might be listening, but the Paladins had left. *This* woman did not need the aid of those armed philosophers.

Chaen said, "I know you can force me to betray my friends. If you do that, you might as well kill me."

The Truthken crossed her feet at the ankle. Her face was pulled awry by an old scar, and she looked as hardened as Shaftal's many vagabonds. She had a dagger in a very old sheath buckled at the thigh. She said, "The task that is assigned to me by the law is not to interrogate you, but to change you."

"Change me into what?"

"That has yet to be decided. My task would be easier if I could reassure you that you will still recognize yourself at the end of this day. But you may not."

"And how is that different from killing me?"

"It is different," said the Truthken, "because you'll be able to start your life again. But this is a waste of time, for you can't persuade me to abandon my duty. Tell me, Chaen of the Midlands, do you have a family?"

Chaen doubted, then, that she was still under the Truthken's compulsion to answer, for she didn't and couldn't reply. Yet the woman said, immediately, "It was the Sainnites that killed them? All of them?"

With the passing years, Chaen had become able to say what had happened so it appeared as if she was done grieving. But this Truthken would see—already had seen—that Chaen lived within her loss like a wild animal lives in the ashes of a burned forest.

"I will never forget what happened to them," she said. Apparently, she could reply without answering, a simultaneous compliance and resistance.

The Truthken said, "Why do you consider *remembering* to be such a virtue?"

"It gives meaning to their deaths."

"What is the meaning?"

"Meaning comes from intention."

"What informs your intention?"

"Rage."

The Truthken's hard, scarred face and terrible eyes revealed a mild amusement. "What is the source of your rage?" she asked.

Back to the same question—and still Chaen must give her some sort of answer. Perhaps her despair could be a kind of armor? She said, "My entire family was burned alive by the Sainnites."

She felt a vertigo. She had declared that she would not forget. And she did remember standing in the children's room beside her son's empty cradle—smoke-smothered, horrified—but how had she survived? How had she escaped when she was trapped like all of them, in the same building and the same fire?

Chaen said, "My son was six months old. I forgot that he was in bed with me, and I went to the nursery to save him."

But she didn't remember what had happened after that awful realization.

The Truthken said, "Your rage has neither matured nor faded, for the air element makes you inflexible, while the fire element makes you unreasonable. Had you not been paralyzed by your dual nature, your vengefulness could have taken another form. In some people, such anger is transformative." So complex and lengthy a statement would require a normal person's full attention, and yet Chaen felt—feared—that most of the Truthken's attention was on something else.

"I am not vengeful!" she said. "I simply want justice!" But this truth seemed insufficient.

The Truthken asked, "Who is the leader of Death-and-Life?"

Chaen froze. She would not betray him. She would not even speak his name.

"I see." The Truthken leaned forward very slightly. Her restraint was horrifying. "Your leader still controls you, but that hold will be unfastened. Everything you believe will collapse. In the wreck of the life you created after the wreck of your first life, you will be a lunatic." She eased back in her seat. "Or, speak freely to me, so I can determine what to preserve, and you will remain a whole person. These are your choices, Chaen of the Midlands."

The room became stifling as the morning passed. Chaen gasped for breath by the open window. The Truthken, impervious to discomfort, sat entirely still, her attention never wavering. Chaen talked listlessly about her life. Occasionally, when Chaen stopped talking, time would pass before the Truthken asked another question. Each silence was excruciating: Chaen's words no longer mediated the terrifying study that the Truthken subjected her to. Surely this cool predator was playing with her.

"And yet you believed your little army could defeat the Sainnites?"

"It's not hard to believe. If one Shaftali out of forty killed only one soldier, we would be free."

"There is nothing simple about your mathematics. As you know."

Chaen felt a trembling, a weakening wall that must not collapse. But she didn't know how to shore it up.

"Were you at the attack on Watfield garrison last summer?"

Chaen answered: she had been stationed in the garden at the outer edge of the garrison, while the bulk of their fighters, hidden on rooftops and in alleyways, guarded the perimeter. In the garden, Chaen had ferried the rockets to the launchers, who seated them carefully in brackets jammed into the ground, aimed them, and held a slow match to their fuses. Hissing like monstrous serpents, the rockets flew upward, dragging long tails of sparks, and exploded, scattering burning rain across the rooftops. Annis's Fire that burning fluid was called: water could not put it out, and whenever it splattered upon a person, it burned to the bone. They burned down half the garrison that night, but when the soldiers attacked the rocketeers in the garden, Chaen and a handful of others could not hold them off and were lucky to escape.

The Truthken said, "That attack was dramatic but unwise; it used more gunpowder than the irregulars normally use in a year, not to mention the rare and expensive ingredients in the liquid fire. Some fifty Sainnites died that night, but so did thirty members of your company. It was a wasteful, impatient attack. Until then, Willis's strategy had been cautious and incremental. What had changed?"

Chaen wiped at the sweat that was dripping from her eyebrows into her eyes. "That was a *year* ago."

"You disagreed with the plan!" The Truthken almost seemed surprised. "You never ceased to oppose it? Were you the only one?" She paused. "You were."

"Why do I need to speak at all?" said Chaen bitterly.

"And the attack on the Children's Garrison—"

"The massacre, you mean!"

"You make my point for me. An entire company of soldiers was there, expecting Death-and-Life Company to attack on that very night. Do you think that was an accident?"

"Someone must have betrayed us."

"Someone *did* betray you. And afterwards, even though Willis was dead, his followers did not abandon their cause. They had believed he was chosen. Now he was dead, yet they continued to believe."

Even after the passage of many hours, Chaen continued to be taken aback by what this woman knew—things that should have been secret, that she knew with detail and accuracy. In fact, the remainder of Death-and-Life Company, devastated by the loss of half their fellows in half a year, had practically been destroyed by Willis's death. Even Chaen, always cynical about Willis's supposed vision, had been stunned. Perhaps she had become a believer without realizing it. Like the others who had yearned for the lost G'deon of Willis's vision, she had detested the G'deon who actually did come out of obscurity, and who, with neither weapons nor army, terrified the Sainnites into submission. That they refused to accept her was a strange contradiction. But that Chaen had been heedless of the contradiction until this moment was the strangest thing of all.

Her voice rasped shamefully. "Who betrayed us?"

The Truthken, remote and indifferent, did not answer.

"*Who betrayed us?*"

The woman crossed her booted feet and stretched back in the chair, rubbing her eyes. For Chaen to be the subject of her unwavering attention was exhausting, but surely the Truthken also was weary with frustration, heat, and attentiveness. Her leg was extended; her dagger practically out of reach; her weight resting precariously on the edge of the chair. If Chaen had ever been so sloppy with an enemy so close, she wouldn't have lived this long. Then the woman reached across her body for the water pitcher.

Chaen launched herself from the chair. Her left foot landed precisely and propelled her forward. Her right kicked the woman's chair out from under her. She grabbed for the dagger—but the woman was not there. Something kicked her ankle. She fell hard to the floor. The woman kicked her in the stomach.

Her vision fogged. She curled around her belly, gagging, whining like a mongrel. In the fog, she saw the Truthken's foot, half an arm's reach away. The woman stood with her weight slightly forward, on her toes, daring Chaen to try again.

She had lured Chaen into attacking her, and Chaen had responded, as stupid as a fish.

"Sit up."

To comply was excruciating. The Truthken regarded her. "You'll live. Go back to your chair."

Chaen crawled. She dragged herself into the chair. She found the Truthken seated again, with a cup of water in her hand. The woman said, "Hadn't everyone in the Death-and-Life Company sworn not to return home? To have no friends, no contact at all with anyone not in the company?"

"Yes," Chaen gasped. She no longer dared to remain silent.

"And yet despite those oaths, one man, who last year was injured in the attack on Watfield garrison, was permitted to return home to die. His home was in the region of Watfield—a family whose young daughter had been taken by the Sainnites in retaliation for the attack, and who were willing to trade information to get that daughter back again."

Chaen vomited a string of yellow mucus to the floor. The Truthken sipped her water, waiting. Chaen said, "Is that what happened? Is that how the Sainnites knew to ambush us at the Children's Garrison? Is that how Willis and the forty were killed?"

The Truthken said, "Yes, that is how it happened. But how was it made possible?"

It was Saugus who had argued that the man should be allowed to return home. He had accompanied him, and had promised Willis that he would make it impossible for the dying man to betray the company.

"None of us had bidden our families farewell," Chaen said. "Few of us even had families any more. We wanted him to be able to go home."

"An emotionally compelling argument." The Truthken's tone was dry as sand.

"Saugus betrayed us," Chaen said.

Expressionless, the Truthken gazed at her.

Chaen said, "Saugus arranged for forty people—members of his own company—to be killed."

Still, the Truthken said nothing.

Chaen was trembling with pain, struggling not to vomit again. "Why?"

"I am a Truthken, tested by Truthkens, bound by vows that I will never break. Do you think I am ruthless?"

"Yes."

"And if I were not bound by vows, what would I be like?"

Fortunately, Chaen needed not answer, for the Truthken continued. "Long before the air witch found Willis, he had made and learned from many mistakes. In Death-and-Life Company, he developed his powers, learned subtlety, discovered his limits, gathered his resources, and planned. When he had what he needed, he began removing impediments: he removed Willis, his inner circle, and any other person in the company who proved troublesome to manage—eventually including you. What remains is a manageable number of fanatical devotees."

Chaen stared at her, hating her, but unable to ignore her logic.

"It's what I would do," said the woman. She filled the cup with water. "For you to faint would be inconvenient. I'm going to give this to you, for you to drink."

Even with this forewarning, Chaen's self-control was tested as the woman stood up to give her the water: The closer she drew, the more Chaen wanted to throw herself through the window, regardless of the iron grate. The Truthken sat down. Chaen drank the water.

The Truthken said, "With too many followers, he would spend all his time managing them, which would be tedious. It's far more interesting and satisfying to control a smaller number of selected people, and, through them, to control events. So Saugus culled the company."

Chaen's trembling fingers dropped the cup. She had said his name? When had she said his name? Then she laughed bitterly. Why should she feel guilty for betraying a traitor?

Suddenly, the sea breeze began to blow, and slammed the door shut. The Truthken blocked the door open with a wedge from the hall. A dust bunny tumbled out the door, and Chaen heard the squawking and banging of a shutter. She heard no voices, no barking dogs, no creaking footsteps or closing doors.

The Truthken poured her another cup of water, and there was the whisper of her breeches and the creak of the chair as she sat down.

Chaen said, "Aren't we finished yet? I gave him up to you!"

"You told me his name. But where is he?"

"I don't know."

"He may be here, in Hanishport."

Chaen muttered dully, "If he is, I guess he'll kill me."

"You don't remember that you saw him in the crowd, the day you were arrested? As you were being escorted to this house?"

Chaen vomited. All the water she had drunk spewed onto the floor. "Don't make me think about it!" Chaen was begging, weeping. She felt a loss—an unendurable loss—but of what? Her awareness spun around a vacancy, sucking into emptiness, like water emptying from a sink.

"Don't think about it," the Truthken said.

Her quiet words yanked Chaen free of the vortex, gasping. "What's wrong with me?"

"Your memories are unstable. You can hold on to nothing. I don't know why. Not yet."

She left the room and returned with a towel that she tossed to Chaen. Chaen wiped her face and dropped the towel on the mess on the floor. She couldn't remember what had upset her stomach, and she didn't want to remember.

Time dragged the afternoon forward, like an old donkey with a heavy cart. The breeze cooled the house; the dull city became noisy for a few hours, and Chaen imagined a thousand brooms wielded without enthusiasm, sweeping up the dirt and debris after the end of a very large party—a party that today was more resented than loved. Chaen curled herself in the chair, trying to ease the ache in her gut.

The Truthken was telling her about Karis, and it became clear how much and how long their lives had been intertwined. The Truthken was the last surviving witness of the moment Harald vested Karis with the Power of Shaftal. She had helped Karis to escape the attack on the House of Lilterwess and had kept her alive, in obscurity, for the next fifteen years.

The Truthken said, "I am only two years older than Karis, but I was given the task of managing her smoke addiction and keeping her alive until someone more worthy to bear the power of Shaftal could be found. Every resource that had survived the Fall was gathered to complete my education, while for Karis nothing was done. They neglected her for reasons that were logically sound but were based on false assumptions. No one seriously considered that Karis might be worthy to bear the Power of Shaftal, not even me. Like Mabin, I was trapped in reality, and when the visionaries told me what was possible, I could not hear them. Well, I learned to listen—but those weren't easy lessons."

She fell silent. At first, Chaen, weary with pain, weak with hunger, bewildered by the shifting landscape of her understanding, could not imagine why this formidable, terrifying woman had decided to deliver this account. Then her sluggish mind managed to have an idea, and she said dully, "To you also she was a false G'deon."

"Yes, and for reasons similar to yours."

"You don't even know my reasons."

"Tell me, then."

"Name of Shaftal—I can't believe I must explain when it is so obvious! She is a Sainnite, and she befriended the Sainnites. Therefore she is not and can't be the embodiment of Shaftal."

"I will grant that your facts are accurate. However, her mother was a Juras woman; so why don't you consider Karis to be Juras?"

"She never lived with them."

"She never lived with Sainnites."

"But the smallest amount of Sainnite blood . . ."

Again, the Truthken sat in silence, but the tendons in her arms looked like bow strings, and so also must the rest of her body be drawn, poised to let an arrow fly the instant her target came into view.

Chaen was the target. The moment she had consented to her impulse to assassinate the pretender, this role had been designated for her, and everyone had subtly yet irresistibly forced her into this position and made it impossible for her to escape.

In every catastrophe, there must be a moment that the victim, having learned the awful lesson that every possible action will only make matters worse, decides not to struggle. When this thought came to Chaen, she realized that the moment of acceptance had passed many hours ago. When she lay on the floor after the Truthken kicked her, she had given up but had not recognized the deadness in the core of her pain.

Chaen said, "If what Seth told me about Zanja's book—the lexicon—is true . . ."

"It does seem to be true. People were here before our ancestors arrived—the border people we have called them, since we have forgotten that it was we who forced them to retreat to the borders. The work of our scholars so far has tended to support rather than disprove this history. Karis, thanks to her Juras mother, is more Shaftali than you or I."

Chaen scarcely heard the Truthken's measured speech. A trembling—a peculiar, awful shudder—had begun in the core of her being, the marrow of her bones—and it became so violent that her chair began to rattle on the floor, and when she tried to grab the chair arm to keep from sliding off, her shaking hand yanked loose again. She fell, and the chair toppled, and still she shuddered so violently she couldn't even sit up. A few words were jerked out of her, like entrails from a fish. "Karis is Shaftal."

The Truthken rose to her feet. For an awful moment, Chaen thought she would kick her again, or even touch her, which would have been worse. But the woman merely spoke. "Chaen of the Midlands, your sentence is finished, and you are free to go."

She left the room. Chaen heard her footsteps creak down the stairs. The door stood ajar, and the sea breeze washed through.

Lying upon the floor, like a piece of debris blown in by the wind, Chaen wept.

Chapter 23

Chaen filled her knapsack and dragged it to her shoulder, and stepped out of prison. She had freedom—but it would curse what remained of her life.

She felt her way down the dim stairs from one step to the next. At the second-floor landing, the sea breeze washed through a dim, barren hall. From below, there arose a cacophony of voices: angry argument, solemn discussion, stifled laughter. Spoons rang dully on pottery bowls, and the scent of food and bread floated up the stairs. Having no choice, she went down into a stair hall crowded with Paladins who ate standing or squatting with their backs against the crumbling plaster. She recognized their voices, but none of them heeded her.

On her left, in a parlor so crammed with people that those on the edges were standing in the hall, people argued about what must be done and why it was not their responsibility to do it. Several talked at once, so angry that they seemed about to start shouting, but the room fell silent when one voice spoke: reasonable, patient, velvet over steel: Emil. "The people of Lalali are our people, and we abandoned them. For that wrong we must make amends."

On the right, in a quieter parlor, people huddled around tables by the windows where the last of the daylight lingered. Chaen felt the G'deon's presence in that room: the weight of her.

Seth squeezed out of the crowd on the left and took Chaen's hand. "The government of Shaftal," she said. "It's enough to make me miss the cows."

"Seth, thank you for your kindness," Chaen said.

"You're not leaving. Not like this, without food or rest."

"I can do what I like. The Truthken has released me."

Seth considered, her grip like a shackle. "I'll go with you, then. I'm weary of these people."

"Seth, your assignment is finished. You need not pretend to be my friend any longer."

"Earth bloods don't pretend." Seth tugged on Chaen's hand. "So, where are we going?"

From the stairway Norina's voice said, "She wants to speak to Karis."

Chaen remembered that she had wanted to do that, but during the journey downstairs her desire had begun to seem foolish.

"Oh, for lands sake!" A cow doctor's patients were large and stupid; far larger than Chaen, but perhaps not any more stupid. Seth easily dragged Chaen into the parlor.

"She's just a metalsmith," said Seth, pulling Chaen into the center of the parlor as people stood up, gathered materials, and moved out of their way.

"Seth," Chaen protested wearily.

"She loves food. She hates bridges. She can't sew but is constantly wrecking her shirts. She nearly got into a wrestling contest with her cousin over who had the rights to a herd of goats. She's incessantly tinkering with things."

Zanja na'Tarwein rose out of the shadows to move a table out of the way. Karis stood up, and Chaen stumbled and fell. Yet Seth remained beside her, still talking, her fierce whisper overwhelmed by the roaring wind.

The G'deon hauled Chaen to her feet. Her big hand touched Chaen's face, and it felt like a blow; then it felt like the sun. Chaen wanted to embrace her. She jerked away, and nearly fell again.

Someone had lit a lamp and brought it near, and the G'deon's eyes became brilliantly, shockingly blue. She said, "What did you hit her with—an ax handle?"

"With my foot," said the Truthken, her presence like a blade in Chaen's back.

"I think you had better keep your distance from her."

"Yes, Karis."

"Yet you remain?"

"Karis, her memories have been damaged somehow. I probably can mend them, with time and her permission. But she's injured in such a way that she can't even remember that she has been injured."

The G'deon breathed in and out. "All right."

The knife in Chaen's back withdrew. The Truthken had left. She could breathe, shallowly, lest the pain in her side become intolerable. Her head had cleared enough that she remembered what she wanted to say. "Karis, I'm sorry for my wrongs against Shaftal, and especially for my efforts to kill you."

The G'deon's body had clenched like a massive fist. "Seven members of my household were murdered!"

Chaen said, "I don't expect to be pardoned. But I'd like to make some kind of reparation."

The G'deon, breathing quickly, gave no reply. Chaen turned to leave. Somehow, she would evade Seth.

But Karis said, "No one leaves my house hungry and weary. You will eat, rest, and leave tomorrow if you wish. Or you can remain here and speak with the healers, philosophers, and visionaries who are gathered here. Perhaps they can help you."

Turning to face her, Chaen lost her balance again and was caught in a rough embrace, with her face pressed to the linen of a carefully made shirt sleeve. There was pleating at the shoulders, and gussets in the collar, and a fraying tear at eye level that someone had better mend before the shirt was washed again. The shirt smelled like dirt, mold, sickness, and sewage.

"Yes, Karis," Chaen mumbled into the filthy fabric.

Seth took her by the arm and showed her the way to the kitchen.

Chaen dreamed that she was drowning.

She awoke to a deep pain in her side where the toe of the Truthken's heavy boot had left a hot, red bruise. Her good shirt had dried overnight where she had hung it in the window, but she could scarcely lift her arm to put it in the sleeve.

She had slept very late; the house was silent and empty. When she started down the stairs, a dog came out onto the landing below and yawned noisily. On the first floor, another dog slept in the parlor, by a sofa on which sprawled a gray-haired Paladin with an open book resting on her chin. Both of them snored softly. In the kitchen, on the counter, there was bread and butter, cherries, and a teapot with the tea already measured into it.

On a folded piece of coarse paper, weighted by a boiled egg, was written Chaen's name. Chaen took the note and the egg outside and sat upon the steps, with the harbor and the road before her. The note, much blotted and spattered from the pen tip catching in the rough paper, read: "Please speak with Zanja about the card-casting. If you won't permit me to correct the damage to your memory, it is hoped that the cards might reveal the knowledge that we lack. I will consider myself in your debt. Norina Truthken, Year I, Day 208, of Karis G'deon."

Chaen tore the note to bits and scattered them on the steps, where she hoped the Truthken would discover them.

She ate the egg and a slice of bread and thought about which way to go, right or left. To both options she felt equally indifferent.

The door opened and Zanja came out with cups of tea. She gave Chaen one and sat beside her. Her feet were bare, and the dry, sandy soil sifted up between her toes. Her sturdy satchel had been on her shoulder and now lay beside her. Her face was austere and remote. A thin braid of black hair lay over her shoulder and looped over the satchel. Her much shorter hair, tied back in a tail, was wrapped with a leather cord.

"The note from the Truthken," Chaen began.

"I know what she wrote. We sat up late, talking about you."

"I'm surprised."

"Norina and I are incompatible. But neither of us will leave Karis. So, with much practice, we have become able to tolerate each other."

"I see," said Chaen skeptically. "About the glyphs—the lexicon you found contains *all* the lost glyphs?"

"Yes, there are a thousand illustrated glyphs. But I didn't find the lexicon—I stole it. I stole it at knifepoint and tied up a librarian."

"I would have stolen it also."

"Others have said the same." She took out her packets of cards and shuffled through them. "After I came back to my own life, I showed the lexicon to some of the oldest soldiers of Watfield garrison." She began showing Chaen some of the cards. "The soldiers told me that this mountain is climbed every year by mystics, and when they can't climb it any more, they die. And this animal is like our ox, used for plowing. The flowers on this vine are used to infuse a spirit that's an aphrodisiac. This building is a place to worship the gods. The fruits being harvested here each weighs as much as a small child. These towers are exactly like the towers in Lalali. Mountains, animals, flowers, buildings, fruits—all are from Sainna. The people who brought the book to this land were Sainnites."

Her hands fell still.

Chaen's hollowed-out sensation became intolerable. The austere border woman sat unmoving with the cards in her hands, looking outward, unseeing. Sometime later she seemed recalled back to herself. She found a card as if by feel and showed it to Chaen.

Chaen recognized it as one of the cards Zanja had cast in the tavern. "The Brothers."

"We've been calling it the Quarrel."

Chaen studied the image of the two men, who stood back-to-back in the road, glaring in separate directions: one dark, one fair, one dressed in white, one in black.

Zanja said, "This card reveals that you had two sons, and only one of them died in the fire. You can't remember the son who survived, and you can't even remember that you have forgotten him. Norina thinks the memory was destroyed by air magic."

"But if I still have a living son . . ."

Chaen looked up from the card. Zanja gazed at her as if expecting something. "What?" Chaen said in confusion.

Zanja said, "Maybe if you look at the card again?"

Chaen looked at the card in Zanja's hand and remembered what they had been discussing. "I have a living son? How do you know?"

"By fire logic."

Stymied, Chaen gazed at the card, afraid to look away lest she forget again. "Will I have to look at this card forever?"

"Norina may be able to repair the damage, if you consent."

"No."

"I wouldn't be enthusiastic about the prospect either. Look at this card." Zanja folded back the sleeve of paper that protected the card Chaen had painted. "This warrior on the riverbank is your living son, the one you can't remember. The drowning woman is you."

"Are you interrogating me?"

"No, I'm trying to understand a card-casting. These are things you don't know either."

"But it's knowledge wanted by the Truthken."

"That's true, but to be owed a favor by a sworn Truthken is no small thing. Once, she made a mistake that nearly cost my life, and she has paid for it with six years of civility."

If Chaen were painting Zanja's portrait, it would be a challenge to capture that remoteness, that exotic face, and the jarring juxtaposition with her plain clothing, her bare feet, and the cracked teacup in her hand. But most difficult to capture would be her profound, scarcely visible sorrow.

"I'm going mad," said Zanja. Her tone suggested that her condition was as ordinary as a splinter in a finger. "Therefore, I have nothing at all to do. Doing nothing is better than listening to the tedious discussions of Lalali's sewage problem, but still . . ."

Chaen laughed, and stopped because it felt so strange, and had to laugh again, and the laughter twisted into a kind of sobbing. Zanja politely didn't notice.

Chaen said, "Can a madwoman tell me how to make reparations? Possibly to gain the G'deon's pardon?"

"I'm just a presciant, not a visionary. I can find my own way through strange places, but I can only find *your* way with the cards."

"Then use the cards."

Zanja cast the cards as she had done before, except for the one she had given Chaen, that was upstairs in her sketchbook. She even used the Quarrel, but Chaen kept her gaze on the card and didn't forget that she might have a living child. Zanja added the new card to the array. "Consider what you see, and then ask a question."

Their teacups were empty; the house's shadow had crept to their shoulders; various people had passed up and down the road; and the blithe cook Chaen had met the previous night returned from shopping, carrying laden baskets, followed by a boy hauling fish in a hand cart. Chaen picked up the card she had painted two nights ago. Her thoughts scattered like dried leaves in wind, revealing a few words, like polished stones, that had been hidden beneath them. "Death of Memory."

"Death of Memory," Zanja repeated. "Perhaps it tells the story of how you lost your memories, and why."

A company of soldiers carrying shovels walked past. Zanja called something in their language, and they looked startled, but a few smiled and one replied. Zanja pinched her nose and made a face, and he laughed. Chaen had never seen a soldier laugh.

"Those soldiers are going to Lalali to dig new sewage trenches." Zanja lay back on the stoop and covered her eyes with her arm.

Chaen picked up the Quarrel again, so she could keep the image before her. "Does your head ache?"

"It's from an old injury." Zanja took a slow breath. "Norina says that on the day you were arrested, as you were being brought to this house, you saw something that comforted you."

"Could my son be here? In Hanishport?"

"That's not a good question. The cards never answer yes or no. Let's ask this instead: Where is Chaen's son?" She immediately pointed at one of the cards already cast. "The Ship of Air." The ship flew high above the earth: a fantastic, puzzling image.

"Is my son an air witch?" Chaen asked.

Zanja sat up abruptly. "If he is, then perhaps he destroyed your memories of him."

Chaen stood up. "Farewell."

"Chaen, wait."

"What should I wait for? For you to tell the Truthken? For her to restore my memories and use them to find and kill my son?"

"You are free to do as you like. But give me my card."

If Chaen returned the card to Zanja, she would forget what she was fleeing and why.

Perhaps the border woman's gaze was not as dispassionate as the Truthken's, but it still was calculating. Zanja said, "Ask where Saugus is, and you can keep that card."

"I would betray him gladly if I could do it without betraying my friends! But they will defend him, and die with him."

"Karis will do everything possible to avoid it."

Chaen, her heart hammering with urgency, tried to think. Zanja must have been considering the same questions: How much would Chaen give up to possess the glyph card? Would she betray the friends she did remember to save the son she didn't remember? If Chaen did ask the question, would Zanja understand the answer? Chaen asked, "Will Karis pardon me? If I betray my friends?"

Zanja did not immediately reply, and her gaze was quite blank. "Yes." She jerked with startlement, then, and put a hand to her eyes. "Yes. Yes."

"Then—where is Saugus?"

The fortune-teller cast a card.

Chapter 24

The empty cup of Zanja's skull was filled to overflowing by a pitcher of pain.

"Will Karis pardon me? If I betray my friends?"

Zanja saw a large room, dimly lit by high windows. Her hand rested on the shoulder of a starving woman who should have been young but was not. She touched the worn, greasy texture of the woman's ragged silk shirt. She felt the dust of a thousand other people, living and dead, trapped there in the dirty silk. She tasted the salt of distant oceans. She sensed the scalding fingertips of slave children unwinding the silk from the cocoons; the tiny lives of the silkworms; the lives of the trees whose leaves they ate; and the life of the soil that fed and stabilized those trees.

"Yes," Karis said with Zanja's mouth and Zanja's breath.

Zanja opened her eyes. Chaen was wending through an appalling labyrinth, one dreadful turn at a time.

"Yes," Zanja said. "Yes."

"Then—where is Saugus?" Chaen asked.

Dazedly, Zanja chose a card.

It was a card from the original casting. It depicted a luxurious room, walled with tapestries, in which a woman sat upon a chair that had no back but had curved armrests nearly as high as her shoulders. Her rich robe covered the entire floor like a carpet. A narrow, winding staircase led to a door that was set in a hillside. The roots of a tree buttressed the walls of the room.

Zanja said to herself, in her native language, "How can I understand this picture?"

"Speaker? Did you call me?"

The boy had been swimming in the Asha River. The city grime had dissolved in its cold, fast-flowing water. He had put on a summer tunic with the woven border pattern of the na'Tarwein clan. His black, wet hair hung nearly to his waist.

"I did call you," she said.

"What is your will?"

"Tell me what this picture means."

The boy examined the glyph card. "It is a burrow."

"Like a rabbit's burrow?"

"It is for those who live among us, underfoot."

"Yet we don't see them. Why is that?"

"Because they keep out of our sight, or they pretend to be what they are not."

Chaen was staring, and well she might, since Zanja was speaking with an invisible boy in an unknown language. Zanja said in Shaftalese, "Chaen, ask me where is this underground room."

Chaen glanced in the direction of Zanja's apprentice, but to her, he was not there. "Where is this underground room?" she asked.

The boy offered Zanja a page from the lexicon. That page showed a farmer, walking behind a plow pulled by the peculiar oxen of Sainna, whose horns covered their heads like helmets. In the turned soil immediately behind the farmer's feet, plants were already sprouting. A river bordered the four sides of the field, floated upon by strange ships, swum in by sinuous fish, and settled by elaborate houses along its shore.

The details may have been wrong, but it was the Corbin River. This farmer could be Waet, plowing the field after which the city of Watfield had been named.

She said, "How can this person be in Watfield? After we have watched for him, sought him, with every power at our disposal?"

"You never looked underfoot," said the boy.

She reached to take the page of the lexicon from him, but her hand closed on empty air.

Chaen said, "I don't understand."

Zanja said, "I know where Saugus is."

"Then I am leaving." Chaen walked away, with the glyph card still held in her hand.

Zanja pounded up the stairs to Chaen's room, grabbed her knapsack, and ran downstairs again to awaken Lil Paladin and ask her to chase Chaen with it. "Then fetch Norina. Tell her to come immediately." She ran back up the stairs, slammed into Emil's and Medric's room, and shook the sleeping seer by the shoulder.

"Mmmph." His eyes cracked open. "What."

"Saugus is in Watfield, in Travesty!"

"Bloody hell," he muttered in Sainnese. "I can't see. Do you see my—"

She shoved his spectacles at him, but he took them off as soon as he put them on and handed them back to her. "You'll need these. For far-seeing."

Zanja put Medric's spectacles in her satchel. She noticed that she had thrown the cards into it without wrapping and tying them. She forced herself to sit at the table to put them right while Medric put on the spectacles for close-seeing and got dressed. Seeming half in a dream, he kept interrupting his progress to give her more things to put in her satchel: a tinder bag, a roll of twine, a mending kit.

The dogs barked. Through the window, Zanja saw Norina running down the road toward the house. Medric was fumbling vaguely with buttons. Zanja did them up for him and then pushed him ahead of her, into the hall and down the stairs, not much caring that he might stumble and fall in his sleepy daze. Norina came in, with the agitated dogs behind her. "Where's Maxew?" she asked. "He's supposed to be watching the door."

Medric sat on the stairs. "Where's Emil? He didn't say good-bye like he usually does." He looked in bewilderment at the sheathed dagger in his hand—Emil's dagger.

Zanja ran down the hall and slammed into the kitchen. "Garland! When did you last see Emil?"

Garland was doing something complicated with a chopping knife, a pile of herbs, and a bowl of salt. "Yesterday."

"He didn't come in this morning for a cup of tea?"

Garland looked up from his work, puzzled, then dismayed.

Zanja left the bright kitchen. The hall seemed shockingly dark. She cried in a panic, "Maxew is Chaen's son! He is colluding with Saugus! And he has taken Emil!"

The ravens lifted off with hoarse cries. One flew up from a branch in a tree near the road to Lalali. One took off from the fallen wall at Watfield garrison. And one flew down from Travesty's rooftop and began croaking at the Paladin who was pulling weeds in the front garden. But the ravens had lost the power of speech, and the Paladin offered the bird a worm plucked from the soil.

She was running down the road, and each step was as heavy and implacable as the rolling of boulders over a cliff's edge. A Paladin ran beside her, imploring her to explain. They were passing the pond where the soldiers usually swam after a day of dirty work in Lalali.

Karis gasped, "I don't know where Emil is!"

"Norina, stop that!" Medric cried.

Zanja staggered. Back in her own skin again, she saw the two of them, mere shadows in the dark hall: Medric sitting on the stairs in a huddle, Norina driving her dagger into the plaster wall, over and over.

Norina stopped. She glanced at Zanja and said, "Karis is speaking with your mouth now."

"Why doesn't she know where Emil is? She always knows!"

"I should have noticed!" Norina began stabbing the wall again.

"Give Zanja your dagger," Medric said.

Norina was never without her dagger, not even when walking from one room to another.

Medric said, "She needs it. The sheath also."

Norina handed Zanja the dagger. Plaster dust shimmered in its rippled surface, where Karis had delicately folded and re-folded the molten metal.

Garland had come out of the kitchen, but kept his distance, as Leeba did when Norina was in a temper. Zanja said, "Garland, I need travel food."

He ducked back into the kitchen.

"No!" cried Karis.

Norina said, "If an air witch has hidden Emil from you, only fire logic can find him." She handed Zanja her belt and scabbard. She was calm now, wound tight as an instrument of war.

Zanja said, "Norina, listen. Saugus has been living with us in Travesty. I don't know how long."

"Then Maxew let him in. And I never set eyes on him. Nor did any law student. He must have entered through the kitchen." She breathed deeply. "The housekeeper, Bran. Bran is Saugus. Karis, did you hear me? I'll write a note immediately for a raven to carry to J'han."

"It's two days' hard flying," Karis gasped.

"Still, it's twice as fast as riding."

Garland rushed out of the kitchen and began stuffing Zanja's satchel with fabric sacks of food. He gave her a water flask with a long strap to loop across the shoulders, and a porringer to hang from her belt. "What kind of blanket, wool or linen?" he asked.

"No blanket." Zanja bent down to check her bootstraps, then Norina caught her arm to keep her from falling.

"Headache?" She knelt to check the straps for her.

Karis made a choking, sobbing sound in Zanja's throat. "Zanja, you must not go into danger! Not when you're losing your mind!"

Norina said, "Madness makes Zanja impervious to air logic. Would you rather send Medric?"

Medric gave her a bewildered look, then seemed to realize that she was being sarcastic.

"How many people will I lose today?" cried Karis.

"You'll lose yourself if you keep running in this heat," Norina said.

"We cannot," Karis gasped. "We must not fail."

"Then send Zanja!" cried the seer on the stairs. "Send her, Karis! Send her!"

The Paladin was asking questions again, in a tone both polite and exasperated. They were walking now, and Karis was coughing from the dust in her throat. "Go," she gasped.

Zanja slung the laden satchel across her shoulders and ran out of the house.

Part Three: Fire

The way of fire is to see and know
Fire with earth can be renewed
Fire needs water to ease its woe
Four elements for balance.

Chapter 25

Tashar's sailboat waited, rocking gently in the quiet water. He packed away the deck covers, stepped the mast, and checked the sail and lines. He made certain the supplies were still in the hold: blankets, tins of water, bags of food. They must travel very lightly. Could they manage with less water? Did they really need blankets? Well, they could always jettison excess gear.

The glassy smooth water began to glow like a lamp chimney of blue glass lit by a brilliant flame. The rising light revealed the hazy city. When the city's business resumed, its loveliness would go unnoticed in the heat and racket. But how beautiful it was, as the white sandstone blushed pink and illuminated flowers flowed like silk over the shoulders of a house. Atop the hill, the House of Lora and the other great houses flared with light, while in the east, not even the edge of the rising sun could be seen—then it appeared, the tiniest shred of brilliance, and sunrise ignited the city. The water's glassy surface crumpled, and the clutter of small boats began to shift restlessly, thumping each other's sides. Tashar heard shoe soles scraping stone. There were his passengers: Maxew, straining like an eager dog, dragging a staggering companion behind him.

It was not Maxew's mother. It was a stranger, who gazed about in childish delight and confusion. Tashar hurried down the dock to help Maxew steer the balky man to the boat. He seemed a witless and ungainly collection of disconnected parts. When told to step into the boat, he stared blankly. When pulled, he pulled in the other direction.

"Just hold the boat there," Maxew said, and, while Tashar held the boat steady with the boat hook, Maxew gave the man a shove. He sprawled into the boat, with his head against the wall of the cockpit and his flailing legs stuck out over the portside gunwale like fishing poles.

"Gah," he said in bewildered surprise.

Three gold earrings in his left ear caught the light.

Tashar said, "We're abducting Emil Paladin?"

"It *used* to be him," said Maxew.

"But what about your—the portrait painter? Doesn't she need rescue?"

Maxew said bitterly, "Whatever happens to her, she deserves."

The light breeze pulled them slowly outward from Hanishport into the bay. Except for a couple of distant fishing boats and two ships that lay at anchor, they were alone. With the rippling water lapping the windward beam, they poked along, running with a luffing sail until they were free of the harbor and could turn more to the north. Then, with a broad reach, they gained some speed, and the ripples of the sheltered harbor became waves that thumped the hull like rough friends.

Maxew, having listened impatiently to Tashar's instructions, perched on the rail when the boat began to heel, and leaned back over the water. The breeze freshened, and the boat raced across the bright harbor, quick and light as a butterfly. Sea birds shrilled, chasing the boat and wheeling away. Tashar asked, "What did you do to him?"

"Broke him," said Maxew.

"Why not just kill him?"

The air witch glanced at Tashar, who didn't like being looked at in that way. He began fussing with a line that had nothing wrong with it.

"Pity, horror, curiosity."

Tashar turned his attention to the streaming telltales. "What are you talking about?"

"Your irrelevant emotions. Our duty is to bring this man to Saugus, without any part of him touching ground, not even once."

Tashar thought for a while, but some of the things he was thinking made him feel wretched, disconcerted, uncomfortable, confused, even nauseated. The more he tried to determine why he felt so awful, the worse the feelings grew. Only when he said meekly to Maxew, "Whatever you say," could he return to his enjoyment of being on the water.

They had a southwesterly breeze, and sailing toward the northeast required some skill and attention. One time that they came about, Tashar, half hoping that the swinging boom would dump Maxew into the cold water, didn't warn him. But Maxew ducked the boom anyway, crawled over the prisoner to sit on the opposite gunwale, and gave Tashar a mocking glance. *I know your thoughts,* he might have said.

One last change of tack brought them to skirt dangerously near the shattered shoreline. Here, where waves broke on black boulders, two ancient buoys wallowed, marking the entrance to a nameless cove. Rocks lurked in the shallow water of the cove entrance, a worse threat than the crashing waves. Tashar used the sight flags planted on shore to navigate. Some of the flags were decoys to wreck or drown unwanted visitors, but he knew which were which.

Now the highland blocked the breeze, and Tashar had to row to shore. He scrambled to raise the keelboard, and they ground into the gravel beach. He said, "I'll go hire some people to carry him. Take out his earrings so they won't be able to guess who he is, not that they'll care."

Tashar took some money from his pouch and waded to shore. Some people of the small, nameless settlement stood at the far end of the beach, watching him with closed expressions. He didn't know their names, and they didn't know his, but they had received and stored his secret shipments over the years. They certainly weren't his friends—but in every bargain Tashar had ever made with them, they had kept their word, and kept his secrets.

"I've got a man in my boat that must be carried to the barn," Tashar said. Immediately, they began to discuss the price.

Tashar wished they weren't standing so close to the drying racks, which were festooned with seaweed and filleted fish. "The man must not touch the ground at all," he said.

These people were completely without curiosity. On his visits, Tashar sometimes had sex with one or another of the women, and they also never asked him a question. A man said, "It's a good four furlongs, I guess, and all uphill. If we can't put the man down to rest, we'll need six people so we can spell each other."

That raised the price by a third. Tashar took out his money and paid them the first half. The six waded into the water, rolled the old man onto a blanket, and lifted him out of the boat in this makeshift sling. Keeping his prisoner in sight seemed to be all Maxew cared about, and he started after them, but Tashar yelled at him to carry some gear, and he hastily grabbed a load of supplies and trotted away with heavy tins of water suspended from his shoulders and baskets of food in each hand.

Tashar dragged the boat ashore, stowed the sail, and secured the decks. It was a sweet boat, the best he had ever sailed. Tashar patted it affectionately to wish it luck and turned away. Laden with supplies, he trudged across the gravel beach, up the steep, winding cliff path, then up the slope of a barren black hillside. Eventually, the smugglers came down the path toward him, and Tashar paid them the other half of the money. Then he found Maxew's water tins abandoned by the trail, and he carried them until he met Maxew coming back for them. The path leveled out, and a barn came into sight, a weathered, sideways-leaning old wreck in the wasteland of an abandoned farm. The smugglers had slung the prisoner from the petrified remains of an oak tree that stood watch near the barn, and he was writhing in this hammock like a sailor in a nightmare.

Maxew wiped his face on his shirt, squinted at the brilliant sky, then looked across the rolling wasteland. "Where are the horses?"

The ribbon of silk Tashar had tied in the top of the tree fluttered weakly in the direction of the ocean. He said, "We don't need them. All we need is a westerly wind."

Their preparations complete, they sat in the narrow strip of shade by the north wall of the barn, waiting for the wind to change. Whenever the man hanging in the tree began to struggle or utter garbled complaints, Tashar would return to worrying about the catastrophes that could befall them. It was like an intermittent fever.

One time, he said, "What about the G'deon's seer? Won't he know where we are?"

Maxew said, in a tone of long suffering, "No, because air and fire are incompatible."

Later, Tashar said, "But if he can't know what you're doing, you also can't know what he's doing."

"It doesn't matter. The man's a fool. It doesn't take magic to see *that*."

"But the false G'deon possesses the power of Shaftal, and could use it against us."

"Emil makes all the difficult decisions—without him, she won't know what to do."

"And if something goes wrong?"

"Whose fault is it that we're sitting here, doing nothing?"

"I *warned* you about the weather, and I *told* you it was important!"

The miserable wait continued. Finally, the tell-tale in the oak tree, which had long hung limp, began to flutter. Maxew followed Tashar to the land side of the barn, where two masts were stepped in deep holes, stabilized by piles of rock, with a rope strung between them like a 30-foot-high laundry line. Earlier, the two of them had hoisted the huge silk bag to hang from that line while Tashar attempted to explain the conveyance to Maxew. The giant wicker basket was shaped like a boat; therefore, the bag was a sail. But Maxew insisted that it looked like a bladder balloon such as children play with on butchering day.

It's a sail, Tashar insisted silently, *and the wind will move us, just as it does on water.* As with a ship, its fire was contained in an iron stove, with wire grates across the chimney to catch the sparks. Fire was a necessary danger, because the silk bag must be filled with smoke or it would not sail. But the silk, painted with many layers of varnish, could ignite like a torch. When Tashar had practiced filling it over a fire last year, on a cold, dry autumn day, it had been an anxious business. But now, with two people to hold the bag over the fire, they could control it better.

Do not be impatient, the instructions said, at least ten different times. Unfortunately, Maxew had not read those instructions.

"The bag has a leak. Smoke is escaping."

"There is no leak. I've checked every inch of its seams."

"Then we should build up the fire. This is taking too long."

"I told you it would be slow!"

"Why didn't we just take the boat? We could go north and then up the river to Shimasal."

"The boat is too small for the open ocean. We'd be swamped before we left the bay."

"And you never saw fit to tell me that?"

Nothing had changed between them. Maxew blamed Tashar for everything, as always.

The bag began to swell, and then it came alive, just like a sail that has filled with wind. Even with the light breeze, the inflated bag strained against its tethers. They must move quickly now, and Tashar was glad he had insisted they practice, although Maxew had sneered through the drills: quench the fire, hitch the wicker boat to its sail, leap in, feed fuel to the stove, then climb out to fetch their prisoner.

But transferring the man to the boat, which they had hadn't been able to practice, proved nearly impossible. They struggled in the sweltering heat, trying one method and then another, while the man grunted and writhed in their grasp. All the while, Tashar was painfully aware of the untended stove and the bobbing sail of silk, tethered only by slipknots. Finally they managed to tilt the man over the edge and scrambled aboard. Tashar yanked loose the tethers.

And waited. He felt nothing. The day was too hot; the wind had died, and they were becalmed; the sail was weighed down by too heavy a load. They would simply hang there until they ran out of fuel.

He noticed that the telltales were fluttering downward. A down-blowing wind? Tashar looked over the gunwale and saw the roof of the barn as if from a low hilltop—a hilltop that gradually grew higher. They had risen so silently and gently that he hadn't even known they were flying.

Maxew actually gave him a look of surprise.

Tashar had long comforted himself with tantalizing fantasies, in which he imagined himself flying across Shaftal in his sky boat, waving to astonished people below as his boat's passenger exclaimed in amazement. Now Tashar stood in the gently creaking boat of woven wicker, gazing over the gunwale at the barren, rocky landscape. No one waved at him; no one murmured compliments. He could only compliment himself, which was distinctly unsatisfying. The barn had disappeared into the bleached landscape, and the ocean faded into a blue haze. He could still see the contorted shoreline of the bay and the haze of smoke that marked Hanishport.

It took a while for him to notice that the telltales flowed upwards now, undulating gently. He reached for the tiller and grabbed nothing; he clasped a line to trim the sails, but this boat had no rudder and no boom. *Trust not the eyes, nor the skin, nor the deep of the gut—trust only the ribbon. When a sky boat's ribbon points at the sky, it is traveling to earth; and when it is pointing at earth, it is traveling to sky.* When Tashar read those lines, he had wondered if the translator had made a mistake. But now he understood: just as they had risen without sensation, so also were they now falling. He opened the stove door to add a piece of firewood, then gazed up at the interior of the bag as it began to fill with smoke again. The sunlight, colored red by the ruddy varnish, gave the appearance of sunrise—sunrise captured in a silken bag.

He looked over the edge, at the long guide rope that dragged below and behind them. The red silk ribbons that fluttered from the guide rope had the same meaning as a sailboat's telltales: they showed the direction of the wind. According to Tashar's document, winds might blow in different directions at different heights, and so it was possible to find a more favorable wind by flying lower—or higher, he supposed. But those ribbons all seemed to be in agreement: their northwesterly course would continue until the wind changed.

Maxew said, "Teach me how to guide this thing, as you promised."

"First tell me where we're going, as *you* promised."

"We're going to the House of Lilterwess."

Older people sometimes mentioned the House of Lilterwess, but their description seemed a child's tale: a house the size of a town, where flowers bloomed and music played year-round, from which a benign and powerful earth witch governed a peaceful land, while talented youngsters learned the arts of the orders they aspired to join, and the wandering servants of Shaftal—Healers, Truthkens, and Paladins—found convivial shelter each winter. "Ridiculous," muttered Tashar.

"No, it lies just west of the Shimasal Road, and north of the Wilton-Hanishport road."

"Are you referring to the pile of rubble where it used to be?"

"That is where old Shaftal ended. There the new Shaftal will begin."

Tashar felt a rising excitement. "And what we're doing now, is that part of it? Part of the new beginning?"

"It is essential! Now tell me how this sky boat works. We need to turn it toward the south."

Tashar looked at his pocket compass, but they were still going northwest. His heart sank.

Chapter 26

In the distance, Garland saw the gates of the garrison standing ajar. Then he spotted a gate guard standing in a strip of shadow near the wall. He couldn't see any longer and stopped to wipe his burning eyes on his apron. He ran again, but the gate guard didn't move or look at him. She was dozing on her feet, propped against the wall. "Soldier!" he yelled.

She swung her fist at him. He dodged the blow, and she stumbled sideways from the momentum of her swing. He flapped his apron at her, crying, "What are you fighting me for? I'm a bloody cook, you lunkhead!"

She blinked at him. "How come you talk Sainnese?"

"I used to be a soldier."

"You're the deserter?"

"You're sleeping on duty?"

"What do you want?" she said sullenly.

"Urgent message for the general."

She waved him in, then shouted after him, "Hey, cook! Why don't you send me a cake, eh?"

Because you're a bloody idiot, he thought.

The garrison was long and narrow, like the spit of land on which it had been built. Within its ancient, salt-rimed walls, the only sound was the shrieks of birds that fought over offal in an alley. The garrison's entire population seemed to be away, working in Lalali.

Garland spotted movement to his right. "Hey! Which way is General Clement?" The old woman continued to limp slowly away from him. She was deaf from cannon fire, maybe. But ahead, a familiar figure stepped out into the road: Bothis, captain of Clement's personal guard. At least General Clement's safety didn't depend on that stupid gate guard!

"Message for the general!" Garland yelled. The captain signaled his people, a door was opened, another beyond it, another at the top of the stairs, and a fourth at the room where General Clement sat beside a mess of papers, rocking a cradle with her foot, the windows open to the harbor. She took the pen from her mouth. "Master cook?"

"General, early this morning Emil was abducted by an air witch." Garland's eyes began burning again. "Norina Truthken asks that you immediately send a mount to Karis on the Lalali road. And prepare to send a hundred soldiers on a rescue expedition."

"Captain Bothis," Clement said. The captain, who had waited outside the door, stepped in to hear her orders. Then he was outside, calling to his people.

"Sit down, Garland." Clement poured him a cup of water. A muscle bunched and released in her jaw. He drank, and she waited. Garland had told her the problem and what needed to be done. Now she expected a more detailed report.

He told her what had happened, and how. He said that Norina was sending an urgent note to Watfield by raven, was summoning the Paladins and councilors from Lalali and Hanishport, and would come to the garrison as soon as she could.

"Is Norina putting my soldiers under her command?" Her tone was neutral; her face revealed nothing; but Garland spoke cautiously:

"All Sainnites are Shaftali now, and all Shaftali must heed her commands."

"What does that mean, *to heed?* Must we obey? Or must we merely listen? Well, I'll ask her when she gets here."

Clement paced to the window. "What plan is this rogue air witch pursuing? For what purpose? Whatever he gains, his way of gaining it seems extraordinarily indirect. Perhaps he dares not confront us directly. On perhaps this is typical of air witches? Did Norina say?"

He said, "Norina Truthken is too angry to think clearly. No one is thinking clearly."

"Well, we have been protecting the wrong person. Emil is the one everyone turns to, and he knits us together."

Garland cried, "I should have told Norina about the spoon! She would have known something was wrong. She would have known I had I let him into the house. But why would I mention something so stupid when she was so busy and burdened? And I kept forgetting about it, anyway!"

"You let him into the house," Clement repeated. "The rogue air witch, you mean?"

"I don't remember doing it, but the only way he could come and go without being seen by the air children was through the kitchen."

The general said, "Norina, well, she's honorable, but still a sideways glance of hers could make an old soldier faint. No one will blame you for what a man of her sort did. So don't take somebody else's evil and put it on your own head."

Garland wiped his face and took a breath. "What should I do now?"

"The companies I've sent for from Lalali—I want the supply wagons loaded by the time they get here. Can it be done?"

"I don't know if the garrison cooks can do it, but I could."

She took an insignia badge out of a bag and gave it to him. "Put that on. For now, you're my quartermaster. Captain Bothis will take you to the kitchen."

Garland had met his father on the day he came to fetch him from his mother's house. He was seven years old—Leeba's age—when he became a soldier, knowing not one word of his father's language, and his father knowing not one thing about raising a child. One day, to chide Garland for being too hurried, his father had told him that cooks never run, just as they never fight. In a retreat, cooks often were left behind and became cooks for the enemy. In a protracted war, cooks might change sides several times. Through many dreary years, Garland had hoped to be left behind in a retreat, until, one day, a couple of years after his father's death, Garland had simply walked away from the garrison. From the day he was brought there until the day he left, he had hated being a soldier.

I'm doing this for Emil, he told himself as the startled cooks opened the storehouse for him and started collecting the hand-carts. For Emil, he surveyed the supplies and allowed the disused millstones of his soldier's mind to grind. He opened his mouth, and orders spilled out like flour.

Clement's signal-man had summoned every soldier in the garrison, and soon a second crew outside was staging the supplies for loading.

"That's too much dried meat," said the chief cook.

The extra meat rations were for the dogs. "Follow your orders," Garland said, and the cook stalked resentfully away.

Karis arrived and began hauling sacks of cornmeal on her shoulder, too impatient for a handcart. Garland's millstones finished grinding, and he went outside to supervise the loading. Three wagons, twelve soldiers, and a couple of dozen soldiers were waiting outside for him. At the far end of the orderly piles of bags, boxes, bottles, and tins, Karis waited, looking away, her arms wrapped around her belly as though it hurt her. The Paladin at her side watched her worriedly. Clement arrived, and a one-legged soldier tried to tell her something, but she sent her away. Then Norina arrived, and Clement looked around until she spotted Garland and gestured with a rocking motion: *Mind the baby*.

"Bloody hell," Garland muttered and went to take the basket in which Gabian slept like a kitten.

Someone was yelling his name—the one-legged soldier. "Anybody know Captain Garland?"

"He's right here!" yelled the chief cook.

The woman staggered around the piles of foodstuff. "I'm to report to you. There are twelve horses here and another eight to come, all fit, rested, and newly shod. The three heavy wagons you see here are sturdy and in good condition. There's a wagon at the barn being loaded with feed, and another that Captains Bothis and Kammer took to get weapons from the lockhouse."

"Uh," Garland said, "Captain Kammer?"

"One of those Shaftali soldiers."

"Kamren, you mean."

"Yeah, Kammer."

"Very good," he managed to say, and the woman limped back to her wagon.

Garland stared blankly after her, stunned and dismayed. The Sainnites had been disarmed for months, and not even Clement wanted to re-arm them.

The chief cook said, "Captain, do you want to review the supplies?"

Every battle, and every other idiotic thing that people did, started like this, with a person telling the others to get started. Garland swallowed. "Start loading," he said.

—∞—

He had found a shady place for the baby and given him a piece of hard tack to suck on. When he heard Gabian cry "Yow!" he turned and saw Clement bent over her son, tickling his stomach. At Garland's side, the chief cook muttered, "Soldiers don't have babies. It just ain't right."

Garland fumbled at the clasp of the insignia as he hurried to Clement. "General, why did the Paladins fetch weapons? Are soldiers going to be killing Shaftali people again? After all the work we've done to gain peace? It's not right!"

"Norina's orders," said Clement.

"And you're obeying her, like a good soldier?"

She gave him a long look. The feed wagon, laden with bags of grain, rumbled past them. The loaders, their work finished, had clustered in the shade to cool off, while the chief cook checked the wagons to make sure the job had been done right, so the tarps could be tied down.

Clement said, "In public, please treat me as a general, and I will treat you as a captain."

He finally managed to yank off the insignia. "I'll talk to you as one citizen to another. Every time someone calls me *captain* I get the jim-jams!"

She didn't take the insignia from him. "To answer your question, Kamren and I both objected to the decision to fetch the weapons. But until we have time for discussion, the weapons will he controlled by the Paladins. Now, regarding your jim-jams . . ."

Garland's heart sank.

She said, "Norina is assigning Gilly to be some sort of captain of Hanishport, and I'm without an adjutant. A hundred soldiers I hardly know are following me on a mission that includes a Truthken, a dozen Paladins, a seer, and the G'deon of Shaftal. I must have someone who speaks both languages and understands both peoples. That person is you, Garland."

In a crisis, a soldier could have said just one thing: *Yes, General Clement.* Garland said, "Like bloody hell!"

—∞—

As Garland left the garrison, a company of hot, grumbling soldiers was arriving from Lalali, with the garrison commander riding behind them and another company of soldiers in the distance. He walked angrily away from them.

When he was still a good distance from the old house, he could hear it groaning from the urgent activity within. As he stepped in the door, a bedroll went bouncing down the stairs. He found Norina in the room she shared with Seth and several other councilors, laying a shirt, underclothing, and spare socks upon a folded blanket. On the table, her map case and various miniature devices were ready to be slung over her shoulder, tied to her belt, or stuffed into her pockets. Emil's dagger hung at her side.

She was trying to be Emil, but she certainly knew she couldn't do it, because she didn't have his heart.

Garland said, "Let me help you with that."

They rolled and strapped the bedroll. Norina said, "You do deserve to remain as the G'deon's cook. You shouldn't have to return to soldiering, not even temporarily. But none of us is doing what we want, or even what we're skilled at."

"But you want me to be what I *hate*."

"Yes," Norina said. "There is no alternative." She had finished filling her pockets. She picked up the map case and went out.

With his gear added to the pile in the hallway, Garland went into the kitchen. He snatched up his spice box, so he could at least make the camp swill more palatable for Karis. The wooden spoon? If there was any combat, he'd need an implement to indicate he was no fighter. He stuck the spoon in his belt, hung his apron on a hook, and reluctantly took the captain's insignia out of the pocket.

Saugus and Maxew must believe that without Emil there would be a collapse. And maybe Norina was trying to prevent that collapse by shifting everyone into new roles.

Sighing, Garland pinned the insignia to his shirt.

What a lot of moving things about was necessary even in a crisis, he thought as he came out into the hall and saw that the Paladins had started carrying the gear outside.

He heard Karis's hoarse voice in the parlor: "But no one can follow her for long."

Near a bright window, Karis and Norina were studying a map: not an ordinary map, but Norina's, so covered with notes and filled with detail that it was useless for finding one's way. It had unrolled itself off the edges of the table and partway across the floor. Karis, who always had odd things in her pockets, took out a bolt and stood it on the map, then put a second one a short distance away. Norina examined the two bolts as though she was about to interrogate them, two upright travelers on inexplicable missions. Someone was following Zanja?

Norina said, "But why has she gone into those woods? They're a tangle, and there's nothing much beyond them. Does she want to make it impossible to follow her?"

Karis didn't reply. She picked up the bolts and put them back in her pocket.

The dogs were barking. Clement entered the house with her baby in her arms. "Madam Truthken, I have two companies here."

Garland went out to distribute to the soldiers two baskets of ripe peaches that he had meant to use in pies. But he soon gave the task to someone else so he could introduce himself and Kamren to the Sainnite captains. Garland knew nothing about those captains or their companies, but Kamren knew how to greet them in Sainnese, and they knew how to clasp hands with him.

Bothis said, "Here comes the Captain of Hanishport. I hope he's still a lucky man. He'll be needing it."

Gilly was arriving in a crowd of Shaftali councilors—the entire Peace Committee, summoned from a meeting apparently without explanation, only to find a hundred soldiers and five laden wagons at the G'deon's door. There being no one else, Garland gave them a hurried explanation, and so suffered the fate of all who bring bad news.

Gilly, at least, was accustomed to crisis. He calmly pulled Garland away from the councilors' agitated questions. With his other hand he tapped Garland's insignia. "*Captain* Garland?"

"Norina has decided that you're to be in charge of Hanishport, and I'm to be her assistant instead of you."

"They're making me the horsefly of Hanishport, eh?" Gilly grinned. "Oh, how I'll make those asses kick!"

Inside, they found Clement faced off with Seth. "I'm going with you," Seth was saying. "Someone in the Peace Committee should be present, and I'm volunteering. I won't stay here and watch the baby, so don't even ask."

Norina said, "Go pack a bedroll, Seth. Do it quickly. Peace Committee, Gilly, I'll speak with you in that parlor." The tangle of committee members gave way before Norina like a knot being cut by a sharp knife. She added over her shoulder, "General Clement, bring Gabian along."

The general said angrily, "Are we also bringing a cow? And stopping four times a day to feed him?"

"I can solve that problem," said Karis, in the other parlor. "Come in here."

Garland, longing to put the teakettle on the fire and pile some pastries on a plate, followed behind Clement. He might as well get used to following her around, he thought gloomily.

Karis said, "Undo your buttons."

Clement did, and Karis put her hands inside her tunic and filled her breasts with milk.

Chapter 29

Chaen rushed through the quivering, rippling brightness of the Wilton Road until Hanishport disappeared and the ocean became a flat horizon. Then she had to stop, and sat on a rest-stone in a shady woodland.

She had no water—just an empty bottle in the knapsack brought to her by a puffing Paladin who had immediately run away again. She tried to recall how far it was to the next watering place, and then tried to remember why she was fleeing Hanishport with such haste and urgency.

Her family was dead; she had betrayed all her friends; and in any battle that had yet to be fought she had chosen the wrong side. Rather than seeking water, why shouldn't she shrivel here in the heat, like meat in a smokehouse?

She noticed the glyph card that remained in her hand: the Brothers. Arin was dead, but he had a brother, an air witch. Chaen remembered nothing about him, not even a face or a name. But he certainly was in dire danger—from one air witch who had subverted him, and from another who would hunt and kill him.

She must have raised her son to be stupid, for he had thoughtlessly destroyed the love of the only person he could have depended upon to help him. She must help him anyway.

First she must devise a method for remembering him, for she could not simply carry the glyph card in her hand until sweat and dirt destroyed it. She studied the image on the card, hoping it would unfold a hidden truth to her, but her fire talent had made her an artist, not a presciant. Well then, she would draw. She took out her sketchbook and began to make a copy of the illustration.

She had scarcely blocked out the shapes and the figures before she began to change them. Arin, at less than a year old, had yet to speak his first word, and had never argued with his brother. So she changed the image so he was a babe in arms—in her arms—and it was she who turned her back on her second son, an older child with his arms petulantly crossed.

That image pierced her heart, so it must be true.

If she left the drawing unfinished, it would nag at her, and she would open the sketchbook and remember. Beneath the sketch, she wrote an instruction to herself: *Flee the Truthken!*

She looked up, startled by a distant sound. Someone was running toward her, coming from direction of Hanishport. She snatched up her belongings and flung herself into a thicket.

As she waited, scarcely breathing, she noticed a faint trickling sound. There was water nearby.

The footsteps drew close, and stopped. She heard Zanja's familiar voice say something in that language she had used while sitting on the steps in Hanishport. Silence, except for panting, then Zanja spoke again. Now Chaen heard the faintest rustle as Zanja stepped through dry leaves. The sound grew close, then drew away. Chaen dared move her head slightly, and she glimpsed Zanja slipping into the woods.

The border woman was not chasing Chaen, but had her own errand, compelled and accompanied by visions, and Chaen needed not concern herself with it.

She found a dribble of a stream, dripping over a tree root, forming a puddle of water that was bitter with oak leaves. Three times, Chaen filled her flask and drank, still hearing only silence where Zanja had disappeared.

She returned to the thicket to gather and pack up her things. She remembered that there was an unfinished drawing in her sketchbook, and looked at it to remind herself what she had been working on. The glyph card was tucked inside. She recalled the petulant boy, her son, whom she had not loved well enough.

Could Zanja be chasing Chaen's son? Perhaps at the behest of the Truthken?

Zanja was known to have prescience. If Chaen followed her, she might also find her stupid son, so she could demand that he restore her memories.

Chaen followed her.

In the clear summer sky, twilight lingered: the sun descending reluctantly like a child who didn't want to go to bed. But in this dense woodland, Chaen was peering through shadows and stumbling over unseen stones and brambles long before the stars came out. By then, the woods were tar black and choked with malevolent undergrowth that slapped her face, caught at her feet, tore at her clothing, and bit her with tiny, sharp teeth.

Zanja left few distinguishable traces, and it was more by luck than knowledge that Chaen discovered a place that her quarry had dug for water in a dry streambed, and some disturbed soil and wilted leaves where she had pulled up and trimmed some smallage, then left a trail of peelings as she ate the root while walking. That first night, Chaen made herself a dry and comfortable bed but paced for hours, fruitlessly trying to scent Zanja's campfire. The simple traps she had set for game were empty in the morning, and she felt lucky to find some edible plants, though the time it took to eat them seemed wasted, because she was no less hungry afterwards. That day, she lost the trail. If Chaen's fire talent had been helping her in this hunt, it seemed exhausted now. Nevertheless, she continued.

As the shadows deepened into evening, she was pushing through undergrowth, seeking any suggestion of Zanja's passage, when a bramble slapped across her eyes. Carefully, delicately, she peeled the thorny branch from her eyes and face, leaving a trail of burning pinpricks. From one eye, tears began to drip. She held out a hand to catch the branches that might slap her again, and stumbled on. She could not remember why.

Her foot sensed an obstacle of tree roots. She stepped over it, and there was nothing on the other side. She fell. A wily hand yanked at her ankle. Still, she fell. A thousand tiny arrows broke in a thousand dry explosions. She continued to fall. A stone mallet smashed her head.

She shouted in the shock of pain, and immediately began to drown—not in water, but in stinking, liquid mud. Her arms trapped by the dense thicket; her feet entangled in tough vines; her pinned head-down on a steep slope by her knapsack; she could scarcely lift her face out of the mud.

She had always planned to die for a cause. To die like this, ungainly, absurdly, and unnecessarily, was unacceptable. Fighting, flailing, shouting, she broke one arm free and at least could support her head and keep her face out of the mud. She lay exhausted.

Time slipped through the woods, leaving no trace. A voice spoke in the thick darkness. "Chaen."

"Zanja!"

She heard a rustle and the soft hiss of the weapon being drawn. The vine wrapped around her ankles snapped like thread. Zanja grabbed and lifted the weight of her knapsack, and Chaen drew up her knees and staggered to her feet.

Zanja said, "Stop following me."

"I can't," Chaen said.

But the space where Zanja had been standing had become vacant.

Chaen touched the throbbing knot on her forehead. She cupped a hand over her right eye, which with every blink of the eyelid was pierced by fresh pain. She worked her ankles, checking for sprains. Then she settled her knapsack and started again through the darkness.

Chapter 28

As abruptly as she had arrived in the city of Hanishport, Karis departed from it. She walked at the head of a column of soldiers, the largest group seen outside the garrison since the truce had begun in midwinter.

The people of Hanishport, being positioned at the juncture of Shaftal and the world, were accustomed to strangeness. Yet they were astonished by the soldiers, who ambled untidily in their undershirts, tunics tied to their bedrolls, calling badly pronounced greetings and apologies to the people they happened to block or inconvenience. At the rear of the column, among the old and ailing, in the cloud of dust and dirt, with the supply wagons nudging at her heels, walked Clement, with Garland beside her. Many accounts of that strange passage would be reported in Hanishport, Clement said, and that could not be avoided. But if any of those stories claimed that Karis had been taken captive by Sainnites, the teller would be deliberately ignoring the evidence.

Clement said that she was afraid for her disarmed soldiers all across Shaftal, whose survival depended on traditions they themselves had practically destroyed. She must hope that the Peace Committee would succeed in quelling the inevitable rumors before they spread far enough to endanger her people.

West of Hanishport, the road was in terrible repair, and Clement told her captains to send scouts ahead to fill potholes and reset cobbles. The column kept a brisk pace now, and the lame, weak, and short-legged soldiers in the rear soon were dirt-pasted and coughing in fitful unison, as though coughing itself were contagious. A green haze of trees appeared in the distance. The column came to a halt, and people hopped into the ditch to build a causeway for the wagons.

Garland noticed Medric standing in the road. The seer, his spectacles encrusted with dust, dirty tear tracks on his cheeks, wore Emil's straw hat, which made him look like a lost and bewildered boy.

Medric and Emil often played frivolous word games with each other, and a person who didn't know them might think they were only bound together by cleverness. But Garland, who for a few months had slept in an attic with them, had seen them early in the morning wrapped around each other like strands of twine and had been awakened during the night by their lovemaking—sweet, fierce, and often interrupted by muffled laughter. Emil and Zanja were the only people who understood Medric, and now he was without both of them.

Garland went over and cleaned his spectacles for him.

Medric said, "It's coming undone, all of it."

His hopeless tone made Garland want to yell at him. He was a seer, for land's sake! Why hadn't he kept this catastrophe from happening?

He said, "You should wipe off your spectacles occasionally, or you'll hurt yourself because you can't see."

"I can't see anyway. These are for reading."

"Where is the pair for far-seeing?"

"Zanja has them."

"Why?"

"She needs them."

Garland couldn't think what to say. He helped Medic across the ditch and left him where he wouldn't get trampled. When the wagons had been gotten safely across the ditch, one of the drivers fetched Medric and helped him into the wagon. What the driver made of his peculiar passenger, Garland could not imagine.

Oh, what a mess things had become! Rather than the orderly progress to integrate the Sainnites into Shaftal, they had abruptly created this mixed company with no planning, no training, and no notice. Here was a cook turned into a soldier, a statesman into a captive, a trickster seer into a dull blind man, a novice Truthken into a liar, and a G'deon into a warrior—a vengeful warrior, Garland feared, if Emil were killed, or Zanja came to harm. The Sainnites' fearful superstitions about magic may have prompted them to slaughter every talented person they could identify, regardless of their harmlessness, but they had been wise to fear the G'deon so much that they didn't attack the House of Lilterwess until Harald G'deon was dead.

What would they do without Emil?

They were crossing roadless landscape now, but the ground was firm, the dry bushes crackled under the wagon wheels, and the soldiers walking ahead of the wagons could find routes that avoided obstacles. Kamren dropped back to the rear, looking for Clement, but she was in one of the wagons, being educated by Seth in how to feed Gabian. He said to Garland, "I want to request that a new group of soldiers be assigned to help us with the dictionary. Do I make this request to you?"

"Bloody hell," Garland muttered.

"Bloody hell," Kamren repeated sympathetically. After six months' study, he could make himself understood in Sainnese, although he had to insert occasional Shaftali words, like raisins dropped into bread dough.

Garland said, "How can you even care about your book of words?"

"Oh, I don't *care*. My heart is preoccupied by worry and fear, just as yours probably is. But we can introduce Shaftalese to another group of Sainnites, and we know from experience that they'll teach whatever they learn to the entire company. It is progress, Captain Garland. If we cease to make progress, then we certainly will fail."

The long day gave way to long evening. They made camp: canvas was hung, latrines were dug; stew was cooked, horses were groomed and fed; wagon axles were checked and greased; blisters were treated; socks were washed and hung to dry; food was served and dishes washed; and more than a hundred beds were unrolled. Ten Paladins and seven soldiers, with Garland sometimes serving as translator, exchanged language lessons over supper.

An uproar rose up on the women's side of the canvas. Garland saw the other captains running there, so he did also. The soldiers, already crowded around the combatants, pretended they couldn't hear the orders being shouted at them, and Captain Washlan began clouting heads.

Norina came up beside Garland. "They should be too tired for such nonsense."

Garland said, "A challenge can't be ignored."

"A challenge over what?"

"Bed position. The best spots are near a window or near the fire."

Norina glanced at the bedrolls, the canvas divider, the sheltering trees. "The soldiers lie on the ground in the same position as in the barracks? And where they lie reflects their status? And now that the captains chose soldiers to be the Paladins' students, new criteria has come into play, and those battles over status must be refought?"

"That's how it works," Garland said.

She rarely looked at him directly, knowing how uncomfortable it made him. But now she glanced at him, sharp and sudden as an ambush. "Then these people are no better than chickens!"

"Chickens?"

"Come with me." The Truthken pushed into the crowd of excited soldiers, who after the hot day's hard work smelled less than pleasant. Though they knew nothing about Norina, the soldiers instinctively backed away from her. In the middle of the crowd, the combatants struggled in the grips of the company captains, shrieking curses at each other. Both women were bleeding from the nose, and their clothing was filthy from rolling in the dirt.

The Truthken's glance quelled even their furious shouts. "The behavior of these soldiers is shocking. Don't they understand what an honor it is to guard the Gideon of Shaftal from her enemies? Don't they realize that this mission is an opportunity to prove that all Sainnites can be of service to this land? It seems that they're proving the opposite, that the Sainnites can be of no use."

Garland translated as exactly as possible for the captains. The two feuding soldiers breathed noisily, mouths open, blood dripping from their chins. Garland added, "Captain Washlan, since these soldiers are of your company, you must answer the questions of the—uh, the enforcer of the law."

"Why is this matter the enforcer's business?" she asked stiffly.

"She outranks nearly everyone, including General Clement."

Still offended, Washlan said, "She is correct that these soldiers put their own concerns above the honor of this company and our people."

Garland translated.

"Will they be punished?" Norina asked.

"Oh, yes."

"Their punishment must not be severe. Karis will feel responsible for every hurt suffered by every member of her company, including these undisciplined soldiers."

Garland said, "These captains will be angered if they are given orders by you. The orders should always come from Clement."Norina already knew that the Sainnite social structure was shaped by hierarchy of command. But it seemed that she had needed to be reminded, for she blinked and said, "Then please make certain that the soldiers aren't punished until I'm able to speak to Clement."

A short time later, Clement lied to the captains that Norina had apologized for interfering. Washlan reported the soldiers' punishment: they had been required to move their beds to the least desirable position, which inconvenienced everyone in the company because all the beds had to be relocated. Also, they had been ordered to clean and mend each other's clothing. Clement approved, and then explained that Norina had interfered because she was concerned about Karis, who was weighed down by worries that ordinary people couldn't understand, and was offended by violence. Garland had never found Karis difficult to understand. However, after attempting for just a portion of a single day to explain these people to each other, he appreciated Clement's skillful inaccuracies, which made sense to the officers and were only somewhat untrue.

Garland made his bed in the first convenient place, and after a sleep that seemed no longer than a nap, awoke to a lightening sky. The Sainnite cooks were putting kindling on the coals of yesterday's cook fires and would soon be making porridge. Across the camp, scattered sleepers were snoring. The horses moved slowly past, hunting for grass. A bird crowed in the distance and another replied nearby. Back and forth they shouted at each other: *Are you still there? Yes, are you?* An idiot's conversation.

What if Emil were dead? Garland's heart was so heavy, he couldn't bring himself to move.

In the pale light, he saw Karis sitting with her back to a tree. A dog lay beside her, and the other was returning from an errand, with Clement following behind, buttoning her trousers. "You were awake all night?" she said to Karis in a low voice.

"So was Zanja," Karis said, as if that were an explanation.

Clement sat beside her, and Karis handed her the baby, who seemed to have spent the entire night in her lap. With some fumbling, Clement got her son positioned on her breast. "By my mother's gods, I wish you had done this to me months ago."

"You didn't ask."

"Why would it occur to me to ask?"

Now Seth came toward them from the direction of the latrines, and Clement said to her, "You could have slept a little longer."

"What, and sacrifice my only chance to kiss you today?" Seth and knelt beside Clement and kissed her fervently

Garland forced himself to get up. He went to the latrines and then stole some water from a grumbling cook's porridge pot to make tea. Now Norina also was sitting with Karis, yanking irritably at her bootstraps. "Tea?" Garland said, and all four women hastily found and held up their porringer.

"Do you still have no idea where Emil is?" Norina asked.

Karis seemed unable to reply.

Seth said, "If you don't know where he is, then he must be on water."

"Zanja is going inland," Karis said.

"But she's also going northward. Maybe she's going to the Asha River."

Norina got her map case and a blanket to protect the map from the dirt, and soon Karis had placed one of her bolts on it to show where Zanja was, and they tried to guess where she was headed. The Asha River did seem most reasonable: Emil probably was in a ship sailing up the coast, and Zanja, having intuited its destination, planned to intercept the ship in the region of Shimasal.

Garland said, "Can't you just ask Zanja what she's doing? She can hear you, can't she?"

Norina said, "No, I'm reluctant for anyone to interfere with her, fire logic is composed of such fragile materials. Is Chaen still following her?"

As a reply, Karis put the second bolt on Norina's map.

Norina said, "She's fallen behind, but hasn't given up. I suspect she can't stop."

A blurred voice spoke from a tangled pile of blankets that Garland had not imagined might contain a person. "But she's drowning."

Norina held up a hand to forestall anyone else from speaking and pointed a finger at Garland. As always when the Truthken noticed him, Garland felt a kind of panic, which was worse now because that pointing finger conveyed so little. Garland said, "Uh, Medric? What did you say?"

"She's drowning," Medric said.

Norina continued to point at Garland. He said, "Who's drowning? Do you mean Chaen?"

Of course the bloody seer wouldn't answer simply, no matter how simple the question. "He killed her memories and left her to drown in time."

Since Emil or Zanja always had to explain Norina and Medric to each other, it was odd that Norina nodded as though she understood his nonsense. And still, the Truthken's finger pointed at Garland. She didn't want to speak, Garland thought, lest air logic interfere with Medric's fire logic in some way. But what question should he ask? What did they need to know?

Well, Medric was a bloody seer, wasn't he? "What is Chaen's future?" he asked.

"Death," said the seer.

Chapter 29

Dawn found Chaen lying on her back as the rising light distinguished tree from sky. She did not recall lying down. The light gradually revealed the peaceful woodland with which she had done battle all night. Birds went about their frantic business. A small red squirrel sprang over her arm. Insects buzzed through the air. A group of deer tread past, silent as cats, scarcely glancing at her.

That day passed in flashes of brilliance and stretches of darkness. Night fell, and still Chaen lay in that place, sometimes sleeping and sometimes not. One time she awoke and saw the moon, floating beyond the treetops like a ship sailing past a peninsula.

A wolf came out of darkness and touched her nose with his. He sat down and uttered a thin cry, and a second wolf came. A dead branch snapped like the breaking of a bone. The leaves of last autumn crackled. A bear, thought Chaen. Wolves and bears in the same glade. This seemed unusual. Like the wolves, the bear walked right up to her. This also seemed unusual. Perhaps Chaen was their dinner. She didn't care enough to ask.

"Oh, for land's sake," the bear muttered.

Beside Chaen's head there was a sturdy boot, a bent knee, canvas breeches with a circular stain. "Shouldn't kneel in mud," Chaen said.

"Mud's cleaner than manure."

"Can't I escape you."

"No, I guess not. Drink."

Cool metal touched Chaen's lip. She turned her head, refusing.

"I can force a sick cow to drink. But I don't imagine it's pleasant for the cow."

This statement seemed both irrelevant and obscure. After some consideration, it occurred to Chaen that Seth might be threatening her.

She put her hand on the flask and accepted some of the water into her mouth. It was sweet forest water, only slightly flavored by tin.

"You're distracting Karis," Seth said, "Lying in the woods like this, helpless as an infant. And she needs all her wits right now."

The dogs grinned amiably, teeth and tongues shining in the moonlight. Chaen sat up, and the night forest spun around her, so it seemed she was surrounded by fifty Seths and a hundred dogs. Well, there were worse things.

Seth continued, "I know you think it's intolerable for me to plant myself in front of you like a stubborn old donkey, but you *really* won't like it if Karis comes after you."

"True," said Chaen eventually. But she suspected there was much that she did not understand.

"So you don't get to kill yourself. Not today."

"I'm not." Chaen considered. "Maybe I am."

Seth handed her something: a thick, dry biscuit. "Eat that."

"I'm contented," Chaen said.

"Indifference might look a bit like contentment, but I still know which is which. Eat the biscuit."

Chaen was feeling exceptionally stupid, but to comprehend the sheer stubbornness of this woman did not require intelligence. She bit the biscuit, and its dry fragments stuck in her dry mouth. She drank water because she had to. She tasted the salt with which the biscuit was sprinkled. Saliva flooded her mouth. She ate several biscuits, and drained the flask.

"Why was I following Zanja?" she asked.

"I guess it's something to do with that son of yours."

"My son is dead."

"One son is dead. But the other has kidnapped Emil Paladin."

"I have no other son."

"His name is Maxew, and he's an air witch."

"I think I would remember if I had a son who was an air witch!"

Seth sighed. She seemed exasperated, but Chaen didn't know why. "Let's go." Seth pulled Chaen to her feet. She picked up the knapsack, which Chaen was surprised to learn had been lying beside her. One dog barked impatiently. Seth wrestled with the pack straps, muttering, "What are you carrying—rocks?"

"Pigments. Oil. Where are we going?"

Seth gestured toward the right, which might have been eastward.

"I'm not going back to Hanishport!"

"Neither is anyone else. Untwist this pack strap, will you?"

Chaen helped get the pack properly settled. Seth said, "We're following Zanja, like you, but at a distance."

"She's impossible to track."

"Well, that's no surprise, I guess. She lived off the land for most of her life."

When Seth and the dogs started off, Chaen followed, unthinking and uncomplaining as a horse led by a rope.

They walked along a deer path at a brisk pace, but could not keep up with the dogs. From time to time, one would come back to check on them, and disappear again.

Then they found both dogs waiting for them. Seth said, "We have to leave the path, I guess."

The dogs led the way through the woods. Apparently, Seth saw well enough to follow them, but Chaen could scarcely see, and her right eye had become so painful that she could heed little else. The forest seemed less dense here, or else the dogs were more skillful pathfinders than she was. The moon set, and the darkness gradually became even darker. Chaen walked into Seth repeatedly.

She walked into her again.

Seth said, "I think we're stopping here."

Chaen heard dry grass crackling as one dog and then the other walked in circles and lay down, panting. The sky stretched over them. Before them lay a rough, flat landscape. They seemed to have walked out of the forest. Seth set down Chaen's knapsack, went off a little way to piss, and returned, grumbling about the stickers.

Chaen said, "I tried to untie the bedroll, but I can't bend over. My eye hurts too much."

"What's wrong with your eye?"

"I think it was scratched by a thorn."

"Keep it closed, then, and don't rub it. I'll look at it when we have some light."

Seth unrolled the blanket, and they lay down beside each other. The ground was hard; the wilted grass a poor cushion. Chaen's throbbing eye filled her entire awareness.

Then the dogs were barking and the sun was hot on Chaen's face. She heard Seth grunt as she got to her feet. "Oh, it's Karis."

Chaen shaded her face with a hand, but she saw only light, streaking and shivering as if on the surface of the river. Was this how a person went blind? She heard voices talking, footsteps crackling in dry plants, and the dogs yelping in welcome.

Seth said, "*Three* more times? Why does Zanja keep switching directions?"

"She hasn't said a single word in Shaftalese." That was the G'deon's distinctive, raspy voice. Close by, boots rattled pebbles. "She shouldn't talk to herself in a language nobody else knows," Karis muttered. "She knows too many languages anyway." The grass blades crackled under the weight of a knee. "All right, let me see." Work-coarsened fingers roughly pushed Chaen's fingers away from her eye.

Then the pain was gone. Karis delicately pulled up Chaen's eyelid. "Huh."

"Ouch," said Seth in an admiring tone.

"Can you pull it out? My big fingers—"

Another voice, flat and lifeless as the clanging of a chain: "I have tweezers."

Karis's big hand clamped Chaen's shoulder. "Be still!"

"Chaen, don't be afraid," said the Truthken impatiently.

Chaen's desperate terror became a peaceful calm, interrupted by flashes of resentment.

"Go ahead, Seth."

Chaen felt a peculiar sensation in her eye.

"That's a wicked looking thing," Karis muttered. Still lifting Chaen's eyelid with her fingertip, she gave a kind of sigh. Warmth suffused Chaen's eye. Karis's face swam out of the light-blur: dusty, sweat streaked, red eyed. The golden land beyond her was glazed with light, but Norina Truthken was positioned so her shadow fell across Chaen's face. Even in her calm, painless state, Chaen could not look at her.

"This was in your eye." Seth, kneeling beside Karis, gripped in the tweezers a thorn as thin as a sewing needle.

Chaen's breath came out of her as though she had been punched. Seth dropped the thorn and handed the tweezers back to the Truthken.

Karis said, "Nori, please give Chaen something she can remember, so she doesn't continue to run wild like this. Do it against her will, if you must."

Now I should be afraid, Chaen thought.

The Truthken said, "Chaen, remember what I am about to say to you. You have a son named Maxew, who is an air witch, and was my student."

Chaen remembered. She remembered all the times people had told her she had a son, and she remembered why she had fled Hanishport, and why she had followed Zanja. Then she realized that her frantic flight and pursuit of Zanja had served no purpose, for the Truthken already knew what Chaen had been desperate to conceal from her. "Please don't kill him," Chaen said.

"I serve the Law of Shaftal." The Truthken added, "Be afraid again."

She stepped away. The sun that blazed above the horizon attacked Chaen with light. She sat up, crying, "But my son is all I have!"

The Truthken, her back turned, began talking to a Paladin. Another fed pieces of dried meat to the dogs. Chaen's heart thundered so that she couldn't think, couldn't imagine what to do, couldn't even breathe. The G'deon rose awkwardly and heavily to her feet.

"Haven't you slept yet?" Seth asked her.

"Zanja hasn't slept; so neither have I." Karis glanced down. "Chaen, come with us willingly, or else come as a prisoner."

Chan knew better than to test the G'deon of Shaftal. "I'll come with you," she said.

Chaen and Seth rolled and tied the blankets, and one of the Paladins took the bedroll. He followed the other, who had already departed with Chaen's knapsack on her shoulders. By the time Seth and Chaen had put on their boots, the others were in the distance. Chaen and Seth followed, never losing sight of them, and never catching up.

A long while later, Chaen asked, "Was my son at my trial? Was he the one who read from the book?"

"Yes, that was him."

"How old is he?"

"Around sixteen."

"He must have been a little boy—six, maybe—when our family was killed."

Seth said nothing. Chaen supposed that pretending to be her friend certainly had been a wearisome task. She said, "It must have been three years ago, when my son was still a boy, that I gave him to Saugus. I don't remember doing it, but I must have. The Truthken should kill me instead of him."

Still Seth said nothing.

"Maybe what Saugus taught him was wrong, but what Saugus believes, I also believed. Now, Maxew is exercising his power in the service of those beliefs. If that makes him a monster, then Norina Truthken is one also."

Seth said, "Do you see where Norina's walking?"

The Truthken had run to catch up with Karis, and a brown dust cloud was settling behind her. Now, for every two steps Karis took, Norina took three. They were talking, and frequently glanced at each other, as people do in an intimate conversation.

Seth said, "For over twenty years she has walked beside her. She was there when Karis was vested with the Power of Shaftal, and if she dies it will be while defending her. I don't know the word for that kind of steadfastness.

"Now, I don't care what you think about Norina, and Norina certainly doesn't care either. But Karis looks after her people—and she's already furious with you."

Chaen thought of a half-dozen ways she could reply, some of them irritable, and all of them dishonest. She said, "I guess I had better learn to guard my tongue."

The sun had risen halfway to its peak when Chaen realized the people they were following had disappeared. Close to her the air seemed clear, but in the distance hardly anything was visible in the fog of dust. Seth stumbled, and Chaen caught her. The soil underfoot had the consistency of flour. They held hands, staggering in the soft soil. Seth had a strong grip, and her skin was leathery, gritty with dirt. Chaen saw shapes in the haze up ahead. Clumps of wire-grass appeared, and the soil became firmer. The distant shapes became a grove of trees. A group of horses, tearing at the tough grass, didn't even look up as they trudged past. Seth said, "I wonder if they found the well."

Chaen spotted another group of horses, and then, under the trees, four wagons. One wagon was being unloaded. It must have become impossible to haul wagons through that soft soil.

"Who are these people?" Chaen asked.

"Soldiers," Seth said inattentively.

One of the people at the wagon was trotting toward them, and it was the Sainnite general: sunburned, sweat-shiny, shirtless except for a milk-stained undershirt. Behind the general came the G'deon's cook, Garland, who had served Chaen the best fish stew she ever tasted. Since that meal, Chaen had eaten an egg and Seth's biscuits. One meal in more than six days. Little wonder she had ended up on her back in the forest, listlessly watching the shadows move.

Garland walked around the two women, who had clasped hands but had not embraced.

"You're starving again, Chaen," he said.

"I can't seem to catch the current of my life."

"That's not a reason to go hungry. Karis and the others went toward the cook-fire for some porridge. Not good porridge." He seemed distressed, but got a grip on himself. "You can wash if you want—there's a good well. Your clothes too, though we may not stay here long enough for them to dry. We only stopped to offload the wagons and organize a supply line, but Karis said just now that Zanja still isn't moving, and since she has changed directions so many times, we'll stay here until we know which way to turn."

"How many Sainnites are here?"

"A hundred and four soldiers, five officers, and—well, Medric, if you count him as one."

"Weapons are what you're unloading over there."

"The Paladins brought them out of storage, in case we need to arm the soldiers. But now that we're abandoning the wagons, there's no choice but to let the soldiers carry them."

"I guess the peace is over," Chaen said. "Give a soldier a weapon, and the weapon will be used."

He gave her a strange look. "Pardon me, but that's not only true about soldiers."

"Captain?" The general had approached them, and seemed to be addressing Garland. "I'll guard the weapons until one of the company captains can relieve me. These soldiers are too unruly. I feel like I'm riding an untrained horse in a parade." She spoke without even the trace of an accent. Then she said a few words in Sainnese, and the G'deon's cook snorted with amusement.

He was a Sainnite.

The general gave Chaen a concerned look. "You're very pale."

"I'm fine," Chaen said. It was the first thing she had knowingly said to a Sainnite.

"If you say so." The woman's tone was skeptical. "Garland will show you where to eat and rest. You may not get much rest, though."

If the general grew her hair longer, she could pass for a farmer. She even had a farmer's cadence, sometimes.

The general added abruptly, "Chaen, I am sorry for what my people did to your family. I truly am. If it could be undone, I would undo it."

She left Chaen affronted by her sincerity.

In the grove, wet clothing hung on laundry lines strung across every patch of sunshine, and soldiers were scattered everywhere, dozing in the shade. Later, when word was passed that they would camp there until morning, Chaen took out her sketchbook and pencils and drew a Paladin and a soldier who sat on the ground facing each other, drawing letters in the dirt. She joined a crowd of naked, laughing women who were pouring buckets of water drawn from the well over each other's heads. Soldier and Paladin alike bore the scars of old wounds. With her own scars from fire and fighting laid bare, Chaen accepted a bar of soap from a soldier.

Chapter 30

Norina's map indicated a well, and finally they had found it, situated in a large grove of trees and wrapped in an apron of grass. It was an island of solidity in an unstable sea.

All morning, they had staggered through soft, fine soil that lay concealed under a thin crust that crumbled underfoot, so that with each step a person sank ankle deep. The horses had groaned in the traces, and the soldiers had groaned also as they put their shoulders to the wagons, only to wind up on their faces in the dirt when the wagons lurched forward. When they reached the well, Clement had called a halt.

Garland had already explained to the captains that the area around a well was a protected place, and that they must not harm the trees. But he was kept busy telling the soldiers what wood they could use, where to build fires so that a much-needed second breakfast could be cooked, where to piss, and how to graze the horses. The scouts returned with discouraging reports of the landscape ahead, and Clement gave the order to abandon the horses and wagons and set up a supply line.

Norina observed dryly, "The Sainnites are better organized than the Shaftali because otherwise they wouldn't survive." She had returned from her side-trip to fetch Chaen out of the woods and was watching the soldiers re-sort the unloaded supplies.

Clement replied, "Perhaps. But it was always an advantage of the Paladin irregulars that they could find food and shelter anywhere."

"Do we even need the soldiers?" Norina asked.

"*You* summoned *us*," the general replied.

"I summoned you because I thought Zanja would follow Emil's kidnappers to Saugus. But now I have no idea what she's doing."

"She's not going toward the Asha River?" asked Garland.

"She's going northwest again," said Karis. "I can't think of a reason for her to take this zigzagging route. It's making her journey twice as long."

Zanja had been traveling two nights and nearly three days. Like her, Karis hadn't slept, but she was sustained by the Power of Shaftal.

She needed to eat more, though—a big woman like her. The porridge Garland had given her waited on a nearby rock, untasted. She gazed away, toward the forest, as if she could see Zanja going steadily, stubbornly, through the woods. The weight of worry and fear was crushing her, Garland thought.

She said, "If we continue northward, we might intercept her. Let's wait where we are, unless she changes direction again."

Zanja didn't change direction until late afternoon, when she turned northeastward again. It was decided to spend the night by the well.

The shadows began to stretch away from the trees like gravy dripping down the edge of a bowl, and the sun rested on the horizon. Garland joined Medric, Kamren, and the rest of the Paladins, who sat near the edge of the grove, passing a flask of excellent brandy that Kamren had been given by a woman of Hanishport. There certainly was more to that story, but Kamren didn't tell it. They all had bathed in cold well water, and the men had shaved. Medric even had dunked his spectacles and set them nearby to dry. "It might be easier to be completely blind than to see so little," he muttered.

One of the Paladins asked why he had given Zanja his spectacles for far-seeing. Probably tired of answering the same question repeatedly, he answered irritably, "Because I myself couldn't be folded small enough to fit in her satchel!"

Garland said, "If Emil was here, he probably could explain to us why Zanja is following such a peculiar course. Karis says she's walking twice the distance, with all her back-and-forthing. Can any of you guess why she's doing this?" That Medric was a fire witch seemed more of a disadvantage than an advantage lately. But the Paladins, with their better balanced fire talents, might understand Zanja.

"She's not lost," Medric said. "Not her."

"But if she's not in her right mind . . ."

"She certainly is not in her right mind. But it doesn't matter."

Lil absently offered Medric the flask, and he turned it away with an expression of revulsion.

Kamren said cautiously, "She's following Emil, but what if—" He stopped awkwardly.

"Emil might be dead," Medric said. "Do you think I don't know that?"

"The fault is mine, Master Seer. I'm reluctant to say the words because *I* don't want them to be true. If Emil is dead, then what is Zanja following? What are *we* following?"

Garland was feeling wretched, a condition they all seemed to share. "Zanja has visions of the dead," he said. "Sometimes she doesn't know where she is. She thinks she's with her people, reliving the massacre. What if she's leading us on a chase after Emil's spirit?"

Medric didn't say anything, and neither did anyone else, until Seth said, "Then perhaps we're wasting our time, but that's no catastrophe, I guess."

"No, but we have a worse problem," said Kamren. "If Emil is dead, how do we manage without him?"

"How does *Karis* manage without him?" said Garland. "Those rogue air witches must know how much Karis depends on his counsel. They abducted him because they thought that without him, Shaftal was as good as lost."

He looked at Medric, who always seemed blank and helpless without spectacles, but Medric's eyes were narrowed as if he were aiming at a target.

Garland said to him, "But Shaftal *isn't* as good as lost."

Medric said, "The air witches may have found Karis predictable—she is an earth witch, after all. But if the air witches think they can predict Zanja, then they are mistaken."

The Paladins gazed at him with some astonishment, but Seth said, "That's either poetry or philosophy, and I think Garland meant a practical question. Can someone replace Emil? So that Shaftal isn't endangered?"

"No *one* can replace him," said Medric.

"But more than one can?" said Garland. "Norina has been *trying* to be him. She's intelligent and she understands people, so that's a start. Clement knows tactics and strategy and how to solve problems, and she's trying to be him also, though I don't think she knows it."

Kamren said, "The Paladins can puzzle through ethics and strive for insight, as Emil always did. And Seth is pragmatic and understands government."

Seth said, "Medric knows the past and is focused on the future. That's the long view Emil valued. And Garland, you care for people like he does."

"It's an Emil committee!" said Kamren. "But to succeed, all of us must think together. Shall we try it?"

Garland could hear the Paladins straightening their backs and stretching out their legs, as though they were heartened by this peculiar exercise. But anxiety scurried through his mind like a stupid mouse in a pantry, which destroys everything it does not eat.

"First, decide what matters," Medric said.

That was exactly right. Emil was always keeping people from focusing on the most immediate or irritating problem, such as a fly buzzing in the window. Garland said, "I don't think anyone has thought about that. Instead, we've been yanked about like a pig by the nose ring. Even the Paladins have."

Kamren said, "It seems more accurate to say that it's Karis who has been yanked about, while we are merely following her—which means we have had a failure of philosophy."

The other Paladins wanted to discuss that statement for a while, and for once Garland wasn't impatient with their digressive habits. They were trying to be Emil in their own way, and he must try to be Emil in his way. What do people need? Well, which people? Not just the people in this circle, or the people who came to his kitchen, but the people of Shaftal, including the Sainnites and the border tribes. And ignore the fly buzzing in the window, he reminded himself.

The people need to trust that Karis acts for the good of the whole. But perhaps she was only able to be concerned about Zanja and Emil.

He said, "Those Death-and-Life people, they are wrong about Karis, but perhaps they're not completely wrong."

Kamren seemed to understand him immediately. "Because Karis is a border woman, a Sainnite, and a Shaftali, she is the only possible G'deon for our time, as Harold must have known when he decided to vest her with the Power of Shaftal. But it must also be true that in belonging to all these people she belongs to none of them, and that having grown up without a family she clings too tightly to the family she now has. For a woman of such strength, she has many weaknesses."

Seth said, "So an air witch, one who knows her weaknesses, can use them to yank her about." She sighed and then exclaimed, "But no one can stop her from doing what she wants, no matter how wrong!"

Kamren said, "Well, no one is born wise, and yet a few of us manage to become so. Emil certainly tutored Karis in wisdom, did he not?"

Medic uttered a snort. "He *tried*."

Garland said, "Shaftal is tutoring her. The land speaks to her. She knows . . ." Even with two languages at his disposal, Garland struggled to express what he had occasionally perceived in Karis, a steadiness and balance, an astonishing ability to know every particular while also knowing the whole. "Her wisdom, it's always under her feet."

In the gathering darkness, he saw the movement of nodding heads. All had noticed those moments when Karis knew the whole and knew what must be done, not from conversation, books, or experience, but from paying attention. Was that what mattered at this moment in history? That Karis pay attention? If so, then an ordinary person, even one as ordinary as Garland, might convince her to do what was natural to her anyway.

One of the Paladins was saying, "If only we could tell her what this Saugus fellow is doing, or why."

"But how can we know that?" Kamren asked, in that way Paladins have of sounding genuinely curious and generously willing to believe anything, no matter how absurd.

Medric said, "Norina is similar to the Saugus, so if she knew what his principles are, she could guess why he's doing what he's doing."

"Principles?" said Kamren.

"All air bloods have principles by which they feel driven to order the world. That's why those students of Norina's cannot endure to be in the same room with a chaotic creature like myself."

Kamren said, "What you're saying was true about Councilor Mabin, who was an air blood. Mabin expected the world to conform to her standards, which made her a restless and dissatisfied Paladin. She hated Karis for being half Sainnite and a smoke addict. She hated Harald G'deon for allowing the Sainnites to become entrenched here. And she hated the Sainnites for not being Shaftali. In fact, if Saugus has read her book, he probably agrees with most of it."

Garland didn't know which book Kamren meant—but Medric certainly had read it, for he had read every written page that was to be found in Shaftal, and constantly hunted for more. Why he had given Zanja his far-seeing spectacles was impossible to explain, but that he had retained the pair he used for reading made sense, for Medric without a book was like Emil without a pen.

"What part of Mabin's *Warfare* would Saugus *disagree* with?" Kamren asked.

Medric said, "I imagine he might hate the part where she advocates minor but persistent actions, designed to wear down the will of a stronger enemy."

"What would Saugus think is true instead?"

"Well, he's an air witch, so he's a bloody egotist, isn't he? He'll embrace whatever truth makes him look important!" Medric made a sound, half sigh and half groan. "How can you keep thinking, without a picture to look at? I should have demanded that Zanja give me her glyph cards! If I must manage without my implements, then so should she. And don't dig me with your elbow, Seth!"

"Then stop whining," said Seth.

This was what happened when people engaged in difficult conversations without proper refreshments. They needed something cold and sweet to drink, but all they had was an empty brandy flask.

"Are we still trying to decide what matters?" asked Kamren. "Are you saying that what matters is that we understand this rogue air witch's principles?"

One of the other Paladins spoke. "No, what matters is that we be able to tell Karis why Saugus is doing these things—why he ordered his subordinate to abduct Emil—so Karis will realize she's being yanked about by her nose ring."

Garland wondered whether, when Paladins converse, they each take roles, like spices in a soup. Perhaps that was how they managed to keep talking as they did, on the same topic, for hours—days—weeks on end. This Paladin kept reminding them of what had been said, while Kamren answered and asked questions. Perhaps another would do nothing but disagree, another would point out overlooked possibilities, another would remind them of tradition, and another would keep mentioning practical problems. Little wonder the Sainnites thought Paladins were peculiar.

"Medric, you're supposed to express Emil's insight," Seth reminded him.

Medric sat silent, but at least he wasn't restless any more. No one said anything for quite a while. Medric said, "I've been thinking about how a bird would explain a fish to another bird: it flies in water; its winds are currents; its feathers are like little, stiff leaves—"

Someone uttered a muffled laugh.

Medric said, "Air magic is the opposite of fire magic. So I ought to be able to guess what Saugus is doing by imagining the opposite of what I would do. That's not insight, though—it's work." Medric sighed. "And it's work I can't avoid. Suppose I were in a position to determine Shaftal's future—well, I *am* in that position, little though I like it. Suppose that, like Saugus, someone of great power, like Karis, was doing something I disapprove of. Using fire logic, I can anticipate that person's every move and impede it. I can guess what she hates the most, and subject her to it. My goal probably would be to isolate her from her powers—not from her element, of course, but from her ability to do anything effective with it. In the end I'd probably drive her away."

"What's the opposite of everything Medric just said?" Kamren asked.

It seemed like an absurd question. But one of the Paladins immediately answered, "Rather than anticipating what she will do, you would force her to do things."

"The things you *want* her to do," said another.

"By making it seem like there's no other choice."

"Rather than make her life unendurable, you would make it inescapable."

"A trap of duty—duty without joy."

"Rather than make her ineffective, you would delude her with effectiveness."

"She would think she's doing something worthwhile, but would be wasting her energy."

"Or perhaps she'd be isolated from herself—from her ability to know what is the right thing to do."

"Isolated from her friends, maybe."

"And in the end—in the end, what? She'd drive herself away?"

"Or she'd be lured too close."

"Too close to what? To her own powers?"

They were talking about Karis! Garland felt an awful sensation, and cried, "Too close to Saugus! Without fire logic to show her another way, and without air logic to protect her from him!"

"Bloody hell," said Medric.

Chapter 31

Just past sunrise, Maxew awakened Tashar by poking a toe in his ribs. He said that during the night they had been becalmed, and he had been nearly mad with boredom. "We must go west," he said. "Today." He lay down and covered his head with the blanket.

The cloudless sky was pale and dull. On a day like this, Tashar's little boat would have remained at dock. Tashar had explained to Maxew that their direction of travel depended entirely on the wind, so he didn't know why the younger man persisted in thinking that Tashar could decide their direction. Yet Tashar's translated scroll had explained that the winds wrapped the earth in layers, so he decided to go upward, hunting for a wind that would take them in the direction they needed. He built up the fire, and the air boat began to ascend.

The landscape below faded as though a thin mist had crept over it, while at the same time the sky overhead turned a brilliant blue, and the air became refreshingly cool. The telltales never indicated the wind Tashar sought, but he remained at that amazing height for much of the day.

Maxew slept.

Their prisoner occasionally opened his eyes or mumbled something. Maxew had not bothered to force him to eat or drink, and soon the old man would die. There was nothing Tashar could do about it.

Their wood supply was depleted. In late afternoon, he decided they'd have to land—and they could choose a landing place no more easily than they could choose a direction of travel. He stopped putting wood into the stove, and leaned on the wicker gunwale to watch for a good landing place, should one happen to appear. The telltales started to flutter upward.

They slowly penetrated the haze. Tashar peered in all directions, seeking landmarks, roads, rivers, anything to tell him where they were. Nothing stood out in the landscape, nothing but black boulders amid the dull green. He couldn't tell if the land was flat or hilly, or whether there were any settlements. Finally he realized that the haze of blue beyond the edges of the land was not sky but ocean. His stomach flipped in a sickening way, as his sense of the world was reorganized. They had made shocking progress eastward—the wrong direction—and the earth was much, much closer than it had seemed.

"Maxew!" he cried. He yanked open the stove door to put in a fresh log. But the fire had burned down to a few embers amid the ashes. He whacked the sleeping boy with a stick, and Maxew sat up.

"We're falling!"

"What? Why did you let the fire go out?"

Tashar flung handfuls of tinder into the stove. He blew to make it flame, but blew too hard, and got a faceful of hot ash. Taking a breath to blow again, he sucked in ashes and began choking.

Maxew shouted at him—angrily and pointlessly. Tashar could not catch his breath, but the tinder caught without his help. He added some small sticks, one at a time, very carefully. An ember was smoking in the wicker near his knee, and he doused it with the last of their water. He carefully closed the stove door and looked up into the silk bag. It was filled with smoke. But on a hot day, only a hot fire could keep them afloat, since the air in the bag must be far warmer than the air outside the bag. He looked at the telltales. They continued to stream upwards; the air boat continued to fall.

Cursing, Maxew shoved wood at him, and Tashar crammed it into the fire box. Now the telltales were flapping, which meant their fall was slowing. More embers fell out. He crushed them with his bare hands.

He stood up and looked over the gunwale. Below them, birds were starting out of the trees, scattering below the basket like minnows in a pond. The air boat's shadow shuddered agitatedly across the treetops. He could not see the guide rope at all. Was it trailing behind them, dragging across treetops?

A hard jolt. Maxew fell into the side with a yell of surprise. The boat heeled wildly, and Tashar was looking directly down at the ground, which was patched with sunlight and shade and a few tired-looking clumps of grass. The boat swayed back, sickeningly, then forward, then back, and then it hit the ground. The stove tipped over. Tashar went over the edge. *I should have lain on the deck,* he thought as he fell. He jolted to earth while the air boat, lighter now that it had lost a passenger, bounced upward. It occurred to Tashar that it would come down again. He scrambled out of its path.

The guide rope, tangled in the trees, had tethered the boat. It subsided gradually and gracefully to earth, and the bag flopped across the treetops like a soft pillow.

Maxew peered over the gunwale. Blood from his nose gushed down his chin. There was a lot of smoke. Tashar ran to climb in and heave the stove upright. Fortunately, its door had remained latched.

The silk settled across the treetops, crackling like taffeta. Maxew crawled out of the boat and lay on the ground. He spit out a mouthful of blood. The old man lay crumpled, mumbling, pathetic, covered by wrecked supplies, singed blankets, and their last two pieces of wood.

No one said anything.

Tashar dragged the wicker boat to a sturdy tree branch and hoisted it with block and tackle so the old man would remain safely above ground.

Maxew, with a black eye and his nose starting to swell, stumbled about with hatchet in hand, picking up bits of firewood. Tashar climbed to high ground with the empty tins clanging on his back, but he saw no sign of water. When he returned, Maxew's pile of wood was unimpressive, and he was sitting in the shade with his head against his knees.

Would people admire this remarkable journey, or just remember this ignominious crash? Tashar was the captain, and this catastrophe was his fault—and his duty to mend. Little though he liked that bastard Maxew, much though he was tempted to leave him, his foul temper, and his hapless prisoner here in this forsaken place, he would not fail Saugus. Nor would he abandon his sky boat. Yet he couldn't help but wonder whether his judgment on these matters was entirely sound, for his dreams of flight seemed real, but his death did not—despite bruises and burns and a devastating crash. But he would not make these mistakes again.

The basketry boat rocked like a cradle hanging from the rafters of a farmhouse kitchen. The prisoner moved restlessly and uttered muffled, guttural cries. "What's the matter with him?" Tashar asked.

Maxew raised his head. There were flakes of dried blood stuck to his chin, and his nose had swollen grotesquely. "We must set forth again."

"We will, but not until the wind changes."

"If you had said that the ship could not be steered—"

"It could—if I knew more about winds . . ."

"Why don't you, then?"

"Because no one knows! And I'm doing the best I can!" He gestured skyward. "There's no clouds, no birds—"

Maxew was breathing through his mouth, and his voice was muffled and hollow, as though he had a head cold. "It's never your fault, is it?"

Tashar took the hatchet and gathered wood. While wandering among the trees, he stumbled across a mud puddle that had been a vernal pool, in the center of which there had survived a bit of water. He waded in, knee-deep in foul mud, and filled the water tins. He took them back to Maxew and told him to first strain the water through a rag, then give some water to the prisoner.

The sun was halfway to the horizon when Tashar noticed a few clouds heading westward at a turtle's pace. With the silk bag spread across the treetops, they built a fire beneath it, filled it with smoke, and went aloft once again.

Chapter 32

Early in the spring, the Two had complained to Norina about how difficult it was to study in the main hall of Travesty, with the noise, the comings and goings, and the frequent interruptions. Braight, although she respected and feared Norina Truthken as she did no one else, had said that the law students should be allowed to keep watch in shifts like the Paladins did. Norina replied that the air students must be under the impression that she considered only her own convenience when she decided how things would be done. Far worse than a remonstration, it was the first sentence of a lecture.

She said, "With enough experience, the heightened perceptions of air witches can be exercised not just on individuals, but on groups. But air children are easily overwhelmed by their own senses, especially since you are painfully conscious that your presence inspires discomfort and hostility in nearly everyone. Thus, air children tend to avoid people, or, when that is impossible, they learn to disappear, so people forget their presence. But both strategies trade learning for comfort. As law students, you must learn to sort your perceptions, to heed what matters and ignore the rest, which can only be learned through exposure. When I was a law student, the school was in the House of Lilterwess, where a tenth of all Shaftali people passed through the doors each year."

Anders calculated that the law students in the House of Lilterwess would have had to cope with 30,000 visitors each year. How could he possibly be congenial to so many: eighty people each day, or four people each hour . . . assuming that he never slept?

Norina's lecture continued. "You must learn more than tolerance. You must learn more than attentiveness. You must learn to notice, even in a crowd, what is not there. Until you can do that, you will only be useful when you control all the conditions, which is another way of saying that you won't be useful at all."

Serrain, the only one who seemed likely to pass such a test, was the only one who could think about what lay beyond it. "Madam Truthken," she had said, "toleration, attentiveness, and heedfulness to the missing—are these precursors to the exercise of air magic on a group?"

Norina had never concealed her reactions from them, though she certainly was capable of it. She showed surprise, followed by wry amusement. "Perhaps. But under what circumstances would it be legal to bend a group of people to your will?"

On a page of Anders's book titled "Unanswered Questions" he had written that question, and he still didn't know the answer. But on the day they found the dead body of Norina's husband, he thought it likely that an air witch could lawfully use magic to prevent a group from murdering a healer.

They had searched again in the room J'han shared with Norina and their daughter but found only some faint stains that Braight said could be blood. They had argued about the meaning of the thump in the night—for if the cleaners had carried out a dead man at night, the law students would not be able to find the body now. Braight said that if there was a body, it would be concealed in the house, entire wings of which stood vacant during this season of travel. "Why bother to carry him farther?" she had asked. So they had searched, fruitlessly, every room of the house, until the Two remembered the seer's tower.

Halfway up the seer's ridiculous hidden staircase, Braight had said, "That is the smell of death."

When they got the trap door open, the miasma became unbearable. The Two fled, Serrain clapped her hand over her mouth, and Braight cried, "Anders! I can't do this alone!"

They had no one in custody whose truths or lies could prove that murder had taken place. Therefore, they must look with their own eyes to see how the man had died. Anders helped Braight to cut the ropes, peel back the canvas that wrapped the body, and examine the dead man.

Life is action, Anders realized, even if that action is nothing more than the moving sparks of thoughts. Death is a permanent inertia, the end of action. J'han's actions had always been rooted in fundamental kindness, yet he also had a toughness, a readiness to do the sometimes hard and brutal work of curing people, or of helping them die. Now he would not take any action again; he was dead.

Surely looking at the dead man's wounds was not the proper business of children! But they were law students. They had studied together the law regarding murder, and thus they knew what was required.

"Let's take some of his hair," said Anders. Pinching his nose made his voice sound like someone else's.

Braight took hold of a blood-stiff lock of J'han's hair, and Anders cut it with his pocket knife.

"I need to be alone now," he said.

Soon after the law school was formed, the six students had agreed upon protocols for solitude. Anders chose the library as his refuge. Other people might be there, but they always were silent and preoccupied and scarcely seemed aware of his existence. Now, with nearly all the scholars and fire bloods gone to Hanishport, the library was quite empty. A book that Emil had been repairing and rebinding lay in pieces, the old boards waiting to be wrapped in calfskin.

Anders sat on a stool in a corner of the library. He thought about death, and then he thought about murder. He thought about the window that had stood ajar in J'han's neat room; the faint scent of soap; one bed, bare to the mattress, while Leeba's bed was carelessly made, as a young child might do it; long, fresh scars in the floor, where someone's hobnails had scraped across the grain. He imagined a row of cleaners standing by with brushes and buckets.

Leeba was not docile or patient. She was persistent and intrusive. After the night of the assassinations, her parents had begun teaching her to protect herself—how to fight, and flee, and scream for help. They had not taught her how to watch her father die.

A prickling in Anders's neck grew into a quivering across the shoulders that crept downward until his entire body was trembling. In his dark, silent corner, he sat shuddering, alone with his sadness and terror.

"J'han Healer has been murdered."

The Paladin nodded politely, just as the two Paladins before him had done; but behind the courteously attentive expression lay incomprehension.

"His body lies concealed in the seer's tower," said Serrain. "If you'll just come with us, we'll show you."

"Oh, I regret that I can't. My duties—"

Anders grabbed Serrain's arm. "No magic," he whispered.

She yanked her arm away. "Magic's been done to them already!"

"And the one who did it will be executed!"

This was an occasion like Norina had warned them of, when it seemed obvious and urgent that they act in ways that seemed natural and easy. "But you must find another way," Norina had said.

"We must find another way," Anders said.

The Paladin was walking away. From previous experience, Anders and Serrain knew that if they called her back they would have to begin again, for she would remember nothing.

"Bran's work," said Serrain in fearful admiration.

How could they make the people left behind in Travesty recognize the crime that they had not noticed when it occurred under their noses?

The big clock in the hall chimed the hour. Soon the people of the house would gather in the kitchen to cook and eat supper. The air children must gather food and slip away before then.

As often happened, Anders had reached a conclusion while he still thought he was considering the problem. He said, "We must go to Hanishport and find Norina."

"But she bid us—"

"Based on a wrong assumption!"

"What Norina *said* was that we must never exercise our judgment!"

"But we have a duty—"

"Students don't have a duty, except—"

"—to Shaftal."

"—to obey!"

The front door slammed open, and agitated voices sounded loud in the empty hall. "—you think you can just float past—" Braight was saying.

"—You don't think anyone should ever do what they're told—" That was Minga.

And Arlis, whom Anders had never heard speak at the same time as Minga, unless he was saying the same words, said simultaneously, "Sometimes obedience might be wrong."

Their efforts to tell the healers what happened also seemed to have failed.

Serrain said in astonishment, "The Two are disagreeing with themself!"

Anders said, "Are you all finished arguing yet? I'm going to Hanishport to find Norina. And I'm leaving right away."

"I apologize for wasting your time," Serrain said. "Of course I will go with you."

"She won't kill all five of us," said Braight.

"She will, if we deserve it," said the Two.

Lacking horse and wagon, the air children followed on foot a road that none of them had ever taken. Even the Two, who had traveled up and down the Corbin River their entire lives, had never set foot on the road that paralleled it. They walked until darkness fell, and slept in a roadside campsite they shared with other travelers, who gave them the remains of a roasted chicken they had eaten for supper.

The next day they walked in the blasting heat of summer, with the sun first in their faces, then burning on their backs. They were learning many lessons about foot travel: wear hats, carry water, don't bring their *Books of Everything,* which they had thought they needed and soon regretted. They passed the Shimasal crossroad and were blinded by the light glaring from the white stones of that famous road. They swam in an inviting pond, and then were too tired to continue, even though several more hours of daylight remained. The next day, they begged a ride in an empty, jolting wagon. The day after that, they were hailed by a soldier who was watching the road from concealment. They knew him, one of the general's guards, who had accompanied her to Hanishport.

The soldier, who knew only a little Shaftalese, pointed northward. "Not Hanishport. That way."

All the air children turned to Anders—even Braight—and waited for him to tell them what to do.

Chapter 33

Chaen hated that she sometimes couldn't distinguish Shaftali from Sainnite. She hated that the Paladins, while teaching some of the soldiers Shaftalese, were being helped to compose a dictionary of the soldiers' language so they and anyone else who desired to could learn to speak it. She hated that Seth had lived with soldiers in their barracks at Watfield Garrison.

Chaen separated herself from all of them, in spite of Seth, who, like a Basdown cow dog, kept finding her and herding her back toward the crowd.

To avoid the soldiers, who made their beds in regimented rows, separated by sex, Chaen lay among the people who orbited or were attached to Karis: the Paladins, the Truthken, Seth, the seer, and usually the baby.

On Chaen's second night as an unwilling member of that strange company, she was awakened by the sound of someone jerking upright. "Zanja," Karis said, not in fear, but casually, as one says the name of a family member, to ask where a piece of clothing is, or whether the chickens have been fed.

Chaen lay a good distance from her, but the night was extraordinarily silent, and the moon had not yet set. She could see the G'deon's shape—tall, even sitting down—and her face, a silhouette against the summer stars. The Truthken lay still, as would anyone accustomed to dangerous living, using darkness for concealment; but of course Chaen recognized her voice, even though she spoke too quietly for her words to be distinguished.

Karis answered, "I heard a voice in the sky."

"A dream," said the Truthken.

"No. I heard it with Zanja's ears."

Another disturbed sleeper had sat up, muttering and feeling around in the darkness.

"Your spectacles are in your shoe," said Karis.

The seer, who never seemed to have anything sensible to say, exclaimed, "How clever of me! Unless I happen to put the shoe on my foot. But I couldn't, because I couldn't see well enough to find my shoe, could I?"

The lenses of his spectacles became visible, dimly reflecting faint and distant starlight.

Norina said, "What voice? What did it say?"

Karis said, "An angry voice, saying, *What's the good of a vessel that can't be steered?*"

"An argument in the sky? It's nonsense."

"It was Maxew's voice."

Medric said, "It's a mutiny, a mutiny in the ship of air. *That* is the vessel that can't be steered. And the one who can't endure lack of control is the air witch."

Norina said, "If I accept the absurd premise of a ship that flies!"

"Be quiet," Karis said.

A profound silence followed, and Chaen did not know what it meant, whether Karis was frustrated by the tension between the incompatible witches, or whether she was paying attention to something no one else could perceive.

Karis said, "I don't know how a ship could fly. But if there *were* a flying ship, I know why it couldn't be steered. A ship in water chooses its direction through the opposition of water and air. If the ship of air has sails, or something like them, it lacks an opposing force to brace itself against. It can only go passively, wherever the wind goes, no differently from clouds or smoke." She paused as though thinking again, then said, "I can't remember the wind's changes of direction these last few days. But what if Zanja has been changing her direction with the wind: back and forth, northwest to northeast? And yesterday, when she started to go due north—even though the wind was more easterly—*that* was when she figured something out. She's trying to intercept the ship, but she may not realize it's passing overhead."

"Like shooting at a moving target," Medric said. "She's aiming at where it—whatever it is—*will* be."

"A flying ship is still absurd," Norina said.

Karis said, "Absurd or not, if it's a ship, it can be wrecked. Medric, how can we do that?"

Norina said, "If it's a ship of air, the seer *can't* know how to wreck it."

Karis said, "A ship that floats in water isn't *made* of water. It's earth floating in water. What we're chasing is a ship of earth, which is floating in air."

"It's of fire also," said the seer, "though I can't explain why or how."

Karis said, "And wind, which belongs in the province of water, carries it and determines its direction."

"So it's *in* air and *on* air, but not *of* air at all!" cried the little man. "All along, we have been using the wrong preposition!"

"I don't care what you call it. How can I wreck the ship without harming Emil?"

The seer said, "Whatever threatens the ship threatens all its passengers, both good and evil."

"Emil is endangered," Norina said, "whether his ship is wrecked or not."

Karis said, "Yes, but I refuse to be the one who endangers him."

"Karis, I'm speaking to you as Emil's friend. He is a Paladin. He would be the first to remind you that one person's life is not more valuable than the whole. Not even *his* life."

Karis seemed to have become of earth, a boulder beneath the trees that sheltered them. "What should I do?" she said in a low voice. No one answered. Perhaps she was asking the plants, the dirt, the creatures that went abroad, all the powers of her realm.

She spoke again, but now her voice was the gravel that slides ahead of an avalanche. "Master seer, tell me, by what means can a ship of air be wrecked?"

"By water magic," Medric said.

That company of enemies and strangers, roused by a bugle at first light, had broken camp so quickly that the cooks served breakfast from steaming pots carried on poles. They had abandoned the wagons and a number of soldiers at the well, but a supply line was being spun behind them. Two of the horses were gone, with two Paladins riding them.

Chaen tried to walk beyond the edge of the main company, but of course Seth found her, gave her a steaming porringer that she said was from Garland, and commended her for walking upwind of the dust cloud.

The porridge was thick and sticky, with a lot of chaff in the grain, but Garland had done something to make it delicious.

Chaen said, "I was awake when the two Paladins left before dawn. Do you know where they're going?"

"I do know, but I can't believe it," Seth said. "Not three months after she warned Grandmother Ocean not to meddle in her business ever again, Karis is asking her for help."

"Grandmother Ocean? That's the water witch? The one who—"

"The perfidious, untrustworthy, wily, ruthless old woman who practically drowned Zanja right in front of me—*twice!*"

"But she's far away, isn't she? South of Basdown?"

"She's far south, in protected lands."

Even on horseback, Chaen thought, it was a journey of at least ten days. "What is Karis asking her for?"

"Oh, *I* don't know! I don't think you *can* ask a water witch for anything in particular. And don't ask me why not, because just thinking about water magic gives me a headache! She'll regret asking that dreadful woman for help."

Chaen, who was unable to escape her own elemental contradictions, thought Seth's aversion was extraordinary.

The sun rapidly grew hot. Somehow this entire company, except for Medric, had neglected to bring hats. The Paladins had head scarves, and many others tied their shirts around their heads, as Chaen and Seth did. But they all wore undershirts, for Garland had warned them that Sainnites never went shirtless.

The dirt underfoot was so dry that the water Chaen spilled when rinsing out the porringer lay on its surface like drops of quicksilver.

Garland came puffing up to them, his captain's badge pinned sloppily to his undershirt and a wooden spoon tucked into his belt. He waved his hand vaguely toward the back of the column. "Seth, general meeting," he said. "Strategy, or something."

"In that dust?" Seth asked.

He gestured helplessly. "She suffers with the lowest soldier."

Seth started glumly toward the rear, but Garland remained. When he had gotten his breath back, he said, "The general asks if you would mind joining her also."

"No!"

"Well, don't pelt cannonballs at me! I'm just giving you a message. She says, if you think all Sainnites are evil and you've got to protect your friends from them—or us, I guess—she understands, even though you're wrong. But if you want your friends to get a chance at mercy, maybe it's time to forget about which side you're on and start trying to make things right."

"Make things right!"

"It's your choice," he said and departed without another word.

In solitude, finally, Chaen could not think about the question that always preoccupied her, how to protect Maxew from the Truthken. Instead her thoughts became stuck in an argument between her air self and her fire self. She should have been relieved, she supposed, by this familiar paralysis, which gave proof that she was still herself in spite of the meddling of air logic. But she was out of the habit of deciding things: her choices had seemed so clear for so long that they hardly qualified as choices at all.

Perhaps she never *had* chosen. Perhaps she had merely delivered herself to a way of thinking that had taken her captive. Perhaps Saugus had brought her into Death-and-Life Company because she already agreed with his views, and so he needed not trouble himself to control her. She had been impatient with the fanatics in the company, nearly all of whom had been betrayed by Saugus and killed on First Night. But how different was she if she made her decisions based on assumptions and principles she had never examined or questioned?

Her fire self was telling her to go to the general's meeting. If she listened without speaking, her air self would be satisfied. She turned her steps toward the rear of the column and soon found herself in the midst of filthy, sweating, swearing soldiers who paid no heed to her except to avoid colliding with her. Every last one of them was limping. Some were white-haired, some had lost hands or arms in past battles, and some coughed in the dust wearily and constantly as though they had a fever in the lungs. Although many soldiers were as big as Karis, none of those giants were in this pathetic, trailing end of the column, and so Karis was easy to spot. Chaen headed toward her and arrived at the same time as Garland and Kamren, who had joined them by standing still while the soldiers walked past them.

"Greetings, Chaen," Kamren said, and added ruefully, "I was trying to make the other day's bath last longer."

"It is a filthy march," the Sainnite general said. She was walking backwards so she could face Karis, and Kamren did so also. Chaen put both the earth bloods between her and the Truthken. She saw that Karis and Clement had recently been arguing. Usually, Chaen was the only one to perceive this sort of thing, but the Truthken certainly perceived it also.

General Clement said, "This is our fifth day. I've got a hundred armed soldiers who must believe they're working toward a goal. Otherwise, they'll invent one, which is sure to be stupid and likely to be dangerous."

She certainly had a low opinion of her people. But Garland, nodding in agreement, said, "They don't carry weapons merely to remind themselves of a philosophical problem."

Kamren laughed so sharply he choked on dust and had to be rescued with a drink of water.

"What am I to tell them?" Clement asked.

Kamren managed to say, "How much time do we have, Clement?"

"Before what? To do what?"

"Before your people break discipline. Without a common language, we can't teach the soldiers to consider the ethics of bloodshed. But we probably can show them how to *avoid* bloodshed, if we have some time with them."

He and the general talked back and forth for a while. Kamren listened attentively, as fire bloods sometimes do. Both of them continued to walk backwards without looking, Kamren because he was a fire blood, the general, possibly, because none of her soldiers dared to be in her way. Clement finally said, "You certainly would *entertain* them. What do I tell them this teaching is for?"

"They are learning how to be of service to the G'deon. Chaen, do you know how many people Saugus can muster?"

Chaen had expected someone would ask her a question like this. Still, she felt disarmed by Kamren's tone of casual curiosity. "Those who follow Saugus aren't evil people," she said. "I won't help you slaughter them."

"That's exactly what we wish to avoid," said the general.

"Return to your garrison, then!"

The general answered mildly, "The Sainnites of Shaftal are the G'deon's to command."

Chaen decided to say nothing more. But after a silence, the Truthken said, "He directly controls forty people at most."

"And how many could he control indirectly?" asked Karis. The baby in her arms uttered a faint yelp, and she lifted the hat that now served the baby as a sun shelter and began fanning him with it.

"It's impossible to say how many are following Saugus by their own wills, and how many are willing followers of the people he directly controls. I know nothing of this man's character, but I suspect that these secondary followers would be kept at a distance, as with the potato farmer in Hanishport who gave Chaen her weapon."

Karis said, "Then I want the soldiers to stay with us. Clem, can't you tell them the truth?"

"You want me to tell the soldiers that we're wandering the hot countryside because we're chasing a flying ship that can't go where it's pointed? They'll think we're all lunatics."

"Blame *me* for our wandering," said Medric.

Chaen had not even noticed the seer's presence. He trudged so tiredly behind Karis that Chaen had taken him for an infirm soldier who was sheltering from the hot sun by walking in her shadow. He said, "Tell the soldiers that my visions are deciding our direction of travel, and that I keep changing my mind. It's *nearly* true, isn't it?"

The general blinked at him. "I will tell them that," she finally said.

Chaen thought the Truthken was puzzled by something, for she had begun paying extremely close attention to each person. She seemed about to speak, but Karis said sharply, "Clement, call a halt."

The general took a tin whistle on a chain from inside her undershirt and blew three shrill peeps that few of the soldiers could have heard. But a moment later, the bugler sounded the same signal.

"Alert? Or at rest?" Clement asked as the soldiers shuffled to a halt.

Karis was peering fruitlessly into the brown haze behind them.

Norina answered Clement, "It's nothing dangerous. Let them rest."

Clement peeped on her whistle, the bugler repeated it, and some soldiers rushed toward the shade of a few nearby trees while the rest dropped their burdens on the ground and sat on them. Four had begun to walk quickly in the general's direction—the officers, Chaen suspected.

Seth grabbed Chaen's arm.

Karis said in a cracked, strained voice, "It's water magic."

Norina said, "I'll go with Kamren, and you can stay here."

"That's very kind of you," said Karis, but she handed the baby to Clement and started walking toward the south, with the seer still at her elbow, and Kamren and Norina behind them.

Then Seth said, "I'd rather see what's coming than stand and wait for it! Come with me, Chaen, will you? To hold me up if I start to fall over?"

They walked southward out of the dust cloud. A pair of horses emerged from the heat waves in the distance and all of a sudden were practically on top of them. The riders staggered as they dismounted, and one fell to her knee. They looked at Karis as though they didn't trust their senses. She took each of them by the hand, and then it was she who staggered, so Norina leapt forward but then stopped when Karis found her balance again.

These same two Paladins had departed hours ago, but now they scarcely seemed the same people: the woman was gaunt, and the man had grown a white beard. They clung to Karis's hands as though the swift current in which they had been traveling might continue to carry them away. The man was the first to let go of Karis. "Lil, we have arrived."

"Have we?" said his companion doubtfully.

"Kamren!" he cried. The two men embraced like friends reunited after a long separation. "How long have we been gone?"

Kamren took a watch from his waistcoat. "Four hours and a half."

"It's been eighteen days," said Lil.

"Lil, Rane, what did Grandmother Ocean say?" Karis was looking very pale.

The returned Paladins both fumbled at their belts to untie flasks that had the natural asymmetry of gourds but were intricately decorated and shone like glazed pottery. The vessels were dressed in delicate fish nets, each knot decorated with small shells that shimmered in the sunshine, their colors alive and unstable like a film of oil on moving water. Karis accepted these gorgeous vessels with reluctance, holding them by the braided cords as though she didn't want to touch them.

"*Stomp on it,* is what the water witch said. Or rather, that's what she demonstrated."

Chaen let out an inadvertent sound. Surely such lovely things had not been made only to be destroyed!

"Stomp on which? Or both?"

"She may have told us," said Lil, "but her speaker, Silver, didn't translate. It doesn't matter, anyway, because she gave us both of them at once, and we can't tell them apart."

"After that, she went under the water and didn't come back up. Silver told us there was no time for us to talk further—we had to leave before the water she had splashed on us was dry. And he said to tell you that Grandmother Ocean is dead."

"She's dead?" said Seth. "How can she be dead if she lives outside of time?"

"Which one do I smash?" Karis asked Medric. The seer pointed at one of the bottles.

Karis gave the other to Kamren and, without a word, turned on her heel and strode off through the dust cloud, up the slope of a nearby rise. Not even Norina followed her, though her gaze never wavered from the furious giant, who had arrived at the top of the slope and now stood still, at the meeting of earth and sky, with the morning's sun still shining on her sweat-glazed back. Karis put the bottle on a boulder, then took the hammer from her belt. For a moment, Chaen could see the tool's heaviness reflected in the swelling of her muscles, not just in her arm and shoulder, but all the way down her back. And then she swung it, and there was a terrific boom, and the pieces of the bottle floated upwards, and bits of stone sprayed outward, raising little puffs of dust wherever they landed. One of the horses gave a jump, and a piece of rock thumped onto the toe of Chaen's boot. But she wouldn't let herself be distracted by the shrapnel, and so she saw what the rest of the watchers may have missed, a little dervish of dust that went spinning away, then disappeared as it flung off the haze that had given it form. But a small cloud, which had been journeying across the dull sky so slowly it practically seemed to be hovering, was suddenly smeared along the edge as if by a painter's knife.

Now there would be mischief, Chaen thought.

Chapter 34

Although exhausted from the day's trials, Tashar stood watch all night while Maxew slept in the bow like the survivor of a drunken brawl and the old man sprawled along one side like a disregarded body putrefying in a gutter. Yet at daybreak, Tashar could turn and turn, until he had viewed the full circle of the horizon, like the rim of a vast round plate filled with greenery, winding streams, miniature ponds, and farmsteads like children's toys in the midst of tiny orchards and fields. The Shimasal Road appeared below them, so straight it seemed to have been laid first, and the hills rose around it like loaves of bread afterwards. And a remarkable wind took them northward, faster than the carts below and steady as the compass. It began to seem that this fair and lucky wind would carry them all the way to Shimasal, where they could hire a wagon and take the road south to the ruins of the House of Lilterwess. Maxew would be furious, but, to Tashar, it seemed like a reasonable solution to their aimlessness.

At around midday, a haze appeared. At one moment Tashar was flying over Shaftal, and at the next the landscape faded away and disappeared. For a short while they floated above the fog, and then the sun and sky disappeared. Only a short time earlier, he had been able to see to the ends of the earth! How could he have been surprised by a fog bank? Had he fallen asleep without realizing it? Well, they must travel below the fog, even though he might lose the wind. He would not stand oblivious again while his precious ship flew into danger.

He banked the fire carefully so he could build it quickly should he need to and kept his face close to the telltales, which otherwise disappeared in the fog. No seaman likes to be trapped like this without landmarks or skymarks. Becalmed ghost ships floated for ages in such fogs, rotten and rusting and empty of life.

The lines were strung with water drops, like a spider's web on a dewy morning. Tashar wiped his wet face with a wet sleeve. The weight of the water alone should drag their ship downward, but the telltales flapped heavily: they were neither rising nor falling.

The old man was not dead after all. He became restless and mumbled indistinctly. He said, "Water." And his tone seemed wrong: not a request, but an announcement.

Maxew started awake. "What!" he said in an aggrieved tone.

"Fog," said Tashar.

He imagined Maxew touching his swollen nose and puffy eye, blinking stupidly as if the fog were in his vision rather than in the air, pulling the blanket around his shoulders, and letting his anger start to build.

"Water!" said the old man triumphantly. He laughed a little: "Ha, ha, ha!"

Maxew grunted with pain, rocking the basket as he staggered to his feet. Tashar spotted his ghostly shape bending over the old man. "What do you know?" he said. "Tell me what you know!"

The prisoner mumbled. Tashar heard a thump, and the old man groaned.

Better he kick him than me, thought Tashar.

One of the telltales swam into visibility, still flapping. There was a brightness above. Tashar looked up and saw the sun, a ghostly, glowing disk that brightened, faded, and brightened again. And suddenly its brilliance blinded him. Blue sky! And against that blue, a massive column composed of clouds.

The fog closed in once again.

There had been something menacing about those clouds. "I have never seen weather like this," Tashar said.

"Strangeness is all that you fear?" asked Maxew.

"I saw something . . . I'm not sure what . . ."

But then he did know. He had never seen that cloud column so close, and had never flown toward it rather than fleeing for shelter in his sailboat. "It is a thunderstorm."

The telltale reappeared in the fog. It was streaming downward. The sky boat was rising.

"Ha, ha," said the old man.

Chapter 35

Zanja's journey had been more stupid than strange. At least twice a day she changed her direction, and once her trajectory doubled back on Chaen, whose dogged pursuit had only been a mild distraction until she took a foolish fall and nearly drowned herself. By the sixth time Zanja changed direction, Chaen no longer pursued her. Sometimes Zanja felt Emil's presence so strongly that she crept through thickets in silence, expecting to encounter his captors in mere moments. Yet his presence always pulled away from her, leaving no evidence—no campfire, no horse droppings, not even an area of trampled grass. It was frustrating—bewildering—disheartening. Zanja, knowing that if she ceased to trust her prescience it would cease to be trustworthy, fought a dreary battle with self-doubt.

She ran out of water and could not find more. Hunger could be endured, but thirst would kill her, especially traveling at this pace, in this heat. At a dry streambed, she moved some large stones with a lever fashioned from a tree branch; the smaller stones she tossed aside; then she dug with her hands through sand and silt, until the soil became mud. As she waited for this little well to fill with water, she dumped the contents of her satchel on the ground. A magpie's collection: twine, though she could not wait for a squirrel or rabbit to wander into a noose; a tinder bag for the fire she didn't need; Medric's spectacles, without which he couldn't see more than an arm's length, while she had excellent eyesight; a sewing kit for mending she would not bother with; a packet of healing herbs labeled in J'han's writing, but no pot to steep them in; and the glyph cards, precious but unnecessary, since her dream guide could answer every question by showing her a page from the lexicon.

Her little well yielded only a slurry, more mud than water. She dipped her cup and drank the mud, then dug the well deeper. Dirt grated between her teeth.

"I'm losing my trust in you," she told her guide, who waited on the far side of the dry stream. He had been walking beside her for days, and his bare feet were not even dirty. He had not eaten or slept, and he entertained himself sometimes by singing the songs Zanja had sung in her childhood.

"If you don't trust me, then you don't trust yourself," he said.

"How can Emil be west of us in the morning and east of us at noon? How can his captors move so swiftly through such rough country? And why are they traveling by a zigzagging route that doubles or triples the distance?"

"They turn like the wind."

"But air witches don't change their minds!"

There was enough muddy water to fill her flask. Since Zanja had traveled beyond the watershed north of the Corben River, she would find no running water until she reached the Asha River, or stumbled across one of its tributaries. Farmsteads with wells could be found along the Shimasal Road, but her quarry had never traveled that far west. Their drunkard's path did tend northward, though it zigged and zagged between west and east. Perhaps Zanja eventually would find herself in Shimasal, or swimming the river. But this afternoon, her eastward journey might take her to the coast again.

Her guide said, "Maybe we will see the House of Lilterwess."

"The House of Lilterwess lies to the south—the only direction we *haven't* traveled."

"Yes, Speaker. But it would be marvelous to see!"

The legendary place had been a ruin for twenty years, but the boy seemed to occupy a timeless world—the world of stories, perhaps.

"Will I need these things?" She gestured toward the pile of useless objects. "Or shall I put the bread in my pockets and leave the rest behind?"

"You will need *some* of them."

Until Zanja could distinguish necessary from useless, she would carry all of it. She packed her satchel again. "So we're turning east again. But if I were to lie down and go to sleep, would they be west of us when I awake?"

"They might be." Tireless and unburdened, the boy stood up and led the way.

—

She went east, and west, and east again, to the eastern edge of the forest, where dwarfed trees kept at a distance from each other beneath big expanses of sky. Here her guide paused to gaze upward. Zanja also looked up and saw three buzzards, their great wings spread to catch the wind, soaring westward.

"The wind has changed," the boy observed.

Zanja gazed dully at the sky. The boy's guidance had always been clear, and Medric had implied she could rely on him. But he was a spirit, like the ghosts that haunted her; he did not occupy the world as she did: change, heartbreak, and uncertainty were unknown to him.

"Is Emil still east of us?" she asked.

"Yes."

The shadows had become attenuated as evening approached. A month after the equinox, those shadows lay west to east with a slight tilt to north and south. She looked at the buzzards again. They were flying towards the northwest.

She said, "In summer, the wind tends from the south. Whether it blows west or east, it also pushes toward the north. What is Emil's direction of travel?"

The boy showed her the glyph for west.

"Is his direction of travel changing every time the wind changes?"

"Yes, Speaker."

Five days of time and energy had been wasted, and it was her fault—not the fault of the guide, who inhabited a world of dreams and symbols; who had never learned how to shoot across the zigzagging path of a rabbit.

She began to walk, not toward the east, but across the lines of the shadows, with the sun to her left. When she glanced back, her crestfallen guide was following her. She said, "Foxes chase behind their prey, following its crooked path, because foxes only know where the rabbit *is*, and cannot guess where it's going. But I can guess, and so we are going northwest."

"Yes, Speaker," said her dream guide.

Once again she entered the deep woods. As the long twilight settled into night, a bank of clouds moved across the sky, blocking the stars. Zanja could not see, and was aching and stupid with weariness. For the first time since leaving Hanishport, she lay down and slept on bare ground.

In the middle of the night, she jerked awake. She thought she had heard a voice speaking in the sky. But the days were past when a raven might suddenly speak to her from the branches overhead; Karis's ravens could no longer talk. In the sky, clouds opened and closed like curtains over a few patches of stars.

Zanja fell asleep again and dreamed that she and Ransel, her clan brother, were standing above the River of Stones, watching the extinction of their people charge toward them. "Those killers will become my friends," she told her clan brother, knowing as she spoke that he was nearly eight years dead. "One day I might be able to prevent this massacre, but I won't take any action."

He looked at her as if he did not know her, as if they hadn't crawled together as infants across the same clan-house floor, as if they hadn't told each other about their trysts, been each other's blade partner, and become *katrim* on the same day.

"My brother," she said in despair, "if you don't know me, then I don't know myself."

The Sainnites overran them, and a war horse trampled her, and with the spikes that bound its hooves the horse shattered her skull.

She awakened herself by her own cry of pain. She clasped her head in her hands and lay sobbing in the leaf mold, among the bodies of her people. The spirit boy, the dream guide, crouched over her. She shouted, "How long must I survive this massacre!"

"As long as your dead lie unburied," said the boy.

She sat up, and the pain was excruciating. She was and was not in the forest, and she could or could not save the life of her brother, who was dead. "Where is he?" she gasped. "Where is he now?"

"West."

"His direction of travel?"

"North."

She staggered to her feet and headed northward, through the dead, trampled, maimed, dismembered bodies: every one of her friends, all of her fellow *katrim*, every member of her clan, all her relations, every member of her tribe. The field of bodies stretched as far as she could see. So many dead! How could she possibly bury them all? "Show me the way," she begged her guide. He went ahead, and she followed, putting her feet where he put his. The dead grabbed at her ankles, saying with their stiff mouths, *Only vengeance will bring peace.*

"That's not right," she said. "For vengeance only made me vengeful."

You could have saved us and you did not, said the dead. *You loved your life more than you love your people. More than the past, which will now be forgotten. More than the future, which will not be remade.*

"I didn't dare! I didn't know how! What Grandmother Ocean did to save her people—how could *I* have such logic?"

They clutched at her. An axe of pain whacked through her skull, and she fell into their bony arms.

The world was wrong, turned sideways and filled up with trees. The boy, her companion, squatted beside her. She saw that his tunic was exquisitely woven, with a complicated, intertwining pattern of blue and orange upon a white ground, the border pattern of the na'Tarweins. She said, "But you are just a spirit. I'm the last—the last *katrim,* the last na'Tarwein, the last Ashawala'i. And I'm a madwoman, lying in a woodland talking to myself."

"Yes, Speaker," said the boy. "You tripped," he added helpfully.

"The dead burden me with their demands and accusations. They grab my ankles and make me fall."

"You tripped over a branch."

She drew up her knees and tried to rise, but pain slammed into her skull. She fell forward again, crying out in agony.

You are not hurt, Emil said. *You remember an old hurt, and that is all. Your pain is just the memory of pain.*

So he had said to her, year after year, reminding her patiently that there was a difference between past and present, reminding her of her living family and friends. By these methods, year after year, Emil had brought her back to life.

She raised her head, though the forest swirled around her. She got to her feet, holding a sapling for support. Slowly, her vision cleared, but she had lost all sense of direction. "Lead me northward," she said.

The boy walked, and she followed. Her water flask felt heavy, but when she raised it to her lips she got a mouthful of wet mud. Some broken pieces of Garland's bread remained in her satchel but seemed too difficult to eat. The boy walked ahead of her, light-footed.

When the dead clutched at her again, she called out to the boy: "I know stories—stories you've never heard—stories from the south, west, and east—stories from far countries. I am a collector of stories."

"That was true of you once, one of the times you were dead."

"It's true now, for I remember all that the storyteller knew. Shall I tell you a story?"

"Yes, Speaker."

She told a story and then another story. She told stories until her voice became like fingers brushing over dry paper. Once, the storyteller's gift had freed Zanja from sorrow. Now it freed her from madness. She did not hear the distant thunder, did not hear it drawing closer, did not notice the wind shaking the trees.

"Zanja, take shelter," said Karis.

She stared at the boy. "What?"

He spoke, and again he was Karis. "Take shelter, Zanja, I beg you. Do it now!"

Fat drops of rain struck Zanja's face. Lightning flashed, and birds startled forth all around her, a shrieking cloud of them, colliding into her and careening away. The trees groaned. The wind attacked in a barrage of dead leaves, broken twigs, green nuts.

"Where?" she yelled.

"Follow me!" The boy ran. She ran after him. A dead limb cracked and crashed down through the canopy. Green leaves filled the air, torn from their stems, then there was a torrent of rain.

"This way!" cried her guide.

She ran: ambushed, pummeled, assaulted by the storm. Now they were climbing. Water poured down the slope. She slipped in mud and fell to her hands and knees. Small stones bouncing in the torrent flung themselves at her. She crawled up the hillside.

"Here!" The boy sat upon a fallen tree and pointed at an old tangle of fallen limbs caught in boulders, roofed by rotted leaves, cemented by old slides of gravel. There was a hole. She crawled in, and smelled the stink of occupation. She worked her way deeper, until her hand touched living rock, and she was in a natural cavity that offered room to turn and sit, with her back against stone and her head pressing the tangled wooden ceiling. She was sheltered, but the storm seemed to be all around her. Thunder boomed and the rock shuddered. Wind roared and the forest squalled like a hunted animal. Rain trickled in, soaking her shoulder. She twisted around to suck and lap water from the rock.

A nose touched her arm. She turned slowly and saw a little fox. "Do you want a drink?"

At the sound of her voice, it ducked back into the burrow, but she saw its bright eyes watching as she shifted out of the way. She sat still until the little fox came out and began to lap water from the puddle. Two more foxes came out of hiding, then a fourth. They were fox children, too young to know that a creature like her could be dangerous. They took turns drinking from the puddle, then began to play, yipping and snarling at each other, chasing each other deep into the burrow and back out again. One raced across Zanja's lap.

A blinding explosion. A jolting concussion of thunder. A net of blue light crackled across the dark den. The foxes dove for safety. Alone, Zanja shuddered with fear. She smelled smoke—and here she lay, buried in tinder. But the smell dissipated. A thousand rocks pelted her hiding place. Some rattled in: lumps of ice. A tree screamed, fell, paused, crashed, screamed again. Then more, and still more, a forest of screams, a massacre of trees, and a sound like the roar of a thousand winds. She shut her eyes, but lightning flashed on her eyelids. She covered her ears, but she heard it in her memory, the bloody, chaotic end of her ancient people.

The rattle of hail became the hiss of rain. Zanja's horror and fear became mere exhaustion. She crawled to the puddle and lapped water like the foxes. Now she needed to piss, so she crawled outside and found the boy still sitting on the log, soaked to the skin, laughing with excitement. The slippery ground glittered with hail. She stripped off her wet clothing and bathed in the downpour.

The boy asked curiously, "Do falling trees always scream?"

"I don't know. I have never seen a storm like this."

"But it was marvelous!"

As the veil of rain began to lift, it revealed a destruction such as Zanja had never seen: trees stripped naked, limbs torn away and leaving raw wounds, trunks snapped in half and folded over, their golden flesh in rags. As far as she could see, the forest had been flattened and torn to pieces.

And nearby, trapped in a tangle of fallen limbs, a shipwreck.

"Oh, by the gods," she breathed. "The ship of air!"

Chapter 36

Tashar huddled in an ice-stiff blanket, shivering in the bitter cold. He had ceased to check the telltales and the firebox, for it had become too laborious and served no purpose. His mind wandered.

Maxew stood up awkwardly and staggered one way then the other. "Do something." Perhaps he thought *he* was the captain, the master of air! Tashar giggled derisively.

Maxew pointed at the telltale. "What that means."

"Up," Tashar said. "Up, up, up."

The air witch leaned over the side and vomited.

If the ship's sides were lower, the spasms of the witch's retching would make him go over the edge and fall to his death in a rain of his own spew. That would truly be funny, the funniest thing Tashar would ever see. His own laughter was funny: *haw-huh, haw-huh,* like a donkey being strangled. Maxew turned upon Tashar, careened into the stove, and fell. He lay atop the old man, gasping like a fish. Tashar laughed until he fainted.

He was awakened by tiny icicles, broken loose from the lines, piercing his skin like poisoned darts. The ship was falling. Its silken sail billowed, on the verge of collapsing. Exhausted and resigned, he fumbled at the firebox. His fingers were stiff and grotesquely swollen. Within the stove he found only embers. He nursed the fire back to life, one twig at a time. He could scarcely see, his eyelids were so swollen.

They had burned through nearly all of the poor fuel they had gathered. The sagging sail continued to billow. He patiently added bits of wood to the stove.

Maxew awakened, groaning. His face was grotesque, puffy even where it wasn't bruised, his eyes swollen to slits. He uttered a quacking sound and flapped his limbs uselessly.

They descended from gloom into darkness. Dark cloud swirled around the little ship, yanking it this way and that, wild dogs fighting over a shred of rotten meat. A terrible light flickered. Something attacked the silk overhead. Then Tashar was hit, and pellets of ice bounced on the wicker deck. Maxew jerked with surprise.

"It's hail," Tashar squawked. At first he had thought they were being shot at.

Lightning cut through the clouds. The crashing explosion of thunder jolted the ship sideways, knocking Tashar onto his back.

Buffeted, swinging, spinning in the grip of ferocious winds, the little ship dodged the powers of the storm. The wind ripped open the silk. Now we are dead, Tashar thought.

A terrific jolt. The stove jumped an arm's length above the deck, and Tashar jumped with it. Again. The wicker squealed. A spear of wood pierced through the deck. The stove lay on its side, spilling hot coals. The ripped silk streamed bravely through the rain, a gigantic, ragged flag. Then a tree grabbed it and fell over with the silk held in its clutches.

Had they landed in a waterfall? To keep from drowning, Tashar covered his face and breathed through his hands. His ears ached. He coughed, and pain stabbed in his ribs.

Time passed.

Unlike Willis, Saugus had been a poor speechmaker, so it was odd that Tashar remembered so vividly every word he ever said. "Some things are right. Some things are true. Some are just. These are the values that make us great. If we allow them to be taken from us, we become like animals who live only to continue living. But if we retain our beliefs without acting on them, we don't deserve to live. Only the cowards have meaning without risk. The Sainnites have made us cowards. If each person in Shaftal, every pig farmer, apple grower, trader, and sailor, acted upon what they *say* they believe, we could be free in a single day! We'd be free of murderers, free of those who collude with them, free of those who say we should forget the blood and injury and sorrow and death that has been visited upon us all these years. The people of Shaftal are cowards, but they will remember their courage when their leaders show them what to do!"

I will be a leader, Tashar thought. He would show the people of Shaftal that belief could become action. He would show them that he could stand up.

He crawled to his knees, grabbed the wicker gunwale, and dragged himself to his feet. With wet hands he wiped rain from his eyes and looked at a nightmare landscape, a wreckage that may once have been a forest. He saw some half-drowned deer in the distance, struggling wildly, entangled in limbs of fallen trees. Rain poured down, making the disaster sodden.

The air boat was wrecked, the wicker deck buckled and shattered, the long rags of the sail entangled in fallen trees.

His beautiful boat! Tashar wanted to weep.

But he was a leader! He crawled out of the basket to see what might be saved. They were trapped in branches, well above the ground. If he put his foot here, and then here, he might manage to climb down. But a branch broke under him, and he pitched into a sodden mess of vegetation that held, then broke, then held again, and broke again, until he landed in mud, buried in wet vegetation, with a cold little stream pouring into his collar. He flung away the mess, dully amazed to find himself unhurt. He seemed to have fallen into a well made up of twigs and shredded leaves. Through the opening at the top, he saw Maxew, water dripping from the strings of his hair. His face was less puffy, as Tashar's also seemed to be, for he could open his eyes fully again.

"What are you doing?" Maxew yelled.

Tashar could hardly hear him. Shaking the water from his ears made no difference.

"The silk!" Tashar yelled. "To keep the food dry!"

He got up and began to force a passage through the wreckage of the forest. It was rough work, and he soon wished he had told Maxew to toss down the hatchet. He broke branches with his hands, trampled a pathway with his feet, and then fell through and sprawled on the ground. He had broken into a pocket in the shattered forest, which felt almost like a house, roofed by silk that diverted the rain, walled by wood, built by a force that had flattened a forest. Safe, dry, on solid ground, he realized how terrified he had been.

He heard a muffled thud and then a clang. He dragged himself to his feet and returned down his path. Maxew was dropping supplies from the wrecked sky boat: water tins, waterproof sacks of food, sodden blankets. Tashar hauled everything to shelter. He had no idea where they were; they might spend days lost in this catastrophe.

Maxew dropped a knife to him and bellowed, "Cut some rope!"

"Why?"

"For the prisoner!"

"Why?"

"Do as I say!"

Tashar was silenced, but in silence he argued with his detested companion: Maxew didn't understand that they could not travel easily through this wrecked forest. To travel while carrying all their supplies and another person was certainly impossible. They would have to leave the old man behind, dead or alive, so why waste effort getting the man out of the air boat?

His resentment grew like steam under a pot lid, but he worked his way through the tangle toward the guide rope, cut it, and struggled for a long time to disentangle it from debris. When he had finally managed to get a piece long enough to be useful, he had to climb back up to the basket, which seemed impossible until Maxew pointed out a limb that went up at an angle and would serve as a ladder. Tashar climbed it—like climbing rigging, which he had used to do for fun when he was young, but he was heavier now, and appallingly tired.

At last he had climbed high enough that Maxew could haul him into the basket. The boy had wasted all that time improvising a sling out of a blanket and the lines that had once secured the sail to the boat. The prisoner's body was a long, unmoving shape.

"How can he breathe?" asked Tashar.

"He's dead." Maxew pushed his wet hair out of his face.

"Why bother with him, then?"

"So long as the G'deon thinks he's alive, he's bait."

"Bait for what? I think I deserve to know—"

"You will shut your mouth!"

Again, Tashar was silenced by air magic. He no longer disliked Maxew—he hated him bitterly.

A dead man is appallingly heavy. Both of them were gasping by the time they managed to hoist the body over the basket's edge. They lowered it to dangle above ground, apparently so that the false G'deon would not discover what had become of her advisor. Then they climbed down the ladder-like limb. They immediately became horribly lost. They could not see the wreck, or the body dangling from it like a fly from a spider's web. They could not see any silk overhead. They could not find the sheltered place where Tashar had taken their supplies. They floundered in one direction and another, staggering through tangles of broken wood and shredded leaves. Maxew shouted in frustration at Tashar's back, "This disaster is your fault!"

"I don't control the wind!"

"You should have brought a compass!"

"I *have* a fucking compass!"

So they continued, breathlessly bellowing at each other as they fought their way aimlessly through the debris, looking wildly around themselves. They were sodden, filthy, and furious; and Tashar thought it was too bad Maxew had contrived to get the knife back, because he wanted nothing more than to murder him.

They would find the body somehow, and bring it to shelter.

They would wait for the rain to stop. Maybe they could even build a fire.

Tashar would get his pistol out, ostensibly to check whether the powder was dry.

Maxew would be very surprised when Tashar shot him.

Lost in vengeful imagining, Tashar was nearly killed when the stove fell through the tangle and landed two steps in front of him. He looked up at the basket overhead, at the charred hole the stove had burned through the wicker deck. He began to laugh, and couldn't stop, until he walked into the dangling rope and fell silent with surprise. The rope had been cut, and the dead man had disappeared.

He felt a wave of relief. "He's gone!" he cried, before he realized Maxew was immediately behind him.

"If I had known you were an idiot—"

"I'm telling you—" Tashar turned to point at the rope.

A person blocked the path—*his* path which *he* had broken through the debris with such effort! He jerked back violently, and his head hit Maxew's battered face. Maxew shrieked.

"Sorry," said Tashar, absurdly.

"Fuck!" cried Maxew, with his hands protecting his nose and tears streaming from his eyes.

The woman blocked the path to the sheltered place where he had put their supplies. Tashar scarcely recognized her. In the Hanishport sitting room, she had been an alien. In this destroyed forest, she seemed to belong: a border woman, thin and wild, ferocious as a forest cat. She spoke. "You should have killed me."

Their water tins were dangling from her hand. She flung them, and they landed with a clanging crash at Tashar's feet. Something about the dagger in her hand turned Tashar's knees to water. He wished his companion was in front of and not behind him.

"Zanja na'Tarwein!" cried Maxew, and his voice tried to be terrible. "You will submit to me!"

She flung a food sack onto the tins. It was the smallest of the sacks and was not particularly full. "When you killed my brother in front of me, when I lay paralyzed with my brains leaking out of my skull, when there were hundreds of you, bearing hundreds of weapons, then you *might* have been able to kill me."

"Do to her what you did to the old man," Tashar whispered to Maxew.

"Can't you tell she's out of her mind? I have no power over lunatics! Pick up the food and the tins, and let's go."

Tashar felt dazzled by anger. "This is *my* path, *my* ship, *my* belongings!"

"You've been robbed, then." Maxew pushed impatiently around Tashar and grabbed the tins and supplies. "That dagger in her hand is Norina Truthken's blade. It's forged with earth power and wielded by a trained warrior." He pushed past Tashar again. "And you want to fight her bare-handed? You'll be dead before you feel the cut."

The woman stood very still, but Tashar had seen enough trained fighters to realize that her stillness meant she was poised to leap forward. And what did Tashar want to fight her for? For a shattered basket, some torn silk, and a dead body?

Maxew had already departed, and Tashar could hear the tins clanging and the branches breaking as he fought his way through the fallen trees. Tashar began to back away.

The woman watched him; and even after Tashar could no longer see her, long after that dreadful storm had passed by, and even at nightfall when he and Maxew fell down to sleep, Tashar could feel that ferocious gaze.

Chapter 37

The storm dragged a mantle of darkness over the forest, its leading edge flickering with brilliant, blinding columns of lightning. Chaen watched the storm in fearful amazement.

"No good comes of water magic," Seth muttered.

Once again, the entire company had come to a halt. The seer stared toward the storms with naked eyes. The Truthken stood beside Karis. The cook, who seemed to have forgotten that he was a Sainnite captain, had put his hand on Karis's broad back.

Chaen could hear a nearby group gathered around a Paladin, reciting words in Shaftalese. She opened her sketchbook and studied her notes about Maxew—more questions than answers. What kind of son was he? How old? Had she ever called him "Max"? How had she raised him without a home or family? When she tried to remember, there were fragments that she knew were important: the pennies that accumulated too slowly, the paintings and drawings done for money, the tedious fairs, the meals eaten among strangers. She remembered the crawling fear that greeted her at every dawn and went to bed with her every night. All this she had endured, for a son who did not want her to remember him, who even now might be falling out of the sky.

Karis snatched the spectacles from Medric's hand and put them on his face. "Don't you see anything?"

He didn't answer.

Karis began dropping everything she carried on the ground. Seth hastily took the baby from her.

"Wait," Norina said.

They argued. Then Karis stood staring at the storm as Norina spoke briefly with Kamren and the Sainnite general. "I'll mark the trail," Chaen heard Norina say.

Chaen grabbed Seth by the shirttail as she passed. "Will you do something with my knapsack? And loan me your water flask?"

Then Chaen was chasing Karis and the Truthken, running through their dust. Norina glanced at her as she drew up to them. "Do you know how to mark a trail?"

"Yes."

"We'll take turns, then."

Not another word was said for many hours.

Karis walked straight as an arrow's flight and never checked her bearings by looking at the sun, at the horizon, or backwards at the hilltop where she had started. She plowed through small shrubs, strode over boulders, and barged across streambeds and rough ground. Chaen followed at a dogged, plodding jog, each foot plopping to ground like a bag of rocks dangling from the unfeeling sticks of her legs. Every hundred steps or so, she and Norina stopped to mark the trail with a cairn of hastily gathered stones. Karis moved away from them so quickly that they then were forced to run full-tilt to catch up.

The distant, gray smear of forest became a scattering of outlying trees that were dwarfed, twisted, shriveled, and even dead in that hostile borderland. As these outlying trees thickened, Norina began cutting blazes into the trunks, and Chaen wrapped her hands in the tail of her shirt, because the rock-gathering had sanded her palms raw. Norina made a very quiet sound—startling because she had been silent the entire afternoon. And then she was running, leaving the marking unfinished. When Chaen caught up, Norina was on her knees. Karis sprawled on the ground, ungainly as a fighter who has been struck dead by a devastating blow.

The Karis lifted her face out of the dirt and spoke, her voice a scraping of fingernails on rough stone. "She has Emil. She has driven them away."

"Is Emil dead?" Norina's voice seemed harsh rather than concerned: she had been terrified, and fear made her angry.

Karis heaved herself to her knees. She wiped her face with the filthy tail of her shirt. "He's dying, but I can keep him alive. Zanja is putting him in earth, so I can reach him."

"At what distance?" Norina wiped the sweat and anger from her face.

"I expect we'll be walking half the night."

"Are you hurt?"

"Not much." Karis rubbed an elbow.

"The next time you need to be inside Zanja, sit down first."

Chaen helped to lift Karis to her feet.

Karis said, "Zanja knows I hear her, but she won't talk to me. What is she concealing?"

"She's probably not in her right mind."

Norina asked Karis for her knife and gave it to Chaen. She said over her shoulder, "For marking trees. Her blades don't get dull."

Karis was already three strides away, while Chaen stood flat-footed.

The dry dirt was pockmarked. As Chaen chased Karis through the woods, the dirt became mud. Whenever a breeze shook the trees, a shower fell, and they became soaked to the skin, slipping in mud, then wading in water. Only two days ago, Chaen had lain in these woods on dry ground beneath a dusty sky, going blind without realizing it. This didn't seem the same forest, nor did she seem the same person.

As Chaen and Norina trotted past each other, marking the trees, Karis disappeared from sight, then from hearing. The trees threw black shadows on the vivid ground. Chaen stumbled through a litter of leaves and twigs torn from the trees by the storm wind that had now passed.

Norina came up behind her. "It's too dark to continue marking the trail."

Chaen carved a second mark across the one she had just completed, signifying the trail's end. "Take this knife away from me—I'm falling in love with it."

Chaen was overwhelmed by her desire to lie down. But Norina set out after Karis, fast-moving and sure-footed, while Chaen could only stagger behind her. Perhaps Norina had been forged by earth magic, and therefore never dulled or lost her edge. Perhaps Zanja, who had scarcely slept or even rested, also was metal on the earth witch's forge.

With the light failing, it had become nearly impossible to distinguish the traces of Karis's passage in the debris. But then Norina spotted some footprints in mud, and they lurched into a run. Karis had continued to crash through bushes and over boulders, but at least she walked around the trees. As twilight became darkness, Norina took a cunning lantern from a pocket and lit it with a match. When she dangled this little light from her hand by its chain, its flame cast just enough light to throw Karis's deep footprints into relief.

Abruptly, they caught up with her. Braced against a tree, she was saying, "Please stay with him. I'll be there by midnight. Stay with him." Then, she was saying, "Return to him. Zanja, I beg you."

Chaen waited with her back against a tree trunk, not daring to sit down lest she be unable to get up, not even daring to shut her eyes lest she doze off. Norina blew out her flame, waited for the tiny lantern to cool, and put it in a pocket.

"She won't heed me," Karis said. "She won't explain herself. She has gone into the woods again."

Chaen asked, "Is she still chasing my son, Maxew? Is he injured also?"

"Maxew and his companion are able to travel. They're going west, and Zanja is going southwest."

Chaen said drearily, "I wanted to be there when Norina caught up to him."

"Well, obviously," said the Truthken.

Chaen had not expected to conceal her motives from Norina. She did wonder why the Truthken had allowed her to accompany them, but now it didn't matter. She said, "I can't go any farther. You'll have to leave me here."

Karis came out of the shadows. Her big, hot, sticky hand clasped Chaen's forearm. Cold water dripped from her hair onto Chaen's face. When Karis drew away, Chaen felt like she could follow her to the end of the earth.

A wind small enough to fit in a bottle had leveled the forest.

They stood staring into the moonlit tangle of fallen trees.

Karis said, with scathing bitterness, "I'm glad that old woman is dead." She stepped forward.

The moon set. Surely the night was half over. Karis continued, inexorable, breaking through the tangle by brute force. Chaen struggled behind her, not weary any longer, but dazed by sleeplessness, so it began to seem as if Karis was not going forward by her own will, and instead was being pulled, like a fish with a hook in its gut. Finally she was landed, in a serene pavilion roofed by varnished silk, walled by damp blankets, warmed by a smoldering fire, and decorated by a laundry line: it even smelled like a cottage on washday. A meal had been laid upon a flattened canvas bag: hard biscuits, potted meat, jam, pickles, a tin of tea, and a pot of water to go on the fire. But there was no smiling host greeting her long-expected visitors.

Zanja might not have been in her right mind, but this haven was a creation of love, not madness.

That message had not been left for Chaen, but only she heeded it. Karis and Norina both rushed to the naked man who slept there in a bed of leaves and twigs. Karis fell to her knees, swept back the leafy blanket, and covered his chest with her hand.

When Chaen had her sketchbook again, she would draw this scene from memory: the dying Paladin, clean shaven, his hair combed back and tied in a tail, his face gaunt and somber but marked by deep lines of joy. She would draw the G'deon, hunched over with her hand upon his heart. She would draw the Truthken kneeling at his other side covering her face with her hand, although she would never flinch from the ugliest of secrets. That drawing could one day be an etching in a book of history, but the readers of the book would only remember the murderer, Maxew of the Midlands, and not the artist.

Karis said, "He has been beaten. Some ribs are broken. He is burned. He has had nothing to eat or drink for days—probably not since Hanishport."

"All this you can heal," said the Truthken. "And yet . . ." Norina took a breath, composed herself, and said, "And yet he's dying."

"I can't even awaken him. I don't know why."

"Karis, if I have any hope of repairing what Maxew did to him, Emil must be aware enough to respond to my voice."

In the heavy darkness Karis was silent, on her knees, holding Emil's heart.

Chaen scarcely knew anything about Emil, yet she had observed the reverence that others held for him. Disguised as a shabby man, he had stood near her, gazing the other way as she prepared to shoot the G'deon with a poisoned arrow. What steadiness that must have taken, to let her commit that crime so he could capture her in the net of the law. And with what insouciance he had bowed to her, like a player upon a stage, when she realized she had been tricked.

An outsider sees from a distance, and sometimes distance is a gift. Chaen said, "Emil must have an injury that prevents him from awakening."

Karis said, "So I thought. But his head isn't injured."

Chaen saw the Truthken grip Karis by the forearm, as if she also could reinvigorate a person by a touch. "J'han has seen people who survived smothering or drowning, but never opened their eyes. They were alive without living. Sometimes their families let them lie in that state for many days rather than permit a healer to deliver to the stricken person a merciful death. They couldn't believe that the person would not awaken."

A tree fell in the distance. There was a startled outcry of birds, and confused small creatures squeaked with alarm and scuttled through the debris. Silence gradually settled in once again.

Karis moved her left hand to Emil's chest and lay her right upon his forehead. "Emil." Her voice caught and tore like a bramble dragging across cloth. "Emil, speak to me. Tell me what to do."

Emil did not answer.

Chaen slept on bare ground. When she awoke, the fire had become ashes, and the stars had disappeared. Toward the east, through the devastated forest, she could see the pink light of dawn. She leapt to her feet, staggered, caught her balance, then heard again the voice she had thought was commanding her to awaken. The voice had been summoning Emil, not her.

Karis lay beside him now, shirtless, skin against skin, with her arm wrapped around him and her face against his shoulder. Every muscle in her powerful back and shoulders was knotted with effort. Norina crouched over the dying man, though her puffy eyes and the black dirt smeared on her cheek suggested she had slept, however briefly. "Remember!" she said, in a voice like the clang of a gong. "Remember the apple orchard, that first spring, when the trees were still in bloom, how you used to take Leeba there and sit with her while you studied philosophy. You said the sound of the bees and the weight of the baby helped you to finally understand Temil's argument about social balance. Remember that, Emil."

Chaen noticed then that Emil's eyes were open, but his empty stare and slack expression only made him seem less alive.

Norina said, "Karis, he is unaware of me."

Karis murmured something, and Norina spoke again. "Remember the night you and Medric made love upon a bed of books, in a storehouse by the river. Remember what you thought, that none of your old friends would understand how you could love a Sainnite."

Norina called Emil again and again, reminding him of something he had done, said, or written. Chaen began to perceive his life: insignificant moments, like when Zanja taught him a word of her native language, significant moments like the night Karis named him head of the council of Shaftal, when that council did not even exist. He had lived a remarkable life, a life of sharp turnings and reverses, of new hopes invented in the cold ashes of old, a life of purpose and understanding, of unsought love and unexpected joy. Yet he had remained true, not by refusing to change but by continually rediscovering his balance. He had lived as a true Paladin. Now the spirit of that joyful, intelligent man was gone—gone beyond reach or recovery.

The rising sun spread a carpet of light and shadow across the pavilion. Karis rose up and stood swaying, and her head pushed the ceiling of stiff silk, and water began to pour over the edge, several arm's lengths away. Chaen put the pot on the fire she had relit. Karis staggered into the tangle, then returned, buttoning her trousers, to sit awkwardly beside the fire.

Her hair had half the forest in it—twigs, leaves, broken bits of dirt and debris, even a spider that made a leap for her shoulder, crawled down her arm, and escaped. Her big hand, injured as she forced a passage through the fallen forest, had begun to drip blood. Chaen made a pot of tea and gave her some. Scarlet drops of blood formed and fell as Karis sat in a sort of daze Chaen recognized, having seen it before. After battle, people were stunned by a fatigue that was like this, a draining of the resources, leaving emptiness. It mattered not at all whether a victory had been won. It felt like defeat.

Wasn't it hard enough, thought Chaen, to merely get a harvest from Shaftal's cold, black soil in time to close the doors on winter and survive until spring came again? Why do we also struggle with each other, over what matters and what things mean, over ideas, for land's sake? Karis lifted her hand as if to rub her face and looked at the blood with surprise.

Chaen said, "You must have hurt yourself when you broke through the tangle."

"Seth will bandage it. She's almost here."

"Shall I pull out the splinters?"

Chaen went to Norina, and the Truthken traded the tweezers from her pocket for Chaen's porringer of tea. The scar that slashed across the Truthken's face made her look cruel and sardonic, but if Chaen avoided looking at that part of her face, she saw instead an unflagging devotion, and inhuman discipline. She saw what her son could have been.

She put a fresh pot on the fire for the people who would soon arrive and sat with Karis's hands spread palm up on her knee, picking out the splinters. After a while, she began to feel a grim amusement. Like Emil, she also seemed to be doomed or destined to a life of reverses, a life that was like a drawing erased and redrawn over and over, until the surface became furry and full of holes. Every time it was erased, there was unbearable sorrow, and yet she drew her life again.

"Are you all right," said Karis, her voice clotted and hollow.

"I've survived worse."

"I'm sorry to hear that."

"Less than ten days ago, I was about to kill you. And now, to know how my son has injured you is breaking my heart."

Norina's voice spoke at a distance. "That guilt is not yours to carry. No one could have raised Maxew better than you did. You pursued the way of least harm, with all your resources and resolve. You found Saugus, and you thought he was like a Truthken. That is a mistake he helped you to make."

And then Chaen remembered a boy who was her son, tense with excitement: "Mother, he is an air witch!" That was all, just a flash of memory, but she could hold it in her mind, and it awakened her heart, so she felt the impatience and terror and hopelessness of her life as the mother of an air child. And she also remembered that she had loved him.

Karis said, "Nori, after Medric has seen Emil, I will let him die."

"It's the right thing to do," Norina said. She rested her hand on Emil's shoulder. Time passed, and then a distant crackling and crashing announced that others were struggling toward them. The dogs arrived first and danced around Karis, so by the time the people came her tears had been licked away. One by one, the Paladins fought into the clearing, wet and filthy, scratched and ragged, red-eyed and resolved. Each one looked at Emil, and each one's face fell. All of them stood aside until Medric entered, holding on to Kamren's shirttail, supported from behind by Garland and closely followed by Seth.

Medric stopped still, his face and gaze nearly as blank as Emil's. Then he shook his keepers loose, stepped over the fire and firewood, as sure-footed as a deer in a meadow, and crossed the pavilion to Emil. Norina offered her hand, but he knelt without assistance and only then took the spectacles from his pocket and put them on.

"Well, Emil," he said, as though they had just sat down for a chat. "What shall the historians say about you? That you died with your life still unfinished? That a boy whom you could have killed one-handed shot you down with his voice? Or will they say that you stood in ecstasy upon your hilltop while a star translated your flesh to light?" He put his bony, ink-stained hand to Emil's face. He stroked his husband's cheek. "Or will they say that Zanja na'Tarwein secretly tutored you in how to find your way back from the land of the dead?"

Emil looked at the seer. His forehead creased. His lips moved.

"I suppose you're calling me a ninny," Medric said.

Emil's much-used laugh lines deepened. "Yes," he said.

Norina uttered a sharp exclamation.

Karis blundered to her feet, turned her ankle stepping on a piece of wood, and caught her balance by grabbing Chaen's shoulder.

"He's lost his syntax," said the seer to the Truthken.

Norina gazed into the silly man's eyes for a moment. She looked down at Emil. "Is that all?" she said.

Emil gazed up at her: serious, thoughtful, and no longer absent. "Surprise," he said. His friends all rushed upon him.

The main body of Sainnites was encamped at the edge of the forest. This Seth told Chaen, after Chaen had startled her greatly by embracing her.

"You don't look like you got much sleep."

"I spent the night sitting upright with water soaking my trousers. Is that a mushroom in your hair?"

They stood laughing, poking fun at each other's disarray.

Seth said, "That emptiness in you doesn't seem as empty."

"I hoped I would find my son," said Chaen, "and I did. I remember his face, and his voice, and a feeling."

"But it might have been easier if you had not remembered. That boy of yours is being pursued by the law and power of Shaftal."

"And he's pursued by his mother," Chaen said.

For a while everyone did what was necessary, and some even did what they enjoyed. They climbed the trees and shouted the measurements of the wrecked air ship to a Paladin who, with a rock for a desk, noted them on a sketch. At the same time, they salvaged parts of the ship and sail and tossed them down to Karis, who made of them an ingenious litter for Emil. From the single pot, Garland served tea, then porridge, then tea again, until all the food Zanja had stolen from the air sailors had been eaten, and even the tea tin was empty.

Emil was heavier than he looked; the litter bearers were weary when they started, and what they traveled through was no woodland but a nightmare. With Medric assigned to carry only himself, Kamren had sorted the rest of them into teams of three: two teams to carry Emil while one team rested. But without help, Medric could not go two paces without falling or becoming entangled. And even six people working together could not easily thread a man through, over, or under the branches, limbs, and trunks of fallen trees. Soon Emil was the only one who had not lost his temper.

The long summer morning had become afternoon when Chaen, who was taking a turn at leading the way, leaned her weight on a stiff branch to widen the passage, felt it snap, and fell into the arms of the Sainnite general who was waiting there with a dozen burly soldiers. Chaen said fervently, "I'm very glad to see you, General Clement!"

"How peculiar that must feel," Clement replied

Karis had sent the dogs ahead with a note to Clement written with pen and paper borrowed from a Paladin, wrapped in a strip of the flying ship's silk, and tied around Feldspar's neck. Seth said, "Feldspar is a follower. With Granite in front, that gave Feldspar some protection, so the note wouldn't be ripped . . ."

Chaen said, "The note reached Clement, and she knew to come meet us, and it was a success."

Seth's shirt was wet, limp, and filthy, and she had tied the tails in knots so they wouldn't catch in the brambles. Her eyes were red with sleeplessness; her weathered, sagging face looked like it might tear up like a rag if she smiled. "We earth bloods do carry on about how things work."

"Sensible effort solves problems. It is a soothing fact."

"It's an obvious fact."

"Not in my life."

"Your life is out of balance, then."

"It certainly has not had enough earth in it." Chaen had taken Seth's arm, without thinking about it. "And I find myself liking that soldier of yours."

"What, because Clement shows up and gets things done?"

"That's a virtue. I never imagined I would ever see virtue in a Sainnite!"

The path narrowed, they crossed a brook by balancing on stones, and she and Seth were separated. After a while Kamren was walking beside her. "Karis tells me your son is traveling west. But you are traveling east."

"That is true, Master Paladin."

He scratched his chin, where his beard was sprouting, more gray than brown. Brambles had snagged his woolen waistcoat, and his shirt was torn open at the shoulder seam. The bottle of wind that he carried at his waist had lost many of its decorative shells. His boots seemed to be made of mud. "What does this mean?" he asked.

Fire people's tendency to perceive significance where there was none could be irritating. "It means you don't have to chase me."

"That's good of you." Truth is, I'm becoming convinced of some things that make me want to stay with you. But I suppose I'll have to make some kind of decision eventually."

Kamren considered for a time. "What I have to tell you would be said far better by Emil. But I must do the best that I can. Saugus, Maxew, and your friends, possibly all the friends you have, pose a grave danger to Shaftal. So long as they require our time and resources in dealing with them, Shaftal cannot recover from this awful history."

"But I don't have to choose one side and betray the other."

"Because there are no sides? You see that now? But those people who do think there *are* sides will call you a traitor."

They took two more steps, or three, certainly no more than four, and even at their slow and shuffling pace not much time passed. Yet Chaen felt like she had traveled a far distance. "I should make some Paladin friends, then, because they don't make people choose sides."

"You have a Paladin friend," he said.

"And I'll accept your friendship gladly! But you have killed people, like I have. You, Clement, Seth, all of you, have killed, or may have killed, my friends. And I have killed yours. Can we forget that?"

"My friend of twenty years was standing watch at the door of Travesty and was the first one assassinated by your friends. We were trading a book back and forth, and she was reading it that night, and now I can't bear to finish it." Then he said, "But if I killed even one person because she was killed, I would dishonor that friendship, and she would tell me so. She would tell me that our war with the Sainnites began long before the Fall of the House of Lilterwess. When they first came to Shaftal, we used coarse tools to separate ourselves from the strangers who were seeking refuge on our coast, and that is how the war began. But even after the Fall of the House of Lilterwess, my friend would say, we should have remembered that it was our duty to know the difference between alliance and truth."

Her glance caught him rubbing his eyes on a sleeve that wanted mending as badly as it wanted washing. He said, "What a maddening life it is, to be committed to a way of living while also remaining open to all possibilities."

"That way seems impossible, actually."

"It's possible if I embrace uncertainty. Your old leader, Willis, when he served under Emil in South Hill Company, was always at odds with him because Willis knew his purpose while Emil lived in doubt. Eventually, both of them found a G'deon to follow. Willis found her in a dream, a G'deon who confirmed his beliefs and fulfilled his desire. Emil found her in reality and every day struggled beside her, in humbling uncertainty, to serve the land. Both Willis and Emil chose a G'deon, but Willis found what he wanted, and Emil was surprised by what he never expected."

"I never believed in Willis's G'deon, and I respected Saugus because he didn't believe in her either. I thought this meant he was a man of principle rather than superstition."

"No doubt he is a man of principle," said Kamren. "But they are the wrong principles."

Chapter 38

At the edge of the woods, the Sainnites had made an orderly and organized camp. There the soldiers, in scattered teams, were practicing a peculiar sort of fighting, with one soldier in each group using weapons to fight all the others, whose hands were empty. The scuffles often ended with jokes and laughter, and sometimes with all of them rolling in the dirt. Many lines of laundered clothing flapped like funeral flags in the sunshine, and a giant stewpot bubbled over with suds, into which a limping old soldier tossed Chaen's dirty shirt. The Paladins who had returned from the woods were bathing and shaving; Karis was pulling on a clean shirt; Emil was being walked like a puppet between two soldiers toward the latrines; and Seth changed the baby's diapers. Chaen wanted to lie down and sleep, but instead she found her knapsack and sat down to sketch the pictures she had been carrying in her memory.

There was a convergence: Garland with a pot—tea, probably; Seth singing to the good-tempered baby; Kamren looking nearly cheerful as he buttoned a fresh shirt; the general, her captains surrounding and then departing from her. Karis had knelt in the shade by a blanket on which Norina unrolled a very large map, and around this the people were gathering. Chaen heard someone calling, noticed Medric wandering confusedly among the trees, and with much effort got up and limped over to him.

"It's Chaen," she said, not knowing if he was too blind to recognize her.

He took her arm. "Did you see that Emil can walk a little, although he's very weak? Garland should make him some of his special porridge."

Medric's filthy shirt was shredding at the hem. His sunburned face had peeled, and the peeled places had been sunburned again. He limped as painfully as the old soldier who slowly and stiffly hung the laundry out to dry. "The cards Zanja cast for you," he said. "Do you remember the one that showed a young man carrying an old man on his back?"

In that illustration, the young man walked naked and barefoot on a steep and stony path, but the old man was magnificently robed, and the pattern of the fabric blended with the background of trees, hills, clouds, and sky. The young man's tongue hung out, and his hair stood around his head in a tangle. The old man's face was serene.

"The Wisdom That Must Be Carried," said Chaen.

"Oh, I like that name! Do you know, some Paladins are fretting that if we think of new meanings for the glyphs to replace the old, then the lost knowledge will continue to be lost. But how did the old meanings come to be known, anyway? People who were like us studied the illustrations for the first time, as we are doing, and decided what to call them."

"What were you going to say about that illustration?" Chaen asked, possibly with too much patience.

"The card-casting didn't reveal your future only. Your question was not just *What should I do?* It also was *What must we do*? For you have become a member of this company, and your future is our future. All of us must carry the burden of wisdom, and that burden will be horribly heavy."

"Like carrying Emil."

"We will carry him, though—and many others as well."

Her heart sank. "But I can scarcely carry myself."

"That may be true. Yet you're carrying me." As if to prove his point, he leaned more heavily on her arm.

At the group that clustered around Karis and the map, many now were sipping hot tea.

"Is that a map?" asked Medric. "What does it look like?"

Chaen said, "It is very intricate. The coastline is like a frayed hem at Karis's knees. The forest is within her reach. The Shimasal Road is a straight line from left to right."

Responding to a question, Karis pointed at a place in the forest, saying, "The air ship crashed there."

Chaen murmured to Medric, "A Paladin's outspread hand is serving as a desk for a pen and ink stone. Norina is marking the place on the map."

"Where is the storm-wrack?" someone asked.

Chaen told Medric, "Karis is showing an area with her fingertip, and Norina is marking it with a pen. The southern point is about a quarter of the way between Shimasal and the crossroad, and the northern point is about halfway. The storm didn't affect any cities or villages, but it destroyed many furlongs of forest."

Watching the Truthken carefully annotate the already much-annotated document, it occurred to Chaen that Norina's entire life was mapped there, on the landscape of the country she served. Karis took an iron bolt out of her pocket and placed it in the area of storm-wrack, perhaps halfway between the shipwreck and the road. She said, "Maxew and his companion are here, heading westward. I imagine they're trying to reach the road."

Norina said, "Can you tell us anything about his companion? Now that you have seen him through Zanja's eyes?" Something in her tone made the listeners shift uneasily. Weary though the Truthken certainly was, she still focused on the two fleeing criminals with the eagerness of a dog chasing a rabbit.

Karis said, "It's the man who met Chaen at the tide clock."

All turned to Chaen, except the Truthken who continued to examine the map. When she averted her unsettling gaze, Chaen realized, it was a kind of politeness.

Chaen said, "His name is Tashar. He's a scion of a great house—of Hanishport—but I don't know which one. Perhaps it's him who watched us through the peephole."

"Lora, no doubt." Norina rubbed her eyes with rough, impatient cruelty. "Perhaps he imported the snake poison."

Chaen said, although it probably didn't matter, "When Saugus recruited Tashar, he had abandoned his family and become a thief. Sometime later, Tashar returned home to his family, and after that we no longer needed to beg for money."

"The House of Lora gave money to Death-and-Life?" asked Karis.

"Well, I assume he stole it from them."

Norina said, "Medric, is it possible that these two young men will lead us to Saugus?"

"They lack vision," said Medric.

Everyone looked sharply at him, and Kamren even smiled and said, "So do we all, Master Seer."

"Yes, but *this* blind man knows when he is blind, and so has carefully chosen which guide to follow. Zanja, *she* has the vision."

"Well then," said Norina, "Where is Zanja?"

Karis took another bolt and stood it on its head on the map. "There. She's going south and west. I don't know why."

Chaen said, for Medric's sake, "Zanja is nearly beyond the stormwrack at the southern edge." She added, "How can she continue to move at that pace with so little rest?"

"By earth and fire," said Medric.

Karis said, "She wept over Emil. She seemed to believe he was lost. She loves him dearly, as she loved her brother who was killed in front of her when he tried to save her life after the massacre. Perhaps she thinks they are the same person, and her brother is killed again. Perhaps she isn't following a vision and is merely deranged. I don't know."

The cook spoke. "Karis, must we decide at this moment what to do next? I think you should rest!"

She looked at him. He stared fearlessly back.

"Garland is correct," said Kamren. "And since it seems that you are driving Zanja even as she is driving you, can't you stop her, so that both of you can rest?"

"Oh, no," Medric said. "Don't do that. It's a terrible idea. Emil would say so!"

Karis looked at the seer, apparently puzzled by the configuration of advisors that surrounded her.

But Norina said dryly, "How many people are required to make one Emil? Is *twelve* the answer?"

"Counting you and Clement, it's fourteen," said Kamren.

"So few?" Karis wiped her filthy face on her ragged shirttail. "Where is Zanja going, Master Seer?"

Medric said, "I can't see the map, but I'm sure the answer is easy to determine. If she was shot from the shipwreck like an arrow, what would she hit?"

The cook, Garland, bent over to lay his spoon on the map, with the bowl at the shipwreck and the handle pointing past the arrow that was Zanja. The map was crowded with details—perhaps not every building and tree in Shaftal, but a good many of them. The area ahead of Zanja contained a scattering of hills with farms flowing between them like rivers. One hill, on the far side of the Shimasal Road, was marked with a few words written in red.

"To the House of Lilterwess," said Kamren.

"Shaftal's broken heart," said another Paladin, perhaps a poet.

Norina said, "A rubble-covered hilltop."

"The Shame of the Sainnites," said Clement. She knelt, and Chaen noticed jealously that her trousers were clean. She rotated Garland's spoon so the handle still pointed at the ruin, but now the bowl lay at the eastern edge of the forest. "We are around here, yes? So we can reach the ruin without going through the storm-wrack."

Norina said, "But we *must* follow the criminals. To do anything else is a disservice to Shaftal. And we don't have any idea why Zanja is going to the ruin. But Maxew and Tashar may lead us to Saugus."

The Paladins murmured to each other, until one said, "Madam Truthken, we Paladins must follow Zanja. But we could divide the company and go both directions."

The general replied, "We could, but there's a cost. If Saugus has as few as thirty followers with him, our divided company won't outnumber him by enough soldiers to capture them without bloodshed."

Garland added, "And two supply lines is unworkable."

Seth said, "Our numbers will be further diminished anyway, since many of us can barely walk. To catch up with Zanja, we'll have to run."

"Who can't walk will be carried," Clement said.

Many of them looked at her, mostly in disbelief. Chaen, having heard Medric say those same words just a short while earlier, looked at him sharply.

Clement spoke in the soldier's language. Garland began to speak, and hesitated. "What the general said is difficult to say in Shaftalese."

Medric said, "Her word refers to a kind of honor that is an aspect of a way of living, a path. If you consider Sainnites to be a kind of order, then you might call it *The Way of Soldiers*. The Sainnites carry each other, and that is both their pride and their wisdom."

One Paladin hastily took out a sheet of paper and began to write on it, using another's back as a table, apparently adding Clement's word and Medric's explanation to their dictionary.

Norina said, "The way of soldiers dictates that no one be abandoned?"

"No one alive."

Still on one knee, Clement turned to Karis. "Madam G'deon, allow my people to serve Shaftal as soldiers. Let us demonstrate what we are capable of."

Karis clasped her big hands and rested them on her knees. Everyone there waited as if they were of one mind, although the elemental contradictions in this group should have made agreement impossible.

Karis shifted her weight. "Maxew could be going to Shimasal or anywhere else. But unless he flies in the air again, or floats upon water, he can't escape me. So let him go where he likes for now. I will follow Zanja. Keep up with me if you can."

Clement said, "Prepare to abandon your belongings. Everything—everything—must be left behind."

The group dispersed. The Truthken began emptying her pockets of clever devices. One by one, she lay them on the map, where the story of her life was inscribed upon the land. Chaen would carry spare socks, of course, as was only sensible, but she needed to think about what else she needed to jam into her pockets. Medric had not let go of her, though, and when she glanced at him, his expression terrified her. If this ridiculous young man was seeing the future, it was a future of devastating sorrow.

A Paladin approached. "Madame Truthken." For a fleeting moment, Chaen saw how tired Norina was. "What has happened?"

"Emil. He says *coming*, and *children*. Then he taps his head and says *air*."

"Air children are coming?" said a Paladin. "Did you send for them, Norina?"

"I did the exact opposite!" The Truthken's face had become the color of sun-bleached linen.

Medric let go of Chaen's arm and walked away.

Chapter 39

After three days of walking, Anders thought it was pleasant to ride. By the next morning, he could hardly endure it. The Two complained about their discomfort, until Braight said that she would kill them if they didn't shut up. The soldier, even though his vocabulary of verbs was limited to *eat* and *piss*, remonstrated with her—not knowing what a waste of words that was in any language—and then, more effectually, reorganized their order of travel, so Serrain and Anders separated Braight from the Two.

Somewhat past sunrise, the shadow on the western horizon had resolved into forest. The soldier, who was walking beside Anders, tapped his foot and pointed. On the straggling edge of the trees, four people stood. Beyond them, a pile of gear and some smoking ashes marked a recently abandoned camp.

Minga shadowed her eyes with her hand. "That's Karis. Norina to her right."

"Karis!" said the soldier, sounding relieved. He certainly had not enjoyed being their escort.

Norina walked ahead of the others to meet them. Norina would not punish him for his disobedience to any greater degree than she punished the others—for she certainly had made it clear that they all were responsible for anything any of them did. Still, it had been his idea to leave Watfield, and it seemed right that he bear the brunt of the blame. "I'll tell her what has happened," he said.

Braight, squinting into the distance, said, "The rest of their party are gone, but those four waited for us. You see how worried they are."

"She's furious," Anders said. "And she's worn out."

"Look deeper," said Serrain.

Anders looked deeper. Norina Truthken was terrified.

Anders's left leg had gone numb, and the soldier had to help him dismount. As he limped to Norina, he saw that all four of them were in terrible condition: Karis was gaunt; Garland's shirttail was ripped; and Medric, sunburned and ragged, normally inscrutable, had become unfathomable.

Anders said, "Madam Truthken, we felt that we had no choice but to disobey your instructions, because we discovered that something awful happened at Travesty, and no one would—" He stopped, for a Truthken's decisions should be so reasonable and principled that they require no justification. He began again. "We realized that Bran, the housekeeper, is the rogue air witch. And we think Maxew is working with him."

"Yes," she said without surprise. "What else?"

He said, "I'm sorry, Norina . . . J'han has been killed."

Norina shut her eyes, then opened them. "How do you know this?"

Anders explained how they had found J'han's body.

"What about Leeba?" she eventually asked.

"All we found was the tail of her toy lizard."

Norina turned away and walked toward Karis. Anders hesitated, then followed.

Norina always told Karis the truth, directly and bluntly, with no attempt to manage or manipulate her. Anders's own struggle to always be forthright with his demanding teacher and fellow students had taught him that this was an accomplishment of excruciating difficulty. But now, as Norina said to Karis, "Bran—Saugus—has kidnapped Leeba," her steady, quiet voice was a kind of lie. Even more unsettling, she did not say the rest.

Anders saw that Garland, who stood beside Karis, was thinking Norina's statement could not be true because she said it so calmly. The comforting nature of that conclusion made it easy for him to embrace it, even though his thinking was flawed.

The seer's thoughts were not perceivable, but he was already weeping.

Karis said, "Leeba is *safe*."

"She's not stating a *belief*," muttered Serrain.

Anders turned and found her and the others close behind him.

"She's stating a fact," said Braight.

"It can't be a fact!" said Serrain.

They observed the adults with great interest.

Norina said, "Karis, Saugus also has killed my husband. The air children are certain."

"J'han and Leeba both are safe in our old house in the Midlands!" Karis was so sure of this fact that Anders actually found himself wondering whether he and the others were mistaken.

Minga said in a low voice, "Something is wrong with her."

Norina, rigid, said to Karis, "Can your raven see them right now?"

The G'deon's gaze veered away. "They're indoors."

There certainly was something not right about Karis, something unclear, but dangerous, and Norina seemed unaware of it. Anders said, worriedly, "Norina? Excuse me?"

Norina said, "Karis, I think Saugus has tricked you. I think he manipulated your memories, so something that happened a long time ago seems like it was just a few days ago. I know you don't want to believe me. Tell me, how many of your ravens are in Watfield right now?"

"Three," said Karis impatiently.

Before this year, the G'deon's ravens had numbered seven, but in recent months, three had been killed—two Karis had deliberately sacrificed to save people's lives, and one had been murdered.

Norina said, "One raven is in Hanishport with Gilly. If one went to the Midlands with J'han and Leeba, as you say, then only two can be in Watfield."

Anders uttered a cry—too late.

Karis lifted Norina off her feet and flung her down. The Truthken fell heavily and badly, and Karis threw herself on top of her. Somehow, Anders reached them—it almost seemed like he darted through the air like a bird—and clutched the G'deon's upraised arm, trying to prevent her fist, big and hard as a smithy's hammer, from smashing into Norina's face.

He truly was flying then, until a tree smashed into him and made him very stupid. The air would not come into his lungs. He saw Norina, sprawled, helpless, pressed down by the weight of the knee in her chest, and in Karis's face was her death.

The seer was shouting and had been shouting, "Norina, stop her. Norina. Stop. Her."

Now Garland grabbed Karis, and dangled from her arm.

"Stop her!" Medric cried as Garland landed at a distance.

Anders flailed desperately. An excruciating pain. His ears rang with a dreadful sound. He could no longer move. Karis also was still as a statue. A murderous statue. What had Norina done? Something horrible—something amazing!

Medric approached Karis. "Is this how an air witch can launch an ambush?" he said.

"Yes," gasped Norina.

"Saugus was alone with her long enough to damage her but didn't kill her? Or walk away with her, like Maxew walked away with Emil? I thought air logic was more logical!"

With some effort Medric pulled down the G'deon's upraised fist. He pushed at her sideways, grunting with effort. "I can't move her. You have to fix what's wrong with her."

"It's not permitted," Norina gasped.

"And you think *my* logic is nonsense? Well! As the G'deon's seer, I predict that after you allow Karis to beat you to death, she will blame you for it!"

Dark spots crawled like beetles across Anders's vision. Norina began to speak. Anders wanted to listen closely, to understand what she was doing. But instead, he blacked out.

Karis was looking down at him with sweat dribbling through the dust on her face. "I broke your collarbone." She helped him sit up. "Can you breathe now?"

"Yes, Karis."

"I'm sorry for hurting you."

"It was not you who did it. Your will was manipulated by another."

"I'm sorry, nonetheless." She got stiffly to her feet and stood swaying. "Anders, are you certain J'han is dead?"

If there was a way to answer that would not cause pain, Anders had not yet learned that trick. "I know J'han is dead. I saw his body. We cut a piece of his hair to bring with us."

Norina lay on the ground, huddled into a knot, her arms clenched over her face like the visor of a helmet. Medric was speaking distractedly in Sainnese to the confused soldier. Garland hovered near Karis, dazed and stricken. The other air children stood in an awkward, fascinated huddle. Anders said weakly, "Braight, give Karis the hair."

He should have worded this statement as a request, but, for once, Braight didn't take offense. She gave Karis the clump of bloody hair that she had carried from Watfield. "Karis, we found J'han in Medric's tower. He had been killed the day before."

Karis said dully, "That must have been the day my raven reached him with the message, which warned him about Bran."

"We did find a raven in one of the Paladin's rooms. We let it out."

Norina stirred. Karis went to her and helped her stand up. The Truthken wiped her face with her shirttail. Again, she had become so calm it seemed a kind of lunacy. They clasped hands and looked into each other's face as though they were going to dance. Karis said, "Could Saugus have done additional things to me? Without me knowing, and without you noticing?"

"Why not?" said Norina bitterly. "He must have done this to you with Zanja in the room. If you had been alone with him, you would no longer be who you are."

"When—if—I lose control again, do whatever is necessary to stop me."

"And negate everything that makes me trustworthy?"

"*I* am not trustworthy if I can be used as a weapon against my friends!"

They were both right, thought Anders. Norina must not exercise her power upon Karis, not even to mend her. But the G'deon of Shaftal must not be subjugated by another, especially not a hostile air witch. "Excuse me," said Anders, and rather to his surprise they both turned to him. "If it is necessary for Norina to intervene, could someone else make that decision? Rather than Norina? Perhaps Medric? Since air logic has no effect on him?"

"You're thinking better than I am," Norina said.

She glanced at Medric, who wiped his tears and said, "Yes, I'll just pretend to be Emil." Karis put the clump of hair into Norina's hand.

"This is J'han's hair, and his blood. He certainly died defending Leeba." Her summer-brown face was awful to look at.

Norina said, "This is what Emil would tell us: Zanja is running ahead of us so she can put herself between us and Saugus. She's doing it to save your life, and mine. For the only way she can stop us from trying to rescue our daughter is by rescuing her first."

Karis trembled: massive, storm buffeted. The Truthken's calm surface shivered as a terrible power swam in her depths. Anders felt his fellow air students shift closer to him. He yearned to huddle with them, for both women were dreadful.

"We will get Leeba to safety," said Karis.

"We will kill Saugus," Norina replied.

Chapter 40

Written by Anders, a student of the Law of Shaftal. If found, please copy this page into my Book of Everything.

Nearly everything was left behind: food, pots, firewood, blankets, spare socks and shirts, musical instruments, books, lanterns, game pieces.

Karis carried only a baby, a hammer, two large iron bolts, and the Power of Shaftal.

Norina brought Emil's dagger, and, in her memory, the Law of Shaftal. She left her *Map of Everything,* and seeing this helped us to abandon our *Books of Everything.* She carried an awful sorrow; therefore I learned that air logic does not preclude love or grief.

Chaen, who is an artist, brought nothing. The heaviest burdens have no weight, she told me, which is a paradox I have come to understand. Her burden was her love for Maxew, her son, a criminal and traitor.

Those who were strong carried Emil. Those who were not strong told him stories. Some stories are light, and some are heavy.

Seth carried diapers: clean at first, then soiled. She carried bandages and ointments, and dried meat for the dogs.

Clement carried seventy soldiers, each with one weapon. The soldiers carried proud traditions that to them were true. And they carried each other.

Kamren brought a bottle that was very light, which Karis hated to have close to her. He and all the Paladins each carried a dagger, pen and paper, and a lifetime of study.

A soldier carried Medric, who carried his spectacles for close-seeing, a pistol, and many secrets.

Garland left a box of spices but brought a wooden spoon and much worry.

All else we left behind.

Part Four: Water

The way of water is to change and sing
Water needs air for its lightning
Water wants fire for divining
Four elements for balance.

Chapter 31

For three days and nights, through twigs and leaves like walls of basket weave, between branches like the turns in a madman's maze, across blockades of tree trunks and barricades of limbs, through shredded drifts that pierced with secret thorns, Zanja had followed her lost son. Her guide was a shape, a voice, sometimes a light. She became separated: part flesh that walked, part mind that slept. Finally, she had left the forest and stood on a hilltop. She had climbed into sunrise.

She saw the House of Lilterwess, an accretion of homes, schools, plazas, refectories, and workshops, each shouldering the next, in a massive cluster of shared walls and hallways, covered by a single, crazy roof. Hundreds of years ago, Zanja had climbed across that roof in pouring rain and entered through a dormer because she had been denied shelter everywhere; even here in the vibrant heart of Shaftal. Like a thief she had slipped into the legend, a place of color and chaos, a town within a house, encircled by gardens, meadows, and a woodland park of ancient cedar trees.

Twenty years ago, Karis, Norina, Councilor Mabin, and a handful of others had escaped through that park as the Sainnites murdered Shaftal's traditions, reduced its government to rubble, and razed the House of Lilterwess to the ground. Now Zanja looked upon a ruin but still saw a place where seers sought both insight and chaos; the Truthkens demanded consistency and honesty; the healers insisted on health and humanity; the Paladins sorted worthy from unworthy, and the G'deon protected and united the whole.

The heat raised a haze over the landscape, and the distant hill disappeared in a brilliant fog of light. The House of Lilterwess was burning.

The houses of Marlin, of Parsa, of Tarwein—all the clan houses—were burning. The heat of the firestorm stiffened Zanja's blood-soaked tunic. She had dragged herself out from under the dead war horse and, on hands and knees, too dizzy to rise, had looked for survivors, but found only the dead. Those who had hesitated were scattered across the summer camp. Those who had fled carrying their children were choking the steep, winding pathway out of the valley and into the forest.

Smoke swept across the meadow. It smelled of blood and death; it roared the story of her people's destruction. And it brought to her the rhythmic cry of a newborn, an infant she had seen in the na'Tarwein clan house, curled like a kernel in a basket lined with carded wool. The firestorm in the village had not reached him.

Her guide, a shadow in the smoke, began to sing in her people's dead language:

Time is the oak tree
That lays down its acorns
The hazel tree
That throws down its nuts.

Time is the dead who enrich the soil
While the corn fields lie fallow.
Time is the mourning songs that won't be sung,
The sorrow that won't be remembered.

Time is the stone river flowing
Past a village of charcoal and ashes.
Time is the summer camp
In which the sleepers do not awaken.

The river will flow,
The nuts will lie uneaten,
The songs of mourning will never be sung,
The sorrow will not be remembered.
You will be a memory of tomorrow.
You will be a ghost of the living.

It was a mourning song of the people, but Zanja had never heard it.

She ran into the firestorm. Her warrior braids fell from their knot, and like candle wicks they caught on fire. Yet she ran through flames to save that wailing infant, to save her clan, her people, from destruction. She ran through the blazing curtain of the clan house, and fire clothed her. She snatched her son from the flames and fled with him. Outside the inferno, she laid him down in a safe place. And then, in agony, she slowly died.

"What is it like to die?" the poet asked.

"Lonely," she said.

Her lost son wore clothing of ashes, and his warrior braids were burning. How could he have survived?

She said, "I never saved an infant from the inferno."

He spoke to her with words of smoke. He held before her gaze a charred page from the lexicon.

It was the Lonely Girl, who sat on an ornate bench, in a fantastic hallway of high, arched walls, with every surface covered by brilliant decoration. In this clutter of color, she was a simple, plain shape: not a vacancy, but rather a possibility. She gazed somberly out of the page, with a curved sword across her knees. Born of a Truthken, raised in a family of elementals, she was a kernel; and they were the protective shell. But they in turn were protected by the harsh, rich land of Shaftal. And Shaftal was a kernel in the world.

Leeba, the Lonely Girl. Leeba, the wailing infant in the burning clan house. The child who must be saved, in order to save everything.

Trembling with exhaustion and fear, Zanja returned to the woods. She used Medric's string to suspend the glyph cards from the branch of an ancient tree, so that water would not destroy her cards again. But in the satchel over her shoulder she still carried Medric's spectacles, Emil's pen that she had taken from his body, J'han's packet of strengthening herbs, and some crumbs of Garland's travel bread. She carried Norina's dagger at her belt, and she carried Karis in her blood and bone.

All else she left behind.

Chapter 42

Tashar dreamed of his marvelous sky boat, flying bravely and beautifully across the sky, gazed at in amazement by all the people of Shaftal, whose cries of wonder rose up like bird calls, until a gigantic, leafy hand reached up from the woodland, snatched the ship out of the air, and crushed it. He awakened, weeping.

Dawn was rising. Humiliated by his tears, Tashar looked hastily at Maxew, but his hateful companion slept undisturbed and dreadful in the pale light: one eye black and swollen, his nose purple, puffy, grotesque.

Tashar got up, groaning, from his miserable bed of leaf mold. He felt like he had been beaten by a gang of thieves armed with staves. He took the ball of string from the bag of supplies that the crazy border woman had thrown at them, tied the string around a branch, and went into the woody tangle. When his string had played out, he followed it back to Maxew, then went forth in another direction. On the fourth try, he discovered a pool that was leaf-choked, scummed over, and crowded with tiny frogs that scrambled over each other in a panic when he dipped fingers in and licked it to check if the water was drinkable.

It tasted of dirt and mold.

In the House of Lora, barrels of spring water had been delivered fresh every day.

He dipped the tin into the water, using his fingers to screen out the creatures and the stringy algae. As he staggered back to his feet, he thought he saw movement, a light-footed shadow slipping into invisibility at the corner of his eye. Then there was nothing, just the tangle of wind-crushed trees, a flash of bird's wings, bright sunrise, and black shadows.

He fled, following the string trail, back to Maxew, who now sat upright, holding his head.

"She's following us!"

"Who?" Maxew's voice was muffled as if with a dreadful cold. His smashed face must hurt awfully, but Tashar could not pity the bastard.

"The border woman! The G'deon's wife!"

"She won't leave Emil."

"Perhaps not if he were alive. But you killed him."

In Maxew's sharp movement, and in the anger that flared in his battered face, Tashar read that he knew he had made a mistake by allowing Emil to die. "If Zanja wanted vengeance she would have killed us already," he said.

"But I just *saw* her."

"You saw your own fear." Maxew got up, awkward and stiff as an arthritic old man. "The sun's still low enough to be a reliable compass."

On the previous day, they had argued all afternoon about their direction of travel. When evening threw some long, eastward-pointing shadows across the debris, they had seen that both of them had been wrong.

They had divided the food, but Tashar carried everything else, because Maxew would have left it all behind. He slung the heavy water tins over his shoulder, put the sunrise at his back, and began the grim struggle westward.

The border woman, the false G'deon's tragic, ferocious wife—Maxew himself had said she was crazy. And in this world of sideways trees that tangled in each other like balls of yarn the kittens had gotten hold of, that insanity seemed reasonable to Tashar. The crazy woman had given them enough supplies to make them think they could survive, and now she was hunting them, and torturing them, for vengeance.

If only she would finish her game! This slow, painful struggle through the unyielding chaos had become unendurable. They should be flying!

Thinking of his lost ship, Tashar felt more than willing to lie down and die; he just needed someone to help him with the last part.

Time passed very slowly. When the sun had finished rising, they stopped to rest and eat. Tashar considered whether to save half of his remaining food so he could eat again in the evening. But if Maxew ran out of food first, he could enspell Tashar and take his share. Tashar ate all the food, spitefully. Maxew lay on his back with a wet cloth on his battered face, oblivious to Tashar's confused hatred.

Tashar said, "She's a witch. She must be."

"Who?" As though their earlier conversation had never happened!

"That woman who's following us."

"She isn't—!" Maxew put a hand to his face—angry speech seemed to be especially painful. "She merely has a fire talent, and it controls her. She can't control it."

"She knew we would crash, and she knew where."

"No, you idiot. We crashed where she already was."

"You're saying that the storm was magical? Then you're the idiot, because no magic controls weather."

"Water magic controls wind, weather, water, time, music, and mathematics."

Tashar had always assumed that water magic existed, but if there were any water witches, every one of them lived in secret. Yet a witch who could control the wind and weather could have lived in luxury in the House of Lora, or any of the shipping houses. A shipping house that was invulnerable to storms and independent of the wind would soon control the entire shipping trade. It would control Shaftal. It would *own* Shaftal.

And Tashar would fly wherever he liked, for he would always be guaranteed a friendly wind.

He was shocked out of his fantasy by a sound, distant but distinct. Maxew sat up sharply.

"A dinner gong?" Tashar said stupidly.

"It was that way." Maxew pointed.

"No, that way."

They glared at each other with hatred and contempt. The gong sounded again, and Tashar started toward it. He felt so indifferent to Maxew that, when he heard him struggling along behind him, he was not triumphant.

That distant gong seemed to be ringing the hours like a town clock. It called Tashar out of the woods; it compelled him over the obstacles and through unimaginable tangles; it blandished him with promises of food, shelter, sympathy, and admiration. That piercing, persistent sound revealed to him his loneliness: the loneliness of hours, of days, of years. No one had ever known or loved him. No one had ever recognized his longing to belong, to know the truth, to do remarkable things, to be courageous. No one but Saugus.

Perhaps the gong *was* Saugus, for only Saugus could call him so steadily, accurately, and clearly.

It was shocking when he burst through the tangle and found himself under open sky—a sky that shimmered with hot light, a light that also blazed below, blinding him so he saw only faint shapes moving about, and a narrow tunnel of brightness, walled on both sides by shadow, with fire overhead. It was an extremely narrow, blindingly bright town, he thought, and staggered into the path of a rumbling wagon drawn by blurry, massive horses.

"Hey!" yelled the driver, and the horses uttered grunts of annoyance as the driver pulled them short. Tashar staggered backwards, his water tins clanging and clattering, and sat on the scalding white stone. He shaded his eyes from the light.

After a while, Maxew came out of the woods and stood beside him. "Huh," said the air witch.

Tashar peered between his fingers at the narrow town, built in a tunnel, with floors and ceilings of fire and walls of shadow. But he saw neither a town nor a tunnel, and instead saw a work camp set up along a stretch of road. He brushed his hand across the stone's surface, so flat and smooth that he couldn't feel the seams. He felt like he had voyaged very far and reached a place he had never been before. But it was just the Shimasal Road.

"Sit there all day, if you like." Maxew walked away.

Tashar got to his feet with great effort and reluctance, and stumbled after him.

"Hie! Hie! Hie!" a woman yelled, and Tashar stumbled out of the way so a team of oxen could haul a massive log past him, to where Tashar saw many such logs piled up, as if in the yard of a lumber mill. Nearby, people collected and stacked debris in stacks, tossing the branches up to people who stood atop the piles.

Tashar followed Maxew northward to the camp that stretched up one side of the road. Neat piles of trade goods, covered by oiled canvas, acted as walls between which more canvas was stretched for shade. In the near distance, people were emptying a wagon of its goods while the driver shouted hoarsely at a sunburnt woman who faced him with her hands on her hips. Closer by, people chopped vegetables and tended huge stewpots. A healer's flag flapped from a sunshade, where a man's blistered hands were being anointed and wrapped. Maxew headed there.

Tashar spotted a wagonload of water barrels, where people were filling their flasks. He began to run, stumbling, nearly falling, but was unable to make himself slow down. He wanted to open a spigot and let the water pour over his body until the barrel was empty. But he merely trickled water over his face and arms, smearing off the worst of the dirt, revealing the red welts and scratches all over his hands and forearms, some scabbed with dried blood and dirt, and some painfully inflamed.

"How long have you been working the jam?" asked a sun-brown young woman who was filling a water jug nearby. "Looks like you've been in it for days." She eyed his bruises and other injuries with admiration. If he weren't too stupid with tiredness to make up a lie or even offer the truth, he could make a friend, or follow her to privacy and learn what farmers know of lovemaking. But all he could think of was his envy of her hat. "Yes," he said.

"How far south does it go?"

He shrugged. "Is there food somewhere, do you know?"

"A load of bread arrived from Shimasal a short while ago." She pointed, and Tashar stumbled away.

He got three loaves of bread and a fistful of dried meat, and no one demanded payment. Standing in the middle of the road, he ate an entire loaf. Then he wandered back to the healer's tent, where he found Maxew flat on his back, with a rag-wrapped chunk of ice pressed to his face.

"Is this your friend?" the healer asked Maxew.

Maxew mumbled something.

"Well, it must be." She said to Tashar, "His nose is broken, but his eye is only bruised. I set the bone, and he needs to avoid vigorous movement for a few weeks."

"I see," said Tashar.

"You were in the storm, your friend said, with the trees falling around you. It's a glad thing you weren't killed."

Tashar had been angry, terrified, desperate, hopeless, and frustrated, but never glad. Even now, with his hunger and thirst satisfied, his face clean, and no need to struggle through that dreadful landscape ever again, he felt only offended and exhausted. "How is it you have ice?"

"Oh, I brought some with me from the ice house in Shimasal. I figured there would be a lot of sprains. There have been broken bones also. People get hot or dazzled or tired, and then they fall. Not many cuts to stitch up, though. The people using axes know their business."

Tashar put a loaf of bread on Maxew's chest, then lay down on the bare, smooth stones. The stones had been cut and laid by a G'deon—the work of a lifetime, it was said. He couldn't remember which one had done it. The white granite was flecked with mica. The Light Road, it was sometimes called.

The encampment awoke with the dawn. The healer distributed liniments to people and draft animals, and the injured people lined up for her to check and rebandage their injuries and tell them whether or not they could work today. Tashar and Maxew found a line of people waiting for porridge. The workers groaned, stretched sore muscles, and spoke longingly of cool drinks: juice, ale, and cider. Mostly they wanted ale.

"Hey," said a woman, as though she were talking to a couple of horses. "You two, you're the ones that came through the woods yesterday?"

It was the sunburned woman who had stood with her hands on her hips while a teamster's horses and wagon were appropriated for the road-clearing. Tashar said, "Yes, madam, and we were astonished to find such a well-ordered project!"

She immediately looked less like a cat getting ready for a fight and more like a cat whose chin is being rubbed. "Can you work?"

"I'm pretty tired, but I'll gladly do whatever I can. My friend has been hurt, though, and the healer doesn't want him to work."

The woman examined Maxew with skepticism. "Today you two will drive the water cart. Tomorrow you'll join a brush-gathering team, if you expect to continue to eat."

Maxew said, in his muffled nasal voice, which made him sound like he had a terrible cold, "How far is the road blocked?"

"Well, if you've got a spyglass, you're welcome to climb a pile and try to see the end. I just hope there are people on the far side, doing the same work we're doing. And maybe it will get easier. The weather-wise people say the cyclone grew weaker as it went south." She shut her mouth then, and Tashar thought she looked aggravated, as if she wouldn't normally exchange three words with people who were stupid enough to get caught in the woods in a deadly windstorm.

"I certainly hope so, madam," said Tashar as she turned away.

"Why don't you lick her hand and wag your tail too?" Maxew said.

"I gained us the right to eat breakfast!"

"Yet you really *are* willing to drive the water wagon. But we're going southward."

"With the road completely blocked?"

"It won't be worse than what we've endured already."

The old man serving the porridge plopped a heavy spoonful into Maxew's porringer, and then another into Tashar's. They stood in another line for cream. "We've got no supplies," said Tashar.

"Well, you get the water, bottom-man, and I'll get the food."

"Why must you always jeer at me?"

"What else should I do? You have no good qualities."

People handed Maxew everything he requested. Within an hour, laden with food, water, and tools, they once again faced the fallen trees, where several teams of sawyers were cutting the limbs from the trunks while a couple of people studied how to attach a chain and the oxen waited patiently. At a wagon with a jury-rigged hoist, a bunch of people hauled on ropes, like sailors raising sail. Someone had made a joke, and they were laughing so hard that they could scarcely pull.

Tashar wanted to go over and teach them a sailor's song, to help them pull in rhythm. But Maxew had climbed over two trees already. Should Maxew be the only one whom Saugus congratulated on his adventure when it was Tashar who had sailed in the sky? He followed Maxew back into the tangle of fallen trees.

Chapter 43

The moon that Chaen had seen from time to time must have set hours ago. Starlight could not penetrate the leafy canopy. She and Seth walked in a crowd that was invisible.

"How will I draw a picture of this march?" Chaen asked.

"You couldn't make it dark enough—not with all the ink in an ink-seller's cart."

"But I want to draw the *feeling*."

"Surely that would be darker yet: death, fear, unimaginable weariness, haunting hopelessness . . ."

"But the darkness moves. It is the bodies of our companions, each one trudging grimly forward. They keep me upright and walking, and I suppose I do the same for them. And I don't even know their names. How can I draw that?"

"I think you may be delirious," said Seth.

"Aren't you?"

"Maybe. I walk around and around my fears, snarling. I jump in and snap at them. Then I jump back."

"Like a dog with a snake." Seth certainly was like a Basdown cow dog: sturdy, bossy, friendly, cheerful, growling or barking when necessary, but fundamentally civilized.

Up ahead, one of the captains gave a call, and the soldiers who were trudging, grumbling, and staggering through the dark woodland voiced a reply. Ahead and then behind, the others repeated the cry. The Paladins shouted hoarsely, but in Shaftalese, "Water, sir!"

Chaen checked her water flask and decided to refill it at the stream they were approaching. She and Seth bumped into the people who had stopped to unbuckle their boots and remove their socks. "Watch out," said Emil at ground level. "Man down."

One of the dogs breathed on Chaen's hand, and she stroked its head. On the first night of this hard march, the dogs had led the way until Karis and the rear party caught up with them. When they stopped for a breakfast of travel bread and water, Chaen discovered that five air children had joined their party.

"You are Maxew's mother," one of them said, and talked with her for a while—stiffly and awkwardly, as though he were practicing a difficult lesson. It was from him that Chaen learned what Death-and-Life Company had done to Norina's healer husband and their daughter, and she was sick with shame.

Chaen took off her boots, hissing with pain when her blistered feet touched ground.

"I am an old woman," Seth groaned. "And with every step I take, I grow far older."

"So do we all," said Chaen. "Even the children."

"Those aren't children," said Seth. "That is the Order of Truthkens."

At daybreak, on the third dawn of the march. Chaen sat upon the ground, eating hardbread and a handful of sweet currants. Nearly a hundred people sat nearby, but not a single word was said, not even by the Paladins. Chaen could hear the general suckling her baby. The Truthken strode past, with death in her face.

The medics were checking everyone's feet, as they did every morning. Chaen pulled off her boots and socks. Karis came and lowered herself heavily to the ground. She lifted one of Chaen's feet and put her rough palm against the blistered sole.

The pain retreated. Chaen's head cleared.

Karis was hollow eyed. Her clothing hung from her frame. Even the bones of her hands were revealed, like stones uncovered by a torrent.

Chaen said, "When people are weary, they lose their will. But not you."

"I am driven—but not by my own will." Her smoke-wrecked voice was a raw whisper. She laid down Chaen's foot and picked up the other.

"Does Shaftal's power never run out?"

"Chaen, I think it is without limits. When Tadwell was G'deon, a water witch goaded him into laying waste to the land, which he regretted the rest of his life. Zanja believes I will do far worse, and is running ahead of me to prevent that."

"Is Zanja correct?"

"Oh, yes," she said. The G'deon of Shaftal was in a desperate, dark mood.

One of the air children approached them, and Karis heaved herself to her feet. A flock of birds that had gathered in a nearby tree made an agitated and contented racket, like market day in a city. Despite the noise, Chaen could hear Karis speaking to the boy in a formal, polite way. It was the same boy Chaen had spoken with the other night, but she didn't know his name.

The boy's back was to Chaen. ". . . Emil Paladin . . ."

"What did he say?" asked Karis.

The boy answered. Karis, looming over him like a tree over a mouse, gazed above his head at Chaen. "Can you do something for me?" she asked Chaen.

Chaen hastily put on her socks and shoes. Her body was like a stream in drought, empty and dry, its secret hollows exposed, its little fishes rotting in the sun. But her blisters were healed and her feet didn't hurt. She followed Karis to a cluster of people that had gathered around Emil. He sat upon his litter, with the general's baby sleeping in his arms. Emil's face was unshaven, but his clothing still was clean, his hair still combed back and tied; even his boots were not dirty. People who had no time to care for themselves were continuing to care for him. His gaze switched from face to face as people spoke, and there was a profound intensity to his listening. If Maxew had intended to destroy the man, he should have undone his ability to pay attention, for that surely was his greatest gift.

Chaen hung back until Karis, who had knelt to draw in the dirt, looked up and said, "Chaen, can you do it?"

"Yes," said Chaen. "What do you want me to do?"

The Sainnite general turned to Chaen with an expression of approval, as though she were one of her soldiers.

Karis pointed at a straight line she had drawn in the dirt. "This is the Shimasal Road." Across the road she drew a mark. "This is the southern edge of the storm-wrack." She pointed to some humps of dirt that she had shaped with her fingertips. "Here is the hill country.

Zanja arrived here yesterday, at dawn. She left her glyph cards hanging in a tree, here." Karis touched one of her bolts, which she again was using as a marker. Then she touched the other. "And we are here."

They were east and south of the hill country. Soon they would break out of the woodland and reach the road.

Kamren Paladin said, "Emil thinks we need to fetch the cards."

"Need vision," said Emil. He had become able to pair a verb with a noun, but, although Norina or one of the air children worked with him night and day, he could do no more than that.

"I gave my far-seeing to Zanja," Medric explained, but Chaen was unenlightened.

Kamren seemed to recognize her confusion. "Some of the Paladins will be diverting northward, to seek food and wagons. You can travel with them for a while, then get the cards and double back to bring them to Medric. The glyph cards may help him see."

"Of course," she said.

Karis said, "Granite will go with you. She'll show you the way back to us." The G'deon's dirty finger poked the hill country. "By then we'll be around here, I guess."

Chaen had been running, or nearly running, then walking quickly, then trudging and stumbling, for many days. She didn't see how she could meet up with the main group in the way Karis was proposing—she simply couldn't move quickly enough.

But Clement was speaking now. "Karis has agreed *not* to employ the Power of Shaftal upon the soldiers, for only if they serve her by their own power will they regain their lost honor. But your honor has been restored to you already."

It had? wondered Chaen.

Karis rose up and took Chaen in her arms. She was overwhelming, and Chaen felt a panic, and tried to yank away. But Karis held her, and laid a coarse hand on the back of her neck, and jolted her with the Power of Shaftal. Chaen heard herself utter a cry, or a groan, and for a moment thought she might faint. Karis said in a low voice, "Sometimes people fall. Are you all right now?"

Chaen managed to reply. Karis released her, and Chaen stood on her own feet. She had been weary for eleven years—so weary for so long that she had ceased to be aware of it.

"Pace yourself," Emil said, very kindly.

The cook, Garland, handed Chaen an extra ration of bread. "The giddiness will pass."

Norina said, "Maxew and Tashar are going south on the Shimasal Road."

Chaen understood immediately why Norina was telling her this. "When will our paths intersect?"

"By the time we reach the road, the two young men will be south of us." After a moment the Truthken added, "I promise you, we are not getting you out of the way so that we can deal with Maxew."

Chaen had needed to hear it said. Or later, when solitude filled her with doubt, she would need to have heard it. This was what air witches did instead of being kind.

Seth hobbled up to kiss Chaen farewell, and then Kamren did also, which surprised Chaen in more than one way.

"You're not coming?" she asked.

He gestured vaguely toward the cluster of advisers. "To replace Emil requires many people. I play two parts: the fire blood and the Paladin." Then he took her to the other Paladins and told her their names, and they set forth, a company of five, one of them the dog named Granite. Chaen walked among them, silent, distracted by wild imaginings of that man between her legs.

Eventually, the giddiness did wear off.

Chaen had been hovering at the edges of the Paladins' peculiar, incessant conversations for days. Much of their talk had been about Sainnese verbs: they were endeavoring to understand how the verbs changed, depending upon how they were used, and how that in turn affected certain nouns that were associated with the verbs. Whenever they thought they had an insight into the pattern, they immediately dispersed among the soldiers to test it.

The Paladin conversations left Chaen feeling ignorant, although her education was no better or worse than that of most Shaftali. Shamed and mystified though she was by the Paladins' communal groping after understanding, she had continued to walk close enough to overhear them. But now they walked in silence.

—w—

It was still morning when they stepped from shade into sunshine, and they paused, dazzled. To their right and left, the ragged edge of the forest wound in and out among corrugated hillsides. A distant spring flashed like a signal mirror.

"I see part of the road." The Paladin gestured toward a quivering of heat waves in the distance.

"If you say so."

"It's a long way yet."

"Should we go through the hills? Or follow the forest edge?"

Granite uttered a sound like a polite cough. Chaen said, "I guess we part ways now."

They clasped hands and separated. Chaen felt a hollowness where her companions had been, and glanced back. The Paladins were tying on headcloths as they trudged toward the hills.

She ran along the tree line with the dog trotting beside her, glancing up at her from time to time, grinning amiably, her tongue flapping out the side of her mouth like a scarlet flag. Chaen could not see far to the west, for the hills blocked the view, but if she were to climb one, she would see the road, and might even see two young men walking down it.

They reached a shelter pine at the edge of the woods. Granite lay in the shade, and Chaen gave her a porringer of water. The dog needed to rest, she told herself. For a long time, she studied the nearby hill, considering whether to climb it to try to look for her son. Birds rustled busily in the tree, and a hawk cried out.

She must have loved Maxew, difficult though that might have been. But her responsibility to Shaftal was greater.

She ducked under the massive pine tree's sagging branches and climbed up a couple of tiers until she could grab a packet that dangled there. She untied the leather cord, unwrapped the oilcloth, and saw the stacks of priceless glyph cards. At the top of one stack, the illustration showed two warriors fighting, with curved swords in one hand and daggers in the other, in identical poses, wearing identical armor. Many other paired fighters surrounded them. Although this was a battle in a war, the fighters stood like arranged statues in frozen, identical poses. "A stalemate," murmured Chaen.

The other card, by contrast, showed a world of motion—a chaos of swirling images—sideways, upside-down, with no apparent rhyme or reason. Chaen glanced away at Granite, who still lay quiet, working her lungs like the bellows of a furnace. When she looked again at the illustration, she realized that these people, objects, animals, and plants had all been caught up and carried into the sky by a terrific windstorm. "The whirlwind," she said. She had seen both cards before—twice, both times Zanja had cast them—but had not had time to study them.

She wrapped up the cards and tied them to her belt and then, for security, tied them with a second cord that she threaded through a buttonhole.

"If you're rested enough, let's be on our way," she said to Granite. "We have a war to fight."

Granite brought Chaen toward the south, along the tree line, sometimes amid trees and sometimes across open land. Chaen was struggling through heavy undergrowth when she heard Granite bark and then splash noisily into water. She pushed through and saw Norina waiting on a stream bank, while on the other side, two companies of soldiers sprawled in a dappled meadow.

Chaen hung her cards, boots, and breeches around her neck, put her arm around Norina's waist, and crossed the stream with her, holding her tightly, hip to hip. On the opposite bank, water sprayed from Granite's coat, flashing in the sunlight like sparks from a fire. Karis stood in the gravel and grass as though rooted there. Of course she couldn't cross through water unless she had no choice—earth witches were like that.

Chaen gave Karis the cards. Karis handed them to Medric. Just beyond them was a clutter of sleeping children. The baby lay under his sunshade made of Emil's sweat-stained straw hat. "May I watch the card-casting?" Chaen asked.

"Zanja cast," said Emil. He had been positioned with his back against a sapling, so he would not topple over.

"She cast the cards already?" Medric said. "Of course she did! No one is a better card-caster—not even you."

Emil shrugged.

"You say it doesn't matter," muttered Medric, picking at the knots. "But you're secretly furious that you taught her everything you know, and now she's teaching you."

Norina said, "Emil certainly is furious. But not at Zanja."

Emil took the cards from Medric and gave them back to Chaen. Baffled for a moment by this round-robin, she untied the knots. Emil put a hand over hers, preventing her from opening the leather wrapping. "What question?" he asked, looking at Medric.

"The question is the hard part!"

Karis gazed at the two men and waited. The woman knew how to wait, and when to stop waiting: a humble hillside that one day becomes a deadly avalanche.

The seer muttered agitatedly. Emil said, "*What*."

"*What*, then. But what *what*? What should we do, of course . . . but it's the next part that matters: In order to *what*?" As the seer dithered and muttered, Chaen noticed that he had been stripping and cleaning his pistol. She knew a little about pistols, enough that she knew this was not merely a pistol in pieces, but one that had its pieces laid out in careful order so it could be put together in moments.

"What do we want?" Medric was asking himself. "Peace? Well, we *have* peace, and yet peace brought a new war. We created that peace as well as anyone could have done it, but still we didn't do everything right. Merely to have the right ingredients is not enough, our intrepid cook would say: they must be composed so the end result has the right balance."

As the seer muttered on, Chaen had begun to hear two voices speaking with his mouth, conversing with each other. One voice said Emil's words: "But not a perfect balance."

"Oh, no," the Medric voice said, "or nothing would ever happen."

"And not the balance that comes from inaction, for without action nothing can change, and we'll end up with a Shaftal like the one in Zanja's story."

"When Raven tricked the hunter into killing and eating him? And the entire world entered a stasis, without birth or death, without mistakes or learning? I like that story."

"Poised," Emil said.

"The balance of poise? Not that I want to shock you by my maturity, but such a balance seems overly influenced by fire logic! If people are always about to jump into something, how can there be time for the earthish things, like planting and making tools and raising children and suchlike?"

"Unity," Emil said.

"*Poised* unity?"

Emil looked pointedly at Medric's hands, and the younger man glanced down and laughed: while he conversed with himself, he also had put together his pistol.

"You're talking gibberish," said Karis patiently.

"Excellent! Perfect! Exactly what we need! Chaen, I am seeking the answer to this question: *What must we do to achieve a poised and unified balance?*"

Emil lifted his hand, which for the entire time had pressed upon Chaen's. She folded back the oilcloth from the two stacks of cards. The top cards now were upside-down. Or rather, the Stalemate was reversed, and the Whirlwind was not. That card must have been reversed before, the first time she looked at it, but because the image was so chaotic, she hadn't noticed it.

Karis stood up and walked away. Kamren, who was asleep in the shade, awoke to her touch. He fumbled groggily at the bottle of wind on his belt.

Chaen said, "I had better wrap the cards up again."

Norina said quietly, "General Clement."

Clement, who lay at a distance, sat up sharply. She looked at Karis, who was now placing the bottle of wind upon the ground, uttered a curse, and scrambled to her feet. Soldiers sleeping among the trees startled awake at her shout.

Karis brought her foot down, and the bottle shattered with a sound like thunder.

Chapter yy

The long summer day had faded into a moonless night. In darkness, Zanja approached the ruin.

The massive stone blocks of the exterior wall were scattered down the hillside, an unintentional earthworks around a battlement of rubble. Behind those blocks, the people of Death-and-Life Company waited for the G'deon of Shaftal.

Zanja huddled at the base of the hill, in the shelter of the first massive stone, and the residual heat in the massive block was like the warmth of a lover's thigh. She could not attack these hardened, skillful fighters and the powerful genius who commanded them. Not when she was armed only with a borrowed dagger and the unsteady flame of her insight.

When she had stood on the rise above the Asha River, watching the soldiers cross the river, preparing to fight their armored horses and lance-bearing riders with the blade at her side and all the *katrim* at her back, that also had been insane, but it was an insanity forced upon them. What lay before her now was the insanity of choice: she must choose to act in such a way that it would prevent Karis from approaching that hill.

She could have prevented the massacre of her people. She could have been less obedient to the will of the elders, and she could have warned them with greater urgency. She could have asked the *katrim* to ally with her, even to help her contradict the decisions of the elders. She could have foreseen that her cousin, in exchange for the smoke drug, had betrayed the *katrim* watch posts and had told the stranger in the woods how to approach the Asha Valley from the north. And when she was abducted into the past, she could have told the future to Arel and Tadwell or demanded that Grandmother Ocean save the Ashawala'i in exchange for the rescue of her own people, the Essikret. But she had not done any of these things.

"Speaker!" called a distant voice.

Her guide's voice came from the cedar park. She crept around the hill to the woodland and spotted movement at the edge of the trees. She followed him deep into the park. She stopped to unstrap her boots and yank off her socks to feel the way over gnarled roots and outcroppings of stone with her bare feet. She felt Shaftal before her and beneath her. She felt the deep roots of the people, Zanja's people, gripped tightly to the foundations of the land, Zanja's land. Shaftal endured, in death and in renewal. The generations made terrible mistakes, and recovered, and did their best.

Karis seemed to be waiting for her among the ancient trees. She said, "Take off your clothes. Lie down and rest."

Zanja removed her filthy clothing and lay down on the soft loam. The quiet power of Shaftal came into her. The fissures of pain in her travel-worn feet knitted together. Her muscles, worn and torn like ragged fabric, were rewoven. She breathed in, and fell asleep.

She slept the remainder of the night and well into the day. When she awoke, Karis spoke with her lips: "Below you there is a foundation of stones on which the House of Lilterwess used to stand."

"I feel those stones, joined to bedrock."

"Those stones were cut and laid by sweat and labor, but by earth magic they clenched the bedrock with a grip that will never be broken."

"So the Sainnites, having won a great victory over powers they desperately feared, tried and failed to move those stones."

"Zanja, something is cupped in those stone hands."

Zanja shut her eyes and saw a series of underground rooms, each one connected to the next by a tunnel. She said, "The House of Lilterwess is gone, but the storerooms survived."

In one of those rooms, a little girl lay huddled in the darkness. They had not even given her a candle. "I know Leeba is there," Zanja said.

Now Norina spoke. "They are torturing Leeba with fear so that Karis will be tortured by fear. What they do to her next will be much worse."

"And then what? Will *you* confront Saugus, and condemn yourself to death?"

The Truthken said, "Yes."

"How does this knowledge help me, Madam Truthken? I already know that I must not fail!"

Karis spoke, and for a moment Zanja was aware of her own lips moving: "Medric says, *What lies far from you is close at hand.*"

Zanja stood up and dressed, hung Norina's dagger at her side, put the satchel over her shoulder, but left her shoes where she had dropped them. She advanced on the ruin of the House of Lilterwess with her feet on the ground.

Chapter 45

Tashar soon fell behind, because Maxew, with his thin, long limbs, could step or climb over the main trunks, while Tashar, being shorter and stockier, was forced to aim for the crowns, where he must step over or duck under each limb.

At midafternoon he noticed some smudges of smoke up ahead. Sometime later, Maxew called that he heard voices. It turned out to be two sawyers sitting upon a log, eating peaches. One was saying that there was plenty of work for everyone, including the Sainnites. The other replied that he would do everything himself rather than work beside those murdering parasites.

The first started to argue, but when Maxew stepped over their tree trunk and continued down the half-cleared road without saying a word, they fell silent with surprise. Tashar picked his way through the crown of the tree, greeted the sawyers, and asked, "Which mile is this?"

"Mile twenty-six."

"The people at the northern side of the jam are at mile twenty-nine."

The sawyer groaned. "We'll be clearing this road all winter!"

"We'll be warm, though, with all this firewood," said the other.

Up ahead, Maxew had gotten onto a wagon's running board, and was waving at Tashar to hurry. Tashar managed a staggering trot on his bruised, aching legs and jumped onto the board as the wagon began to roll away. "Why such haste?"

"I should have been there yesterday."

"For what?"

"I can't say."

"You don't know!"

The wagon, laden with tree limbs, jolted over debris as they passed the various stages of road-clearing that they had passed through in reverse that same morning, and the same sorts of labor-hardened people and draft animals that leaned patiently into their yokes beneath the hot sun. This labor camp was larger but more ramshackle, with mismatched teams, all kinds of wagons, and a collection of much-used tools, barrels, and food, all marked with the glyphs of the farmsteads to which they belonged. Surely these farmsteads could ill afford to be without these workers at this time of year. The road-clearing seemed a heroic effort, as memorable in its way as the legendary shipwreck rescues that were recounted in Hanishport taverns during the long, slow days of wintertime. *I should stay and work,* thought Tashar.

The wagon stopped at the limb dump, where on many sawhorses the fallen trees were being cut for firewood. Maxew hopped off and walked away, and Tashar followed several steps behind him, ashamed of his misery.

"Where are we?" asked Maxew.

"Mile twenty-six."

Maxew glanced at the sun. "We can be there by sunset, but we must keep our pace."

"Since you won't tell me why we're in such a hurry—"

"Exactly. Should Norina Truthken get hold of you, you'll babble everything."

"A Truthken will get the truth from you as easily as from me."

"Not nearly as easily."

"Why don't you just enslave me to your will? Is it that you'd rather harangue me? Maybe to keep from haranguing yourself?"

"What we're doing is important! If the operation succeeds, it will end the necessity for us to live in secret as though we are the wrongdoers and not the wronged! The Power of Shaftal will belong once again to Shaftal and not to these leaders who are misleading us into injustice!"

"What is this, a recruitment speech?"

"We're going to capture the false G'deon, make her subject to Saugus's will, and thus use her power to destroy the Sainnites—since she has refused to do it herself."

"What?" cried Tashar. He found himself gasping for breath. "That is—that plan is—audacious!"

"It is," said Maxew smugly.

"If we can force her to do what she should have done long ago, then of course we must. But how is it possible? Can't she destroy anyone who even attempts to capture her? Isn't that why we decided to use poison to assassinate her?"

"Saugus can control her. But Karis has been guarded by presciants, and such people are nearly impossible to take by surprise. You've seen yourself what Zanja is capable of."

"You *knew* Zanja would follow us?"

"She was supposed to follow us."

"Emil was not the bait for Karis, but for Zanja?"

"She took the bait, didn't she?"

"Then—we were supposed to kill her, weren't we? So Karis would not have her presciants?"

"Some aspects of the plan weren't entirely successful."

"What's our hurry, then?"

"At least try to do some thinking on your own! Emil is dead, we've separated Zanja from Karis, and the seer is an idiot. But if Norina and Saugus confront each other and I'm not there, both of them will die."

Tashar said spitefully, "Then you should go slowly, shouldn't you! For once you help him to kill the Truthken, you'll be more trouble than use to Saugus."

"Is that what you think? That people are nothing but tools to him?"

"I was just making a joke—"

"Hold your tongue!"

Tashar's words stuck in his mouth like nut paste.

"Stand, traitor, where you are," said the air witch.

Tashar could not move.

Once, a fey wind had yanked the tiller out of Tashar's hands, dumped him into the cold water of the harbor, and carried his boat away without him. Now he felt like that: stunned, embarrassed, dismayed, terrified, and yet laughing at his predicament.

Maxew yanked the last full water tin from Tashar's shoulder and trotted away without another word.

Tashar lost his sense of time. Eventually he saw three people coming down the road—footsore travelers, he thought at first, all dressed the same, which seemed odd. When they were close enough to greet him, they were close enough for him to see that they were Paladins in ragged shirts, earrings glittering below filthy headscarves and daggers at their belts. By their battered appearance, they may well have been following him all the way from Hanishport.

They took him by the arms, one on each side.

One woman asked, "What's wrong with him?"

"His muscles are straining—but he seems rooted here."

"Then it's air magic."

"This is Maxew's companion?" The woman peered at him. "What was it like to fly?" she asked.

"Feel how hot he is. He's been standing here for hours."

"That's a cruel way to kill a man."

"Let's put him in the shade, at least."

They carried Tashar to the road's edge, then dragged him into a thicket. They were able to adjust his position for him, so they could leave him sitting, with his back supported. But when they tried to give him water, he couldn't swallow. "We'll return in a while," the woman said.

Tashar sat where they had left him. Afternoon began to feel like evening, and the wind began to blow.

Chapter 46

Zanja crept up the hill, often hiding in plain sight. After many hours, near the crest, she lay face down on the ground, her black hair wrapped in a mud-smeared head cloth, her dark face hidden in her plant-stained sleeve, trapped by a group of four that had begun to play a dice game on the hilltop just above her.

"Hsst!"

She uncovered one eye and saw the boy perched on a massive foundation stone. "He's coming," he said.

Zanja covered her face. The boy began humming. She could remember some of the song's words, and made up the rest.

> *Time is a* katrim *who waits and waits and waits.*
> *Time is a shadow turning slowly with the sun.*

The dice players spoke in deferential murmurs. She heard a voice as soothing as a snake bite. "He should have been here yesterday, at the latest."

The boy said to Zanja, "You never liked Bran."

Zanja mouthed two words against her shirt sleeve: "*Shut up.*"

Bran—Saugus—joked with his people. They laughed eagerly. That the man craved and enjoyed such deference should have been shameful.

Zanja's guide said, "He's studying the landscape. He's looking down the road, which is completely empty. Now he's looking at the sky."

"Did you notice that a storm is brewing?" Saugus asked.

A dice player stood up. "*Another* storm? That last one was dreadful."

"So I have heard. But the cellars didn't flood."

"No, Saugus. Just a puddle at the door where the rain came down the stairs."

"We should bring the powder kegs into shelter," Saugus said.

The boy snorted derisively. "They're picking up their playing pieces as though their lives depend on it!"

And they would die for him and think it was a choice. Zanja lay flat on earth, tense with fury.

"He's still there," murmured the boy. "Studying the storm, irritated by your presence . . . but he doesn't seem to know it. He thinks it's the weather that's unsettling him, or that laggard he's expecting: Maxew, I think. There—he is leaving."

Zanja breathed in, and breathed out. When she was calm enough, she advanced to the top of the hill. Now the fortifications concealed her from anyone above her. A person approaching from below might see her, but she could hide in the afternoon shadows.

She dared turn and look at the view that Saugus had been studying: the white, vacant glare of the Shimasal Road, the forest a smear of green beyond the hills, the boiling storm that cast a rapidly growing shadow on the land. She saw a bolt of lightning, brief and startling as an insight.

People moved past on the opposite side of the barrier, carrying something heavy. Someone shouted and was answered by laughter. Distant thunder rumbled, and the air began to move. That breeze would bring the storm directly to this hill.

The boy, standing on the massive stone, held up a page from the lexicon: the Whirlwind. It signified a loss of meaning, a tearing loose of all connections, a rending and reversing of every idea, the severing of every love and friendship, the reduction of purpose to lunacy.

Emil probably was dead, as was J'han. Leeba would be killed, and Zanja would die trying to rescue her. Norina would die in a duel with Saugus, and Saugus probably would survive because he had a plan. Medric, Garland, and Clement would be killed for being Sainnite. Karis would survive in such servitude that her years of enslavement to the smoke drug would look like freedom.

Zanja huddled in shadow, weeping, as the whirlwind charged the hill.

People began shouting, chasing hats and belongings. Loose canvas flapped like torn sails. The sailing ship climbed a spilling mountain of black water. An old woman stood upon its plunging decks. She looked across the sea, the land, the waterways, the mountains of Shaftal. Zanja, crouched in a corner by a mountain of stone, scarcely kept her balance, but Grandmother Ocean remained steady, peaceful, and unconcerned upon that tossing deck. She glanced at Zanja and laughed at her despair.

A lightning strike, a concussion of thunder, a joyful shout from the crew, and Zanja ducked her head as water began to pummel her.

Karis spoke. "Zanja, except for two guards at the entrance, all others have taken shelter underground."

Darkness had come with the storm. Without the sun, Zanja was lost. "Karis—I saw Grandmother Ocean."

"This is her storm," said Karis.

Zanja breathed out. Her trembling stilled. "Harald G'deon," she said, "he chose his successor wisely."

With weary, fearful sorrow, Karis said, "I hope so."

Zanja was alone, but she had remembered that a ghostly army was being dragged behind her, the whole pattern that was implied by her small, ragged piece of carpet. She rose and moved upward among the massive stones, following pathways made by the hill's other occupants. She found two people who sheltered beneath a flapping roof, watching the road for lost souls, guarding the stairs to the underworld.

She found a place to take shelter from the gale, close enough to hear the guards shout to each other above the roar of wind. To pass them unnoticed was impossible, and to fight them both—two fighters more hardened and experienced than she—was foolish. She waited, and the storm waited with her.

"A strange storm," said one guard, in a lull. The other said that he had expected a summer storm, of the sort that passes quickly, with a clear sky in its wake. But now it seemed likely to last all night.

"Here comes another downpour."

Rain washed over them. Zanja's only shelter was her own back. With her head on her knees, she sang silently:

Time is a storm that never ends.
Time is a witch who pays her debts with rain.

Sometimes she heard bits of conversation: the guards telling each other about battles they had fought when they were Paladin irregulars in one or another of the militias that had formed to resist Sainnite rule. They had never learned the first lesson of the true Paladins: the only good battle is the one that is avoided.

She heard a thud. A warped door was wrenched open on squawking hinges. Dim light from a lantern glittered on the rain.

"I was afraid you'd fallen asleep."

"I've been about to piss myself for half an hour."

"Drink less, then." The newcomer climbed up to the guard shelter, and one watcher departed down the stairs, presumably to use a bucket latrine.

Zanja had been waiting for one of them to step away, but the wait seemed wasted. The watcher returned, and the other left. That one returned, and all three of them lingered, saying ordinary things that they all knew to be true. Sometimes she saw their heads nodding in rhythm. Even if they fell asleep, she could not slip past them—not through that squawking, crooked door.

Upon the Shimasal Road, sodden boots stumbled over flat ground.

Zanja's hands clenched into fists. Rain-blinded people from her ghostly army crashed into her.

Someone tugged her out of the way. Karis said, "Maxew has arrived at the House of Lilterwess."

Norina's voice: "Trust Zanja, and keep walking."

In her own wet skin once again, Zanja wiped rain out of her eyes and stood up. She stretched her legs. Her satchel had become heavy with rain. In the shelter, the guards' aimless talk had become a tense silence.

A distant voice called, weakly.

"That's him!"

"Is he hurt?"

"Can you see him?"

"Coming toward us from the road."

All three guards left their shelter, cursing the coldness of the rain, and hurried down the hillside. Zanja ran to the doorway, ducked under the sagging, rain-filled canvas roof, and descended cracked and canted stone steps illuminated by a lantern tucked into a niche. The door with the squawking hinges had been left half ajar. She slipped through and descended into deep darkness, feeling the way down slippery steps to the uneven stones of a laid floor. She sensed shelves and bins looming in thick darkness. She heard the breaths of many sleepers, and the muffled ticking of a clock. She smelled wet laundry, cooked fish, and pungent pistol oil.

She followed the passage between sleeping people and their bags, weapons, and boots. She passed through a dry sprinkle of dirt that was trickling through the rotten ceiling boards. She put her hand on a heavy, closed door and knew its history: acorn, sapling, tree, and then thick oak boards strapped with iron. Now the wood was returning to earth, its bolts rusted away, its hinges turning to red dust.

Karis was in Zanja's hands. The iron submitted to her, and the wood was healed. Zanja swung the door silently open, slipped into the passageway, and shut the door again. With Zanja's mouth Karis whispered, "More people are sleeping in the next room."

"And one of them is Saugus," Zanja replied.

"We must go through."

In the next doorway, all that remained of the door was some spongy splinters underfoot. Zanja should never have uttered the air witch's name, not even in a whisper scarcely louder than a breath. She had awakened Norina that easily many times. She stepped in, terrified, remembering how she said to Leeba, *Never scream or yell from fear—it only makes you more afraid.*

This room was drier than the last, and the company's food stores were here, hanging from the ceiling beams in oilcloth bags. The powder kegs were here also, lined along the wall. A dozen more people slept here. One was turning restlessly: Saugus. Zanja raced to the far door and again was able to open and close it with no sound. Yet she continued to flee, down the short passageway, to the next, empty room. There she forced herself to pause, to slow her thudding heartbeat. But deep breathing only made her dizzy.

She crossed the room to the next door and stopped short in dismay. She could hear the mutter of voices. A few ghostly traces of light slipped through the cracks. That guarded passage would be similar to the others: two body-lengths' long, one wide, with beamed ceilings and walls of mortared stone. Two body-lengths separated Zanja from Leeba.

She could not think what to do. She felt strangely light-headed, her heart pounding as if she had stood up too suddenly after a long illness. How many people were in the passage? If she opened the door, what then? She must not, dared not, could not fail!

Something poked her left arm. She turned sharply, lost her balance, and staggered into nothing. She felt the poke again. Karis! Why had she become so stupid? Poke. She shuffled to the left. Poke. She shuffled forward. The palms of her hands were tickling. She pressed them to the wall.

A wall of stone and mortar, with earth behind it, thicker than Karis was tall, more stones and mortar on the other side, and then the next storeroom. The mortar was weak, and it powdered at her touch. Zanja dug her fingers around the edge of a stone, pulled it out and managed to lower it to the floor, though it probably weighed as much as Leeba. She staggered dizzily and cracked her head on the wall. She pulled out another stone and put it atop the first, giving herself a platform to kneel on. She pressed her hands to bare soil.

Between each particle of dirt there were channels: the pathways of earthworms, of ants, and of roots that had rotted away. She slid a finger into one tiny passage, claiming room from other passages that were equally tiny, claiming more room, making her own passage larger until her head and shoulders could enter the earth and she could wriggle through it. The weight of earth pressed upon her. There was no air. Lungs aching, she wormed through the wall. She struck stone with her bruised head. The far wall? And her arms were trapped at her sides.

Her ears were roaring. There was a sick pressure in her temples. She wiggled her legs, which moved the soil a little further, just enough that she could bend her knees and creep backwards to the empty store room and kneel on the stone platform, gasping.

Muffled voices spoke. Too far way to worry about. "Bad air," Karis gasped. "Smothering. Must go forward."

Zanja wiggled back into the earth, this time with hands reaching ahead of her. When she touched the rock wall of the next room, the mortar dissolved into limestone and sand. She pushed the stone desperately, and it fell. Sweet air poured into her tunnel. She breathed. Her first clear thought was that she should have swooned a good while ago. And if she had fainted, Karis would have fainted with her.

Leeba lay utterly silent, possibly sleeping, possibly frozen with terror.

"Leeba, it's me. I've come for you. Don't make a sound. Stay where you are."

Zanja pushed out another stone, which should have thudded to the floor so loudly that a person would have to be deaf not to hear it. But it landed almost soundlessly, and when Zanja dragged herself into Leeba's dungeon, there were no stones—just mounds of gritty dust. She ran into the room, dropped to her knees, and grabbed her daughter.

"I didn't scream," said Leeba.

Chapter 47

Tashar slept.

"Here he is," said someone.

He blinked his eyes vigorously, but the darkness didn't go away.

People dragged him through long, whiplike stems that slashed at his face. Other people in a wagon bed hauled him aboard. He noticed the flickering flame of a lantern with its dirty chimney girded in rusty iron hanging from a pole above the driver. He heard people talking, hooves scraping on stone, harnesses rattling. He smelled wood and burlap. Someone put a folded sack under his head.

Later, it began to rain.

Later, a voice commanded him to awaken.

He jerked upright. "The bastard!" he cried.

Five sodden, solemn children gazed at him from outside the wagon. "He means Maxew," a girl stated.

"What did Maxew do to him?" asked a boy with wet hair in his eyes.

Two soldiers swam out of the rain. They yanked Tashar from the wagon. He staggered on stiff, numb legs and fell to his knees. The rain opened like a curtain, and a woman stood there. "Return to Hanishport," she said.

"I will." He would have said anything to make her go away. The rain flapped like a blanket, and she disappeared.

The children drew around him, peering at him with great interest.

"He doesn't mean it."

"He won't do it."

"But it doesn't matter."

"Karis can find him."

"Then he should do as he was told."

"It's only reasonable."

"But Madam Truthken, he could flee on a boat."

"Good riddance," said the Truthken, who appeared and disappeared again in a gust of wind.

"If he flees, he can never return. Does he know that?"

"He knows now."

"Go away!" Tashar cried.

They disappeared. When the rain opened again, he saw two soldiers hoisting the children into a wagon. A huge woman strode past with a man riding on her back, who said, ". . . must be another word. Your language doesn't seem able to express how much I appreciate . . ."

People stretched a tarpaulin over the wagon bed to shelter the children from the rain. A soldier handed a babbling baby to one of the children.

Someone helped Tashar to his feet. He gaped at her: it was Maxew's mother, in sodden shirt and dripping hair.

"Can you tell me anything about my son?" she asked.

"That bastard," he croaked.

"Does he only exercise his power *upon* people? Will he never do it *for* them?"

Tashar laughed at the idea. Maxew's mother, who didn't seem to have been joking, walked away.

A voice shouted words Tashar didn't understand. Everyone in the road stopped still, and by that stillness he realized how much activity, and how many people, had been around him all that time. The voice shouted again, and now everyone replied, hoarsely, fiercely. Some cried their answer in Shaftalese: "Yes, General!" The horses groaned and began to pull, and the people groaned and began to run.

A Paladin ran into Tashar. "Pardon me," she said over her shoulder. "Get out of the way."

Tashar shuffled to the road's edge and stood there, stupid as a sheep, while history passed him by.

Many hours passed. The rain stopped falling, and the sky was riven by cracks that for a time hovered over him like a net of black lace, until the clouds started to glow, and the net became a cloud-clotted sky. He saw tall grasses strung with glittering beads. He saw stands of trees, and streams swollen by rainfall. But the sun had not yet risen when he heard a distant yell of rage, metal clanging on metal, and the brisk announcement of a bugle.

Tashar stepped off the road and tried to run toward the sound, but soon he had to walk again, although he was gasping with excitement. How hopeless he had felt throughout that wet night. He had thought that everything he had done and sacrificed had amounted to nothing. But he was not too late! The fate of Shaftal had not yet been decided!

He pushed through a stand of trees and came out near the base of a hill. Although many of the walls had tumbled down, crescent-shaped terraces climbed the slope like gigantic stair steps. No one had looked after these gardens, but the plants were green. A mossy stream that waterfalled over and meandered along the terraces was too decorative to be natural. The hilltop, slopes, and spiral road were cluttered with massive stone blocks: the remains of the House of Lilterwess.

Upon one of those blocks at the hilltop, a soldier stood, her gray uniform gilded by a foolish sun. She was watching the battle, which Tashar couldn't see. Near the soldier stood the bugler, whose instrument flashed as he raised it to blow a signal. The soldier must be the general. Excited, Tashar ran toward her. He scrambled onto the first terrace, then was slogging through the wet tangle of the lowest garden. He fought through: waist deep, then chest deep, in leaves so shiny they seemed varnished, among sweet-scented flowers that were twisting open in the sunlight. Then he stepped into an emptiness he couldn't see and fell into an invisible pond. Insects exploded upward, black clouds of gnats, darting blue jewels of damsel flies. The vines that had grabbed each other across the pond now held him upright in the warm water, where, assaulted by the sewer stink of stagnant mud, he could see nothing but leaves.

He felt somewhat discouraged. He pushed away the vines that blocked his view. The general was bent over, speaking with someone Tashar couldn't see. Then she spoke to the bugler, and he blew another signal. Between Tashar and the hilltop, a clump of people staggered into view, their arms wrapped around each other like lovers. They stumbled out of sight before Tashar could figure out what they were doing.

Then he noticed a person who, like him, was creeping toward the Sainnite general, but she was following the wall of the highest terrace. In one hand she carried a dagger and in the other a pistol. When her face turned toward the vivid light of sunrise, Tashar recognized her as a member of Death-and-Life Company. After the massacre at the Children's Garrison, she had spent the winter huddled in a dark corner—or so it had seemed to Tashar, in his sporadic visits to the house in Hanishport. But now she was intent, fearless, focused as a predatory cat.

He saw movement between two of the massive stones. A man slipped out of the shadows and dropped down behind the woman. She whirled on him, dagger in hand, and three more people jumped down behind. One grabbed her fighting arm, one grabbed her pistol arm, and the third, a very large man, wrapped his arms tenderly around her from behind. She yanked her dagger hand free and swung awkwardly at the first man. The weapon he raised to block her blow looked like a giant cooking spoon. It broke into pieces. One of the others yanked her arm backwards, and her dagger went flying. Gunpowder exploded, and the pistol ball screamed as it ricocheted from stone. Tashar kept his eyes on the flying dagger. *There,* he thought, when it landed. *There in the next terrace, near the pine saplings.*

The general coolly ignored the skirmish immediately below her. The group struggled and stumbled about until they had bound the woman's arms behind her back. Three dragged her away, while the fourth remained behind, scanning the gardens. He did not spot Tashar in his stinking hiding place. Now he picked up the pieces of his spoon, climbed the wall, and disappeared between the stone blocks.

Of course, the general had not left her back exposed. Though her guards had borne their prisoner down the road that spiraled the hill, others probably remained. Tashar decided not to attack the general. But he did retrieve the dagger.

Chapter 48

Leeba clung to Zanja. "I did everything you taught me," she said. "But they caught me anyway."

"But Leeba, you did well. You were brave!"

"Why did it take so long for you to come?"

"I have been running day and night to come to you. I have hardly rested. But I was far away from you."

"Where is Karis?"

"She is inside me," Zanja said, "and she is coming."

"And Daddy? Is he coming?"

"I don't know," said Zanja. She felt certain that J'han was dead, and it seemed likely that Leeba had seen him die. "Leeba-love," said Zanja, like J'han had always called her. "Leeba-bird," like Karis. "Hay child, ink child, dirt child, Little Hurricane." One pet name for each parent, to remind her of them.

Leeba lifted her face from Zanja's shoulder. "What are we going to do?"

"We'll escape together. Walk around this room with me, and I'll try to think of how."

With her daughter's hand in hers, Zanja walked the perimeter of the room. This stone floor, like the others, was rippled with age, but the wall stones were so tightly fitted she could hardly distinguish their edges. The only egress was the door to the guarded passage.

She could put Leeba where the door would protect her when it was opened and attack the people who came in, possibly injuring two or three of them before the rest recovered from surprise. She could put Leeba into the worm-tunnel and push her into the adjacent airless room—but only if that room had a door to the surface.

She tried to imagine the space, as she had done before without effort, but now she could not do it. "Boy," she said in a low voice, but Leeba answered.

"You're talking in your people's language again."

"I'm calling a friendly spirit for help."

"Come help us, spirit!" Leeba said.

The boy didn't come.

Zanja said, "My sight and my insight both are gone. I need to see."

Leeba said, "Then we need Medric."

"Leeba, what a ninny I am! I have his spectacles!" Zanja's satchel still hung across her shoulders, sodden and heavy. She dumped its contents on the floor, for it was halfway filled with dirt.

"You sounded like Medric, just now," Leeba said.

"That was the spirit talking. He speaks with my mouth, and sometimes he sounds like people I know. I found the spectacles. I'm putting them on."

"Now can you see?"

Medric stood before her: bright as flame but casting no light. Sunburned, dirty, and unshaven, he gazed inquiringly at her.

Zanja said, "What can a fire witch do to an air witch? I need to know!"

He answered, "I do tend to get the missing bits at the last possible moment, don't I? Well, what does the card-casting tell us?"

Zanja's dream guide was there, with the lexicon, a huge, heavy book that he held up to the seer as though it weighed no more than a sheet of paper.

"Are you here, Medric?" Leeba asked.

"I am here, dirt child!" said Medric. "Don't let go of Zanja. Don't let go at all, no matter what happens. Can you do that?"

Zanja saw Leeba, bright as day, with her rabbit peering out of her pocket and both her hands clenched in the canvas fabric of Zanja's breeches. She seemed as confident and fearless as Norina.

Norina, Zanja thought, and drew her dagger.

Medric said musingly: "Since air bloods are incapable of *unreason,* what is the *reason* they find fire logic intolerable?"

Norina stood rigidly still, her formidable self-control barely adequate to manage her impatience. "Surely we don't need to discuss this *now.*"

"But we do," the seer replied, "or else we can't continue."

Norina said, "Fire logic is maddening because it has no facts, purpose, or method. And yet, despite its lack of underpinnings, more often than not fire knowledge turns out to be accurate."

Zanja found Emil's pen. And he was there, the suave and somber chief councilor of Shaftal; the shabby tool seller who had wandered the land, seeking the wisest, most knowledgeable, skillful, and respected people of Shaftal; the commander of South Hill Company; the young Paladin who yearned to be a scholar. He was the Man on the Hill, and his star-pierced heart was too bright to look at.

Emil said, "Madam Truthken, your truths rise out of facts and reason. The truths of fire bloods not only lack facts and reason, but sometimes are true in spite of them. Thus, the very existence of fire logic constantly challenges the certainty of air logic."

"And so fire logic awakens air witches to humility," said Medric wickedly.

Leeba said, "Emil is here, and Norina. Is Daddy here?"

Zanja had found a packet of healing herbs and a piece of waybread, but neither J'han nor Garland had appeared. So she tore open the packet of herbs and dumped them in her mouth, and they were damp enough thanks to the rain that they didn't choke her as she swallowed them with the waybread, and a fair amount of dirt.

"Philosophy!" said Garland. "Eat *that* when your belly is empty, and see what it gains you."

"Garland!" Leeba said.

"Jam buns," he replied. "I promise. As soon as I have a kitchen."

"I am here, Leeba love," said J'han.

"Daddy, the people hurt you!"

"Yes, they hurt me," he said. "Listen, Leeba. This is important. Every single day of your life, remember that I love you."

Zanja put her hand on Leeba's shoulder, and it was Karis's hand. Karis said, "I'm sorry, Leeba-bird. Some things I cannot fix."

J'han said, "Leeba love, sing a song for me—the song of the four elements."

In a thin, wavering voice, Leeba began to sing:

> The way of earth is to make and till.
> Earth needs fire to enrich its soil,

Earth wants air so its storehouse fills,
Four elements for balance.

She must have learned the song in school. Zanja had never heard it. She sang,

The way of air is to judge and prove
Air by earth can be beloved
Air needs water so it can move
Four elements for balance.

Medric spread his long fingers and gathered up the lexicon and the dream guide. Zanja saw her lost son's laughing face, and then the book and boy were crumpled into a ball.

"Boy," she said, but he was already gone.

"Now, Emil," said Medric, "the fire."

Emil pierced his own heart with his pen, so it burned with starlight. With that he lit the crumpled stuff of intuition, and Medric's hands were filled with fire.

Leeba sang,

The way of fire is to see and know
Fire with earth can be renewed
Fire needs water to ease its woe
Four elements for balance.

The way of water is to change and sing
Water needs air for its lightning
Water wants fire for divining
Four elements for balance.

"Now, Zanja," said Medric, "water, earth, and air."

Zanja dipped Norina's dagger in the fire. The dagger became the flame, and the flame became a dagger of light that rippled like water along the wavemarks in the steel. The flame burned in Zanja's trembling grip, and it was much too late to pass that awful weapon to someone else.

Leeba sang,

> Four enemies, or four friends
> Four elements to tear and mend
> Four elements to begin and end
> Four elements for balance.

The door opened.

By the light of the lantern held up by the first man, Zanja saw three people, but several others stood behind them.

"Hold on, Leeba," said Zanja and backed away until the wall was at her back—the outer wall, the foundation wall, which with stone fingers gripped the bones of the earth. She heard a distant, muffled sound of shouting.

The man with the lantern cried, "Saugus—there is a woman with her!"

His surprise reminded Zanja that she was standing in darkness, armed with a dagger, clutched by a child, talking with spirits. But the spirits remained.

"We left the door unguarded for a little while to help the boy up the hill."

"But she couldn't have passed us in the hall," objected another one of the guards Zanja had squirmed past.

The front lantern briefly illuminated the wall, but Zanja's tunnel had closed, and no one heeded the missing stones.

"I was going to warn you," Maxew said. By the light of a second lantern in the crowd, Zanja glimpsed his swollen nose and the shredded hem of his sleeve.

Bran—Saugus—said, "How ironic it is that your arrival, Maxew, distracted the guards so that she could get in."

The young man said sullenly, "Everywhere we went, she arrived first. And she is out of her head too."

"Fire bloods can be difficult to hinder. But now she's trapped. Hold up that light."

The lantern that shone on Zanja also illuminated his face. He looked at Zanja as though he would only be satisfied if he could kill her a dozen times, in a dozen different ways. Norina had often looked at her in that way.

"What arrogance," Norina said.

"Disagreeable," said Garland.

"An ass," said Emil.

"A ninny," said Medric.

Maxew said, "She's crazy!"

"She has spells," said Saugus correctively. "But Norina could reach her, and so can I. Zanja na'Tarwein, I know how you entered these cellars. But how did you enter this room?"

Zanja felt Norina's twisted, predatory smile upon her own face, and the rogue witch's gaze was like a dissecting knife trying to cut a block of granite.

"Ask again," Norina suggested. "But you never ask a question twice, do you? As a point of pride, a display of petty power."

"Petty?" cried the air witch in a dreadful voice. "Every moment, every day, I serve only Shaftal!"

In her life of hairpin turns and gaping canyons, Zanja had often been astonished; but never more than at that moment, hearing Saugus say those words. He served *only* Shaftal. He was not like herself, who served her fear of losing her second tribe as she had lost her first. Nor was he like Emil, whose humility concealed his vanity, or Medric, whose desire to understand events was driven by desire to control them. J'han and Garland both managed other people's lives because it helped them to feel more comfortable, and Karis used her vast powers to insulate herself from fear. As for Norina, wasn't her devotion to the law merely a convenience?

But Saugus, his love for Shaftal was pure. He did not struggle with an unclear vision; he was not weighed down by affection and tragedy, nor was he entangled by history and tradition. He had never known doubt. Zanja was too broken to know what was right. She certainly should obey him.

"Zanja, lay down the blade," Saugus said.

Medric and Norina grabbed Zanja's wrist. They could not fight her for the blade—they weren't even there—yet they could help her to lift the dagger and fling it at Saugus.

It struck him in the chest and fell harmlessly to the floor with a ringing sound. Startled, Saugus stepped backwards, striking Maxew's smashed face. The young man shrieked with pain and staggered into a woman with a lantern. The shadows spun. The glass chimney shattered on the floor. The spilled oil caught fire. Everyone began screaming, shouting, rushing to pull Saugus out of danger. Somehow they knocked him over, and his clothing exploded into flame.

Karis flung Leeba into Zanja's arms and shoved both of them into the wall. The stone dissolved: a glittering powder sifted down between her and the burning. Then the flames dissolved. The earth's great weight squeezed the breath from her lungs, the sound from her ears, and the light from her eyes. Something scraped down the length of her body; something shattered across the top of her skull.

Hands gripped under her armpits. She entered the light of dawn. In a shouting circle of Paladins and soldiers, Karis hauled her wife and child out of the ground.

Two soldiers grabbed Zanja, with Leeba still clinging to her neck, and dragged them both away—Zanja gasping, coughing, spitting, choking out some words in Sainnese: "Bloody hell, I can walk!"

"General's orders," one snapped.

They hauled her far from the battle, to the swale that rose up to the park, dropped her in the meadow, and left. Nearby, in the shade of the cedars, cooks, medics, and farmers seemed to be improvising a hospital.

Zanja lay in soft, wet grass, coughing until she could breathe. Then she sat up and brushed the soil from Leeba's eyebrows and eyelashes. Leeba grinned, her small teeth very white in a face brown with dirt.

"You lost a tooth!" said Zanja. "You're getting very old."

"You are the dirtiest person in the history of the world."

"Except for you, Hurricane."

"Where did Karis go? Is she all right?"

Zanja peered over her daughter's head at the struggle on the hilltop. Karis was a wild-haired titan with a fierce dog at either side. A man charged her with an ax in his hand, but one dog grabbed his leg by the calf, the other bit his forearm, and Karis punched him. The attacker twirled away, blood spraying from his smashed nose, and landed untidily among the stones. Someone tripped over him. Then a couple of soldiers grabbed him by the arms and legs and hauled him away.

"Don't worry about Karis," Zanja said. "Only an idiot picks a fight with a metalsmith."

Chapter 49

Tashar had worked his way toward the north side of the hill, where the steeper slope dropped into a swale. On the facing slope, just beyond the hill's shadow, was a collection of wagons. At least a dozen draft horses were calmly tearing up the grass in a field so lush and green it even looked appetizing to him. Various people—Shaftali farmers, by the clothing—were stretching tarps between wagons to make sun shelters. A pot had been hung over a brisk fire, but no one was paying attention to it.

He crept in shadow, sneaking up the hill along the old spiral road. As he drew near the crest of the hill, the bugle uttered a brassy cry, and a few fighters shouted a hoarse answer.

Now he saw the battle, and his excitement drained.

It didn't seem like a battle at all. People, mostly soldiers, but Paladins also, were clustered around what seem to be a hole in the ground, from which smoke drifted. There was a flurry of activity, but by the time he could distinguish what was happening, all he saw was a passive prisoner being escorted away. Off to one side, a group of soldiers seem to be chasing someone in and out among the blocks. In another place, the false G'deon talked with a Paladin, and a couple of large dogs panted beside her. Blood dripped from her right hand. A man, one of Willis's old lieutenants, was being carried away, his head bobbing loosely and his mouth slack, his face blood smeared.

Tashar felt a dizzying, spinning sensation: his sky boat caught in the storm, falling, caught in the heavy grip of the tumbling trees, smashing and torn to shreds. His foot slipped, and he grabbed wildly at the stones, at the gravel, at the sky, but could get no purchase. Then he was giddily clutching the tilting earth. Oddly, he thought about his mother, who had abandoned him to the care of a disapproving family and taken a boat somewhere. In his mind, she had always been a romantic wanderer, enchanted by the horizon. But maybe she had just been disappointed.

He stood up cautiously. No one had even noticed him. The calm, efficient business on the hilltop continued. Tashar's faintness certainly was from hunger. What should he do now? Was anything left at all?

He turned away from the hilltop. He noticed, at the near edge of the swale, that a woman sat with a child in her arms. It was the woman who had stolen his sky boat and made him feel like a coward. The G'deon's wife.

He had stuck the dagger in his belt, but now he took it in his hand.

He slithered down the steep slope, crossed the spiral road, and more cautiously crept down the slope again. He heard the child ask a querulous question, and heard the murmur of a reply.

"They'll be sorry they made her so mad!" he heard the girl say.

"She won't want to forgive them," said Zanja na'Tarwein.

"She shouldn't."

"She probably wants to hurt them like they hurt you," said the woman.

Tashar could not hide from view, but the woman's back was turned to him, and the girl was nearly invisible in her lap. With the ground nearly level, and the wet grass silent underfoot, he approached them. He heard the girl begin to weep: not the shrill, temperamental cries Tashar was accustomed to hearing in the House of Lora, but a heart-broken wail.

"I'm so sorry," said the woman. She was crying also. How dared she weep? He wasn't weeping, even though he had lost his sky boat and upon the hilltop the brave members of Death-and-Life Company were being captured and hauled away like dumb animals.

He charged her. In his mind's eye, he slashed the blade across her throat. But her forearm somehow got in the way, and instead he sliced a long piece of flesh from her arm. He glimpsed the little girl, white-eyed with terror.

The child would be so easy to kill! Yet somehow the girl had been flung away, and the woman, scrambling on one hand and two feet like an insect with half its legs pulled off, was impeding him, blocking him, forcing him to strike again at the bloody, bare bone of her arm. His weapon stuck in the bone and nearly slipped out of his hand. The famed fighter, Zanja na'Tarwein, had not even managed to get to her feet! If he thrust down at her back, and remembered to angle his blade so it slid between her ribs, he would pierce her lungs and might even pierce her heart.

He felt a glee, like when he was sailing tight to a brisk wind, with the boat leaping from the waves and the sun shining in the spray so he was flying through rainbows.

Then something punched him in the chest, and he fell.

"Zanja," Emil said.

She looked at him, and he was smiling wryly at her. "Am I dead again?" she asked.

"Alive," he answered. "Bleeding some."

She heard a troubling sound, the hysterical cries of a child. "Leeba!"

"Safe," Emil said. "Safe. Safe."

He wasn't wearing a shirt. He was hurting her arm. She looked down and saw his shirt padding her arm, sodden with blood. He pressed it with both his hands. I really should lie down, she thought. But she was already lying down.

She turned her head and saw Medric with Leeba in his arms and a pistol in his hand. She saw a dead man who had a neat, black hole burned in his shirt. He had been trying to kill her, and she didn't know why. But he was solemn, and quiet, and would never explain himself to anyone.

Chapter 50

When that motley company left their belongings on the edge of the forest, they also had left behind some twenty soldiers who were strung like beads along the supply line. These soldiers hauled the belongings back to the wagons, then drove the wagons by stone roads westward and then northward until they stumbled upon the main company. The air children received their *Books of Everything,* Norina her maps, the Paladins their notes for the dictionary, and Chaen her sketchbook. She immediately began to draw.

Eventually, she and her sketchbook would go to Watfield, where the artists who lived in Travesty would teach her how to turn her drawings into etchings to be printed in a broadsheet distributed throughout Shaftal. A year later, those same etchings would be in Medric's book, *A Hinge of History: The Last Year, and the First.* That book would be printed and reprinted until every village had at least one copy. But Chaen merely drew the pictures because her memory felt overfilled. She never imagined that, for the rest of her life, she would never be far from a print of those drawings.

Chaen drew two people carrying a burned woman through the doorway to the cellar as soldiers hurried down the stairs to help them. Norina studied the faces of the people, members of Death-and-Life Company, then said to Chaen, who stood beside her, "Something has happened to Saugus—he may even be dead."

Chaen drew Karis, who was approaching them with her dogs and Paladins, blood dripping from the broken knuckles of her right hand. "Leeba is safe," she said to Norina, who heaved a breath, as though she had not breathed at all for many days.

Chaen even drew herself, a shadow in the smoky cellar, facing a thin, gangly young man of knobby bones and little muscle, like his father had been when Chaen first loved him. She grabbed Maxew's bony arms and said, "I told them I could convince you to surrender."

He had made a strange, barking sound—perhaps it was laughter, distorted by smoke and despair. "Surrender for what, Mother? Only death lies before me. Death and nothing else."

"You know nothing of what is possible," she said. Then she knocked him down and threw herself upon his chest, so he couldn't use his voice of command on her.

But she did not draw how she begged Karis for his life, or how Norina took Maxew's will into her control and led him into the darkness.

Chaen drew Saugus, contorted by pain, dressed in the ashes of clothing, among charred blankets that had been used to smother the flames. His flesh was gruesome: vivid red, leathery white, and charcoal black. And yet he was alive enough to utter a wheezing whine of pain. In the drawing, Karis knelt beside Saugus on the smoking stones, numbing his agony with one hand while with the other she passed Norina the dagger she had plucked from the ashes.

Norina spoke a few formal words and then killed him. His blood welled sluggishly from the large veins of his throat, flowed thickly between the floor stones, and stained the knees of the G'deon's breeches. This Chaen did not draw. Nor did she draw how she had lingered beside the dead man and thanked him for his right and kind actions that few would remember. Saugus had not been evil—not always—but how could that fact be portrayed in a picture?

She drew sleeping people—Sainnite, Paladin, and farmer—scattered across the swale while draft horses grazed among them, as Seth and a medic went from one person to the next with baskets of unguents and bandages. In the foreground lay Zanja and Medric, with Leeba between them. Emil watched over them, resting his hand sometimes on one, sometimes on another.

Emil had beckoned Chaen over. "You, Paladin, become," he had said.

"I don't understand—"

He took her earlobe between his fingers, then touched his own, three-times pierced.

"Become," he had said.

This was the day Zanja realized she had become a legend among the Sainnites. She walked among them where they sprawled upon the hillside in their filthy, sweat-stained uniforms, their socks and boots scattered about them. She had run an army into ground and now walked through that toppled forest of Sainnites, barefoot, not even limping. Wherever she went, their gazes tracked her.

She saw Clement uphill, with her baby son's head inside her tunic. She already had mastered the trick of holding that wiggling body to her breast and gazing into his milk-drugged eyes, but she looked from Gabian to the exhausted soldiers, and that sight also seemed to content her. Of course, Clement's struggle on her people's behalf hadn't ended, but it certainly had changed. She raised a hand to Zanja as she passed.

Beyond Clement, upon the hilltop, farmers recruited by Paladins were cooking a gigantic meal in pots they must have borrowed from every nearby kitchen. Zanja spotted Garland talking shyly with a farmer.

Zanja had heard that Garland had protected Clement with a wooden spoon. She should talk to him soon, but not now. The farmer he was talking to pointed northward and made a gathering motion. Were they talking about picking berries? Zanja continued across the slope as Garland and the farmer walked away together. He also wasn't limping.

Among the cedars, the members of Death-and-Life Company sat in grimly muttering groups, apparently under the impression that the rope strung through the trees was the walls of a prison. Two flags of torn fabric fluttered, tied to the rope at an arm's distance, and on each flag was painted the word "door." An air child ducked under the rope, between the flags. "Zanja na'Tarwein."

"Yes, Anders."

"Please, will you speak with Norina?" He pointed.

Norina Truthken sat at a distance, her back against the ancient trunk of a cedar, gazing blankly toward the ruin of the House of Lilterwess. Zanja said to Anders, "Yes, but why?"

He said, "Zanja, I am just her student. You are her friend."

Norina turned her head as Zanja approached. Her bristling hair was stiff with sweat and dirt. Her hand was clenched in a white-knocked fist. The dagger Zanja had flung at Saugus lay beside her, black with soot and blood. Zanja took and cleaned it, using water from her flask and the ragged tail of her bloodstained shirt. She polished it until the wavering folds in the metal were visible again. She said, "Your student, Anders, he'll be head of the order someday."

Norina answered dully. "I hope he doesn't realize it. Just as I hope the air children don't realize they are teaching him how to lead them."

"He said I am your friend."

"Then it must be true."

And indeed it was true, after a fashion. Medric claimed there was a long history of friendship between air and fire elementals, but Zanja believed that, as with herself and Norina, friendship merely had turned out to be the most reasonable, though not the easiest, alternative. Fire and air didn't want or need each other, according to Leeba's song—except for balance. But balance was crucial.

Zanja said, "What's in your hand?"

Norina unclenched her fist. There lay a lock of J'han's hair—brown, ordinary, stiff with blood. "I never understood why people save the hair of the dead."

With no little effort, Zanja put an arm around her.

Norina began to weep. It was terrifying. Fortunately, it didn't last long.

She said eventually, "Thank you for rescuing and defending our daughter."

Zanja dried her own tears. She knew all about how grief would continue. Every day they would miss J'han's sturdy patience and gentle humor, and they would never cease to feel that loss. She said, "All of us rescued Leeba, even J'han. Norina, can Emil recover?"

"Yes, don't be concerned about him. Maxew shattered Emil's patterns, but he didn't destroy the pieces. It's a good lesson for my students, to put those pieces back together. And if they ever are tempted to engage in such destruction, they'll remember what it costs."

A wagon was arriving, laden with loaves of bread and yellow rolls of butter. Zanja stood up, for she was ravenous.

Norina also rose to her feet. "You haven't talked with Karis yet."

"No, the little time I've had with her, when she wasn't healing me she was crushing the breath out of me." And Zanja had a new scar, another of the many that marked where Karis had healed her, leaving a scar so that Zanja could read the script of her own history.

Norina said, "Karis wants to go with you to the Asha Valley."

"To the mountains? She can't leave Shaftal!"

"That's true, but not in the way you mean. Wherever Karis goes, Shaftal goes with her. By her presence that place would become part of Shaftal, and from then on it would be under the G'deon's protection. And the Law of Shaftal will apply there, so if you go there with her, I'll be needing a map."

Garland was at loose ends, and didn't like the feeling. Some people had tasks, but no one needed his help. Despite his pain and exhaustion, he couldn't bring himself to lie down and sleep like so many were doing.

A collection of young farmers, gathered under the shade of the beautiful cedar trees, raptly watched the activities on the hilltop, where Karis and some giant Sainnites were moving an enormous block of stone. Garland wasn't sure what they found so interesting. One of the farmers said, "Do you know what they're doing?"

She repeated her question before he realized she was talking to him. "They're uncovering a well. I guess it's blocked and buried, but we need water or else we'll have to move all these people somewhere else." He gestured toward the company collapsed upon the hillside. "That would be difficult."

She had approached him to converse better. She had a pointed nose and eyes with flecks of gold in them, and she held a half-finished hat in her hand that she had been weaving out of wet straw. "That's too bad," she said.

"What? Why?"

"We hoped they were rebuilding the House of Lilterwess."

"Well, they might be. Karis might start thinking that the stone she moves should be moved some more, and when she gets it to the right place she'll be so happy that she moves another one. And before you know it, she'll have built a building."

"So you know her."

"I'm her cook. She sharpens the knives when they need it."

"So you're her husband?"

"I don't think so."

The farmer burst out laughing. "Wouldn't you know if you were?"

"Not really. Ours isn't the usual sort of family, I guess. Is your farm close to here?"

"Not very close. Why do you ask?"

"Because I need help getting some food for these people. The soldiers' supply wagons won't be here for several days. We can't ask the three nearby farms to fed more than a hundred people for that long."

"I can help you, then. I was hauling supplies to the road-clearing camp, and I know which farm can spare what. I know where the orchard fruit is coming in. And the berries too. You might have to send crews to pick the fruit.

"That can be done, once our people have had a bit of a rest."

"So let's go. We can return with tomorrow's food before dark."

"Aren't your horses tired?"

"I was driving a borrowed team last night. I only just fetched my own horses from the pasture where they've been resting since the night before last. I'll get my horses and meet you at the wagons."

She picked up her sack of wet straw, gestured a farewell to her friends, and walked down the hillside, whistling from low to high as if it were a question. By the time Garland reached Clement, the farmer's horses had come to her and nuzzled in her shirt until she found a handful of oats in her pocket for each of them, which they chewed happily while she clipped the leads to their halters.

"Her horses like her," Clement observed. "That's a good sign."

Garland felt a rising flush, but she wasn't even looking at him. "General, I'm going out in the countryside, I'm not sure where exactly, to get food for tomorrow. I'll be back before sunset."

"Very good, Captain."

As he walked away, Clement called, "Garland, find a way to tell her you're a Sainnite. It won't get easier with time."

So the first thing Garland said, as he got into the wagon beside the farmer, was, "I might need some help with talking to your neighbors. I'm pretty good with the language, but there's a lot I don't understand about farmers, since I spent most of my life in a garrison."

She tutted to the horses, and they started forward. "They won't be hard to talk to. If plowing wasn't such hard work, they'd have started plowing the fallow fields already, just in case the G'deon needs a larger harvest in this place." She was nut-brown, barefoot, sturdy as the horses in her team, dressed in plain work clothing like everyone was, except for a blue, tasseled cord that decorated her hat. Her eyes were as brown as the rest of her, and they were full of laughter.

He felt a sudden, overpowering desire to cook something for her.

"I'm Terys." She said offered a work-hard, strong hand for him to clasp.

"Who has the best butter around here?" Garland asked. "And who's likely to be able to spare some flour? Or cider?"

"The cider has turned to vinegar by now, but I know where we can get some excellent beer. Butter and flour, those are easy."

By the time the wagon reached the road, their route had been entirely planned, and Garland could have crawled into the wagon bed, and even if the road wasn't famously smooth he still could have slept like the dead.

But he perched on the bench beside her, because he wanted more than anything to watch how she held the reins with thoughtless competence and to hear her tell about how things had been before the Fall of the House of Lilterwess. Of course she had just been a baby, but she retold the stories of her elders with hearty humor. "The music, the arguments, the liveliness of the House of Lilterwess! The entire household turned out in spring and autumn to help with the planting and harvesting. Our kids could go to school there in winter, and there was always a healer within call. And the Long Night parties—those are legendary."

As she drove the horses directly into a pond that had appeared, tucked between hills like a wonderful secret, she said, "Every single person will ask if Karis has come to stay."

"I'm afraid Karis keeps her household in Watfield."

"In that place called Travesty?" said Terys with laughing sarcasm. "She can't like it much."'

"It does have an excellent kitchen."

"An excellent kitchen is important, but you can build one of those anywhere."

The horses were drinking, with deep, sucking sounds. Terys took off her hat, her longshirt, and her breeches, and jumped into the water. Garland, having grown up with the rigid separation of the sexes that prevailed in the Sainnite garrisons, had never gotten entirely accustomed to seeing naked women. But even among the Shaftali, who were casual about nudity, he was fairly sure that when a grown woman like Terys took off her clothing in the presence of only one other person, it meant what he hoped it might mean.

He tore off his filthy clothing and jumped in. It was cool, and rather murky, and little fishes began nibbling on his toes almost immediately. Terys splashed him with water, and he splashed her back, and he felt dizzily, ridiculously happy.

Lookouts posted at the crossroads began to direct messengers up the Shimasal Road. At a table constructed of wagon boards and boulders, sheltered beneath an ancient oak tree, the government of Shaftal began to operate at one end and the command center of the Sainnites functioned at the other. There Garland met daily with the region's farmers, who continued to provide fresh food to this strange encampment, even after the supply wagons arrived. There Clement dispatched work parties of soldiers—those who had recovered enough from boosters and exhaustion—to assist in clearing the Shimasal Road. There Emil, never without at least one unnaturally attentive child at his side, began to compose letters, with Zanja or Medric as his scribe. There Karis, usually with Leeba in her arms or clinging to her leg, occasionally sat down long enough to eat a meat, hear a report, or offer an opinion. There Chaen sat with her sketchbook and pencils, composing her vision of history. And there people gathered to paint funeral flags for the pyre, even though all but Chaen were strangers to the dead.

The air children marched the demoralized prisoners to the funeral, then marched them back to their air-logic prison. A messenger reported that J'han's body also had been put to the pyre, because of a note Anders had left at the home of one of the city elders in Watfield that explained the strange and awful situation at Travesty. Chaen's son sat in the same cellar room in which Leeba had been imprisoned, visited only by Norina, given only a single candle for light. Every sunrise, people sleeping in the lush grass groaned, put their shirts over their faces, and fell asleep again. Karis and her company of giants, having uncovered and rebuilt the well, moved other massive stones as well, just for the fun of it, some speculated, though Garland claimed he knew exactly what

Karis was doing. A cobbler arrived, and a blacksmith also, and people and horses were re-shod. There was an orgy of mending, accompanied by many negotiations over the possession of needle and thread. Leeba sometimes could tolerate being out of contact with Karis, and one afternoon she even played for a while with some farm children.

A day was set to return to Hanishport. Chaen, still undecided about which direction to turn, discovered that everyone assumed she'd continue to assist in rehabilitating Death-and-Life Company. She'd get food and shelter, Seth pointed out, and that logic proved impossible to argue with. She sought out Anders, whose awkward and unnatural politeness she found endearing, and told him she'd continue to serve as a friend to the prisoners. He thanked her very much and promised to tell Norina of her decision.

So she would go back to Hanishport. But she reminded herself that she could step off this path anytime she wanted.

Chaen awoke before dawn because she heard Sainnite-shod horses arriving. Some day, she thought, that sound might cease to seem ominous. She lay awake, her bones aching, troubled by someone's snoring, uselessly wondering if she would be able to watch quietly while her son was executed for his crimes.

As the light rose, the camp became boisterous. Everyone packed and loaded their belongings, and bid farewell to the farmers who had supplied them with fresh meat and vegetables. Chaen sat with her knapsack at hand, her blankets rolled and tied. With her sketchbook across her knees, she drew what she could remember of Maxew's face. She kept an eye on the hilltop, where the Paladins had been bathing. When they hastily started down the hill, still buttoning their waistcoats and tying back their hair, Chaen stood up. She felt like she was diving into water so deep that it crushed her lungs. Seth came up and clasped her arm. Chaen said, "If I stand still, will I stop time?"

"Chaen, you must show him that, even if all else ends, love endures."

"That might be the last lesson of his life—and I'm afraid he won't learn it."

"But Norina learned it," Seth said. "So can he."

They walked to the table, where Karis, Zanja, Emil, the air children, and a collection of witnesses had gathered. Norina approached, with Maxew following jerkily behind her, as if he resisted every step.

Norina muttered a command, and Maxew halted. He stared at the children, who stared back at him. Norina began to explain the rule of law. Chaen finished drawing her son. He had a chin like hers, eyes like his father's, wavy light brown hair like most Midlanders, and anger and arrogance that were his alone.

When she glanced up from the page to check the length of his nose, Maxew was looking at her. Her heart recalled him, a boy both wise and stupid. Perhaps she had loved him by effort of will, but sometimes, surely, she had loved him with pride and hope.

Norina was saying, ". . . therefore, I cannot permit him to speak for himself. But we have witnesses to his other crimes."

Maxew looked away. Chaen corrected his nose in her sketch, but she could not easily depict what she had seen in her son's eyes. Angry pride, yes—but also the burden of his solitary days in the lightless cellar, the only place secure enough and solitary enough to imprison a person like him. Had he, after all, been able to learn something there?

Norina paused. "To my students, I say this: one day, each of you will be confronted by a decision that requires you to put the needs of the land above your own need to be right. Until you can accept that humiliation, you cannot be a Truthken."

Zanja na'Tarwein's self-control certainly rivaled Norina's, but Chaen saw an ironic expression briefly cross her face.

The Truthken said, "Emil Paladin, it is time for your testimony."

Emil rose to his feet, and in sentences that now had two levels of complexity, recounted what Maxew had done to him. Then Zanja stood up and said some of what he could not remember.

When she had finished, Norina said, "By my vows as a Truthken, I declare these statements to be accurate and truthful. Do the witnesses have any questions?"

One of the farmers, who had been supplying food to this unexpected crowd, and was now recruited into this alien proceeding, asked uncertainly, "Madam Truthken, did you say that the penalty for these crimes is death? The boy can't make the choice? But that isn't how the law works."

"You are correct. But since air witches can't be changed, and can only be imprisoned under cruel conditions, they must be put to death. So says the Law of Shaftal."

"But he is so young!"

"Yes. His judgment isn't fully developed, and he acted under the influence of an older air witch who is now dead. Nevertheless, he has unlawfully used air logic."

The farmer subsided, still unhappy.

Norina turned to Maxew. "Maxew of the Midlands, by the Law of Shaftal, I condemn you to death."

Chaen dropped her pencil. "Madam Truthken!"

Maxew, pale as milk, turned a startled gaze on her. Chaen directed a thought at him: *Allow me to rescue you, stupid boy!*

She said, "I am Maxew's mother, and he is the only surviving member of my family. During his childhood I could not give him the life an air child needs, and I helped him become criminal. Therefore, I ask the G'deon's clemency."

Karis rose to her feet. "Madam Truthken, I have been consulting with the children of the new Order of Truthkens. They have suggested that Maxew be given a choice. He may die, or else he may choose to live for five years with a spike pierced in his heart. That will enable him to roam freely while his life is in my hands."

She took the spike out of her pocket. She had made it from the two bolts, which she had melted down and pounded into an ugly, sooty thing. She placed it on the table, and the Truthken put her beautiful dagger beside it.

Norina said, "Maxew, which do you choose, the spike or the blade?"

Chaen became a Paladin. First she lived in Watfield, then in Kisha, and finally in the House of Lilterwess as it was being rebuilt. During the winters she helped copy the glyphic lexicon, and during the summers she traveled, often with Seth and other members of the Peace Committee. Occasionally, in places that violence had not yet been replaced by reason, the Paladins had to fight. But in most places, the old ways had persisted or at least had been eagerly reinstituted. Some members of Death-and-Life Company became Paladins. So did some soldiers, including Clement.

Five years passed. Maxew came to the House of Lilterwess and was accepted by the Order of Truthkens. Karis pulled out the spike that she had pounded into his heart. Then Maxew visited Chaen. He had grown to be as handsome as his father, but was far quieter. Chaen's memories of their life together had long since been restored, although those memories would always seem distant to her. She was no longer the bitter, grief-raddled woman who had willingly joined the infamous Death-and-Life Company. She and Maxew both had developed detachment and restraint.

Now they would once again spend a winter under the same roof, and eat and work together as did everyone in that rebuilt house, who crowded together in a few rooms and worked together to build a few more rooms that they would occupy next winter.

Some buildings, Chaen thought wryly, are never big enough. Some buildings are always being built.

Four elements to begin and end
Four elements for balance.

As green summer began to dance with golden autumn, Zanja returned home to the landscape that haunted her dreams, to the mountains that until then had marked the northern border of Shaftal: a shadow, a wall, a perilous obstacle. She led a small party of Paladins and pack horses through the foothills to the narrow pass scoured through the rocks by the Asha River—which eventually would meander placidly across Shaftal's flatlands to the sea but here was a crashing torrent. Their precarious path climbed the precipice, with mountains above and river below, and soon even the horses were groaning with pain as they toiled nervously and wearily upward.

After climbing for many days, they stood looking back at the path, which wound among ridges and rock falls, and soon disappeared entirely from view. The plunging river also disappeared behind a fold of the vast canyon and did not reappear until it was merely a flash of silver among the foothills.

That mountaintop was a harsh, astoundingly beautiful place. Even the sunshine felt unfamiliar, said Zanja's companions: brighter, purer, immoderate. Zanja wondered if Karis might be disoriented by the height. But Karis was smiling, her eyes teared only by wind, her hair blown back from her face. Leeba, riding on her shoulders, raised her arms to feel the power of the wind.

Now they walked downhill more than they went up, and sometimes even walked on the level for short stretches. As the path became easier, Zanja felt both dread and eagerness, as though she simultaneously remembered and had forgotten what had happened in Asha Valley.

"Am I going mad again?" she asked.

Karis said, "Shall we turn back?"

"What?"

"Well, I insisted on this journey. Of course, you're a helpless ninny who cannot say no."

Zanja pretended to be seriously considering this statement, until Karis laughed. "The closer we are to the valley, the more peculiar I feel. But let's go on. If I'm to lose my mind again . . ."

"If it happens, at least you're with your tribe." Karis gestured toward the busy camp, which was being set up in one of the few halfway comfortable places on that difficult trail, near a spring-fed pond of crystal clarity, sheltered from the wind. The Paladins drew water but didn't allow the horses to drink directly from the pool; for, like the Ashawala'i, they treated such springs with reverence. One Paladin had put Leeba on horseback and was teaching her to ride.

Zanja said, "This is my tribe. A very peculiar tribe, of disparate people whose beliefs are so complex they must be recorded in books, and a whole class of people must be devoted to keeping track of what the books say."

"A strange tribe," said Karis agreeably. "With many peculiar members—like you, and like me."

Two days later, they reached a place where the path wound between two high pinnacles. Atop one of these had been an outpost, where the *katrim* had kept watch on the pass. It was the farthest limit of the land that the Ashawala'i considered to be theirs. From that outpost, the watcher could signal watchers farther down the path, giving warning of a stranger's approach from one peak to the next, all the way to the valley.

As she had always done, Zanja cupped her hands around her mouth and called in her native language, "Greetings, my brother or sister! It is I, Zanja na'Tarwein, returning home again!"

In a moment she heard the echo—her own voice, shouting that greeting back at her.

Then the mountains spoke again: "My sister! Zanja na'Tarwein! You have been gone a long time!"

Zanja staggered.

"Who's that?" cried Leeba.

Karis, a massive tension, said to Kamren in a low voice, "It's just one person."

"One person in such an advantaged position—"

Zanja, feeling astonished, angry, and stupid all at once, said to them, "It's a *ghost!*"

"It's a real person," Karis said. "Zanja—is it someone you know?"

"It's Torel na'Parsa," she said, and fainted.

When her head cleared, Karis was holding her by the armpits, saying, "Reply to him, before he shoots at us."

She managed to call, "May I climb up and speak with you?"

He showed himself: a thin-legged silhouette in warrior's braids. "Climb up."

When the mountain fell on Zanja, and when her beloved brother was killed before her eyes, Zanja had felt like this, as though her thoughts could not attach themselves one to another. She felt a trembling in her bones, as if they might shudder into dust. She unfastened her belt, from which now hung the new dagger Karis had made for her in the smithy yard of Hanishport. "Hold this for me, Little Hurricane." For Leeba was pinched with fear, clutching Karis's leg with both hands, like a toddler. "I'm going to climb up and talk with him. He's a *katrim* like me—a friend I have known all my life."

Leeba said, "But they're all dead. You said so."

"I don't understand how he could be alive, but I'll ask him to explain."

Karis said, "If you fall, I'll break your head myself."

Generations of *katrim* had crawled up that rock face, and the route of hand- and footholds was easy to see. Zanja climbed up, then Torel clasped her wrists and helped her onto the ledge, where there was a simple rain shelter of wood and hide, a basket of supplies, and a rolled sleeping rug. "How can you even be alive?" they both said.

She said, "My brother, I thought I was the last of the Ashawala'i. I was taken prisoner, and I would have died also, but that woman down there—the very tall one—saved my life, for she is an earth witch. Since then, I have lived with her and her people."

Torel said, "Zanja na'Tarwein, why are you bringing these strangers into our country?"

"I have been haunted—maddened—by memories of the massacre. So my friends offered to come with me, to help me bury the bones of my people. They thought it would give me peace."

Before, Torel had been younger than she: energetic, impulsive, not considered trustworthy. But now he looked old, and he was trusted with this guard post, where the first and most important decisions were made. "Your friends are carrying weapons."

"They are *katrim* of Shaftal. But their blades are tied in the sheath."

He said, "I will say this, Zanja na'Tarwein: You are dead. I saw your body. We sang your spirit into the land of the dead. We burned your body and buried your bones."

He spoke with a stunning certainty, but how could what he said be true? She said, "I feel like I have died many times. To come back, to be alive again, has seemed so difficult that I have been tempted to stay dead. But I did survive the attack on our people."

They stared at each other, until Karis's raven flew up from below and hovered above them, looking at them curiously. Karis still could see and hear whatever Zanja saw and heard, so the raven was a signal from her, a question: *Do you need me yet?*

"How did you survive the attack?" Zanja asked. "On that night that filled the Asha Valley with bodies, and our village was burned to the ground?"

"Of course, we did as we had practiced—as you had insisted. The children and young people ran to take the path behind the village, with some *katrim* to protect them, and the skilled adults that had been chosen by the elders to go with them and teach them. *The kernel of the people* you always called them."

"*I* called them that? *I* insisted?"

"Yes. Your plan—which many mocked—it saved the people. More than half of us died—but many hundreds survived, though we live in the shadow of hunger."

A trembling came over her. She knelt so she wouldn't fall. "But how did I know?" she said. "How could anyone have known?"

Torel did not seem surprised by her behavior, or by her ignorance of her own life. "You knew from a song—a mourning song. One day you overheard someone singing it, and you said it was a message that predicted the doom of our people."

"What song?"

Torel sang:

> Time is the stone river flowing
> Past a village of charcoal and ashes.

Time is the summer camp
In which the sleepers do not awaken.

The voice of Zanja's dream guide had been sweet when he sang her this song, but Torel's was cracked and tuneless. He sang as one who had survived; who had fled catastrophe and returned to destruction; who had rebuilt in the ruins and planted in the bones. He sang as one who knew exactly what the song meant.

Zanja said out loud in Shaftalese, "Karis, my people have survived, but they are starving."

The raven turned into the wind and soared down to the pathway. When Zanja climbed down, she spotted Karis on her knees, writing a tiny message with ink she had made from spitting on an ink stone.

"Grain?" Karis asked, when Zanja stood before her. "Preserved meat? For how many people?"

"Four hundred and seventy, he says."

Karis said wryly, "I should have brought Garland to tell me how much food. And Medric, to do the ciphering." She wrote another sentence, which Zanja read upside-down: "Five hundred people to survive until the pass is clear in spring—two hundred days." She wrote her name, and Kamren took the paper, which he carefully folded into a strip, to be sealed with wax and tied to the raven's leg.

"You don't look well. Are you all right?" Karis asked.

"I need to ask Emil and Medric a question."

"What question?"

"Am I alive, or am I dead?"

Leeba, pressed against Karis's side, said irritably, "That's a stupid question."

Torel had climbed down to the path and was approaching. Karis heaved herself to her feet. To him she must seem monstrous: gigantic, with hair like a bleached shrub, eyes like pieces of sky, and muscles like boulders. Torel stopped in his tracks, as would every watchpost *katrim* they met that day. But each time Zanja would convince the *katrim* to let them pass, and each time she would feel her alienation anew. Either her people were no longer her people, or else she was no longer herself. As she walked, she saw many, many paths: the paths of her companions, of the Ashawala'i, and of herself. It seemed impossible for all of them to go the same way, at the same time, when each of them had arrived by such disparate routes.

They made camp in a lush meadow with a brook running through it, and it would have been difficult to say who appreciated that grass more: the horses, which had eaten only oats for many days, or the people, who were bruised and sore from many nights sleeping on beds of rock.

That night, Zanja dreamed she was walking down the dark hallways of Travesty. She needed to find the library, but every time she took a turn that seemed correct, she wound up in an unexpected place: in rooms and halls she had never seen before, or in rooms that were familiar and yet alien—the kitchen, with its pots empty and its stoves cold; the cloak-room with its hooks unused and not even one shoe on the shelf; her own bedroom, filled with broken furniture and strangely cold. She felt desperate and heartbroken, and shouted for Emil in the empty, alien hallway, though she knew he could not hear her.

"You have had this dream before," said a young *katrim* of the Ashawala'i.

"I don't think you're correct," she said.

"Many times you have tried to follow the path to the Asha Valley. And many times that path has turned away."

"Are you saying that the valley and Emil's library are the same to me?"

"Yes, Speaker."

"Why am I having this dream?"

"Because you think you are going home."

"Why can't I find the way?"

"It's this way," he said.

He led her to Emil and Medric's bedroom, and opened the door. She flew in and landed on the back of a chair, and then remembered she had been there all night, sleeping, with her feathers puffed up. She said, "Medric, I have become a raven."

Medric dropped his book—the lexicon, which was huge and heavy, and made a tremendous thud. Emil jerked upright in bed.

"Zanja is in the raven," Medric said.

Emil peered at Zanja. She had been roosting in a dark corner, and he couldn't see her there, so she flew to a bedpost that was lit by Medric's lamp. "Is that all?" Emil said. "And why is that surprising, when a great deal of what we've seen is simply impossible?"

Medric said, "Because I believe she may be dreaming. This *is* surprising, since you and I are awake."

"I was trying to go home," said Zanja-the-raven.

Emil gazed at her thoughtfully. "And now you're here. Why is that, do you suppose?"

Medric was trying to pick up the book, but apparently it was too heavy to lift. He got on his knees on the floor and began turning the pages.

"My dear, what has happened?" Emil asked her.

"I don't know the answer to that question."

"Why not?"

"There are too many paths. I can't follow all of them. I thought this would be a simple journey."

"But you are in the maze." Medric tilted the book so Emil and Zanja could see the page, which depicted a hedge maze, with several people and various creatures, including a small white dog, wandering through it. Zanja had studied that illustration, trying to find the way from one end of the maze to the other, but after many attempts and much wasted time had never succeeded.

Zanja-the-raven said, "My people entered through one opening, and I entered through the other. Our paths will never intersect."

Medric blinked at her, and his lenses flashed much more brightly than the dim candle flame. "You found a remnant of your tribe!"

"Yes—and they say they survived because of me. They tell my life story, but it's a life I never lived. And apparently, I died in the massacre. Many of them died who now are alive. This isn't my tribe. It's the tribe of a woman whose name was my name, but who was not me."

She heard the familiar rasp of Emil's hands rubbing his unshaven face. "My dear," he said rather plaintively, "that isn't how it works."

"It's water logic," said Medric.

"Water logic?" Emil looked sharply at him, then at Zanja, and she saw the spark of candle flame in his eye. "What was the name of that Ashawala'i speaker you met two hundred years ago? Arel? When you traveled through his time, you didn't dare to reveal your people's fate to him, but you feared he had realized so much that he might guess the rest. Surely Tadwell decided to give you the lexicon because of Arel."

Medric cried, "Oh, Zanja, you are an excellent thief but a dreadful liar! And that failure saved your people!"

Emil said, "Arel must have done something—and perhaps you can discover what he did—"

"He was a poet," Zanja said. "He made a song—a song that would be sung by one generation after another, until I heard it, and by fire logic understood what it meant."

"But *you* never heard that song. It was heard by the Zanja who died. Oh, but these thoughts are too difficult to think at this hour!"

"You're saying that I'm forever an exile from my people."

"Not *exiled*," Medric said. "That's the wrong word. You're *estranged*, or *alienated*."

"Oh, Medric, but not from us!" Emil cried.

"I have you now," said Karis, with her arm around her.

The stars whirled, and slowed, and became still. They lay together in the meadow, with a few accuser bugs creaking in the distance, the horses chewing their cud and sighing with contentment, the Paladins sighing in weary sleep, and Leeba breathing quietly, pressed against Karis's other side.

The next day, the Ashawala'i elders met Zanja and her companions at the fork of the path, which at the left went to the village and at the right to the lush flood plain of the valley. The elders—little older than she—drank the Paladin's tea, talked for a long time, then granted her party permission to take only the right-hand path and make no attempt to cross the river or go to the village. So Zanja returned to the Asha Valley, but would never go home. This decision seemed right and wise, and she accepted it without complaint.

"I might as well get the people tired of staring at me," said Karis, and took the horses to the riverbank to drink, where she checked their hooves and legs, then let them loose to graze, and all afternoon sat on a rock in full view of the opposite bank, doing the mundane work of checking, mending, and dressing harnesses. When Zanja joined her to say that supper would soon be ready, a good many people were still standing and sitting on the opposite bank, watching Karis in amazement.

The young children had grown bored and were playing in the water, but the older children seemed unable to play. Many of the adults supported themselves with staffs or sat on the ground doing nothing.

"They starved themselves to the point of death so that the children would have enough food," said Karis.

"They used to grow a sturdy kind of corn, and various vegetables, and they cut hay for the goats, whose wool they spun and wove into garments and rugs. I don't even see any goats, and the farmland lies barren. Maybe the starving people killed and ate the goats, along with the seed corn."

"I notice that the forest within a day's walk of here is mostly nut trees, then it gives way to mostly pine. Over many generations, your people must have planted a nut tree every time they cut down a pine, so the nut trees could be a hedge against famine. But the mountains offer no salt, no metal, hardly any flat land, a slow, wet spring, and a very short growing season. That corn your people managed to grow under these conditions, there's nothing like it in Shaftal. We can't bring in some sheep to replace the goats, either—sheep are too stupid, and too destructive. So, early this spring, before the planting begins, someone will have to visit the other mountain tribes, with salt and tools to trade for pregnant goats and seed corn that will thrive in the mountains."

"Do you mean to say that I'll be returning here with the first supply train in the spring?"

"Well, you still are the speaker of the Ashawala'i," Karis said.

This was their shared destiny, thought Zanja. From the Asha Valley south to the grasslands, from the eastern coastline west to the borderlands, until she and Karis were very old women and Leeba's children had borne children, until Karis handed over the load of power and knowledge to the next G'deon and then died, until Zanja lay down and died beside her they would think together like this, mulling over serious questions, working their way slowly toward equally serious answers. It would be a good life—sometimes significant, often surprising, and perhaps never again as perilous as it had been.

Zanja said, "And so my life will have turned completely inside-out and backwards. I'll occasionally visit my mother's people, but my home will be Shaftal."

"Oh well," Karis said. "You'll get used to it."

A short while later, a small group of people arrived on the opposite shore and came down to the river. Some took off their tunics and put them on a raft to keep dry, and some sat on the raft. Zanja said to Karis, "They are na'Tarweins."

"Of course fire bloods would be the first to cross the river and meet the strangers. Well, I'd better go tell the Paladins we have supper guests. But we don't have enough soup bowls to go around . . ." Karis walked off, talking to herself, hauling an armload of harnesses. She certainly would have resolved the bowl shortage by the time she reached the camp.

Zanja stood alone, waiting. The swimmers entered the water and began pushing the raft across the water. One person in the raft held a baby: she was Zanja's sister's oldest daughter, and in her arms was a grandchild. The young woman probably had volunteered to allow her baby to be held by Karis, to determine whether the alien earth witch's powers were benign. Perhaps the baby was sickly, and the baby's mother was insightful and reckless.

The others sitting on the raft were people Zanja recognized, but the four youths in the water would have been very young children when she knew them, and they had changed too much.

One of those four swimmers could not pay attention to his task. His curious gaze reached beyond the water, beyond Zanja, perhaps tracking the shape of the giant as she strode away across the meadow, or perhaps yearning farther, toward the strangers' camp, or farther still, toward the mysterious land of Shaftal. Although Zanja didn't know the boy's face, that eagerness, that yearning toward the alien and unknown, that was familiar.

Then the knowledge of what had happened in the last two days came over her: the loss, the bewilderment, the weary ache of old wounds. Standing on the riverbank, waiting for these members of her lost family, soon to be eating supper with her people past and present, she looked toward the high bank from which she had once watched the doom of the Ashawala'i come across the river. She had thought she was to witness the end of everything.

It had been the end, and yet it had not been. She began to weep, but it was only sorrow—familiar, endurable sorrow, and extraordinary gladness. Her people's years of starvation, like her own summers of madness, had ended. Perhaps their paths through the maze could not converge in the past; but they had converged in the present.

The small contingent reached the shallows. The swimmers began walking, and their lithe bodies slowly rose out of the water—the boys with chests beginning to broaden, the girls with breasts starting to take shape, their brown bodies cloaked in long, black, wet hair. The curious boy looked at Zanja—a respectful, hopeful, hungry look. Suddenly she remembered his name: Brama, son of Sarja. He had grown to look much like his mother.

And then she recognized more than his face. She knew him: her dream helper, her lost son, a fire blood selected by the elders and chosen by the owl god Salos'a to be a crosser of boundaries. The boy would be the next Speaker of the Ashawala'i. The na'Tarwein elder stepped into shallow water and waded to dry land. He had come to ask Zanja to accept Brama na'Tarwein as her student. Zanja would accept him, and, for the boy, in that moment, everything would begin.

Acknowledgments

My wife, Deb Mensinger, deserves my most profound thanks, but I feel unable to begin to list the reasons, for fear that I'll never finish. My longtime friends and advisors, Delia Sherman, Rosemary R. Kirstein, Didi Stewart, and Ellen Kushner, have given me priceless support and intelligent and thoughtful commentary on various drafts of this book and the Elemental Logic series, and I hope I have managed to give them equal value in return. My most profound thanks to Gavin J. Grant and Kelly Link of Small Beer Press, not only for giving this final book a home, but also for devoting so much time and energy to helping it to be a better book, and for reprinting the entire series which, for a while, seemed in danger of disappearing entirely. Thank you above all to the many who waited patiently for me to finish this book, while I wrote and rewrote it in hospitals, hotel rooms, coffee shops, airplanes, trains, and any other place that happened to be handy. I wish the writing hadn't taken so long, but it is amazing that I managed to do it at all.

About the author

Laurie J. Marks (lauriejmarks.com) is the author of nine novels including the Elemental Logic quartet, *Fire Logic, Earth Logic, Water Logic,* and *Air Logic.* She lives in Massachusetts, and works at the University of Massachusetts, Boston.